WHERE
THE
RAIN
CANNOT
REACH

WHERE THE RAIN CANNOT REACH

A NOVEL

ADESINA BROWN

atmosphere press

To my mom—
thank you for the time, space, and freedom to create.

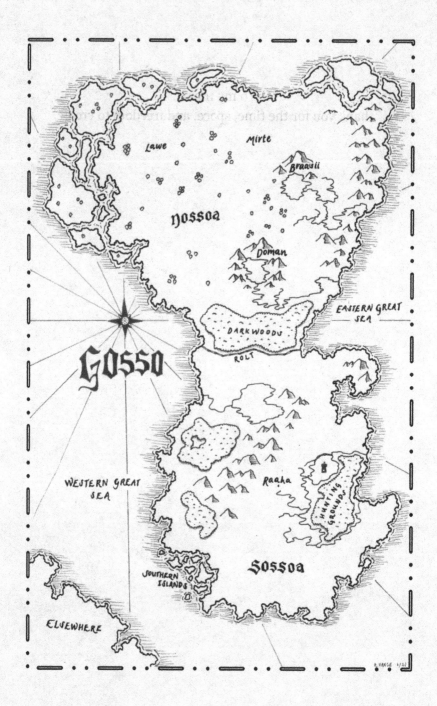

Lawe

Mirte

Braauli

Nossoa

Doman

EASTERN GREAT SEA

DARKWOODU

ROLT

GOSSO

WESTERN GREAT SEA

Raaha

HUNTING GROUND

Sossoa

SOUTHERN ISLANDS

ELSEWHERE

R. VANCE 4/22

BEFORE

Through the thicket lay a crying child. Stuck in time though
she was, the child was no more than three years of age. Her
black hair flowed over her golden-brown skin; her knees
tucked into her chest to hide her eternally tear-stained cheeks
from a harsh world. The child could no longer cry for her
parents, who she had forgotten long ago, and still she sobbed
over a future lost far too soon. Just a little thing, with only the
missai birds to watch over her, until a kind hand reached out
and awakened her to a new world.

NOSSOA

ONE

Tair lay in the grassy green hills of Mirte, her unruly black hair a halo around her. Airy blue cloth draped her form, which she soon discovered was a serious miscalculation as great gusts of wind rippled over her body. Mirte's late-winter, early-spring days were quite warm, but the temperature swiftly dropped as night set in. Tair wondered how much time she had left before the cold forced her inside. Unperturbed by the weather, the Elven children around her danced a well-known choreography and sang the same songs they had for the past fourteen years Tair had lived in the land. Songs that reminded her of childhood and innocence and, unfortunately, alienation. After all, she was the only Human in Mirte, the last valley under solely Elven control. It had been that way since she had first arrived when she was five years old, and it had stayed that way her entire life.

The days were shorter that time of year and the skies grew darker earlier. That day in particular, a storm rumbled in the distance. This only sent new life into the Elven children, who squealed and skipped alongside one another, a Northern

3

Elvish tune of thunder and lightning on their tongues. She took this as a sign to head back inside: while Elves were particularly fond of rain, Tair preferred observation from indoors. Two Elven children followed as she started back for her cabin in the distance, picking at her clothes all the while. They giggled when she smiled down at them, almost half her size already and bound to tower above her in their years to come. Even now, she felt herself an outsider; though they had grown up with her in their community, she was still an unusual sighting.

The children remained at her heels as she neared her front door. As an offering, she pulled out a small silver taper candle. The little Elves gasped, grabbed hold of the candle together, and happily set off on their way to show their friends what they had received. The Elves of Mirte exchanged and accepted gifts for all kinds of occasions, and they particularly enjoyed gifts that symbolized fire. A silver candle like Tair's was a clear request for privacy when she knew her words would not do the trick. Tair had learned at an early age to carry offerings with her, if only to avoid a negative reputation among the Northern Elves, who already had a rather low opinion of Humans.

As did all other races, and rightfully so.

Upon opening the door to her cabin, a glass stein shattered next to Tair's head. She shrunk back, shielding her eyes on instinct. It had just started to rain now, and a bit trickled down her back as she stood on the threshold between the cabin and the stormy valley.

Silaa laughed as Shianna pulled Tair inside and shut the door behind her. "Oh, Tair! Are you okay?" Shianna cooed, in her most loving tone.

Shianna was, perhaps, one of the only beings in Mirte who understood Tair's racial isolation. Being a Dwarf, she stood out not only in height—only meeting some of the eldest and tallest Elves' waistlines—but also in build. Not all Dwarves, she often bragged, could have achieved her immense size. She took up as much space as physically possible, and then even more in personality. Her dark skin glowed with the light of the fire burning in the hearth. It was as though wherever Shianna was, light followed. She wore a thick quilted top and pants, both of which had been worn by her grandparent during the Doman War.

In her early years, Tair looked to Shianna as a guardian, and then as a sibling as she grew older. By then, she was better equipped to recognize the Dwarf's faults. Nonetheless, Tair held plenty of respect and admiration for Shianna. She cradled Tair's face in her strong, warm hands and checked for any nicks or cuts, even as Tair reassured her that she was not hurt. The Dwarf was admittedly overprotective.

After seemingly satisfied with her inspection, Shianna let go of Tair. Silaa teased, "We have to be more careful with her. You know how fragile Humans are."

Tair huffed. She hated to think of herself as fragile, a word Elves like Silaa loved to use in reference to her and her kind. Then again, as far as anyone knew, Humans possessed no magic to defend themselves with—Tair included.

Shianna frowned. "I didn't know she was coming back so soon. I wouldn't have thrown it." Why Shianna had thrown a stein in the first place, Tair did not know. One thing was for certain, though: Shianna and Silaa were never truly violent with one another, but the two did play some childish games that resulted in an inordinate amount of destruction. It was not uncommon for them to spar, break delicate things, and start (somewhat) mild fires, if only because they were bored.

"I'm fine," Tair mumbled. She toed around the shards of glass in the entryway as she headed to the kitchen to get herself a shot of Elven *arne*.

Something was telling her it would be a long night.

Silaa was almost a foot taller than both Shianna and Tair, and her light brown skin radiated just as much firelight as

Shianna's. The Elf had been one of the first to greet Shianna upon her arrival all those years ago, when Tair was around seven years of age, and the two had been nearly inseparable ever since. That was how it went with mates, Shianna had explained to a rather intrigued young Tair who had not quite understood what it meant to be someone's mate. It was undeniable that the two made a beautiful pair. In contrast to Shianna's tight-fitting battle wear, Silaa always wore loose clothing that nicely suited her curves. Truthfully, if Tair had been attracted to anyone in her youth, it was that older Elf. She had, on occasion, had to draw her eyes away; mating was a serious thing in any realm and, though it never demanded monogamy nor eternity, more dependent on a deep feeling of connection than on a particular style of relationship, Tair would have never challenged Shianna to be with Silaa. After all, Tair was only a child when her infatuation began, so she would not have had a chance; as she grew older, Silaa became less attractive to Tair, if only because she began to feel more like family.

Still, Silaa's knowledge of Tair's childhood crush was something she loved to lord over the younger Human. As such, Tair often stayed out of Silaa's way as best as she could. Tonight, arms wrapped around Shianna from behind as she watched Tair down a second shot of *arne*, Silaa winked at Tair. She teased, "Hope you can control yourself after all that."

Tair huffed and went for a third shot out of spite. Her tolerance was not usually so strong, but that night she barely felt the alcohol's effects.

Only a week before Silaa had moved in with them, Tair had expressed her childhood crush to the Elf, a declaration she later regretted. A two-centuries-old Elf calmly explaining to a Human child why they would not be mates, why they would *never* be mates, and why that confession would one day be a great source of embarrassment still humiliated Tair. It was a moment that, she discovered as she grew older, she could

6

never quite outlive. As though it heard her frustration, thunder clapped outside.

Shianna chuckled, full-bellied, at something Silaa whispered in her ear, and the two collapsed on the cushions in front of the fire. Tair set about looking for a snack. Just in time, Alyn arrived back, soaked in rain and a bundle of food in his arms.

Tair helped him carry all the foodstuffs into the kitchen. When he laid eyes upon Shianna and Silaa, who may as well have already taken each other's clothes off, he gagged. "Do I have to ask again that you two not... *integrate* in common areas?" Tair could hear the shiver in his voice.

After one final kiss, Silaa sighed, "You ruined the fun." They both sat up and straightened out their clothes.

"Well, I'd rather that than have to witness your private relations," Alyn muttered. Alyn was Fel, the result of a Faery and an Elf mating. As he explained it, Elves and Faeries had a whole slew of physical differences that required they reproduce in other, more creative, and more magical ways than other races, in the rare cases they reproduced at all. Alyn claimed that all Fel grew up with a natural misunderstanding or otherwise an aversion to the overt nakedness and sexuality of others. At the very least, they believed such acts were meant to be confined to private settings between consenting adults. That could not have been true for all Fel, Silaa once argued, because those that had passed through Mirte in the past were some of their most overtly promiscuous visitors. Alyn himself had many partners with whom he strictly avoided emotional bonding; unlike the Fel Silaa spoke of, though, Alyn shared only the vaguest details. Silaa liked to tease him by asking where he had been all night, or where he was going at the end of a long day, and Alyn would only mutter something indistinct and hurry away. Though they all had a pretty clear idea of who his three or four partners in Mirte were, they still relished in feigning ignorance, which always turned his pale

7

cheeks the shade of a ripe tomato.

Fel were immediately recognizable—which was perhaps why they were the only mixed race that had their own defined identity term. Alyn, like all Fel, was the same height and build as any average Human. Unlike Humans', however, were Fels' sharp features; their ears came to a piercing point, their jawlines and chins were severe, and their skin was devoid of melanin, no matter the complexion of their parents. Most other Fels' additional features were also blanched of color, but Alyn was distinct with his black hair and dark brown eyes set beneath contrastingly white eyebrows.

In Northern Elvish, a language only employed by the Elves of Mirte, Tair asked Alyn how he was feeling: *"Eesu-mapii shon?"*

Alyn simply nodded and sent the question back to Tair, to which the Human responded with a similar nod, though a little more enthusiastic than her counterpart. The question often did not warrant nor necessitate a verbal response, but that night Tair found Alyn rather curt. Usually, he had at least one story for her: a conversation he'd had in passing, a new type of bird he had observed, the changing in the weather, or some other mundane topic he had spun into a poem or a song or tale. He was an adventurer, after all; he loved to indulge in the little things that made each land, and all his experiences in those lands, unique.

Tair took a step back as Alyn set to chopping up the vegetables for their dinner. As much as—or perhaps more than—he loved adventures, he *adored* cooking. And, because the rest of them thought themselves more suited to eating, they let him. Tair asked, "What do you have planned for tonight?"

"Some sort of stew," Alyn answered absentmindedly.

"Some sort of stew?"

Alyn nodded.

Tair folded her arms across her chest. She could sense that

his mind was elsewhere. Perhaps his favorite part of preparing meals was the opportunity to obsess over all the ingredients and spices involved, as well as divulge his inspirations. Alyn had been almost everywhere on the continent of Gosso, save Sossoa (though he still wanted to venture to the land, no matter if it would cost him his life); as such, he had tasted thousands of different kinds of food from countless cultures. Still, the best recipes, in Tair's opinion, were the ones that came to Alyn in a dream, often beautiful to look at and consume all the same, and rich both in texture and in flavor. Tair's mouth watered just thinking about it.

However, her hunger was not enough to distract her from Alyn's unnerving behavior. Come to think of it, he had been more detached the previous couple of weeks, but that night he seemed particularly removed.

Tair did not want to push him. Instead, she asked, "Need any help?"

Alyn nodded, handing her some *spi*, a leafy vegetable native to Mirte, and potatoes to cut up for the contents of the stew while he worked on the broth. He usually started with a water base as it was the quickest and most accessible broth base in Mirte but, if he wanted to treat his housemates, he went with something thicker. They all particularly enjoyed *camiit*, a type of root that, when cooked down, produced a thick texture that tasted like childhood to Tair. Apparently, that night was a special occasion; Alyn placed a few ripe *camiits*, their bitter skin peeled and even more bitter core pitted, into boiling water.

When the broth was ready and Alyn and Tair had both finished cutting up the vegetables, they placed each of the components in the pot. Alyn softly sang one of his many original songs as he went about spicing the dish. This song was not about joy and love, which he often sang when cooking so as to put the supposed "right energy" into the cuisine he fed his friends, but rather one of sorrow:

9

Hear the water rage,
Feel the first light—
But sing! our songs of old;

Hold our forgotten
as you hold our seasons past,
And may the Suns rebirth you
So we may find you at last...

Tair could not place why this particular tune had come to him. She was certain it had been lazily translated from a language unknown—as though he wanted to ensure that Tair could fully understand it. As though he was trying to send an unspoken message that spoken word would not be able to accurately express.

Even more disturbing, Silaa and Shianna were typically excitable—if not rambunctious—as they waited for dinner. That day, though, they sat (mostly) in silence, finding far too much interest in the bowls of stew being set down in front of them. With the food dished out and distributed, the four of them gathered around the low table in front of the now-dim fire and began eating. In between bites, Shianna, Silaa, and Alyn all kept glancing at one another, on the cusp of blurting out whatever they were hiding. Their strange behavior unnerving her, Tair's heart started to beat rapidly in her chest. As delicious as the stew smelled, as much as it filled her with nostalgia, as loudly as her stomach growled, she could not will herself to eat it. Finally, when she could not take it any longer, Tair asked, "What's going on?"

Alyn tentatively met her eyes. He swallowed his last bite of stew and spun a little cloud of smoke from the tip of his finger—one of his nervous ticks. With a slight hitch in his voice, he said, "We have to leave tomorrow before dawn. I wasn't—we weren't sure how to tell you."

Tair laughed. In a wave of relief, she took a bite of food.

What a comfort Alyn's ridiculous words were! It must have been part of some elaborate joke, which she believed until, after a few spoonsful of her stew, she realized that everyone else in the room remained silent. They had not found Alyn's statement nearly as funny as she had. She forced herself to swallow before she asked, "What are you talking about?"

"We're leaving tomorrow before the Red Sun rises," Alyn repeated, casting his eyes into his lap.

Now, Tair did not laugh; now, Tair wanted to vomit. Or, she was about to vomit, the desire and the instinct muddled. Her skin felt clammy when she balled up her fists. Alyn was not joking. And, as much as she had accepted that she would have to leave Mirte at some point in the near future, she never expected that she would have to leave on such short notice. Nor did she expect that Alyn, of all beings, would inform her in such an abrupt, careless way.

She did not know what to say. Shock was an overwhelming emotion, so all-consuming that any verbal reaction felt wholly inappropriate. As such, the next words that came out of Tair's mouth surprised her, if only because they had never come to mind before that moment: "How am I meant to say goodbye?"

Shianna and Silaa sat still and silent as they watched Alyn and Tair. They were not surprised by Alyn's statement. Indeed, it seemed everyone in the room was more familiar with the trajectory of Tair's life than her. Noticing Alyn's struggle for an amicable answer, and confirming Tair's fears, Silaa stated, "You're not."

"But I..." Tair leaned forward onto her knees and gripped the small table situated in the center of it all—the table that they had eaten at and laughed around and danced over for years. The table that she had carved her name into the underside of when she was young—she felt the ridges of her name in their Northern Elvish characters even now. The table that she would have to say goodbye to, too. She welcomed the splinters in her palms, the only things grounding her in a reality she was having a hard time accepting. If she had known this was her last day, she may have relished in the children singing, or sat out in the rain despite her aversion to it, or requested that they eat in the common hall amongst the Elves she would have to leave in a matter of hours. She might have savored this land and its community for all they were to her.

All they were ever going to be, apparently.

Unable to come up with anything coherent to say, Tair stuttered out, "This is the only home I remember, the only home I know. They have—Silaa, you know—there are specific traditions for saying goodbye, all of the rituals and celebrations and...I was supposed to get all of that. Now—"

Alyn gently cut her off. "It's for the best, Tair. We don't have three weeks to say goodbye, not as you would like to. If we don't leave now—"

Silaa found coddling unproductive. Exasperated, she interjected, "You always knew this was coming."

"And that's supposed to make it less painful?" Tair snapped. Silaa's mouth hung open, looking for the words, while Alyn shifted in his seat on the floor across from Tair, uncomfortable and unsteady.

Good, Tair thought to herself, *I hope this hurts you as much as it hurts me.* She asked aloud, "How long have you all known today would be my last day?"

"That's not important—"

"*How long?*" Tair shouted. She never raised her voice, especially not with these three that she considered family, but she felt it warranted given the circumstances.

"We always knew," Alyn admitted slowly, "that today would be your last. We had always planned on it being this way."

Always...*fourteen years* they had known they would tear her from what she had come to see as her homeland? From what they had told her to adopt as her homeland? Indeed, Mirte was more of a home to her than Sossoa. Sossoa, founded in the aftermath of the Doman War about five hundred years prior, and founded on the genocide of all non-Humans who had once inhabited the lands south of the Darkwoods, had been and was still a homogenous nation of Humans. It was where the majority of contemporary Humans resided and, unfortunately, where Tair had originated. She had no memory of nor connection to Sossoa—and she did not want to be connected to the land, knowing its history and what had been done to create the nation. Tair, feeling both hatred toward and abandonment from her technical homeland, had come to see Mirte as a naturalized homeland—but even within the safety of Mirte, her family had *planned* to cause her undue pain. Planned to betray her. Her chest tightened and her eyes blurred over, though from rage or sorrow, she could not tell. She stood, paced back to the kitchen, and took another shot of *arne* to dull it all. Apathy was much easier to control than the crushing panic that threatened to overtake her.

Silaa, in her own way, tried to console Tair. "We know this is difficult—"

"Difficult?" Tair spat. "What if I told you that you have to leave the only home you've ever known within hours, not knowing what would become of you in the days and months to come? Not knowing *why?*"

Shianna paused, bit her lip. Tair knew she had crossed a line when the Dwarf whispered, "Tair, you know both Alyn and I have gone through exactly that, and for you, no less. All of you—all of us, too, have been kept in the dark about all the reasons *why*, but we also know the importance of what we must do. We know it is difficult, yes, but we only know that because we have been through precisely what you are going through."

Tair winced. They had always taught her that she was no more "chosen" than anyone else, for everyone had been chosen in their own mind, for better or worse. Tair was no stranger to *worse*. After all, much of her life had been shaped by some still unknown, incomprehensible greater duty to a land and a kin that had once abandoned her. She had only rarely admitted it to herself, but she knew too that Sossoa would demand her eventual return—for what and why, she still did not know. No matter the secrecy, she had been told that she was not unique in her responsibilities, her path, her life, but that she was precious all the same. It was a dizzying mindset to grapple with. Nevertheless, Alyn, Shianna, and Silaa had all had to make sacrifices for what they believed to be a higher cause, had to make sacrifices for Tair, especially. In fact, Tair was the only one in the room who did not know what true sacrifice felt like. Not yet, anyway. Not until today, thunder echoing outside and rain pounding at the walls of the cabin.

Tair knew hers was not a fair question, not when she had a moment to reflect back on it. But if they knew the true pain of sacrifice, why not prepare her for it? Why inflict upon her any pain at all? Tair would never be able to comprehend the pain of their losses, but this was undoubtedly a betrayal. She managed a quivering, "Why?"

So much for not appearing fragile.

Forever able to switch between compassion and diplomacy at a moment's notice, Shianna said, "You know what we three are here to do. We're your protectors, Tair. If the specific moment of our departure from Mirte had been widely known, it may have compromised your safety—*our* safety. Then what would all of these years of isolation and hiding have been for?"

"So you decided to protect me from myself?"

After a moment, Shianna gently nodded and explained, "We were the only ones in possession of this information. Had you known even a day earlier, you may have compromised your own safety by saying goodbye too early, or handing out too many gifts. Someone would have caught on."

Alyn, in his silence, did not seem as sure of their choice to lie to Tair. Clearly, though, he had agreed, which hurt Tair more deeply than she could have said.

"I could have been smart," Tair managed. She felt like a child again, explaining why she was accountable enough to gather that week's food supplies on her own. She continued, "I'm"—she cleared her throat, squared her shoulders—"I'm responsible, and you all are supposed to trust that—trust *me*, just as I am supposed to trust you. How am I meant to trust you after this?"

Shianna hated hurting Tair. Apparently, that still held true; she winced at Tair's pointed words.

As the Dwarf fumbled, it was Alyn's turn to take over again: "We decided that perhaps this minor pain could have spared you further harm. There are Humans who have wanted you dead for a long time, Tair—Humans who have known what you represent and want that destroyed. You still have so much more life to live, so much more to give and to do."

"Yet I do not remember consenting to give any more than I already have, or do anything more than *live*. Now, this homeland I have come to claim as my own, this culture that feels like my own, this community I am most familiar with— you're telling me I must leave all of that so suddenly, without regard for who might be hurt in the process?"

"Elves will undoubtedly be hurt by any way you choose to leave," Silaa offered. Her tone was softer than Tair had ever heard. As if speaking to an inconsolable child. Tair blinked back tears. "Even with goodbye rituals, there is always a great deal of pain—and plenty of concentrated attempts to convince the being who wishes to leave of all the reasons that they should stay instead. I know you are aware of the ways in which they might convince you to do so?"

Of course, Tair was aware. She had only ever witnessed one departure ritual in all her time in Mirte, which had lasted five weeks and had resulted in the Elf staying in Mirte after all. Following that, there had been another five weeks of celebration and joy—all of which was terribly exciting for a ten-year-old Tair to witness. Yes, Tair was conscious of the ways that the Elves of Mirte maintained a strong, insular community through bombarding their members with an almost suffocating degree of love...

But she had wanted all of those ceremonies and rituals, too, if only as proof that she was loved and needed by the community she had grown up in. A community that she had always felt herself an outsider to. Now that she was apparently leaving for an undefined amount of time, she wanted to feel important to them. She deserved to feel important to them.

Tair clutched her stomach. The stew was coming up. Her nausea was overwhelming—a mixture of the heavy food, the alcohol, the nerves. She squatted down on the floor. She heard Shianna rush over to her; the Dwarf placed a tentative hand on Tair's back, which Tair swatted off before realizing she needed Shianna's help to stand up again. A bead of sweat rolled down her forehead as she stood and sighed, "Tomorrow morning?"

Through blurry eyes, she saw both Alyn and Shianna nod. Silaa was in her own world, her back turned to Tair.

"Where?"

"Oh, Tair!" Shianna exclaimed, far too joyful for a night Tair knew would always haunt her. She said, "That is the best part, if there can be one. Everything may feel awful right now, but I promise you it will all be resolved when we arrive back home—to Doman!"

The true ancestral homeland to all kind—now, a homeland to only Dwarves—or so the creation legend went. Doman was ruled by Dwarves, for the vast majority-Dwarf population, and located just north of the Darkwoods. According to Elven lore, Doman was a place of great magic and impossibility. True or not, Elves often spoke of Dwarves as mythical creatures, perceived to be so entirely separate from their kind that Dwarves were deified. It was commonly agreed that, at the dawn of creation, Doman birthed the First Five Dwarves, then the Second Five Faeries, the Third Five Elves, and then the Fourth Five Humans; eventually, as they grew in population and became distinctive in identity, Fel. With that tale in mind, the Elves of Mirte believed that Dwarves, being the closest to the dawn of creation, possessed spiritual and magical abilities that later creations either felt an echo of (amplified, in the case of the Faeries; dulled, in the case of the Elves; and somewhere in between, in the case of the Fel), or could not grasp at all (in the case of Humans). There were plenty of lies and plenty of truths out there concerning Dwarven capabilities but, ever since the trauma of the Doman War, their kind had been secretive of their magic, only daring to use it in the presence of other Dwarves within Doman. Even under the most comfortable conditions, their use of magic was infrequent and fearful, which made it less potent than it would have been prior to their pain. All this magical secrecy led to a variety of responses: from the capture, imprisonment, and torture of Dwarves who had wandered too far south into Sossoa; to the assumptions of Dwarven wisdom and magic that made them into celestial beings amongst the Northern Elves of Mirte, and then everything in between. In Mirte, it was common advice to seek out a Dwarf for answers to existential and spiritual questions. At that point in time, that Dwarf was unfortunately Shianna. For better or for worse, the resident Dwarf of Mirte was expected to provide an appropriate answer.

This, of course, was a great source of stress and frustration for Shianna, who did not have the solutions to all of life's problems and did not feel as though she possessed any greater spiritual knowledge than anyone else, particularly the Elves of Mirte. In fact, she had told Tair once that she had little to no connection to her magic, having been trained since she was young to suppress it or otherwise hide it if only to keep herself and those she loved safe. Tair wondered how true that was. Either way, even though she did not have most of the answers that Elves sought, Shianna was still expected to answer—honesty a gift of its own among the Northern Elves—but all her answers were careful and cryptic. She never knew whether or not her response would be perceived as fact, thus altering the course of Elven spirituality for the considerable future. Worse yet, the mythology surrounding Dwarves often created strife between Shianna and her mate. Silaa, though conscious of the inaccuracies of such stereotypes, sometimes slipped and turned to Shianna to solve her deepest troubles, beyond what a traditional mate would ask of their partner. Throughout the years, Silaa had gotten better about listening more to Shianna and her needs but, whenever the challenges proved too great to bear, Shianna requested distance. Silaa respected this, of course, and Tair had witnessed their partnership grow stronger because of it. That did not downplay the great emotional fatigue it caused Shianna, though.

The second legend that pervaded Elven perception of Domani Dwarves was that of war. In any non-Dwarf culture, there came differing tales of Dwarves' tendencies toward conflict. As allegedly the most magical beings in all the realms and then as producers of some of the most innovative weaponry, Dwarves had been posed as quick to prove themselves, quick to fight. In attempt to dispel this myth, Shianna had explained many times to Tair and any curious Elves who gave her audience that Dwarves did indeed have plenty of weapons, but that did not necessitate that they wield them. There were plenty of false tales circulating in Mirte, but the most common one Elven children learned was that the Doman War had begun when a Human spilled cold water onto a Dwarven bladesmith's axe as he was in the middle of crafting it. The reality was far more complicated, as reality often was, Shianna had told Tair. Truth was, Dwarves and Humans had peacefully coexisted in Doman for three centuries, after the mountains had birthed the Fourth Five, Humans, into the world. The exact incendiary moment was unknown, but after so much peace and seemingly without cause, Dwarven children began disappearing in the middle of the night. When they were later found, Domani Dwarves discovered that Humans had been extracting magic from their stolen children, and then indoctrinating those children into a Domani Human lifestyle. The Dwarves confronted their Human kin—their community members, and families—but many Humans claimed no wrongdoing by fault of having been given no magic to begin with and so needing it to survive. Thus, the Doman War began. Thousands dead but, ultimately, Dwarven authority over Doman had persevered. Knowing now the repercussions of softness and laxity, it was only right that Dwarves innovated in the fields of battle and self-protection.

They did not seek to destroy, but to preserve.

Even then, Shianna still would not have been considered a pacifist, not unlike many other Dwarves. Besides herself, Tair had never met anyone who she would have truly considered a pacifist; where she would have let herself die before she took up arms against another, Shianna would have instead caused great harm to anyone who would try to hurt her, hurt those she loved, or even hurt a passing stranger. Shianna had said it was the same for many Dwarves; they would not consciously allow for injustice to continue. Shianna herself was rather averse to complacency, often saying that nonparticipation could have far worse effects than active participation. *It is in the refusal to defend others that one loses their ability to defend themself,* she had said on occasion.

Now, Tair saw in the Dwarf a wicked duplicity. Shianna had not decided to defend Tair; instead, she had knowingly caused harm. Tair had once accredited all her sense of trust in the world to Shianna, but clearly that trust had been misplaced. She winced when she realized that anything she might have shared with Shianna throughout the course of her life could have very well been knowledge to Silaa and Alyn as well. They knew more of her and her own life than she did, so it was safe to assume that their horrible secret necessitated a breach of her privacy as well. Here was the culmination of their long-conceived betrayal, feeling deeper and more invasive with every moment that Tair thought. And thought.

It was not Shianna alone who bore the brunt of her anger, acute as the pain of that betrayal was. Silaa was to blame, too. Her usual passivity meant that she knew what was bound to happen, but saw no reason to question it, no reason to stop it. Silaa was one of theory over practice, words over action, which had caused some struggle between her and Shianna in the past. Even still, it hurt Tair to think that Silaa did not question her usual apathy for her sake.

And then there was Alyn, who only sat and anxiously wrang his hands, probably to keep himself from spinning another wisp of smoke from nothingness. Alyn had always said that he had taken Tair on as his responsibility to protect her. She was three years of age when she was found in the Darkwoods and five years of age when they both arrived in Mirte, after a couple years in Doman where they carefully deliberated her safety as a Human outside of Sossoa. Ultimately, it was Alyn's honor, he claimed, to take responsibility for Tair. He taught her how to communicate with the Elves, taught her which gifts would be best received; he cooked and cleaned for her; he bathed her, despite his aversion to nudity; he made spoken and unspoken sacrifices for her; he loved her.

Or, at least, he was supposed to love her—like a child, like a sibling, like a friend. Now, though, Tair feared Alyn only viewed her as the first; an irresponsible child, incapable of understanding the weight of her own life and too stupid, apparently, to be worth the effort of explanation. He was meant to protect her, and yet he hurt her all the same. Maybe he should have been protecting her from himself.

Shianna still awaited Tair's response, but when Tair

looked to the older Dwarf she could not convince herself to feel excitement. Yes, there was a dull sense of childlike wonder for the places she would see along the way, the beings she would meet, and the experiences she would be able to call her own; like she had dreamed when she was a child, she would now have her own stories, just like Alyn. And, besides, she supposed a journey to Doman was a return for her, too, in a way, having apparently spent ages four and five there before Alyn brought her to Mirte. True as that was, she never would have dreamed of adventure had she known it would come to this. She never would have thought of home in Doman, home in Sossoa, had she known it would mean a violent uprooting from Mirte. Try as she did for words, she had nothing to say to those she considered family but who had betrayed her all the same. She soundlessly left the kitchen and shut her bedroom door behind her.

In the silence of her sparsely decorated room, Tair realized that much of her maturation had invited a kind of push-and-pull of knowledge, a push-and-pull of relations and reality. In Mirte, she was raised to believe the same truths Elven children believed. Then, at the end of the day, Shianna would ask Tair what she had learned and proceed to alter or undo much of that education. In her early years, Tair wondered why Shianna did not just remove Tair from general education in Mirte and teach the young Human herself, which Tair had privately hoped for so that she would not stick out so sorely amongst the Elven children; in her later years, Tair understood that it was Shianna's way of ensuring that Tair always challenged what was portrayed as truth. Tair was ultimately grateful for this, but she often found herself confused over what to believe—or, rather, *who* to believe. Doman was a land of magic and spirituality, according to the Elves of Mirte; Doman was also Shianna's home, a nostalgic land of peace and bounty. Ultimately, Doman was a land for the Dwarves. Yet again, she would be an unusual sight, alienated amongst those she desperately wanted to connect to but who probably had far worse perceptions of Humans than the Elves she had grown up around.

And why Doman? What new betrayals awaited her there? So much of Tair's life remained hidden from her, and so what laid before her was life not yet lived, a life that she did not know if she could ever confidently claim as her own. Whether she liked it or not, that life was about to begin—just as life in Mirte died.

TWO

They had been walking for three and a half days before they arrived at Braasii, the waterfall-capped mountain between Mirte and Doman. From the lake at the base of the mountain, the Braasii River flowed out to meet with the other, smaller rivers in its path toward the Eastern Great Sea, passing through the Faery-ruled Ika-Ika Mountains along the way. Braasii's location, so accessible from the coast and near fresh water, invited cross-racial, cross-cultural interaction; now, the mountain was perhaps one of two known places in the world where all races coexisted—the second being Lawe—though this coexistence was not always peaceful, with no governing bodies to regulate such peace. The mountain itself was ruled only by its economy and no particular governing body, having little else to offer but trade and shelter. Of both, it had plenty. A winding path led up the western side of the mountain, up and up until, short of breath and physically fatigued, Tair, Shianna, Silaa, and Alyn finally reached the opening to a grand cave. Inside was a vast open market lit by torches and candles. Elves kept booths next to Dwarves; Faeries and their Fel children sold herbs and tinctures; even Humans, though far fewer in population, traded their crafts.

Tair did not remember her life before Mirte, which meant she did not remember her parents nor her infancy in Sossoa. Her memory lacking, it was as though she had never seen another Human. As such, her gaze lingered on her kin longer than anyone else in the market—intrigued or stupefied, she did not know. After feeling betrayed by Shianna, Silaa, and Alyn, all of whom she considered family, the Humans all around her provided a new definition of family. Accustomed to embracing what little family she had, Tair had never truly considered that kin could also include those who *looked* like her. Physical resemblance was something she did not share with Shianna, Silaa, and Alyn, but she had always understood that family was chosen; family was those she cared for and who cared for her in turn. Family did not betray family.

And yet.

Tair watched as her small family wandered away, all distracted by a Dwarf doing cheap card tricks at another booth. She did not follow them. She did not *want* to follow them. In fact, if she had it her way, she would have liked to disappear into the crowd around her and never return, which she privately admitted was a bit melodramatic. Given the circumstances, she felt it warranted. Mirte was isolated and homogenous; Tair belonged to an even more insular and distinctive group within Mirte; and then, to make matters worse, Tair was the only Human in the land. She was far too accustomed to singularity. Braasii, then, offered a whole new world of anonymity and freedom, both of which she had never experienced. As she scanned the market, looking for an out (if only temporary), Tair found an elderly Human beckoning her over. Almost on instinct, Tair weaved her way through the dense crowd until, finally, she arrived at the jewelry stall. Long chain necklaces with clear gems, rings with massive crystals, and gold and silver cuffs were strewn about, with little attention paid to organization. Tair tore her eyes away from the chaos and met the older Human's. Their eyes were just like hers: big, brown, and curious—with short eyelashes to boot. Tair had always felt her eyes to be rather abnormal in comparison to the Elves of Mirte, whose eyes were narrower, like Silaa's. Her eyes also did not match Alyn's, small and piercingly black; nor did they resemble Shianna's amber jewels. No, this Human had *her* eyes. Tair grinned despite herself.

The Human stuck out their hand and said something that Tair did not recognize: "*Aesolo-aso. So ahrra-aso ano?*"

Tair furrowed her eyebrows. She did not recognize the language, so she figured that the older Human was speaking Sossok, the official, constructed language of Sossoa. Though Tair had never seen the gesture before, she took the Human's hand in her own, if only to make her confusion less obvious.

They frowned at Tair and repeated what Tair was still desperately trying to translate.

Tair took a slight step back, embarrassment and fear coursing through her; embarrassment because she did not know the language of her own kind; fear because she knew, in her lack of knowledge, she had inadvertently revealed herself to be unlike other Humans. Perhaps Tair's family had been right to conceal certain information from her—she clearly was a little more irresponsible than she let herself believe. Still, her curiosity took precedence, and, even if she had stayed with Shianna, Silaa, and Alyn, she knew she would have forced them over to this booth despite their likely protests.

Tair wondered why the three had never taught her Sossok. The language was deeply rooted in the Human atrocities against all non-Humankind, but it was also a tool for survival for any Human, and especially a tool for the ever-vulnerable Tair. If they were so worried for Tair's safety, why had they not prioritized her cultural and linguistic familiarity with her kind, too? When they accepted the responsibility of a Human child, why did they not also take on the responsibility of familiarizing themselves with Human culture?

Tair did not have time to feel the anger bubble back up within her before the Human asked, "Nossok?"

Tair nodded, grateful that they had caught on.

"Hello," they said with a smile. "I asked how you are, though perhaps the moment has passed. My name is Moss. And yours, little one?"

Tair distantly noted that the Human did not introduce themself with their pronouns, so she assumed the Nossok neutral for them. When she introduced herself with a simple "Tair," she realized that she, too, did not include her pronouns, though she never minded how others referred to her. Instead of focusing on this minor detail, Tair found herself distracted by Moss's use of *little one*. In Tair's internal translation, the term closely resembled the Northern Elvish word *sitafei*, which she had only ever heard in reference to a beloved relative. Her cheeks and ears warmed.

Moss apparently found Tair's name hilarious. They put a hand on their robust belly and threw their head back, their long graying hair falling over their shoulders as they did so. Tair feared that this would draw too much attention to the pair, but no one paid any mind to the hysterical older Human and their customer. In Mirte, laughter always drew a crowd of curious Elves. Tair felt herself truly in a different world.

Moss said, when they realized Tair was not laughing with them, "No, little one, what's your chosen name?"

"My..." Tair swallowed. She knew the more questions she asked, the more she revealed herself to be unlike other Humans. Instead of revealing that she did not know what a chosen name was, she stopped herself and tried, "Tair is my chosen name."

Moss looked incredulous. They sarcastically said, "Yes, and Missiomisa is *my* chosen name." Moss glanced over Tair's shoulder, as if in search of her caretaker. Tair squared her shoulders and stood a little taller in hopes of seeming more capable. Moss recognized Tair's defensiveness, cleared their throat, and continued, "I'm joking. Just...all Sossok Humans I know have chosen names, usually from the natural world. For instance, my grandchild's name is *Opamaas*—Boulder in Nossok. You know, like those big rocks."

"I know what a boulder is," Tair mumbled. Moss had most likely lived a whole life around other Humans before their arrival in Nossoa. A life Tair would never truly experience, not like the rest of her kind. In Mirte, she had been an outsider, and even now, with another Human, she was still an outsider. Tair's heart clenched; she did not feel Human, and that was the most frightening thought of all.

If she was not Human, what was she? *Who* was she?

"Little one, I did not mean to insult you," Moss hummed. Their voice was like sugar dissolving in tea—or, perhaps, like a soft stream over a patch of moss. Tair relaxed a bit as they continued, "And, who knows, maybe things have changed since I lived down south."

Without thinking, Tair blurted, "In Sossoa?"

"Well, yes. That's where we're all from," Moss said as a fact. And it might as well have been fact; Humans were the only race living in Sossoa, and it had been that way for over five centuries at that point. More accurately, all *contemporary* Humans had originated from Sossoa. All the land had once been free to all the races, until the Doman War and the establishment of Sossoa. With Sossoa came the swift imprisonment and genocide of all non-Humans living south of the Darkwoods. In Tair's knowledge of Nossoa, there were no non-Humans who had escaped the founding of Sossoa to tell the tale of the horrors committed. There were fewer still in Nossoa who had lived through that era to speak on the atrocities, save Prime Eslania and other elders of Doman or the eldest of Faeries and Elves who isolated themselves to Lawe. By Tair's lifetime, it was a well-known fact that non-

Human races were not welcome in the Human land. Though she knew she would one day have to return to Sossoa for some mysterious reason no one would explain to her, Tair had never felt any true desire to journey to the land. Having been raised by and having spent most of her life around non-Humans, Tair was fearful of what such a homogenous culture would look and feel like, and at whose expense.

Tair nodded as she thought, not sure how to respond.

Moss seemed to understand Tair's unfamiliarity with Human culture and thankfully offered a part of their life's story without prompt. The older Human said, "I came to Braasii after my grandchild Boulder was born, maybe twenty years ago now. Once the first grandchild is born, grandparents are free of any responsibility to their children, parents now themselves. I decided I wanted to see more of the world, which of course came at a cost. One day I hope to return, but..." Moss shook their head after a moment of silent contemplation. "Well, I'm sure you know that Sossoa has been a brutal world since its founding, and I do not wish to return there as it is now. Though I have heard some hopeful whispers that this regime is nearing its end..."

Tair nearly gasped. Were the rebels truly so strong? There had been so little news of the Sossok revolution that had traveled to Mirte that Tair had almost thought it all to be a hoax—and so, then, would her own role in that rebellion have been a falsity. Maybe it was less that she thought it was a rumor, but that she *hoped* it was a rumor. Nonetheless, Tair felt some degree of pride that the rebels were accomplishing their goals, estranged from them though she was—pride that there was even *talk* that they could oust the most oppressive and violent regime the continent had ever seen. And, somewhat selfishly, she was also glad to know that her abandonment to the Darkwoods had borne some fruit. All her childhood loneliness...for freedom. For her kind's freedom, she supposed.

"With that," Moss continued on after they cleared their throat, "is there anything I can help you with? You must be a very special child to be out here on your own."

"I am not on my own," Tair quickly clarified. *And I am not a child*, she wanted to say, but she knew that would have been childish. Either way, she had to protect herself, unsure of whether or not Moss was a Sossok spy, or otherwise wished her ill. Even if she had remembered meeting any Humans before Moss, Tair had been taught not to trust them—taught not to trust her very own blood.

Moss hummed and nodded. After a moment of thought, they said, "Well, I don't mean to draw you from your party, but I do feel ill from the insult I have caused you."

"No insult unto mine," Tair said, but instantly regretted her Northern Elvish phrasing as Moss's face contorted in confusion. Clearly, this was not a common sentiment among Humans. Tair attempted to correct herself with a simple, "It's no worry."

Moss smiled and said, "I would like to offer you a gift to express my grief and, perhaps, protect you in your journey." Before Tair could object, Moss pulled out a pendant of a broken red crystal that had been pieced back together with what appeared to be gold. The pendant hung on a matching gold chain. Tair's eyes widened as she looked between the pendant and Moss. The older Human said, "I hope you will accept this as a gift of gratitude for your forgiveness."

Before Tair could accept the gift, Shianna had come up from behind and swatted the pendant out of Moss' hand. It hit the floor with the sound of broken glass, but Tair was relieved to see it intact. The crystal's resilience surprised her, though not enough to distract her from her shock at Shianna's actions—why, she wondered, did conflict have to be Shianna's first instinct?

The Dwarf's voice was low and serious when she told Tair, "Do not accept gifts from *Humans*."

Not quite offended but clearly seeking apology, Moss asked, "You would scorn me for my ancestors' mistakes?"

"I would scorn you for your current misgivings," Shianna said as she pushed Tair behind her, "and, yes, I would scorn you for your ancestors' *mistakes*." She spat the final word— the evils Humanity committed were certainly more than mere mistakes.

Silaa came to Shianna's side as Alyn pulled Tair a little further back from the altercation. No matter the ruckus they created, the crowd bustled on around them. It was hard to hear what the Dwarf and Human said to one another from Tair's vantage point. After a few moments of clearly heated dialogue, Moss threw up their arms and smirked. As if in announcement to the entire market, they shouted, "It was only a humble offering! We may all walk away unscathed." Wandering eyes from both patrons and merchants came to land on the altercation.

Shianna pushed Moss back, softly enough to not throw the older Human off-balance but harshly enough to indicate threat. Recognizing an eventual escalation, Silaa placed a gentle hand on Shianna's back. She guided her mate away from Moss, through the crowd, and into a sparsely populated pub located in a pocket of the market. Alyn followed the Elf and the Dwarf, and Tair begrudgingly trailed behind him, struggling to keep from glancing back at Moss.

The bar was filled with Elves, a kind of comfort Tair had not known she needed in that moment. Her whole life had been spent around the kind, so three days without an abundance of familiar faces felt like weeks. Alyn indicated to the bartender to start a round of drinks as the four of them chose a table in the farthest corner from the entrance. Shianna and Alyn huffed as they sat down, nerves still running high. Silaa watched her partner thoughtfully, while Tair looked to everyone for some kind of explanation.

Tair understood her fault; she should not have left the

group, and she certainly should not have approached a random Human, not when she knew the threat they could have posed to her and those she loved. As Alyn and Shianna had both explained many times, Tair's lack of knowledge of Human culture would have been a clear indication that she had not originated from Sossoa. Obviously, their warning had not been without merit.

Still. Conscious though she was of her mistake, Tair wondered why it warranted such an extreme reaction. After all, she figured, it was at least *partially* their fault for not teaching her how to be safe around, or even knowledgeable about, her kind. Shianna, of anyone, must have understood the feeling of recognizing one's own kind and feeling drawn to them, despite advice against it. The Dwarf had been isolated from other Dwarves for eleven years, living amongst Elves who held her up on an impossible pedestal and also responsible for a child of the very kind that had once been, and continued to be, an enemy to Dwarvenkind. Even though it had been dangerous, one moment with her own kind felt like a homecoming she had never previously known possible.

Shianna, Silaa, and Alyn all poured out a shot of *arne* and then set the pitcher in the middle of the table. Tair glanced at the alcohol but did not drink it. Instead, she folded her arms over her chest and patiently awaited explanation.

Finally, after some minutes of quiet drinking, Shianna said, "You cannot speak with Humans without one of us present, Tair."

"I *am* Human," Tair muttered. Even as she recognized and understood Shianna's worries, she disdained the thought that she would not be able to speak to her own kind on the rare occasions that she encountered them. These three had taken her from the kin she had adopted, the Elves of Mirte, and then denied her the kin she was born into, Humans. Tair resisted the urge to dull the edge of her frustration with alcohol and pushed her small glass away from her.

"You are both Human and non-Human," Alyn offered. "You have a...a complicated identity, as I am sure you understand. You simply could not see the harm in it."

Silaa scoffed and downed another shot, then refilled her small glass before she said, "You're being too gentle with her, Alyn. She is no longer a child. She did not see the harm in it because we did not *teach* her to see the harm in it." Then she turned to Tair to say, "You have been sheltered, Tair. It is not your fault, but you are not like them and, for the time being, you cannot find shelter amongst them. That Human, though we cannot know their intentions, could have used the pendant to lure and abduct you. Even that may be too generous—they could have done far more nefarious things to you, all in the name of Sossoa. You must understand that Shianna was protecting you the best way she knew how."

Tair tried to stop herself from rolling her eyes. Shianna gently repeated, "We are here to protect you. You have to believe that we only wish the best for you."

"I have to believe that? Really?" Tair scoffed. "Just three days ago now, you uprooted me from the only home I've ever known without a care as to how I might feel about it. Now you expect me to trust that you want the best for me? One thing is for certain, I am the only one here who knows what it is to be abandoned by your own kin and then raised by and amongst those who have no regard for the culture, the life, you are missing out on in the process. And you expect trust? Now?"

Shianna stared into her lap; Alyn spun his empty glass on the table; Silaa was the only one who dared meet Tair's eyes. She said, "We should have taken further responsibility for finding ways to connect you to your kind."

Tair shook her head. "It's not so simple. It wasn't until now that I realized how much of myself I am missing due to negligence—due to *your* negligence. I had this one opportunity to discover a *small* part of myself..."

Alyn, ever curious, asked, "Discover what?"

"Moss said that all Humans choose their names, and that all their names reflect the natural world." Tair frowned, taken aback by the fact that this was the most significant issue to her and not, say, the apparently upcoming demise of the Sossok empire.

Shianna gently questioned, "Would you like to choose your name?"

This, Tair knew, was the most confrontation she had ever had with her family—and it felt *good*. She did not know that there was so much trapped within her until it all started pouring out. She was disappointed, though, to realize that Shianna had, with one simple question, trivialized everything she had said. The issue was not that she had not had the opportunity to choose her own name—in fact, she had never really thought about it—but rather that a chosen name was another aspect of her Human identity that had been denied to her. How old were Humans when they chose their names? How did they decide what part of nature to make a part of their identity? Why had Moss chosen to associate themself with the moss plant? Tair wondered who she would be with a new name. Really, she wondered how important a name was in the grand scheme of her life. All she knew was that this detail had stuck with her.

And still a name was not the crux of the matter. Tair shook her head again. "That's not the point."

"Well, then, what would you like to know about Humans?" Shianna asked, a tinge of defensiveness lacing her voice. As a Dwarf, her opinion on Humans was biased at best, bigoted at worst, which Tair knew was justified for far too many horrible reasons. Even then, Shianna had the most knowledge of Humankind of the four of them.

And she had kept it from Tair. Tair had never considered asking questions about her Humanness, but this was in an effort not to offend. She had learned there was simply some information she would not be privy to, like what she was meant to do when they arrived at Doman—what she was meant to do when she eventually had to return to Sossoa. She had learned not to question her racial identity and had inadvertently categorized her own kind as hidden knowledge.

Overwhelmed and frustrated, Tair answered, "I don't know yet. Perhaps you should have asked sooner."

They stayed the night at the Eeg Inn. The space had been carved into the center of Braasii and claimed to have space for all, regardless of race or creed. "Faery nests, too!" they boasted on the small sign just outside the main entrance. Their hospitality ended at their entrance signage, though; the old Elf who ran the inn was rather frustrated by the fact that they had to find room for four guests at a moment's notice—especially four rather irritated and intoxicated guests who only planned on staying one night. All four of them were also terribly filthy, coated in sweat and grime from three days of travel without wash. The innkeeper did, however, take a particular liking to Shianna and Silaa. The pair apparently reminded them of themself and one of their late mates. Shianna laid on the charm and managed to negotiate for two separate rooms, both of which needed to be more thoroughly cleaned before they were ready for new inhabitants, Tair thought. Shianna and Silaa had a room at the end of the hall, and Alyn and Tair were a few rooms down. The "doors" were actually simple cloths, probably to increase air circulation throughout the mountain; as such, Tair could hear Shianna and Silaa enthralled in one another, giggling and moaning and making all the sounds Tair had previously been able to shut her door against back in Mirte.

Alyn and Tair, on the other hand, were careful to tiptoe around one another. They had lived together as long as Tair could remember, but they had never shared a room. Even when she was a child, she knew not to bother Alyn when he shut his bedroom door—no matter how pressing the issue. One night around the age of nine, Shianna had been away with

Silaa somewhere in the woods south of Mirte, and Tair had cut her hand on broken glass. Rather than disturb Alyn, she rinsed and bandaged her hand on her own. The next morning, as Alyn rebandaged her hand, he thanked her for her respect of his privacy, though he did suggest she find an elder Elf if it ever happened again. Now, they shared a space and Tair wished desperately that Shianna had negotiated for three rooms instead of two.

"It's nice here," Alyn mumbled. He sat on the edge of his bed, closest to the cloth sheet that acted as a door, and ran his hands over the knitted blanket. Tair was surprised to hear him speak. Still harboring anger from earlier, she remained silent in (admittedly childish) defiance, but also in an effort to create some semblance of privacy in such close quarters. They still wore their clothes from the day, soiled with sweat and alcohol and conflict. Alyn added, "It's comfortable, though surely different than what we are used to."

Tair shrugged. "It's familiar enough to me."

"Yes, you never added much...personality to your room." Alyn cleared his throat and twirled his finger. A small cloud of smoke spun through the air and very slowly dissipated, trying to find its way back out of the mountain's halls. "Why is that?"

Tair scoffed. This was the most Alyn had said to her in weeks. Upon reflection, his silence had grown as their departure from Mirte neared. She felt some degree of pleasure knowing that he felt guilty for his actions. For a moment, she had forgotten the depth of his betrayal.

Only for a moment. Tair maintained her silence.

Alyn did not repeat his question. Instead, he said, "I appreciate a nice room. Mine was very pleasant—not that you ever saw it. I suppose it is the Faery in me."

Tair was curious, she had to admit. It was a quality Alyn had instilled in her. She was willing to quell her curiosity when it came to her own life and where that life was going; however, when it came to other cultures, she could not help but wonder at their customs. She cleared her throat and prompted, "Nesting?"

Alyn perked up at Tair's inquisition, her first word since they arrived back from the pub. "Yes, nesting! I don't remember telling you, but nesting is quite important for Faeries. Usually, Fel can be indifferent to the practice, but I was very close to my Faery parent, and he strongly encouraged nesting. My Elven parent...well, he is very adventurous. I suppose I have a little of both of them: I love to travel but I take pride in creating safe spaces for myself."

Tair had never heard about Alyn's parents, not really. If she had, it was only in passing, and never open to further question. As much curiosity as he had for other cultures, he was very protective of his own origins. Presented with such a rare opportunity, Tair absorbed every detail that she could. She sat on the edge of her bed facing the wall, and finally answered, "I didn't decorate my space much because I knew we would leave as soon as I felt settled in."

Alyn coughed. Cautiously, he asked, "Is that so?"

"Well, it came true, didn't it?"

"You tell me."

Before that last day, Tair had never truly felt settled in. But the morning of what she considered to be the worst day of her life, she had woken up with a particular lump in her throat and a tightness in her chest when, for the first time ever, she realized that Mirte felt like *home*. At least, as close to home as she would ever come. She should have known something was wrong. All her life, she had kept what she felt was a healthy distance from the Elves in her community and only deeply connected to her small family of Shianna, Silaa, and Alyn. Beyond them, she made a point to weaken her memory of specific names and learned, too, not to reveal much about who she was, why she was there. Unfortunately, as the only Human in Mirte, she always drew attention to herself; fortunately, as the only Human in Mirte, Tair was also the sole authority on

Humanity, which she often used as an excuse to remove herself from communal activities. Excuses as to stamina or fatigue, excuses of cultural or philosophical differences... anything that got her out of integrating into a community that she knew she would one day abandon—a community she desperately wanted to be a part of and feel important to but knew she could never truly integrate into, whether it was her choice or not. She bit her lip as she wondered who she might have become had she embraced the only land she remembered as home.

She stopped herself. That potential Tair was a fantasy. However she felt now, she knew this severing from her adopted homeland would have been worse had she *known* Mirte.

Alyn cleared his throat, yet again avoiding telling Tair something. After a few minutes of silence, he said, "I know it is important to feel like you've found your kin. I hoped we could be that for you by default, but sometimes you need to look another being in the eyes and recognize them as you might recognize yourself."

Tair, still facing the wall, glanced at Alyn. He rustled around in his jacket pocket as he thought, and then added, "Perhaps I was not thinking clearly, but I went back to that Human and retrieved the pendant for you. I wasn't able to get the chain from them as their prices were rather steep after our altercation but..."

The red crystal rested in his outstretched palm, the familiar gold lacing gleaming in the lantern light. Tair turned to him, transfixed on the object that had meant so much to her yet caused so much strife. It reminded her of Mirte, where gifts were more than mere objects. Where colors were more than simple perception. Red, she had learned, was the color of independence and love. The crystal was so precious that she hesitated to take it from his hands, so she cradled his cold hand in her smaller palms. Finally, she took the crystal between her fingers and turned it into the light, savoring the warmth it garnered after a few moments in her possession. Not knowing what else to say, Tair smiled at Alyn and bowed her head as she said, "Thank you."

"If you're worried about...whatever Shianna and Silaa were worried about, I took it to a Faery to get it cleansed—as cleansed as it can be, that is. That's important, anyways. Keeping stones cleansed." He returned the smile and tucked his chin to his chest. "I hope we can someday prove ourselves to be kin again—despite our differences in blood and our disloyalty to you." He met her eyes when he added, "Though I want you to let me know if you ever need to be Human."

After nearly a lifetime in Mirte and two nights sleeping in the dense forest between there and Braasii, Tair was quite accustomed to the Red Sun waking her. However, when she rose in Braasii, there was neither the Red nor Yellow Sun through a window or hanging overhead to indicate the time of day, and there was no one demanding that she be awake at a particular hour. She yawned as she sat up. With a sinking heart, she wondered if life within mountains meant an inherent absence of natural light. Perhaps it would be the same in Doman, but Tair could not say for sure, having little knowledge as to how light—or really anything at all—functioned in Doman. How long would they stay in the unfamiliar land? How long would she have to go without the suns?

And, again, those questions: why Doman? Why now? What fate awaited her there?

In attempt to run from her anxieties, Tair jumped out of her bed—but far too quickly. All the blood rushed to her head at once. Once her vision had cleared, she dragged on some clothes and placed the crystal Alyn gifted her in her pant pocket. This was all a struggle in the dark; Tair and Alyn had put out their lanterns the night before and only the light from the hallway illuminated the small space. She did not bother re-lighting the lanterns, though; in a moment's time, she was out to greet Silaa and Shianna and inquire as to whether or not they had seen Alyn that morning.

Tair had expected herself to be hesitant at the thought of seeing Shianna and Silaa after their conflict the night before, but her legs carried her forward with a level of confidence that her mind could not yet muster. She wanted to foster that feeling.

The Dwarf and the Elf were not difficult to locate. Tair heard them stirring in their room as she approached the sheet that separated their space from the hallway. Shianna threw back the sheet when she heard Tair approach and pulled the Human into a tight embrace. Tair let her hands hang by her sides. Though Tair could not say the same for herself, Shianna rarely held grudges, and she *never* got hungover. In fact, Tair often found Shianna more pleasant after a night of heavy drinking.

"Come in, come in!" Shianna beckoned. Silaa, her nudity only half-covered by a thick blanket, smiled at Tair from inside the room.

Tair frowned as she looked upon the scene. Confident though she wanted to be, she more desperately wanted to be out of their company. "I'm just looking for Alyn."

Quickly, Silaa said, "Oh, he's out with some Fel he met over breakfast. You know how Fel get when they find each other. Like, 'no one else understands me,' or whatever. It's very dramatic."

Tair understood Alyn a little better after their conversation the night before, however brief it was. Now, she saw more clearly that he must have been indulging in the embrace of his own kin after so long surrounded by Elves, just as Tair had tried to with the Human Moss. He had been surrounded by a kind who only saw and vaguely understood one part of him for so many years. Tair stomached her annoyance from Silaa's comment and asked, "Have you both already started your day?"

Shianna glanced back at Silaa. Where Tair expected a suggestive smirk between the two, she saw only worried eyes. The Dwarf quickly altered her expression with a smile as she repeated, "Come in."

Tair shifted her weight. Shianna looked over Tair's shoulder, and then adjusted her gaze to meet the Human's eyes. Tair said, "I suppose I should eat before we depart, too, if everyone else has started their day."

Shianna finally took it upon herself to pull Tair inside the room. She shut the curtain behind the flustered Human, as if it would ever serve as an effective barrier. Silaa sprang up from the bed, evidently clothed from the waist down, and pulled on Shianna's quilted coat from the chair to the side of their shared bed. Though fastened tightly at the waist, the fabric was much looser on her than it was on her mate. Shianna shoved all of their belongings haphazardly into the satchels they had taken with them from Mirte. Tair watched all of this unfold in silence, the mates erasing all trace of themselves from the room. They then pushed Tair down the hall back into her own dark room and the three of them stood inside for a moment, quieting their quickened breaths as they listened for any sounds outside the room.

Tair started, "What—"

Shianna and Silaa shushed her. For a few minutes, the only sound came from their short breaths and the occasional shuffling of feet in the hall. Tair, having earlier believed that Alyn had found safety amongst his kin, now worried for him. There was something going on—and Alyn was the only missing piece.

Silaa snapped. A little white light emerged at the tip of her index finger and illuminated their worried faces—illuminated, too, Alyn's absence. Tair had preferred the darkness. At least there, they could hide from their current reality.

"We cannot find Alyn," Shianna whispered, though anyone could have heard what she was saying through the flimsy curtain.

Tair furrowed her eyebrows—*cannot find him?* It was not like him to disappear without warning, as adventurous as he was.

"No, we can't find him, Tair," Silaa hissed, as though she could hear Tair's thoughts. "He didn't check in with either of us before he left this morning, and we all know how heavily you sleep. All his stuff is still here, right?"

Shianna then rustled around the room, aided by the light Silaa provided. The Dwarf pulled Alyn's travel journal out from between the mattress and the frame. She held the object carefully; Alyn kept few personal possessions with him, but a notebook was one thing he never went without. No matter where he went, even just to gather food for the next meal, he brought his journal. He said he wanted to share it with his parents when he reunited with them, wanted to leave some proof of his existence behind when he died.

Shianna put the notebook into her own satchel. If there was one item they would all protect for the missing Fel, it was his journal. Shianna continued, "This is not a safe place. Those who live here...those who visit...What did you say to that Human?"

Tair was taken aback. She could not see how the two issues were related. With her arms crossed over her chest, she huffed, "I didn't do this."

"I'm not—"

"She's not saying that," Silaa took over, probably for the best. "Share what you told the Human yesterday."

Tair resented the implication of fault but detailed her conversation as best as she could remember. Shianna had Tair repeat the bit about the chosen names. Tair obliged: "She thought it was funny I had chosen Tair as my name. She said Humans chose names to reflect the natural world, but I promise I didn't ask her any further questions. I was careful."

Shianna cursed under her breath as Silaa palmed her forehead. Finally, as Tair began to worry that she had made a grave, irreversible mistake, Shianna said, "I knew something about the names was bothering me. We should have given you a name..."

Shianna trailed off in contemplation as Tair frowned. She asked, "*Given* me a *chosen* name?"

"We should've had you *choose* a name," Silaa corrected Shianna, "for our travels. That's a small detail that immediately differentiates you from the rest of them."

"Them?" Tair frowned.

"Please, Tair," Shianna groaned.

Tair hung her head and muttered, "You think it had something to do with Moss?"

"Alyn may have just left to explore without telling any of us, but we all know that is unlike him," Silaa said. Shianna was silent, a mode which Tair knew she reserved solely for planning. Silaa continued, "Someone could have taken him because they thought they could get to you, but it is not your fault."

Where she briefly could not imagine herself at fault, guilt now clouded her thoughts. For clarification, Tair asked, "*Thought* they could get to me?"

Shianna considered her words for a moment before she clarified, "We've always had a plan. For all of it. Some parts of it, you have not been privy to, as you know. We knew that, if one of us was compromised, the others would have to move on."

"Not for my sake," Tair insisted with a scoff. She could barely stomach the thought that her safety would surpass any of the others'. Her circumstances were different than theirs, perhaps held a different weight, but she still would have readily given her life for any one of them. As much as they had tried to steer her away from any ideas about being "chosen," they also treated her life with a care that they did not afford themselves. This was one moment where, given the chance, she could prove that she did not view herself in a superior light; whatever fear she experienced for her own safety and what a breach of that safety meant on a greater scale, she would overcome it in order to save Alyn—to save any one of them.

Neither one responded to Tair, though. She looked to Alyn's bed—the bed where he had sat the night before, where he offered a bit of compassion to her in a time of grief, where Tair even more thoroughly understood that they were not as different as she had originally assumed. Once she had gathered up the courage, she announced, "If you both do not mind, I would like find him."

THREE

They were thorough, but Braasii was a heavily populated maze and no single face—and especially not the face they were looking for—could have stood out in the crowd. Eventually, they had to pay for a bigger room at the Eeg Inn, where they stayed in case Alyn came looking for them. Besides, they needed the space (and the time) to recuperate at the ends of their long days of searching. Even Shianna, who had been to the mountain on a few separate occasions, admitted that Braasii had changed so drastically since her visits that the realm was as new to her as it was to Tair and Silaa.

The times when they thought they had finally found Alyn—in conversation with a merchant, or out for a drink at a pub—it turned out to be a different Fel or a Human with dark features. Tair made the latter mistake too often, still growing accustomed to the fact that other Humans existed outside of her imagination. Their eyes particularly drew her in. Every Human she encountered had her eyes, sometimes different in color but always similar in shape and, Tair privately noted, always the same in spirit. They all contained parts of what she saw in herself but had never been able to name after so many years isolated from her kind. Tair wondered if she would ever be able to look at another Human without the childlike sense of wonder that was inherent to recognizing oneself as a part of a larger whole.

On the third night without sign of Alyn, Tair sat in the pub they had all spent their tumultuous first night in, hoping the Fel might miraculously appear beside her, and then they would be able to continue their journey. Not that Tair knew where that journey was taking her, but at least it would not have been as stagnant as her current reality. At the bar, Tair nursed a glass of the cleanest water she had ever consumed, which she assumed had come from Braasii Lake. She was careful not to intoxicate herself in those days; though she probably would not have been able to—nor have particularly wanted to—put up a fight, she wanted to be as aware of her circumstances as possible.

Out of the corner of her eye, Tair saw a Fel sit down at the bar. They had black curly hair just like Alyn's, rare amongst Fel, as well as poor posture just like Alyn's and similar mannerisms...Tair rushed over to them and exclaimed, "Alyn!"

The Fel jumped back. Tair met their fearful eyes and realized that she had disturbed an otherwise peaceful night for them. She excused herself, gave them a loose coin she had in her pocket to buy their first drink, and hurried back to the Eeg Inn.

When she awoke the next morning, Silaa and Shianna had already begun their search. Lacking motivation and fearing the worst, Tair spent hours lying immobile in bed, desperately trying to recall one positive memory of Alyn that to hold onto if she never saw him again. It proved to be quite the difficult task. Losing Alyn shrouded her memory of him in a thick haze. *No*, she reminded herself, *I have not lost him*. Rather, Alyn was, in that particular moment, lost. She gripped the red crystal he had gifted in her hand and traced the gold laced all throughout the rock with her thumb. Thankfully, Shianna did not take it away when she had discovered Tair with it, despite her abhorrence toward Moss and the thought of trusting any gifts from the Human—from Humans in general. The Dwarf had understood that, if nothing else, at least Tair had one reminder of Alyn.

Seven nights later, still with no sign of the Fel, Shianna, Tair, and Silaa all felt trapped in Braasii. Their lack of success weighed on them and, as such, they made a collective decision to toss out their "no alcohol" rule. As unwise as it was for Tair to drink, as unwise as it was to cripple her awareness, she would have accepted the repercussions of incapacitation. If nothing else, she would be able to, for one moment, forget her guilt and fear and, sometimes, grief. The three of them had overheard talk of a pub carved into the northwestern side of the mountain and set upon it as their destination late one night. Torrential early spring rain poured down outside, which made their brief trip outdoors tumultuous, to say the least. They were very grateful and very wet when they finally arrived inside—where they were the only non-Fel beings. All conversation halted, patrons distanced from one another, and the bartender shot them a glare, though the smirk on their face was unmistakable. Almost perturbing. Regardless, the three intruders were too distracted by their own problems to notice (and too accustomed to Fel company to think their arrival odd), and so they claimed the only available table at the front. Silaa went to buy them all something to drink while Tair and Shianna sat down. Rain from the pub entrance licked at their ankles; a cold breeze beat at their backs.

Conversation quietly resumed around them as everyone settled into the strangers' presence. After a few minutes, all of the Fel patrons returned to their varying degrees of normalcy. Silaa finally seemed to be able to communicate with the bartender, though apparently through a thick language barrier.

Finding opportunity in this uniquely private moment between herself and Tair, Shianna ventured, "We have not included you in many decisions over the years."

If Tair had a drink, she would have spit it out. *No kidding.*

"It was for your safety, we thought back then," Shianna continued.

"Oh?" Tair leaned in to hear more as the volume in the room increased.

But before Shianna could continue, Silaa came back with three bowls of some unfamiliar fruit. Tair and Shianna frowned at each other in confusion and then directed their questioning looks to Silaa. The Elf smiled and shrugged. She said, "Apparently, *arne* means something different in whatever language they speak." She popped a piece of the cubed pink fruit into her mouth, closed her eyes, and said, "You *must* try this."

Shianna ate a piece. She sank back in her seat with a smile, arms limp at her sides and a soft moan escaping from her mouth.

Tair tried a small bite, a little warier than her companions but always willing to try new foods, another quality Alyn had instilled in her. The initial flavor was flowery though slightly more bitter than expected. The aftertaste, though, was precisely like the *pasu* cakes in Mirte: all sugar and no substance. It was wonderful. Tair ate her bowl in a matter of seconds, just like Silaa and Shianna, before she began to feel the relaxant properties. She felt at peace in the room, but not in control of that peace. With an unintentional smile spread across her face, Tair asked, "What was that thing?"

"I don't know, but I want more," Silaa mumbled through lazy lips. She squinted her eyes at Tair's hands on the table and asked, "Have you always had, um...like a bird...claws? What a funny word...claws..."

Tair glanced at her nails and found them appropriately filed, one thing she found comfort in controlling. The drug apparently affected Elves and Humans in different ways. And, again, in different ways than Dwarves.

Shianna stomped her feet on the floor, leapt up from her seat, and danced in a little circle despite the absence of music. Tair laughed, which the Dwarf took as a prompt to lift Tair from her seat and twirl the two of them around the pub. None of the other patrons paid any attention to either of them, more comfortable with the strangers' loopiness than with their sobriety. Perhaps the three posed less of a threat this way. Tair eventually got Shianna to sit down again, though now in a fit of laughter, and realized that she was the most in control of herself of the three. With that responsibility, she went up to the bartender to ask for some water for the table.

"They're funny, your friends," the bartender said. The psychoactive fruit in her system must have made her think the Fel, who once had a heavy language barrier with Silaa, spoke Nossok, without even the slightest accent to indicate where they might have come from. Tair thought it strange—everyone she had met from Braasii and the immediately surrounding lands had a distinctive accent, their pitch usually on the higher side.

After what felt like a few seconds of deliberation but was, in reality, a few minutes, Tair decided to ask, "You speak Nossok?"

They seemed taken aback. "Of course."

"She"—Tair gestured to Silaa—"said you didn't know what *arne* is."

They smiled. "Yes, she said that."

Tair blinked and thoughtlessly explained, "*Arne* is an Elven liquor."

They laughed, full-bellied. "Yes, yes. It certainly is."

"Well then..." Tair braced herself on the bar stand as she inexplicably teetered on the smooth rock floor. As her eyes began to blur over, Tair muttered a weak, "What was that? Who...? Who are you?"

The bartender handed Tair a glass of water, which she gulped down without question. Over the sound of her thirst, she heard the bartender say, "That was *pitai*, and we..."—the patrons of the pub joined in to simultaneously say—"are Faeries."

When Tair finally awoke, she did not know where they were, but she was thankful that her headache was gone. It was damp and dark, with only a single candle in the corner to light the scene. Shianna rattled the bars that blocked them from escaping into...nowhere. The bars blocked their access to a cave without a clear exit. Silaa groaned under the candlelight and—

Alyn, gaunter than before and almost sickly, laid sprawled out across the floor. When he noticed Tair had opened her eyes, he said, "All together again. I was wondering how long it would take you all to realize my capture."

"Stop bringing that up—we could not have known," Shianna snapped, balling her fists at her sides. She did not like being confined nor having her loved ones confined, and she undoubtedly blamed herself for failing to protect everyone. In fact, Shianna was *unaccustomed* to confinement, since Domani Dwarves had done away with "cages," as she called them. She shook the cell bars yet again and shouted for someone to let them out, then mumbled, "It's not like these Faeries were particularly boastful about their conquest. They're *your* kind—you understand them. Just tell them to let us go."

On Alyn's behalf, Tair retorted, "Faeries are as much his kind as Elves."

"They're *both* part of my lineage"—Alyn shot a look both their ways—"but that does not mean these particular Faeries are any more intelligible to me than they are you. They're strangers to all of us." He spun his index finger. Where usually this action produced a ring of odorless white smoke, Tair noted that nothing happened now. The cave had probably been enchanted to limit its prisoners' magic.

Shianna groaned. By the tone of their bickering, Tair knew that they had already had this same conversation several times before she awoke.

Tair barely paid their bickering any mind, still adapting to the reality of Alyn's presence. She wondered how long she had been unconscious, completely unaware of the fact that they had found him. Of course, Tair had not expected it to go this way; the Fel looked as though he had not eaten in days, his lips were chapped, and his normally curly hair was limp with oil and sweat. Even still, they had *found* him. As much emotional turmoil as they had caused Tair in recent weeks, she was grateful to have her family whole again.

Tair's legs ached more than anything else, though she could not place why. When she applied pressure to them, she realized that she had been bruised at some point—whether she had fallen or been intentionally injured, she did not know. She nursed her wound as she asked Alyn, "How long have you been here?"

Alyn huffed. "I suppose as long as you all have thought I was missing"—Tair estimated ten days—"plus the additional time you were unconscious. It feels weeks longer when you do not have consistent meals or water."

Apparently, Shianna had not thought to ask Alyn about his physical conditions when she had regained consciousness. Indeed, it seemed that she had not even thought about her own hunger until Alyn mentioned his, something that Tair felt true for herself, too. Now, Shianna was curious; she asked, "How long have you been without food?"

"I've slept twice now since my last meal of bread and that horrible fruit," Alyn answered. Tair deduced that Alyn had been subdued in the same way the rest of them had. Perhaps the Faeries had masked themselves as Fel to draw visitors in; the race was so exoticized that many sought them out simply to observe, almost like one would marvel at a mystical animal. Of course, Alyn, Silaa, Shianna, and Tair, had all fallen into the trap for completely different reasons.

"What about water?" Tair asked. Her throat was incredibly dry. So dry, in fact, that she considered lapping at the conspicuous puddles on the floor. She shook the thought out of her head. Those puddles were probably not water, she realized as her nose attuned to the faint scent of urine and feces and blood.

Tair nearly gagged and tried to focus instead on a much more positive circumstance: they were all together. Well, they were all *imprisoned* together, but the exact details did not seem to matter so much as the overall state.

Alyn took a moment to answer Tair's question. "I'm not sure." He sat up with a grunt and wiped his dirtied hand on his already filthy tunic. He reeked, but Tair could not say she smelled any better. Alyn continued, "I think I've slept three times since the last offering of clean and unlaced water. Liquid is not as hard to come by—in whatever form it comes." With a wince, he gestured to the puddles at the floor of the cell.

Shianna and Tair gave each other horrified looks. Silaa sat silently in the corner with her hands wrapped around her knees. If Shianna was doing poorly, Silaa was in another realm of suffering. The drawn-in eyebrows, the tight lips, and the resting flex in in her jaw—Silaa was confident and collected, but it was clear to Tair that confinement had severely impacted her mental state. In her first words since Tair awoke, Silaa asked, "What do they want with us?"

Alyn shrugged. "I know almost as little as you all." He crossed his arms over his chest, revealing a hole in his top and an open wound at his side. Despite their circumstances, it did not look infected. He seemed like he had more to share, so his three cellmates gave him the silence to share what he had gathered so far.

He continued, "I do not think they are malevolent, though I could be wrong. They have taken care of my wound." He pressed into the open, though clearly healing, wound without the slightest wince—he felt no pain. "I imagine they would not care about my health if they wanted to hurt me. Perhaps we have just stumbled in at the wrong time, or they think we're someone else."

Shianna derided, "What, they're looking for another group made up of a Dwarf, an Elf, a Fel, and a Human?"

The Dwarf sat down next to Tair. She had been on her feet for hours, it seemed, as she rubbed at her bare soles. All of them were barefoot and...in different clothing than Tair had remembered them in last. In fact, none of their clothing seemed to be in their usual style. Averse to discomfort, Silaa regularly wore light and loose clothing, but she now wore something tight and conservative. She struggled against the fabric. Alyn, on the other hand, always wore black, no matter the occasion, a kind of ritual for him. Now, he wore all white, and his usual jewelry on his neck and wrists was absent. Shianna often stuck to clothing that prepared her for any circumstance—which meant she was always ready for a battle, as she never knew when she would have to defend her loved ones. Now, though, she wore clothes closer to Silaa's preferred style.

And Tair...Tair wore a *dress*. If any of them knew Tair, they would know that she never, ever wore dresses. She thought them impractical and representative of a freedom she did not have, not when her whole life had been pledged to a cause she did not even thoroughly understand yet. The embroidered dress she wore now was nice enough, though covered in various stains and quite ill-fitting.

As though it had once belonged to someone else.

"Whose clothes are these?" Tair blurted.

This took everyone by surprise.

"You say they're not malevolent," Tair said slowly. "Then whose clothes are these, and why are we wearing them?"

The others began to pull at their apparel, nearly disrobing to ease their discomfort.

Tair did not know when the authority had fallen on her, but she suddenly found herself in command of the room. Once their initial stress had passed, they all turned to Tair to hear whatever theory she had developed—whether or not such a theory existed. As they did, she smiled at her chosen family, nearly forgetting where they were, nearly forgetting how they had gotten there, and nearly forgetting how they had taken her life away from her a little under a fortnight earlier. Just nearly.

Tair replaced her smile with a frown. "I don't mean to make this already uncomfortable moment more uncomfortable, but we could have gotten to Doman safer had we asked for help in Mirte."

Silaa nodded in agreement before Shianna shot a glare her way. Tair grew curious as to what Shianna had been about to say before they had consumed the psychoactive fruit, seemingly near apology. There were more pressing issues at hand, though—like their *lives*—so Tair decided to put aside her curiosity for a later moment. Instead, she said, "It seems like none of you planned for something like this. And now I have to get us out of it."

Though they had all turned to Tair for guidance, Silaa clearly doubted the younger Human. She asked, "And how do you think you'll do that?"

Tair paused. The weight of this new responsibility was almost crushing; not only did she not want to be responsible for any harm that might come to her and her family, she also did not want any harm to come to their Faery captors. She owed them nothing, really—after all, they had drugged and imprisoned her and those she cared about—but she also abhorred violence, a quality Alyn that had instilled into her and one that Shianna had made entirely unnecessary, forever ready to fight for her family at a moment's notice.

"I don't know too much about Faeries," Tair started. "And, even if I did, I would not have any information on these particular Faeries, isolated as they are. And still..." She swallowed, hoping that her next words would not cause any more harm.

It did not take long for the Faeries to check in on them. After all, they had been making quite a ruckus for what felt like an hour, in accordance with Tair's plan. If they were truly trapped in some alternate dimension accessible only to these Faeries, as Tair had reasoned, their captors would have felt a disturbance in that dimension with all the shouting and banging on the cage. From there, the prisoners were meant to subdue one of their captors and bargain for their release. Sure enough, after all their noise, one exasperated Faery appeared in front of them. Their pale blue skin that somehow provided its own light to the small cave, a bald head, and piercing green eyes. They were also only tall as Tair's hips, though undoubtedly an adult. No matter their size, they clearly held all the power in this situation, and Tair wondered if subduing them would even be possible.

The Faery peered up at them all with a mischievous smirk so similar to the bartender that Tair now understood the truth of all the tales she had heard in her youth: Faeries could mimic the appearance of any race. She would have been amazed had she not been imprisoned.

The Faery said, "We're not liking the noise."

Shianna scoffed, while Silaa mumbled for the group, "We're not liking being imprisoned."

"Forgive her," Alyn covered. He did not need to take responsibility. In fact, they had all appointed Tair to lead, but Alyn gave himself the responsibility to communicate between his family and their captors. This was probably for the best, anyway; Tair herself had very few distinct encounters with visiting Faeries from the Ika-Ika Mountains, with Faeries in general. Though she hoped never to be captured by Faeries again, she did make a mental note to ask more questions about Faerykind, as she meant to with Humankind, too. Unfortunately, Alyn was the only resource Tair had. Thinking it unreasonable to ask him to divulge all his cultural knowledge, especially since he was rather private of his background, Tair decided she would either learn in her own time, or she would let the topic come up naturally, at Alyn's pace.

Alyn continued, "We would just like to know why you are holding us here, if it please you all."

The Faery laughed, which shook their whole body up and off the floor. When the apparent comedy of the circumstance settled, as did their feet on the floor, they said, "If we told you, the Mountain would find out!"

"The Mountain would find out?" Tair echoed, unable to contain herself but knowing that each moment was precious if her hastily constructed plan was going to work.

The Faery nodded. "That ruins everything."

Shianna shook the cell bars; Tair could *smell* the anger on her friend. The Dwarf snarled, "Listen, I don't care what it ruins. I demand you release my friends and me right now—or you are going to regret the outcome."

Tair looked at all of their clothes again, then looked to the Faery telling them that they could not know what was happening lest it spoil something in (or for, she supposed) the Mountain. Her clothes, along with Alyn's, were a little tattered and bloodied—but Tair now realized then that it was not her blood. Shianna and Silaa...their clothing fit awkwardly and had been brought in or stretched out in places that did not fit the curves of their bodies. Gathering what little information she had, Tair resolved, "You're going to sacrifice us."

When the Faery said nothing, Tair immediately forgot her plan, replacing instead with fear. Shianna and Silaa looked to her, horrified, while Alyn kept his eyes trained on the Faery on the other side of the bars.

"You're going to sacrifice us," Alyn repeated. He accepted this resolution very quickly for having believed their intentions kind-spirited an hour earlier. Perhaps he had thought the same thing but did not want to worry his companions. Perhaps he did not want his companions' first impressions of Faeries on their journey to be a negative one. No matter what he thought, which Tair could have never known, he did ask, "As you have made clear, you can neither confirm nor deny this fact, but may we find a middle ground?"

The Faery paced in place, spun around, and shouted out. A few seconds later, two more Faeries materialized around them. The three spoke in a hushed foreign language that even Alyn, who claimed to know almost every language in Nossoa, did not seem to recognize.

The Faeries nodded after a moment and spoke in unison: "The Mountain will still accept you as suitable sacrifices, if your deaths will not bring great harm our way. We only act in service of what provides us life and cannot defend against an organized force. We hope you accept these terms."

The admittance that they were not strong enough to overwhelm armies was certainly a show of vulnerability by the Faeries, but it did not immediately help the four prisoners' circumstances. Tair's death would not have brought armies to Braasii; her still unknown role in the Human revolution, she thought, could have been replaced, and no rebel would have left their own cause to fight in a foreign land for one small being, as she was. And, if not Tair, they were out of luck. Alyn slumped to his knees in exasperation, struggling to come up with some sort of compromise that would not result in their untimely end.

When all hope was lost, though, Tair was surprised to hear Shianna clear her throat. Though the Dwarf hesitated, she masked her nerves, breathed deeply, and said, "Should you kill me, great harm would certainly come your way." A pause. Tair blinked, looked to Alyn or Silaa for explanation, before Shianna continued, "For I am Prime Heir Shianna Kasgan of the First Family of Doman."

The cell dematerialized around them, back into the bar they had originally stumbled into. And rightfully so; the world had crumbled around them. Alyn, Silaa, and Tair were bound to chairs in this reality, but Shianna stood freely, her head hung to her chest. After the darkness of their imprisonment, the midday light from the entrance to the pub was a harsh yet welcome presence.

The light was not nearly as disturbing as the fact that a once-familiar being had suddenly become a stranger. Shianna had *never* slipped, *never* mentioned being of royal blood—and, it seemed, she had never even divulged her well-guarded secret to Silaa. The Elf looked at her mate with large wild eyes, a red hue spreading across her face as it often did when she was angry, which was rare.

Alyn looked between Shianna and the floor. Calculated. Silently connected the dots. Tair wanted him to scream, wanted him to share what raged on in his head; Tair wanted someone to make what felt like a dream into reality.

Prime Heir. Shianna was next in line to the throne of Doman. When the current Domani Prime died—when Shianna's *parent* died—the Dwarf Tair had known for over a decade of her life would rule an entire kingdom. Despite her sameness in circumstance, imprisoned by Faeries like the rest of them, Shianna had become incomprehensible in a matter of seconds. The Faeries, nervous and silent, bowed in her presence. The way the captors now viewed the captured was a radical mismatch to the Shianna that Silaa, Alyn, and Tair had always thought they knew.

Tair's throat was dry from a mixture of dehydration, screaming, and shock. Still, she said, "You must be joking." The Human could not control herself nor the words that slipped out of her mouth, dangerous though they were. If Shianna was lying, then they probably would have been sacrificed in seconds, without the slightest chance to protest. The Faeries tentatively met Shianna's eyes, searching for proof just like Tair.

Shianna cleared her throat and flipped down her bottom lip for all to see. Permanently etched into that sensitive peace of flesh was the Domani symbol that the Dwarf had drawn for Tair many times when she was younger. Shianna's words still echoed in her mind: *Only those with royal blood may don this symbol.* Mesmerized, Tair had looked to Shianna with wide eyes and questioned for hours about the pain level, the particular reason for the symbol—had asked why she could not have one. Surely, she had argued, the Dwarves would know that she, a Human, was not actually of royal Domani blood. There was something sacred about it that Shianna could not— rather, would not—explain. Tair was ten years of age then. She didn't blame herself for her foolish questions, though she did curse herself for never asking to see Shianna's inner lip. All the details the Prime Heir had provided about royal life had led the young Tair believe the Dwarf had just been well-educated, or simply connected to the royal family, perhaps as a committee member or an aid or a counselor—something predictable, reasonable, easy.

Not royalty herself.

The Faeries bowed their heads again when they recognized the symbol. After all, Doman was the strongest standing kingdom in all of Nossoa; their royal sigil was similarly as distinctive. It was irrefutable: Shianna was Prime Heir to the throne of Doman.

"You will release them," Shianna commanded, her tone foreign to Tair's ears. It demanded respect, even and deep as it was, and she enunciated each word as though she had been trained to speak without mistake. Did she make a conscious effort to make mistakes in the past, or had she now accessed a part of herself that had laid dormant for years? Tair—and, she imagined, Silaa and Alyn, too—now questioned everything the Dwarf had shared about herself and her life before Mirte. The weight of every word had just been increased a hundredfold. Tair felt lightheaded.

Their chairs and binding disappeared beneath them. They all fell back, then stood on wobbly legs, dusted themselves off, and stood a few feet back from Shianna.

All were silent, patient for Shianna's next words. "No harm will come to you, and word of your transgressions will not be shared. All we ask is you release us without harm."

In unison, the Faeries nodded, creating a path in the crowd straight to the world outside. Shianna glided out, stood at the opening, and turned back to her family, who stared at her incredulously. After a few moments simply watching one another, the three ran out with her before the Faeries changed their mind.

They had their priorities straight, after all.

Their priorities also included cleaning themselves, changing into familiar clothing, and eating—all in that order, even though their stomachs growled louder for proper nutrition with each passing moment. They knew they could not stomach anything with the layer of filth that shrouded them. When it came time to eat, they did so while overlooking Braasii's waterfall and lake. They took comfort in the horizon—the relative smallness of their being—and avoided the questions that accumulated in their minds. There would be a time for all of that, but now was the time to nourish themselves.

Tair started to make a list of questions she would ask as she stuffed her mouth. They had picked up some sort of Elven sandwich from one of the vendors in the market—a market in which Tair could no longer place Moss. She barely thought about the older Human now, though, focusing instead on the spicy meal she hastily consumed. Next to her, after having finished his own meal, Alyn kept the mountaintop from feeling too silent. He talked about his own kidnapping and then about the mundane, like the pleasant, cool weather that evening. He interrupted a lot of important questions that sprang to Tair's mind. *Who else knew?* was pushed aside for Alyn's "Oh, and then the weather! I just loved the weather in Mirte, didn't you?" Or, *why couldn't you have trusted us? At least Silaa?* was crowded out by, "The further south we go, even just in Nossoa, the colder it gets. Always a trade-off." And so it went. Tair would have stopped him if it had not been so nice to have some degree of mindless noise to keep her from becoming too overwhelmed by her thoughts.

Alyn continued on in his unreciprocated conversation and, later, song. He improvised some tune about the mountains and Faeries and, Tair realized after a few minutes, he was telling the story of their collective capture. Never too soon for a ballad from Alyn, she supposed.

When they had all finished their meals, though, Alyn did not feel such an incentive to continue talking. He straightened his shoulders, cleared his throat, and took a sip of water. His attention was on Shianna instead of the horizon, instead of the setting Yellow Sun just in front of the still-looming Red Sun.

In a hushed voice to match his disbelief, Alyn asked, "Prime Heir Shianna Kasgan of the First Family of Doman, huh?"

Shianna scoffed. "You do not have to say the whole thing." She shifted where she sat, bringing a knee up to her chest to have something to wrap her arms around and comfort herself. Tair had expected the Prime Heir to be larger than life itself, as such a title suggested, but Shianna just folded in on herself. Indeed, Tair had never seen Shianna so nervous about anything, and they had lived together for the better part of eleven years.

Shianna added, "I do not identify with...all of it."

Alyn raised an eyebrow. "And which parts do you identify

with?"

Shianna shook her head and muttered, "It wasn't meant to come up like that."

Silaa huffed and asked, "How was it supposed to come up, then?"

Shianna winced. After a moment of opening and closing her mouth, she simply chose not to answer the question, fair as it was. Had Shianna thought that she would not have to say anything until they arrived at Doman and everyone began treating her as royalty—as who she truly was? Or would she have told them earlier, when they were planning to leave Braasii, knowing her companions—her family, really—could refuse to continue onward with her? Whatever her plan was, she did not share; instead, she told them they could ask any questions they liked. If Silaa's question had been evidence enough, though, the Dwarf felt no obligation to reply. Tair wondered if that was a learned diplomatic tactic. Really, she had no knowledge of how any of this worked, as a similar political structure had not been employed in Mirte. Doman was unique in many ways, but their monarchal government was especially new. The First Family of Doman still ruled, the legacy of their essential role in the Doman War still holding fast centuries later. Chief among those who had brought about Dwarven success in the war was Doman's first Prime, Sasnakkna Kasgan—who Tair now realized was the famed grandparent Shianna always spoke of.

Shianna waited for questions. Unfortunately, in that moment, Tair's list left her, her questions so blurred that none stood out. In all honesty, she wanted this all to be over with, so that things would get back to normal. Whatever normal was now.

Alyn started with, "How will we be expected to treat you in Doman?"

"Hopefully no different than you already do," Shianna answered hurriedly. "I never told anyone because of the kind of behavior that comes along with being around...someone in my position. It's tiring. I wanted something different, at least for a little while."

"Eleven years is not 'a little while,'" Silaa scoffed.

Alyn moved on to say, "Just because you do not want us to treat you differently does not mean we will not be expected to. I do not want to offend anyone."

"And if you offended them, they would come to me or the Prime."

Silaa, whose eyes had been trained ahead for the better part of ten minutes, whipped around to face Shianna. With all the malice she could muster, she said, "When? When did you think would be the appropriate time to tell us what we all rightfully deserve to know? Tell *me* what I deserve to know? How long until you thought to tell the truth? Until they sat me down by your throne? Until I inevitably had to take on responsibilities I never consented to but am obligated to simply by association?"

Tair had not totally considered Silaa's position as Shianna's mate, but she understood the fear in a newfound obligation that she never chose. Silaa and Shianna had often spoke of where they would end up after all of this was over, after they had gotten Tair as far as they could and had completed their mission—when they could finally sit back and know that the future held only sunrises and sunsets, and then a final sunset. Now, it was clear that Shianna would never get a break from a life of danger and obligation; she was bound to it as much as she was to Silaa, for better or for worse. The mates had always indulged in the fantasy of a simple life.

And that had been stolen from Silaa.

"I had to do the same," Shianna said, a little defensive. "In Mirte. I never chose to become a spiritual leader, but your kind pressured me"—Shianna stopped herself. "But I was pressured into it. I, too, had to take on responsibilities I did not foresee."

Silaa glared. "It's not the same, and you know it."

"I wanted to live a normal life," Shianna muttered.

"At whose expense?" Silaa said. "Your life is not just *your* life, Shianna. Your life is mine and it is all of ours, too—and you have wrapped us up into something from which we can never escape. You have no right to manipulate us and expect no repercussions. You know I was already reluctant about Tair, this risk"—Silaa gestured to the Human she spoke of—"and I would have never considered *this*. You've compromised all of us; you've compromised our lives. *My* life." The Elf shook her head, mumbling, "Eleven years...*eleven* years..."

Shianna's arrival had come a few years after Tair had settled into her childhood with Alyn and into life in among the Northern Elves of Mirte. The young Human had made some loose acquaintances but knew that she was somehow different from the other children. Somehow. The details had been fuzzy. It was only when Shianna arrived and later brought Silaa into Tair's life that she had begun to understand, at least to a minor extent, her role in the larger scheme of things. One night, she had stayed up late to eavesdrop on adult conversation, her healthy curiosity regarding the mates Shianna and Silaa getting the best of her judgement. She stood behind her bedroom door, left slightly ajar, to listen to the quiet voices in the next room over.

Shianna and Alyn's voices had been hushed as they spoke to Silaa. The Elf had recently moved into their modest cabin in Mirte's southeastern lands, away from her family home, after having just declared Shianna her mate. The two were happy, so in love that they were nearly blind to conflict. Every small disagreement had been insignificant, every quarrel just another minor obstacle to move around. Tair had derived great pleasure from seeing Shianna in such a joyous mood. The one being she had looked up to and trusted most was thriving—and she could not have thought of a better thing than that at nine years old.

"We have something to tell you," Alyn finally said. Tair had almost thought they had left the room, quiet as they were, but Alyn's serious voice cut through the silence. Actually, he used the voice that the young Tair had thought he only reserved for the rare occasions that he scolded her. He was rather gentle with her, she had noticed when she compared herself to the other Elven families she had seen in Mirte. Alyn only ever stopped Tair when she was doing something that might have caused her, or someone else, harm. Tair was careful, though, and she liked that Alyn trusted her. Now, with this tone equipped in a conversation she was not meant to be a part of, she was both captivated and a little frightened. She pressed her ear more firmly against the crack between the door and the doorframe, never minding the discomfort it caused her.

"So serious," Silaa teased, but Tair heard her shift a bit in her seat after a beat of silence. "So serious" had been right.

"You have asked about Tair for quite a while, why we have a Human child in our care, why she's our responsibility to protect," Shianna said slowly. At the mention of her name, Tair sat up. "We suppose, now that you live with us and we have claimed one another as mates, that we owe you an answer."

A silence had settled over the room and Tair longed to be with them. She wanted to see their faces; she wanted to understand why a conversation about her needed to be had without her. Instead, she had shut her eyes against the darkness of her bedroom and attempted to open her ears wider to listen for anything she was missing.

It was Alyn's turn to speak. "I first heard about the child when she appeared in the Darkwoods a little over six years ago. A Human child abandoned in the Darkwoods would not have come from the insular settlements just to the north of the forest, and the Humans of Lawe and Braasii would have no reason to venture so far south to desert a toddler. We knew the child had to have come from Sossoa." Tair furrowed her brows—she had been told that she had originated from one of the Human settlements north of the Darkwoods that Alyn spoke of. Accepting that Alyn, Shianna, and Silaa were the closest to family she would ever get, she had asked few other questions about her biological family. To know she had originated in the land everyone only spoke of with contempt, to have been abandoned by that land and the Humans that lived there, and then to be found in a place shrouded in so much mystery and magic...She shivered but kept listening.

Alyn continued, "She was found and rescued, of course, and brought to Doman to determine her fate. They had considered elsewhere, but it is the most central location in the realm and the Dwarves did not want to discuss the fate of a Human, to discuss what that Human *meant*, if not on their terms. I traveled there and was met by some other Fel, some Elves, some Faeries, some Humans and, of course, Prime Eslania of Doman." He paused in anticipation of Silaa's questions, a million of which raced through Tair's own head, but the Elf did not interrupt. Alyn continued, "In order to protect the child, we were contained to a small, trustworthy council. Many passed it off as a hoax, others had little care for the child, but I, like some others, have heard rumors for generations..."

Alyn had remained silent for a few minutes after he trailed off. Tair worried that he had heard her shift where she sat on the floor—Fel ears were sensitive, she had learned—but he must have chalked this up to her kicking in bed. He seemed to seriously consider what he would say next, eventually deciding to say, "I have known for a long time what it would mean for a Human child to be left in the Darkwoods on their own. The oppressed, subjugated, enslaved Humans of Sossoa"—Tair heard the Fel shiver—"were finally prepared to enact serious change. Rebellion. Revolution. The child would be the first sign to Nossoa to prepare for turmoil and, eventually, unity. From there, the Humans would work to grow their ranks, strengthen their numbers, and eventually move to overcome their oppressors. In the meanwhile, the child would have to be protected, so that the first phase of—how should I put this?—an intellectual revolution could be completed."

Silaa did not respond. Tair was in shock, desperate for the tale of her own life to continue. She did not know what intellectual revolution meant exactly, the words foreign together and still foreign apart, but it sounded terribly exciting if only because it was unknown.

Shianna said, "I had been...working with Prime Eslania for years, and after a while I decided I would join the Fel—join Alyn—to protect the Human child in Mirte. It bodes well for future Dwarf-Human relations and, well, we all know the evils that have been and continue to be perpetrated in Sossoa."

No, Tair had thought in her young age, *I do not know*. Of course, she did not voice her interjection.

Shianna continued, "It is time for a change, and they cannot do that without any and all the help they can get. Protecting Tair is protecting a possibility—protecting a future for unity and liberation and peace."

Silaa suddenly jumped up to pace as she thought, frightening Tair enough that she knocked her head against the door. It slammed shut. Alyn shuffled over and softly asked through the door, "How long have you been listening?"

Tair answered in a whimper, rubbing her forehead.

"Come out," Alyn whispered, and Tair obliged. She faced the three older beings, looking up to them with wide, inquisitive eyes. Was she really the fated child that had been spoken about for generations—and why her? What was she really—*who* was she?

Glancing down at the child before her, Silaa asked, "And why is she *our* responsibility?"

Alyn answered, eyes locked on Tair's, "Because we could no longer accept complacency."

Eleven years Silaa had known what Tair meant, who Tair was—and, for eleven years, Tair had believed that was the height of the information she had to keep hidden about her and her family. She had believed that was all that she needed to know—at least until they arrived at Doman, where she knew even more was waiting to be revealed. Apparently, though, Shianna had her own secrets. She had never worked for Prime Eslania; she had been the Prime's *child*, the Prime Heir. Shianna had educated and politicized Tair—but had left out a key detail as to her own political role in the world. Offering her own interjections to Tair's education, Silaa had sometimes cut in to denounce royalty and its role in a liberated world. No wonder Shianna had always gone silent at Silaa's ideological interruptions; she was a part of the very structures her mate wanted to dismantle. Whatever Silaa had reluctantly signed up for, she had never been prepared for this. None of them had.

"It's not that simple," Shianna offered after her mate asked her why she did not see the hypocrisy in a fight for a new, free world while she was entrenched in a traditional, rigid one. Tair had wondered similarly in the past: what role did any attempt at governance play in a world so varied, so diverse? Unfortunately, Shianna did not answer in the philosophical, but the personal: "There are things I mean to challenge when I return to my responsibilities—things that would be easier to challenge when older generations have passed and no longer seek comfort in centuries-old structures."

Silaa scoffed. As she had expressed many times, she believed there would never be a time without those who desired to maintain the "old world," as it were. Rather, those birthing the new world had to give those attached to the old the respect that accountability and change afforded. No room for excuses, she always argued.

Shianna ignored Silaa's scoff and said, "As time went on, I did not want it to change us. I love you. I love what we have." Tair considered the use of love here, nearly weaponized on

Shianna's tongue. The Dwarf said next, "Since the day we met, we knew we were mates. It is something we can never rid ourselves of."

Untrue, Tair thought, *and unfair*. She knew that, if this hurt Silaa enough, she and Shianna could have performed a ritual to sever ties with one another.

Shianna finished, "This is merely...a complicating factor."

Without a word, Silaa stood and walked away from the group. She muttered some obscenities to herself as she stormed off, down the side of the mountain and retreating back inside.

"I understand why you did it," Alyn, ever the peacemaker, said. Almost inaudible, he added, "But it may have been information that we all had a right to know, especially me. I could have helped you." Though less shrouded in anger, he followed after Silaa.

When they had both gone, Tair finally asked, "What were you going to say—before we ate that fruit?"

"What?" Shianna had not expected that. She shifted to look Tair in the eyes, but Tair did not return the attention.

Tair clarified, "You said you had not included me in many decisions over the years, for my safety. And...you seemed like you had more to say before Silaa came back with the fruit."

Shianna chewed on the inside of her cheek, thinking a moment. Then she said, "Yes, we have not included you in many decisions over the years. I think you understand why that is, but that is no excuse as to the pain it has caused you. As much as we want you to be this...*beacon*, as much as the world needs that from you, we have not truly let you *feel* that responsibility. Of anyone, I understand what it is to have a duty no one thinks you are prepared for, but you have to accept, nonetheless. And we must accept it. For your pain, though, I wanted to apologize: *Rak grasora'a*."

Following Shianna's Domani apology, which always held more weight than any Nossok apology, the Human and the

Dwarf sat silently for some time. The Yellow Sun descended for the night and the Red Sun chased after it. Bugs chirped from the forests below. A *missai* bird flew overhead with those eyes all around its head, able to see the skies above and the ground below all the same. Those birds were particularly magnificent to Tair, and always had been; their multicolored plumage was thick, their feathers long, and their talons were obviously sharp, even from miles away. Tair's last memory of the bird was vague, harbored from a life she could not remember; they were distinct nonetheless, rare as they were. One of the Elven Elders explained to her that the birds signified a need for the observer to pay attention to the world around them, to take nothing for granted. Tair took a deep breath as the bird flew into the distance, long wings distinct against the starry sky. She could feel Shianna watching her in wait, perhaps expecting an acceptance of her apology, or expecting everyone she loved to leave her.

Tair maintained her reflective silence. She had a strange sense that she did not *want* to know what else Shianna was hiding, nor what those lies meant for Tair herself. Instead, she wanted to live in the lie of temporary ignorance a little longer. There, she did not have to anticipate; there, she still had some degree of agency over a life that she rarely felt to be her own.

Tair eventually said, "It has been a long day—a long couple of weeks, really—and you all have hidden a lot from me throughout my life. I understand some things and others...I do not. I know there is more for me to learn, only to be revealed when you finally decide I am capable of understanding. I have accepted that I have to wait, and I have come to expect the lies—or the delayed truths. Silaa and Alyn have not. This news is a greater shock to them than it might be for me. You're different now. Or, you've had this different aspect added to our image of you." Tair took a deep breath. "I'm just tired, Shianna. I'll begin to try to forgive you tomorrow."

The Red Sun set; the moon rose, full and bright over Braasii; and, no matter how their lives changed, the world did not. The two let the night pass them by without another word.

FOUR

Their slow journey to Doman continued the next morning in relative silence—save Alyn's singing, of course, which was its own kind of silence. They only took two breaks the first day: one to replenish their fresh water and then again when Tair's legs tired. Unfamiliar with (and truly unprepared for) such extensive physical activity, Tair held the group back. They might have made it to Doman in half the time if not for her, for which she did not feel guilty. If they were going to uproot her from the only home she had ever known, the least they could do was go at her pace. Later, when they decided it was time to make camp, they found a natural clearing in the forest. Tair, unexpectedly comfortable on her makeshift bed of blankets, promptly fell asleep to woodland sounds echoing all around her. In the early afternoon the next day, when the Yellow Sun began to rise in front of the Red, Shianna woke the snoozing Human before they all set on their way again. The days passed.

Tair grew to enjoy the silence that the forest brought. There was a kind of clarity and awareness there, one which she had previously been unaccustomed to. Much of her life had been crowded by noise—noise meant to hide the silence beneath the surface. Alyn singing, Shianna educating, Silaa teasing...In the woods, Tair found herself contained only to her own mind, which was the only place that now felt like her own, unseen and unknown to anyone but her. The relative stillness also provided the necessary space for Tair to try to forgive her family; unfortunately, in the middle of their fourth day heading south, the silence broke.

"Just as Alyn, I have been wondering," Silaa said, in her first words since their departure from Braasii, "what will be expected of us in Doman."

The whole group stopped and turned to face her where she stood at the back of the party. The Elf was distracted by the canopy above, denser and darker in than the woods that lived between Mirte and Braasii. The Red Sun and Yellow Sun shone down in tiny rays across the forest floor. One soft ray fell across Silaa's face. As beautiful as she looked in that moment, Tair knew she was angrier than she let on, asking the intellectual questions before the emotional ones.

Tair wondered which were more important.

Shianna beamed, Silaa's first words since Braasii more than welcome. She inched closer to Silaa but stopped herself when her mate flinched back a step. The two were nowhere near emotional intimacy, let alone physical. Shianna looked around, eager for any degree of forgiveness, and suggested, "Perhaps we can break for lunch while I answer your questions?"

Shianna grinned as her companions cautiously drew in around her and sat on the cool forest floor.

So it went; she answered their questions. Or, at the very least, she answered Alyn's questions, though Silaa had started the conversation. Doman, though a monarchy, was not a rigid bureaucracy. Even if it had been, Shianna insisted that her family treat her no different than they had those eleven years they had known her. She explained that she and the Prime acted more as figureheads with practically permanent places in an otherwise representative government. Each year, the inhabitants of Doman voted on whether or not to oust the family; each year, their power was only strengthened. Tair did not know if she agreed with this system; in Mirte, all matters were decided by an ever-shifting council of Elves who were most directly affected by the given issue. She had never seen any problem with the way the Elves governed themselves. As she familiarized herself with the rest of the world, though, she recognized how many different, organized systems were put in place to keep communities and community members under control. Except, of course, in Lawe...and, of Elsewhere, no one knew.

Despite Tair's wariness, Shianna insisted that the Kasgans were well-liked, both due to their legacy and their continued commitment to the betterment of Domani Dwarves. Shianna, a particularly active participant in liberating oppressed Humans in Sossoa, was viewed as a respectable Prime Heir to her parent. Revolutionary spirit was embraced among Domani Dwarves; even still, there were certain systems, like the monarchy, that none dared rebel against. Perhaps they did not know of a better option, Tair thought privately, though she could not have said what that way would have been. Never mind her own politics, Tair was glad to know that Domani Dwarves widely celebrated Sossok revolutionary efforts. Any attempt to weaken Sossoa, especially after the Doman War and the subsequent genocide of non-Humans in the southern realm, was commonly seen as appropriate retaliation for both the past and the present.

And, of the revolution, Shianna claimed that it was relatively strong—and safe, at least for now. The divided worlds of Doman and Sossoa had always been intimately linked and became even more intertwined the more power consolidated in Doman and the more power weakened in

Sossoa. Their separate but shared goals intrigued Tair—though she was more intrigued by the Human rebels, who had grown up in Sossoa without non-Humans but somehow understood that unity across races and borders was an essential part of revolution.

Shianna went on to clarify that no one need expose who Tair was to anyone outside their small group, save Prime Eslania. Shianna explained that she had, at least in part, hidden her own identity so that she would not have been associated with Tair in those early years. Secrecy had to be employed at many different levels, which was also part of why they had chosen to sequester Tair away to Mirte in the first place; Northern Elves were unconcerned with Human revolution and had little knowledge of the legend that would have followed Tair anywhere else. Evidently, it had been a smart choice, as none had ever questioned the true nature of Tair's inclusion in the community, abnormal though it was.

Still, in Doman, many Dwarves were going to be suspicious of a young Human living in their midst after so many years of deliberate separation—suspicious enough to harm a Human, Tair did not know, nor did she want to ask. She had no doubt that some would be wary of her. What worried her more was the Domani involvement in the Sossok revolution; preparing to support the Human rebels in any way they could, they also undoubtedly had enough knowledge of the rebellion to know its origins. With that, Tair wondered whether anyone would recognize her as the very Human whose abandonment to the Darkwoods had signaled the start of the revolution. No matter her precarity in circumstance, Tair knew Shianna would protect her. Tair also knew that part of Shianna's protection involved lying, a tactic she would involve Tair in, too. Tair was to pretend to be a liaison between Doman and some falsified Human settlement north of the Darkwoods, seeking support and peace and collaboration. She was only meant to share that information if directly asked.

Also in the information Shianna shared was the particular geographical organization of Doman. Prime and Prime Heir regularly lived toward the top of the tallest and centermost mountain, to the north of the lake. To journey to that final destination was going to be unlike anything Tair had ever experienced—or Silaa, for that matter. There would be some physical struggle to overcome as they all adjusted to the altitude and life within mountains, making their ascension through the mountains rather slow (but worthwhile, Shianna claimed).

Apparently, Shianna said, everything would be easier to understand when they arrived. She then turned to Silaa to say, "As my mate, they expect some things from you as well."

Silaa averted her eyes.

"I won't allow them to test you," Shianna offered, "and you do not have to take on a political role—in fact, I would urge you not to. The Dwarves would not trust you to know us, to know our politics and traditions. We have some...problems with Elven perceptions of our kind. Still, they will know you are my mate. They will want to know how suited you are to that role, and they will expect you to behave accordingly, even if you feel betrayed right now."

The Elf scoffed. "Then it is a test."

"Not if I can help it."

A silence fell over the group then, but after a moment Shianna returned to an explanation of Domani affairs. Alyn asked some questions about meals, clothing, ritual; he wanted to know as much about Domani culture as possible so as not to insult anyone who could later blame his mistakes on Shianna. And, as for Tair, she had entirely different questions on her mind—questions about her own life and her responsibilities, of Doman and the timing of their departure from Mirte. It was not the time to ask those questions, she thought, fearing that Shianna would have brushed her aside.

Shianna's dismissal would have hurt more than not

knowing, so she kept silent.

That night, a little further south, Alyn built a fire with twigs and other scraps Shianna had gathered. Silaa had successfully scaled a nearby tree and remained up there, desperate for time away from the beings she had spent the past eleven years with. She was clearly willing to forgive, or at least consider reconciliation; otherwise, Tair thought she could have very well turned back to Mirte. Tair herself might have returned to Mirte—if the destination they sought now did not contain all the answers she had been waiting for. Not brave enough to turn back, Silaa stayed nearby to maintain physical closeness, but refused to participate in any acts of kinship, while Tair sat with Shianna and Alyn to eat and sing.

Well, Alyn did most of the singing, and Tair sometimes hummed along if she recognized the tune. The moon and stars shone down on them, and they lost themselves in trying to find constellations. Alyn called one *Faery's Breath*—an arrangement of six stars that looked more like a pyramid than a breath to Tair's untrained eyes. For a moment, her world moved with ease.

Only for a moment.

Silaa nearly fell from her perch as she scrambled back down to the group. In a hushed though hurried voice, she said, "I saw someone—some*thing*, maybe—moving in the distance. We're not alone."

Then Tair heard it: the rustling between the trees, the quiet crunch of a twig underfoot. Tair was not sure where the sounds came from. She felt terribly jealous of *missai* birds at that moment, their many eyes able to see in even the darkest nights. Right now, all they could do was blindly spring into defense. Shianna readied herself for action as Alyn moved to Tair's side. In all truth, Alyn would not have been effective as any kind of defense—or offense, for that matter. He would have gone down kicking, that was for sure, but Tair never thought of him as a fighter. He was certainly too understanding to fight anyone without asking questions beforehand. *Why do you want to fight right now? Where is that reaction coming from? Is there another way we can solve this problem without our fists?* He was an explorer, after all, and there was not much left to explore if he killed everyone and everything that had made his journey the slightest bit difficult. Still, the Fel appeared to be more than prepared to fight. Tair wondered which of his stories he had watered down to instill pacifism in her.

For her part, Silaa seemed *anxious* to fight, almost desperate for someone to direct her rage toward. Tair wondered at Silaa's instinct and quickly reflected on her own; she would not have intentionally harmed anyone, so she was thankful that her family was ready to fight for her when faced by an external threat. Then again, could she accept that their fight could cause another harm—or even death? She could not have killed for herself, nor did she believe she could have killed for anyone else. The thought that someone would kill for her frightened her far more than the foreboding threat that stalked through the woods toward her and her family. She bristled in the cold, trying to see through the thicket, but the firelight infected her vision and she could only hear as much as her ears were capable.

A high-pitched whistle sounded and then, following immediately after, a low hum erupted. The hum got louder and louder until—

Tair was sure that whoever was out there stood just beyond the next line of trees. They were surrounded, no doubt—and what could they do about it? Tair looked to Shianna, surprised to find the Dwarf relaxing as the sound grew nearer. In fact, she began to join along in the hum herself, almost overcome by pleasure. Finally, she gasped, "I am home!"

From the thicket emerged about ten to fifteen Dwarves.

Skin just as dark or darker than Shianna's and hair braided into too many styles to identify, they all resembled Shianna in the way that only Dwarves from Doman could; they were her kin. They moved in closer to Shianna, who welcomed their company, but paid little mind to Alyn, Silaa, and Tair, who had each transitioned from battle preparedness and fear to intense curiosity in a matter of seconds. Of all the information that Shianna had hidden from them throughout the years, she had never veiled her love for her kin, which meant her companions simply had to trust that they were in safe company. That was not a difficult task to achieve, what with all the joy and laughter in front of them, all the exchanges of adopted pronouns and tales and gossip, all in Domani—a language and culture that Shianna had undoubtedly yearned for. She had spoken Domani with Tair throughout the Human's childhood, but Tair never had true fluency, which only came from shared experience. Now, Shianna was among those who understood her and her origins, who communicated like her, who *looked* like her. Knowing what that felt like, even to the smallest extent, Tair understood Shianna's loneliness even deeper.

Tair also began to understand—and only *began*, she emphasized for herself—why Shianna had not told them about her origins. They would not have understood what it meant to be a Dwarf among Elves, even more to be the Domani Prime Heir in Mirte, founded on a completely different political structure. However they may have treated her would not have compared to the comradery she was accustomed to. She had said that all the information she provided them would be easier to comprehend when among other Dwarves, and she was right. Tair saw how she moved with them, how she conducted herself, how she shared time and space with them all. The Human, the Elf, and the Fel could only watch until Shianna was able to set aside her excitement and make room to introduce the three of them to her kin.

"We have arrived at the outermost defense line of Doman,"

she explained, arm wrapped lazily over the shoulder of another Dwarf with a full beard and long, braided hair. Their styling was different from anything Tair had ever seen, and she supposed then that self-expression would be different from what she had learned in Mirte.

"I have lived and trained with everyone here"—she looked around lovingly—"since I was young and, oh, I have not laid eyes upon any of them in years." She leaned over to poke the one who sat at her feet in their ribs and they doubled over with laughter. They all experienced such joy in one another's company—a joy Tair once had with her family but now felt much harder to access.

Shianna nearly sang as she introduced her family of over a decade to her family of centuries: "Alyn, the Fel, was one of my closest friends in Mirte. The Human is...here as a diplomat to meet with my parent." Shianna, drunk off the presence of her Dwarven family, only just caught herself before she blew their cover in a matter of seconds. Tair also noted that her introduction as "the Human" earned a mixture of glares and soft, curious glances from the group. Tair felt more anxiety from those varied looks than she had when she felt her life threatened moments earlier. Shianna continued, "And Silaa is the Elf, my mate."

The Dwarves all grunted simultaneously. Tair started at the noise, but realized it was one of acceptance and not of upset as she had previously come to understand. They all watched Silaa with keen eyes, watched her calculated movements around the fire, and willingly pressed their foreheads to hers when she offered hers to them. When she had finished, one of the Dwarves asked no one in particular, "An Elf?"

Shianna nodded. Her hands roamed over her friends as she refamiliarized herself with them. Touch was clearly an important part of their relationships to one another. She kept her eyes trained on Silaa, though, just as the others did. They seemed to move as a unit—as a family, as kin. Tair shook the jealousy from her mind.

In Nossok, another Dwarf chimed in, "Wait until she has to explain that to Omma!"

And the group erupted in a hysteric fit of laughter.

The Dwarves had taken them to a Domani base about twenty minutes further south. There were plenty of rooms and plenty of beds, having once been a Domani military barrack in those early, nervous days just after the Doman War. It now served as a lazy defensive line and, evidently, housed some of the Dwarves Shianna loved more than life itself—and Dwarves who reciprocated those feelings in turn. Tair wondered if this was going to be the case as they moved through Doman proper. How loved was Shianna really among her subjects?

Tair also wondered how much the Dwarves of Doman would embrace *her*. It had taken about two hours for Shianna's Dwarven family to accept Tair, at least as a part of the background. It also may have helped that Tair had tasked herself to individually make acquaintances with each Dwarves. Some were intrigued by her and kindly introduced themselves, but there was certainly still hesitation when it came to her presence amongst them.

On Silaa's part, she had apparently been able to get over her conflicts with Shianna for at least one night, or at least for a couple hours before they were finally able to rest their heads. The next morning, Alyn and Tair had awoken with the Red Sun and were in the middle of drinking a morning cup of tea when Shianna, Silaa, and two of Shianna's friends stumbled out of a room down the hall. They all wore a variety of clothes that did not correctly fit any of them. Tair's private assumptions about Shianna's relationship to her friends— *friends?*—was correct, it seemed. More than that, Tair was relieved that Silaa and Shianna had returned to a degree of their normalcy; the mates already had enough to work through as it was.

Rather in Silaa's fashion, Tair teased, "Have a nice night's sleep?"

One of Shianna's friends—Sano, he went by—laughed as he placed a hand on Silaa's back. Sano had been kind to Tair when she first introduced herself. What she did not expect was to have Sano share his whole life story with her only moments after meeting: how he first discovered he was *konos* (one of the Dwarven gender identities Tair had learned about that same night); how he discovered his sexuality among his friends, Shianna included; how all of his faith in the potential of Doman and the Domani monarchy had kept him alive on multiple occasions. What he did not talk about, it seemed, was his familial history. In fact, not a single Dwarf mentioned their families. That was to say, they did not mention their *biological* families, which was perfectly comfortable for Tair as she knew so little about her own. Even Shianna had not divulged much of her family history as Tair grew up. Of course, that may have been because she had been hiding a serious detail about who she and her family were. More than that, though, it seemed that it was Dwarven custom not to attach so much to blood relatives, but rather to claim collective ancestors and chosen family. Tair noted several times that they all claimed Shianna's grandparent, who had helped to win the Doman War, as their own, referring to her as "our grandparent," rather than "Shianna's grandparent." It took a moment to understand it all, especially as Tair's grasp of Domani was mostly conversational and had been confined to a completely different context. To complicate matters, these Dwarves' use of Domani was mixed with Nossok; just when Tair thought she understood what someone had said, they added something else that had her stumbling to translate.

Silaa kissed her mate, indulging in their moment of calm. The fourth one—Nomos, recognizable mostly for their braids that nearly reached the floor—simply watched the three of them together and hummed a song.

Alyn caught the tune and exclaimed, "Oh, I know that one!" He stood from his seat, almost knocking over his tea, and began to sing with Nomos. Alyn took Nomos's hands and the two swayed together to a song only they recognized.

Tair looked at the scene with delight and amusement, both of which she had not felt for what felt like quite some time now. As happy as she was, she could not have helped but feel a little excluded, unsure of how she fit in and unsure of if she would ever fit in anywhere. This was their world; yet again, she was a Human observer. An outsider.

Down the hall, she heard another room open. From within, the one Dwarf Tair was simultaneously elated to see and actively avoiding emerged: Bonn. Bonn was *ashonke*, they told Tair within moments of meeting one another. Tair had not been quite sure why those were the first words the Dwarf had shared with her, nor did she know what it meant. She later deduced that *ashonke* was yet another Domani gender identity term, like *konos* or *ijarak* or any of the new words Tair had learned the night before. Bonn thankfully helped Tair and explained a bit about the ever-changing nature of gender in Doman and in the Domani language. In the time since she had arrived at the outskirts of Doman, Tair herself had made plenty of mental notes of her own about how gender expression and identity functioned this culture, seemingly holding more importance among the Domani Dwarves than it ever had amongst the Northern Elves. Tair now knew well enough not to assume anything about Dwarven identities. She had wished, in an admittedly lazy way, that Shianna would have just explained it all to her before their arrival, but she was also pleased to learn it on her own—and, perhaps too, from Bonn.

Bonn was also the only Dwarf who looked at Tair with something deeper than disgust, something deeper still than curiosity.

They smiled as they sat down and moved their chair closer to Tair. Though nothing had happened the night before (as much as Tair thought something was about to happen—as much as she privately *hoped* something would have happened), Bonn exhibited a kind of physical closeness that Tair was unaccustomed to. Tair, in a part of herself she could not quite admit to yet, liked Bonn in a similar way to how she had once liked Silaa. Now, though, there was something different. Tair tried to deny it, averting her eyes from Bonn's in attempt to distract herself from the Dwarf's, averting her attention too from their endearing gap tooth, their full lips, the sharp line of their jaw, the soft curve of their neck...

"Is something wrong?" Bonn asked. Recognizing Tair's discomfort with physical intimacy, they leaned back and ran a hand over their bald head. The Dwarf's voice was deeper than Alyn's—deeper than Shianna's, even. A little smokier. Tair did not want to lose herself in thinking about their voice. If she were to do that, she would have to admit to herself that she was dedicating an inordinate amount of attention to this being who she had developed too much of a liking for in far too little time. Nevertheless, Tair noted that Bonn had a slight accent in Nossok, though they had probably had just as much experience with the language as Tair.

Then she realized that she probably had an accent in Bonn's ears, too, which made her blush.

Tair decided not to answer. Meeting Bonn's eyes, she asked instead, "How long have you known Shianna?"

Bonn took the hint, folded their arms over their chest, and looked to Shianna dancing with her mate and Sano while Alyn and Nomos sang. They said, "I've known her the shortest amount of time relative to the rest of them." They paused. "Since I'm the youngest."

Tair was curious. When she imagined herself with Bonn (which she did not, of course, though in the most hypothetical sense she *did* fall asleep conjuring up ideas of what life might look like and...). When Tair imagined herself with Bonn, she did experience a little hesitation when she came to the topic of age. Though Shianna, Silaa, and Alyn were significantly older than her, they only appeared about ten or so years older. As a result, Tair had placed a barrier between herself and Bonn, unsure of whether or not the Dwarf was two years older than her or two *centuries*. And, with Shianna's age in mind, and her kinship to Bonn, Tair's hesitations only grew stronger. In attempt to seem casual, she merely said, "Oh?"

A small smirk spread across Bonn's face. They did not look at Tair directly, but the Human still felt observed. The Dwarf said, almost too quiet to be heard over the singing, "I believe a fair approximation would put me somewhere in my twenties. We do not pay as much attention to age as you might, but maybe...well, maybe that is important to you. I don't know much about Humans."

Tair wanted to say that she did not know much about Humans, either, but was distracted by the information that Bonn had just shared. *Twenties.* They were significantly younger than the rest of the Dwarves—and, coincidentally, quite close to Tair's own age.

"They all took me in as their kin when I was young, and Shianna left not long after that. I matured apart from her but love for her has always been a part of my life. She was somewhat of a character in a legend, and yet she is here, right in front of my eyes." Bonn gestured out to Shianna, who was now dancing around with Alyn.

Shianna had always been a part of Tair's life, so much so that Tair could not imagine someone growing up without her—like a child finally realizing that other children had parents and families of their own, or that their parents had once been children, too.

Tair understood what Bonn meant, though. Over the course of a few weeks, Shianna had gone from one of Tair's most trusted confidantes to *Prime Heir* to an entire realm and culture. She was no longer Shianna, but something warped—a character in a distant legend.

Tair nodded, though she was not sure if Bonn saw out of the corner of their eye. The Human asked, "Do you know what they are singing?"

Bonn shook their head, then abruptly grabbed Tair's hand and led her outside without explanation, which surprisingly did not alarm the Human. In the daylight, the barrack looked more like a castle. The two came to sit in a patch of grass a little distance away, but not far enough that Tair lost sight of the building they had originated from. Tair felt an odd degree of relief to be alone together—or as alone as they could be, with song still following them outside. That relief dissipated when Bonn released Tair's hand and said, "Tell me the truth. Who are you?"

Tair blinked. "I'm Tair."

"Yes, but..." Bonn glanced over their shoulder and made sure to angle themself so that they were positioned in front of Tair, in case anyone was to look out the door for either of them.

"I'm a liaison," Tair quickly said. Shianna only wanted her provide answers if asked, but Bonn's skepticism felt like an unspoken question. Fumbling, she said, "Between a settlement north of the Darkwoods..." *A name!* Tair thought. If she was truly meant to embody who she said she was, then why did she have so little specifics? Shianna's lies throughout the years must have taken a lot of focus, she realized.

Tair cleared her throat, then continued, "I'm just a liaison."

Bonn frowned, then smirked. "Who are you *really*?"

Tair had hoped that her vagueness would strengthen their lie. She breathed easy with the resolution that they did not necessarily have to be lying in order for Bonn to wonder who, exactly, they all were. Still, Tair took a little too long a pause before she tried, "I don't know what, uh, identity term to use—

is that what you mean?"

Bonn narrowed their eyes, but their shoulders relaxed. They recognized Tair's discomfort and were not going to press. In a way, the Dwarf seemed to be testing Tair—for what purpose, the Human did not know. They said, "I'm not sure about the terms Humans use."

Tair was not well-versed on that either, having been raised in Mirte her whole life, only ever speaking Nossok, Northern Elvish, and some Domani. She admitted, "I didn't know there were so many terms for oneself."

"One's gender is not their self," Bonn gently clarified.

Tair nodded. Language would be a precarious thing between the two, what with such different upbringings. She did not want to get anything wrong, not in this new land, not with Bonn. Tair was intrigued by Bonn in many ways, but she did find their confrontational curiosity to be contradictory to their desire to have a conversation in private. Then again, if they had confronted Tair in public, it might have been disastrous. They cared for her enough not to compromise her safety—or so Tair hoped.

Bonn was now sitting closer than Tair would have thought comfortable with a stranger, and she secretly wished they would close the gap, move a little bit closer, maybe...

"I still wonder..." the Dwarf began, suddenly standing and beginning to pace. "I don't know why you're here with Shianna, why you've all shown up so randomly, why you have so many among you, yet seem to be in hiding...Can you explain any of that?"

Tair hesitantly shook her head. As best as she could avoid it, Tair did not want to lie, and she certainly did not want to invite further questioning. She herself was not even sure of what was off-limits to share, since much of the information about her own life was still a mystery to her. In all truth, Tair did not know why they were on their way to Doman at all—if she was so important to Sossoa, why not send her straight there? Other questions of the future constantly filtered through her mind, but Bonn was looking for an explanation of the present. Tair could have told Bonn that they had all met in Mirte, but why would they have been in such a reclusive Elven valley? Why did they need to leave when they did? And, if Tair used the lie that she was a diplomat from a Human settlement in southern Nossoa, why would she have come to the northeast of Doman on her way to communicate with the Prime? Silaa could easily explain away her position as Shianna's mate, but Alyn and Tair did not have such an easy excuse. Tair left it to Bonn to come to their own conclusions, however fantastic those turned out to be.

Bonn maintained a defiant silence, so Tair realized that they were not pleased with such a simple answer. She shrugged, trying to appear indifferent, and said, "Ask Shianna."

"She could better explain your own life?" Bonn met Tair's eyes, which was when Tair realized how orange they really were. She did not think orange eyes were possible and, yet, there they were, staring into her own brown eyes. These orange eyes were the piercing color of the sunset or a cool fire or...they were *passion*. If Tair could make passion any color, she would have made them Bonn's eye color.

Tair averted her eyes, both self-conscious and steadily becoming uncomfortable from Bonn's confrontational gaze.

Bonn said, "I asked you for a reason. You are more approachable than Shianna."

Tair shook her head with a small chuckle, "I think she would be more than happy to answer any of your questions." Partially because Shianna knew the lies—and knew *how* to lie—better than anyone else, and partially because Shianna loved catching her friends up on what had been happening in her life since they last saw her.

"Who would be more than happy to answer your questions?" Alyn's voice was immediately recognizable behind

Bonn, who had begun to pace again. He approached with a wry smile on his face and his hands clasped behind his back. With Alyn amongst them, Tair noticed her height in comparison to Bonn's; the Dwarf was at least a head shorter than both her and Alyn.

"Shianna," Tair said, her eyes on Alyn and Bonn's eyes on her. She felt a shiver run down her spine.

"Ah, yes," Alyn affirmed. "She would love to answer any questions you have." He began to hum the same song they were singing inside earlier, tapping his foot in the moss beneath him. He was upbeat, an emotion Tair had not seen him exhibit in quite some time. Things felt cheery.

Tair grew even more uncomfortable.

"Well," Alyn began softly. "We have to keep on our way to Doman."

They were not, Shianna insisted, going to leave as abruptly as they had from Mirte. Evidently, Shianna had different standards for her own circumstances than Tair's. The Human did not particularly feel the need to voice her discontentment with Shianna's hypocrisy—after all, it was not *entirely* discontentment. She enjoyed the Dwarves' company (and one particular Dwarf's company), the general merriment in this reunion, and the stable roof over their heads for one more night before her life undoubtedly changed again.

Tair downed her beer in seconds, earning much applause. She could feel Bonn watching her from across the room, like they had the night before, and somewhat enjoyed feeling watched. She felt that her life mattered to someone, even if she barely knew that someone. Strangers though they might have been, Tair had to admit that something was different with Bonn. The Dwarf had kept their distance after their conversation earlier that day, but they still kept an eye on Tair. When Tair was not in the room, she could hear, distantly, someone asking around for her. Now she was five drinks in, happy and impulsive. She strolled up to Bonn, squared her shoulders, and cleared her throat.

Then, Tair said, "What's your problem with me?"

Bonn laughed with their whole chest and then repeated their question from earlier, "Who are you?"

"Ask Shianna," Tair said automatically, though her intoxicated mind wanted to say, *None of your business*.

"I want to hear it from you," Bonn hummed. Their voice was deeper than before, so their attempt to err on the quiet side failed. They leaned forward onto their knees and peered up at Tair from behind rather long eyelashes.

Tair scoffed, stumbled over her words, and took another sip of her refilled drink. *Who was she?* That did not feel like an entirely fair question. Tair herself did not even know the answer, so what right did Bonn have to one? Through the fog of intoxication, she knew Bonn was challenging her—but also offering her this strange opportunity to craft this entire new self, the self she *wanted* to be. Nevertheless, too tipsy and too stubborn, Tair did not want to answer with her heart and instead slurred, "Why don't you figure out for yourself?"

"I intend to." Bonn smiled, stood from their seat, shouldered past Tair, and began to make their way across the room. On instinct, Tair followed until the two were face-to-face with Shianna, who stood close to the low firepit in the center of the room, her arms wrapped around Silaa's hips. The two were not talking, merely nudging and kissing and laughing. Tair knew that the mates had drunk more than her, otherwise Silaa would have been sulking again. Tair knew Shianna's status as Prime Heir was going to take more time to accept than Silaa had been provided—than she provided herself.

Bonn said, "Shianna, I will return with you four back to Doman."

Shianna turned her head to Bonn but her eyes followed shortly after. A wide grin spread across her face as she dragged a finger down the side of Bonn's face. "The baby!" If her skin were not so dark, Tair was sure Bonn would have blushed at Shianna's nickname. Tair indulged in seeing the Dwarf lose their self-assuredness, their eyes downcast and a slight, bashful smile on their face, if only for a moment.

Shianna then remembered what Bonn had said. She considered a moment, then answered, "Okay...why?"

Bonn answered, "I intend to join your group."

Join? What was there to join? Bonn had a particular way of talking that Tair had not yet grown accustomed to. Joining their group could have meant too many different things. Tair's inebriated mind trailed away from her...until she could no longer find a precise reason why, exactly, Bonn joining them would have been a bad idea. In fact, the more time she spent with Bonn, the more she began to relish in the feeling of attachment that blossomed in her heart—which also seemed to be the case for Bonn. Tair clasped her hands in front of her chest in a mock prayer. Bonn cocked an eyebrow at her.

Shianna resolved, "You may join us, but you will probably have to ask me again when I'm not..." She burped, long and loud. The room erupted with laughter.

The next morning, Shianna was not happy to discover the decisions her intoxicated mind had made for her. On her own principle, though, she always trusted the choices her inebriated mind made, believing herself uninhibited by the concerns that would normally hold her back from a potentially good decision. Regrettably for her, this was a big decision, a *bad* decision, to make—and Tair could tell that she wished to revoke it.

Even if Shianna had gone against her own principle, Bonn was not going to take no for an answer—especially after they told all of their and Shianna's family that the *Prime Heir* had trusted them as a part of her group, and that they were headed to Doman to be formally recognized as a soldier and defender of Doman. This was nowhere near the truth, of course. It seemed that Bonn was coming up with their own lies, practically a key trait in Tair's family.

Everyone cheered Bonn on—except, of course, Tair, Shianna, Silaa, and Alyn, who all knew this meant much more than just someone joining them on their journey. Every decision had to be made with a particular care, as they all had direct repercussions on the fate of an entire realm—and all the Humans who lived there. They had all been sworn into secrecy for over a decade; each day since they had left Mirte, that secrecy crumbled more. There were risks that they had to actively avoid, including inviting practical strangers into their lives.

No matter, Shianna was not going to negate her poor decisions; Bonn was not going to back down; Tair was not going to object; and Silaa and Alyn were not going to voice their opinions too enthusiastically without inviting suspicion. Privately, Tair was glad that Bonn was joining them. All Tair had with her family was history; all Tair had with Bonn was the *present*.

When the four original members of the group had gathered in the den in their last few moments before departure, Tair had to feign anxiety, if only for appearance's sake. Not particularly curious about the answer, she asked "What are we supposed to tell them when they start asking questions?"

Shianna dropped her head into her hands. Silaa placed a hand on her mate's back. Shianna flinched at the touch but welcomed it anyway. Their tenuous normalcy in the barrack was already dissolving. Without Shianna's friends, this support structure, to hold them together, Tair worried who they would become.

Shianna finally decided, "We'll climb that mountain when we have arrived at its base."

Tair scoffed at the expression; quite literally, they would have to answer that question when they reached Doman. Even though the mountains loomed over the small outpost Shianna's friends occupied, they seemed distant and impossible. Tair began to wonder as to why all of Shianna's friends were here, so far from the rest of their kind, why they had all carved out this small part of the world for themselves.

Shianna had always been so proud of her home. Was this the home she held so much love for, or was it the one yet to be discovered?

Alyn said, "I think we'll need to have a better idea of what we're going to say than simply leaving it up to instinct. Our lie leaves too many gaps to be filled by suspicion." Alyn was gentle in his suggestion. He did not want to contradict Shianna in a place where her status as Prime Heir was becoming increasingly present. Alyn did not even understand the rules of decorum; Tair did not know if there were any rules to begin with. Yet another mountain to climb.

Silaa dropped her hand from Shianna's back and the Dwarf pulled her head out of her hands to peer up at her friends. She took on a kind of new air: one of authority, power, responsibility. These were qualities she had always had, of course, but they now felt like they were coming from the Prime Heir of Doman, rather than Shianna. She said, "You do not have to worry about that."

It was Shianna's responsibility, then.

Bonn arrived, almost as if on cue, with a pack strapped to their back and a tentative smile on their face. They had more belongings than Tair, Alyn, Shianna, and Silaa combined—all of whom had to leave their entire lives behind in different ways and take only the essentials. Essentials, Tair discovered for herself, included food and clothing. Bonn's essentials, though, included nearly everything they considered their own in the outpost. They bent a bit from the sack on their back but tried to keep their posture straight. Tair held back her laughter.

"Ready?" Silaa asked in jest.

Shianna dropped her shoulders as she settled back into a more casual demeanor. Tair caught glimpses of this constant battle between what—or *who*—came naturally to the Prime Heir. Around Bonn and the other Dwarves, she dropped any expected formalities entirely—Tair first saw it the night before when they all began to say their goodbyes. Even as they set off to their rooms to gather their belongings, Shianna had carried an air of freedom that existed in stark contrast to the image she faded in and out of as they neared the mere *concept* of Doman. She was practicing, Tair knew, for the real thing.

"We should hope so," Shianna added. She patted Bonn's cheek, less than a slap but too rough for Tair to have taken with such a shining face.

Bonn lavished in it. They nodded once, and they all set off for Doman.

FIVE

Tair was relieved to find that their journey to Doman was relatively short, only about a three-hour walk south from the barrack. By then, the Yellow Sun was slowly rising overhead, and two guards saw them emerge from the thicket, then guided the group onward. Soon, they arrived at the base of the mountains, of which they traced the perimeter until they came to an opening that revealed the Doman Lake. Having lived to the west of Mirte, Tair did not have much familiarity with the ocean, but she knew that this lake could have been likened to a sea. She no longer felt the common approximation of Doman as the origin of all creation to be too far off. The greatness of the landlocked water was enough to convince her of the impossibilities of the world. Some Dwarven children, their distinctly Dwarven feature their abnormally large ears, played on the lake's shoreline, unsupervised and carefree—though aware not to wade too far into the water, Tair noted. The mountains sprouted up like trees from the lake, peaking higher than the unaccustomed eye could comprehend—than Tair could comprehend. Just as Shianna had described many times, the tallest mountain reached the clouds. From there, the other mountains descended by height and formed a natural border around the pristine water. Where Tair expected raging waters and wild wind, there was a kind of calm that could only be created in a vacuum of sound. Carved into the sides of the mountains were plenty of Domani symbols, as well as a few ledges from which Dwarves fished. Everywhere she looked—the very tops of the mountains with dim fires or standing at the very opening she found herself in at that moment—Tair found guards protecting the realm.

"Isn't it beautiful?" Shianna choked out as she dropped to her knees, overcome by the incontestable majesty that was her homeland. The two guards that had led them there ran up to her and tried to help her up, but she batted them away. On the brim of her eyes were tears—*tears*! Tair realized then that she had never seen the Dwarf cry. As expressive as she was with her emotions, those feelings never manifested physically. Now, Shianna could barely contain herself.

Tair shifted her weight but did not move away when Bonn approached at her side. They said, "She truly has not been back for eleven years?"

Tair shook her head no.

Bonn huffed. "I don't think I could do it."

Tair doubted that she could become so attached to a place that seeing it would bring her to her knees in total awe. Doman suddenly felt suffocating, representative of a home Tair felt she would never find. The sky, unconquerable and infinite in Mirte, was now invaded by mountain peaks. The lake, too, swallowed up what could have otherwise been a wide expanse of land, an expected sight for Tair after a childhood in an unending prairie. In her mind, the world was an endless valley set against a similarly infinite sky. At least the forests they had traveled through felt familiar. Doman contrastingly cut up the land, broke it into pieces, and declared itself the logical limit to the world. However long their time in Doman would be, which she still did not know, she already felt stuck in this isolated realm.

A tear escaped her, too.

Bonn had turned around to wait for Tair to proceed with the rest of them, who had continued ahead without her. Tair defiantly wiped the tear from her eye and strode forward.

Shianna, followed by the two guards who had accompanied them thus far, led them on the final steps of their journey. She moved with the confidence of someone in the absolute comfort of home. Even Silaa knew to take a step back, falling in line with Alyn. Where Tair had expected some improvised song from the Fel, as he often provided, Alyn was silent and awestruck. The Fel, despite having been to Doman before, still could not comprehend the world before him. Tair felt herself desperate for a song, desperate for some element of familiarity in this unfamiliar place.

The smallest mountain—but *mountain* nonetheless—had a large sigil drawn near the base, just up to standard Dwarven height. When Shianna pressed her palm there, the rock opened to reveal a narrow tunnel. The passageway led to a steep staircase and then to a great, empty hall. It was remote, elaborate, and *aged*. Tair had never felt so thoroughly the continuation of time as she did inside that first mountain. The walls had been established some millennia before, weathered by change and constant care. Tair looked around for the light source, only to find it too far overhead to distinguish what exactly produced it. What Tair did notice was that the light fabricated precisely the same quality and warmth of light as the two suns outside the mountains. When Tair breathed in, all she could smell was...bread! Oh, she had not had bread in weeks. The Elves were not as fond of it as Shianna (and Tair, admittedly) would have liked them to be, so Shianna often resorted to cooking loaves of her own in their small cabin in Mirte. Well, she baked as often as Alyn would allow; he very much appreciated being able to provide food for his family, perhaps to the point of self-importance. Tair simultaneously longed for the comfort of both familial and communal meals in Mirte and longed for the food that was to fill her stomach in this new land.

Besides the smells, the actual interior of the hall was luxurious. Everything was some shade of red, which amongst the Northern Elves meant love and independence. Tair wondered what it meant in Doman, important as it seemed to be when every rug and flag and cushion and table ornament had some shade of the color in it. The throne at the head of the hall was large enough to distinguish itself but modest enough to give the sense of equality. A Dwarf who closely resembled Shianna sat there, arms outstretched, and face weathered by scars and wrinkles: Prime Eslania, Shianna's parent.

Prime Eslania, or Omma as she was more colloquially known, had all the regality that one expected of a Prime and all the warmth one expected of a parent. Her skin was a little lighter than Shianna's, her stature a little wider, and her smile the exact same. She had one large scar that traveled from her cheek down to her neck that suggested she had lived through great pain. She did not stand from her seat when Shianna approached, but the two still embraced a long while, comfortable in their reverential silence.

When they pulled away from each other, Shianna's eyes were puffy and red, her cheeks stained with tears, still an unfamiliar sight to Tair. Shianna did not bother to collect herself before she said, "This is Omma—Prime Eslania Kasgan of the First Family of Doman."

Omma. Not "my omma." Shianna did not possess her parent; the Prime was everyone's Omma. They still held onto one another's hands as they stood facing their meager audience: the two guards, Silaa, Alyn, Bonn, and Tair. It was then that Shianna as Prime Heir settled into reality. Tair could see it in the way the Dwarf held herself, the way she related to her parent, the comfort and joy she felt in this incredible world of impossible responsibility.

Alyn bowed low to the ground, a formality he imposed upon himself. For Alyn, first impressions were incredibly important, as they were for any traveler. Though he had met Omma, it had been many years prior—and a lot could change in that span of time. A lot had already changed. Shianna and Omma chuckled the same chuckle and urged him to stand up. With an almost audible gulp, Alyn said, "It is a true honor to once again be in your presence, Prime Eslania."

Omma smiled. Tair struggled to think of her as "Prime Eslania," almost as much as she had a hard time conceptualizing Shianna as "Prime Heir Shianna." They were Omma and Shianna, respectively. That was the familiarity with which they held themselves. Tair began to understand why the Dwarves of Doman might have had a hard time voting them out.

"Please, you know we do not relate to such frivolous terms," Omma said, her Nossok thick and accented. And for good reason; those older than three centuries, both in Doman and in the entire realm of Nossoa, had not grown up with the common language. Dwarves like Shianna, around 150 years of age, or Elves like Silaa, slightly older than 200, had been raised on the language. Alyn's Nossok came naturally, the first language he learned as a child in Lawe, nearly 100 years ago. Before their lifetimes, though, there had not been any reason for a shared language. In the early days just before the formalization of Nossoa, it had become increasingly apparent that all beings of the realm would have to cooperate with one another and create a world that was *theirs*—one which the Sossok Humans could not deny them, and one which they could defend as a collective. Language was one of the first steps toward unity, offering a common identity to its speakers. A shared language was also a response, one which said that Sossoa was as separate from Nossoa as the spiteful Humans who had founded the nation had intended. Omma had been at the devising of Nossoa and the Nossok language around 250 years ago. As such, she must have already had a distinct way of speaking and pronouncing certain sounds, no matter if she helped form the new language or not. Now, at Tair's formal introduction to the Prime, Omma was over two and half centuries older and had lived with Dwarves who would have only spoken Domani with her. The Prime's *s*'s were especially punctuated, Tair noted.

Before anyone else, Shianna introduced Silaa. Omma smiled ear to ear and stretched out her arms again for embrace. She did not have as adverse a reaction as Shianna's friends had teased she might. Even still, in that embrace with Silaa, Omma did not rise.

Having already met Alyn and Bonn and, of course recognizing her own guards, the only stranger left in the hall was Tair. Well, stranger now. The Prime had met Tair when she had not yet established a distinct identity, being only three years of age; in the presence of one another now, Tair felt herself rather inadequate. She held all the weight of Human history in Doman, as well as the weight of the unfolding history of the Sossok Humans' revolution in the present day. As much pressure as she felt, Omma looked upon Tair with kind eyes and a gentle smile. Bonn seemed particularly curious about this special treatment.

Examining the range of interactions she had seen performed with the Prime, Tair decided to try them all: she bowed like Alyn and then approached for a hug like Shianna and Silaa. Omma held Tair tight, which was when Tair realized that Omma was paralyzed from the waist down. Though she tried to hide her surprise, she was caught before she could change her expression.

"Some things go with age," Omma said as she gestured to her lower half. "I am grateful that the one thing that has not gone is my life." She winked and flashed another smile.

Omma's eyes casually scanned the group. Landing on

Bonn, she asked, "What brings you here, *rakr kaako*?" *Our child*, Tair translated to herself. Not only did Shianna not possess her parent, but apparently none possessed their children, perhaps belonging to Doman on the whole.

Bonn dropped to one knee despite the explicit request for informality. They maintained eye contact with the Prime as they said, "I have returned home in the hopes of developing further responsibility for our sacred realm by protecting your child, my future Prime, if you believe me to be worthy."

Omma considered this for a moment. She undoubtedly knew all the lies they would catch themselves in if she said yes; even still, she seemed just as endeared to Bonn as the rest of them. Tair still could not understand what particular qualities the Dwarf held that made them so appealing, but each moment she became more determined to find out.

Though it was clear Omma approved of Bonn, she was unable to express her affirmative answer before a Dwarf dressed in a long silver robe emerged from behind a large red velvet tapestry that hid a tunnel just behind Omma. They had the lightest skin tone Tair had ever seen on a Dwarf, somehow lighter than Alyn's, and no hair on their face or head. Even without eyebrows to convey shock, it was clear to Tair that they were surprised to see a Human—or surprised to see Tair in particular, she did not know. She shifted where she stood.

When their initial shock had subsided, the Dwarf said, "Greetings to all. I am Denon, Counselor to Prime Eslania." Their Nossok was *perfect*. They had to have been just as old (if not older than) Omma, so they could not have grown up with the tongue. Knowing that, it would not have surprised Tair if they had played a part in creating the language. The Counselor clearly prided themself on formalities, unlike their counterparts, and bowed low to the ground in front of the small crowd around Omma.

Bonn frowned and whispered into Tair's ear, "Detestable Denon. He resists change at every turn." Tair registered both the appropriate pronouns for Denon and the undeniable contempt in Bonn's voice when they looked to Counselor Denon—contempt which Shianna, too, was unable to hide. A scowl spread across both Bonn's and Shianna's faces, though Shianna covered hers better with a tight smile. Conversely, Counselor Denon did not hide his grimace toward the Prime Heir.

Alyn did not seem to notice the disdain. Presented with the opportunity, he mirrored Denon's bow, demonstrating his respect in a way he believed most suitable. The Counselor took this response in stride, squared his shoulders, and smirked at Alyn—he must not have gotten that introduction often. Tair did not know who to side with, unaccustomed as she was to this kind of formality and bureaucracy.

"Well, it seems that I have arrived just in time for the reunion," Denon continued. "I was informed that the Prime Heir had returned, and I wanted to find her before she...What is it that you do again?"

Shianna bristled at what Tair felt was an entirely unnecessary taunt.

"Forgive me, your role simply must have slipped my mind. It has been too long," Denon said.

"Oh, Denon, just long enough," Shianna muttered. As much as she missed Doman, she clearly did not miss this Counselor. For the first time since they arrived in the hall, she dropped Omma's hand and went to stand by Silaa.

Denon smiled a wicked smile and said in a far too cheery voice, "Prime Eslania, we have other matters to attend to at the moment. A family reunion may have to wait." He bent down to Omma to whisper in her ear. She thought for a moment before nodding.

"I think," Omma said, "a family reunion is precisely what I must attend to at this moment. In fact, I would like to speak with the Human and my daughter, alone."

Alyn perked up as Silaa stiffened. For Alyn, this private

moment would serve to prove that his responsibility for Tair had been adequate—that he had been the appropriate choice for the task of raising her. For Silaa, this privacy was a clear demonstration of the kind of responsibility Shianna held as Prime Heir. Bonn, to Tair's side, looked between the Prime and the Human. Tair did not know when she would be able to divulge all of her secrets, but it was becoming increasingly apparent that she would not be able to lie to Bonn forever. Despite the general interest in what their conversation would entail, the hall cleared out, except for Denon, who stood by the Prime's side.

"That includes you, Counselor," Omma clarified.

Shianna grinned and waved a slight goodbye as Denon retreated behind the tapestry. When the click of his heels down the long, hidden corridor had died down, the great hall was silent, though this silence was not nearly as comfortable as those Tair had endured in the forests between here and Braasii. Tair cleared her throat, and the sound echoed all through the walls. She placed a hand over her beating heart if only to will it silent.

Omma did not notice. Instead, she smiled even wider and said, "It has been so long since I last saw you. How you've grown! Come here again, let me look at you."

Tair did as she was told. Omma took Tair's face in her weathered hands. More distinctly now, Tair found that the Prime smelled of burned wood, of fire. Though she could not place Omma in her childhood memory, Tair recognized the Prime in a deeper way. She was a part of Tair's family, too, if only distantly. Omma looked at and spoke to her like a grandparent might have spoken to their grandchild. Tair smiled in the Prime's hands. It was the closest thing to a family reunion Tair felt she would ever receive.

Omma released Tair's face. The Human took a short step back, and Shianna a step forward. The two stood over Omma as she said, "You have had quite the life, quite the journey...I remember when you were only a child, when my legs still allowed me to chase you around. Shianna was away then, and much too big to be chased, anyway."

Shianna scoffed.

Omma smiled at her child, then turned to Tair to say, "I trust you have had the nature of your significance explained to you. To avoid repetition, though, what do you know thus far?"

Tair willed herself to speak but could not muster the words. The right to divulge knowledge of her own life was being presented to her for the first time, and she did not know how to react.

Shianna recognized Tair's hesitation and said for her, "She knows she is a symbol of Sossoa's future and, of course, what that means for her position in the affairs of the world—what it might mean for her own future."

Omma hummed in consideration. "That seems quite vague, Shianna...is that truly all? You have hidden a lot from her, I suppose."

Tair laughed but quieted herself when Shianna glared at her. It was true; a lot had been hidden from her.

"That is what she knows for now, yes..." Shianna paused and looked down at her feet. "That is what she knows, and what Silaa knows, as well."

"Your mate knows?" Omma was clearly startled by this information but quickly plastered on a practiced, neutral face. "You must know the danger in sharing such information, Shianna."

Tair had never heard Shianna's name uttered with such scorn.

"You must be joking," Shianna said. "I only recently told her that I am Prime Heir—if I had hidden all of this information about Tair, I don't know...I don't know if she would ever return to me. Can you imagine the pain?"

Omma said, "You know I can."

Shianna nodded curtly.

Though curious, Tair wanted to get back to the topic at hand—what, exactly, had been hidden from her? In her most polite voice possible, she began to ask, "What..." She paused. Ever since they had left Mirte, she had known that she would not like what her life had in store for her and, in attempt to hide from that truth a little longer, she had kept silent. The Human exhaled before she asked what she knew would undoubtedly change her life forever:

"What else should I know?"

Omma shifted in her seat. She winced a moment but breathed through the pain. Shianna did not bat an eye. She must have seen Omma's pain just before her departure for Mirte and did not think it cause for immediate concern.

Omma released a long breath and said, "As you probably know, a little over sixteen years ago now, you were left in the Darkwoods. There had been legends that a Human child's appearance there would be a sign that change was on the horizon—that the Sossok revolution and unity of the two divided realms neared. That was a long time ago now, but these things take time to plan and execute. Alyn, one of the only beings who wholeheartedly believed in all of this—and, frankly, one of the only beings in Nossoa who cared for the fate of the Humans at the time—took it upon himself to take charge of you, and clearly he did not fail in his task."

If Alyn has been trusted to raise me, why is he not trusted to be here, now? Tair wanted to ask. She was not worried, though. In fact, she felt an almost foreboding sense of calm as Omma spoke—a calm too closely tied to what Tair feared would turn to turmoil.

Omma continued, "It has been a long time, but it seems that things are coming together now. The revolution is stronger in the minds of the Sossok and has roots across the realm—across all the realms on Gosso. The King's health has been failing for quite some time, and his successor—the King

Heir—will be sworn in not long after his parent's death. In the past, that period of succession has proven to be a loose thread in the fabric of Sossok politics. That loose thread has been waiting to be pulled for years, for centuries, and there is only one Human who may be able to pull it. Someone whose return would be celebrated, someone who would immediately gain Usnaso's trust and use that trust to more swiftly bring an end to his life."

Tair nodded, curious and patient.

Shianna looked away.

"Of course," Omma said, "that someone is you."

Of course? Mirte and Braasii both had made it abundantly clear to Tair that reveals such as this were not jokes—and still she wanted to laugh. This feeling quickly dissipated when she saw the grave look in Omma's eye; Tair—believing herself incapable of intentionally causing physical harm, and never trained to fight nor kill—was meant to assassinate King Usnaso.

Tair almost fell over. Before it was too late, Shianna caught her. She slumped in Shianna's arms, the world blurring before her eyes. Though choked (by laughter? by tears? Tair did not know), she managed to say, "You expect me to kill a Human."

"The King, yes," Omma corrected, her expression neutral and unreadable.

Not just a Human. The King of Humans—or, at least, the King of Humans in Sossoa. King Usnaso was responsible for generations of harm and hatred, signed into law and with very real repercussions on Humanity, on the whole of the continent, perhaps on the whole of the world. Any ordinary being could have easily acknowledged and helped others heal from the harm they caused, but a *king*? When a king caused harm, there was no apology great enough to make up for the lives lost, the families broken, the culture changed, the damage done. Even still, Tair did not know even a quarter of the evils King Usnaso had committed, with so much of her knowledge of Sossoa rooted in the past—in war and genocide and pain, in homogeneity and isolation. All of those existed in their own ways today, but Tair was not intimately connected to that contemporary violence. King Usnaso especially was the largest gap in her knowledge of the kingdom, beginning and ending at the simple fact that he was cruel enough for Sossok Humans to rebel against. She could not have imagined that *this* was why she had been taken to Doman. She could not have imagined that *this* would be her role in it all.

Had she known any more information on King Usnaso, would this task have been any less laughable—any less shocking? Had she known any more information about King Usnaso, would she have told Moss that the rumors were true— that the Usnaso regime was ending, and that she was meant to end it? No, she could not imagine a version of herself who took this news in her stride, nor any version of herself who would have flaunted the task. Even in her wildest imagination, she could not visualize a dagger in hand, a vile of poison tipped into a drink, a noose tightened around a neck. She could not kill; if there were to ever be a version of Tair who *could* kill, it would no longer be Tair, she thought. Her mind and body were still as they contemplated the movements that it might take to overcome her morality and take the life of another. That may as well have been a scene in one of those tragic Northern Elven plays—and never something she could do herself.

More importantly, Tair thought, she was not Sossoa's savior. She had not been raised in the land, nor had she experienced even a fraction of the injustices that Humans who lived there had—that Humans who lived there were fighting against. Some days, she barely felt Human at all, stuck between so many racial and cultural identities that did not allow space to describe her particular and complicated history. Identity fractured or not, Tair still felt that she had no claim to King Usnaso's life, no claim to any personal hatred toward him. As much as she had not wanted to intrude in the affairs of Domani Dwarves, if only in acknowledgement of the harm her kind had caused in the past, she surely did not want to intrude upon Human affairs and claim their struggles as her own.

Despite Tair's stunned silence, Omma continued, "You will travel to Rolt"—the Sossok border that divided Humankind from the Darkwoods and Nossoa—"and inform them that you have escaped after having been kidnapped at a young age by us, the Domani Dwarves. The King, hearing news of this, will embrace you as a representation of non-Human vice and will have no choice but to turn his troops against us. While he is distracted by the preparations for war, you will kill him and, if you're able, the King Heir."

Not just the King then. The King Heir, too. Omma was instructing Tair to kill *two* Humans. Tair's mind slowed, the world seemingly coming to a halt around her.

"I meant to share more of Sossoa and the language, of the revolution on the whole, for which you will have a tutor, but it seems..." Omma paused. "It seems that this news is overwhelming you already. Had I known you were so ignorant of your fate, I would have chosen to divulge this information in a different manner, perhaps over a longer span of time, but I am not the one who raised you," Omma said with a slight edge to her voice. Shianna grunted. "I am sure my child had her reasons for her secrecy."

Shianna knew then. Shianna *knew*. Three betrayals in less than three weeks' time. And what of Alyn? Silaa? No, Omma's phrasing was clear, Tair hoped: *I am sure my child had her reasons for hiding this information from you*—it was an acknowledgement that, at least in Omma's eyes, Shianna was the only one who had known the whole truth. Tair shoved Shianna off of her and steadied herself on her own. She straightened out her tunic, brushed off her pants, and held her head high. With the most confidence she could muster, Tair said, "I refuse."

Omma furrowed her eyebrows and glanced at Shianna, who stood openmouthed and staring at Tair. The Prime, clearly confused by Tair's response, asked, "What do you mean, 'you refuse'?"

Tair braced herself and said, "There is a lot I have been forced to sacrifice simply by fault of birth, and I know there is more I must do. Still, I do not have enough of an emotional tie to Sossoa to claim it's rulers' lives; I do not have the skills to carry out an assassination; and my own morality would not allow me to commit such an act of violence. I must refuse." She bowed her head in conclusion.

After some silence, Tair looked up. Omma stared back, then placed her forehead in her right hand, her left gripping onto the arm of her throne. She muttered to Shianna, "Have you truly not taught this child to fight? To kill?"

Shianna did not answer, watching along with Tair as Omma's face scrunched up in a way that made her scar seem even more pronounced. She took three deep breaths, her back rising and falling such that Tair thought she might take flight. Finally, her face relaxed and her breathing evened again. She said, "You think your morality greater than the lives of your kin—of the beings of all the realms?"

"That's not—" Tair started to respond.

Omma put up one finger and said, "You seem to think your aversion to taking the life of an evil Human even greater than the good lives such a Human has taken. You seem to think that there is no need to fight if you do not have a personal tie to the pain that being has caused. Against my child's advice or otherwise, you believe that you have been particularly chosen for this task, as if you have been put into this life simply to carry out the wishes of those around you anymore than the rest of us have. Tair, little one"—Tair bristled—"we all have a role to play. Some have died if only to get *word* of King Usnaso's transgressions into Domani ears. Some have sacrificed their and their families' freedom if only to ensure that your very identity not be revealed. So many have chosen this fight, so many have *been* chosen for this fight; it is only a matter of degree."

"You made a distinction there: so many have *been chosen*," Tair dared, "and so many *have chosen*. You want me to make this choice, but you also tell me I have not been particularly chosen. Which am I, then, chosen or chooser?"

Omma's face again contorted into frustration as she shook her head. There was a sort of unattractiveness to Omma's features when warped by irritation, but it somehow made her more charming. Tair could not help but think of the Prime as her Omma, a parent or grandparent of sorts. In this way, she found it rather difficult to hate this Dwarf, even now. When her face had relaxed a little again, Omma scorned, "Shianna, you have made this nearly impossible. She knows nothing of anything, she cannot even *think* to fight, and yet you claim to have told her of her role in the world. Why would I have sent you to Mirte if not to prepare her for this fight?"

Shianna winced and tried to explain herself. "She was a child. She...I didn't want to hurt her."

"You may train children without hurting them," Omma said, which Tair wholeheartedly disagreed with. She did remember, though, one day about a year after Shianna arrived. The Dwarf had taken Tair a little farther north for what she had called an *adventure*. It was a pleasant enough memory and contained Tair's first memory of the ocean—but there was also that odd moment when Shianna tried to teach Tair proper footing for a fight. Tair recalled none of what she had been taught, but she did recall collapsing into a fit of laughter with Shianna after she fell the umpteenth time. She had proved useless in a fight and, apparently, Shianna had given up trying after that.

Stuck between her parent's scorn and her own parental instinct, Shianna only nodded and said, "I just...I did not want her to carry this burden, Omma."

"You did not want her to carry this burden, and yet she carries it. At the very least, you could have..." Omma sighed and shook her head. She would talk to Shianna later, apparently. She winced as she shifted in her seat once more to turn to look at Tair. "Some have chosen, some have been chosen, and you are amongst the latter—but make no mistake, you are no more chosen than anyone else who has been chosen. I promise you this: every being to walk Gosso, to walk the entire world, has been forced into a life they would not have imagined for themselves."

Tair folded her arms over her chest.

Omma said, "You are the only Human who could ever get close to King Usnaso without raising suspicion, but you are not singular in the sacrifices you must make to fulfill that task. Your parents, too, had to make hard choices—choices their world also forced upon them. Evidently, they did not refuse as you have."

Her parents. Tair had not considered her parents. In all honesty, she rarely considered her parents. Once she had discovered that she had been left in the Darkwoods as a defenseless child, she definitively decided that she hated them. Decided that, if given the chance, she would decline any opportunity to meet them. Omma claimed that Tair had a responsibility to Humans because her parents had also taken on a grave responsibility years ago—as if that alleviated the horror of what she was now tasked to do. Besides, Tair did not agree that her parents had no choice in the matter of their child's life. If they had truly loved her, could they not have gone with her to Nossoa? How thoroughly had they processed the fact that Tair, their child, would have to represent an entire revolution? Did they know what she would be tasked to do—did they know she would be tasked to kill? Whoever they were, they had sacrificed her to be a pawn in the revolution, not knowing if she would even survive the Darkwoods long enough to fulfill her role. As far as Tair knew, she appeared to have been in the Darkwoods for two days, guarded only by some enchanted stone to keep rooted in place until she was discovered—until someone external to, and able to view, that ring was able to release her. She had been left to starve, or otherwise dehydrate to death—and who was to say that a soldier of Rolt could not have discovered her first? Her parents had left so much up to chance.

They had left Tair's *life* up to chance.

If only in hopes of a better future. Tair shook the growing feeling of empathy from her heart.

And what had Tair really expected when she thought of a return to Doman, a return to Sossoa? She knew she would have had to return to the latter some point in her life, if only because she assumed the Humans who had abandoned her would recognize their mistake following their revolution and *want* her back. In her brief imaginings of returning to Sossoa, it was to a welcoming extended family of Humans more than it was to her particular biological family. Though she had acknowledged and wondered at that eventual return, she never thought it would look like this. Look like *murder*. Perhaps her own narrative of her future was naïve, childish. She bit back her tears. Had she left Mirte believing that she would ever experience any true degree of freedom? Was the value of her freedom anywhere near the value of her entire kind's freedom, a kind who had apparently rejected her before she could feel herself a part of them? She had no answers to her questions, as she often found to be the case. Yet, now it was different; now, Tair did not want to wait for the answers to come to her through experience. She wanted answers.

And was that not the root of this conflict in her mind? She had been *told* the answers, by Omma, by Shianna, even by those who had not known but had participated in the construction of Tair as she was, like Silaa and Alyn. Everyone was invested in their own truth, no matter the lies they had to tell to maintain their truths. When Tair had finally chosen her own answer and refused the task set to her, she was told that she was wrong, selfish, just as evil as the two Humans she was meant to kill.

She was only going in circles now, her new questions leading back to the same old questions and on and on. The path had been carved out by everyone and everything except her and her own two feet. There was no right path, no right answer, that led to anything but pain, either for herself or for the world. Tair hung her head in her hands as she paced in front of Omma and Shianna, reassessing all that the Prime had shared.

This was the information she had: King Usnaso was evil and dying; the King Heir was evil and very capable of continuing the legacy his parent had left for him. Was the son, then, not a worse offender? Was he not worthy of being the primary target? After all, he had the most potential to cause future harm. And then, who was she to know his future? Who was she to even *consider* changing the course of his future? The revolution was at its strongest point in almost seventeen years but was still unable to access the root cause of their revolution—unable to access *who* they were revolting against. Tair was meant to remedy that, having been deserted in the middle of the infamous Darkwoods, all in the hopes of an unknown, but hopefully better, future. She was merely a pawn waiting to be played, and here was her final play. In order to free her kind from generations of oppression, Tair would have to kill the King and King Heir who, until now, had been unkillable.

Tair, slightly enraged and wanting to lash out, started first with this: "And where were you then? After the Doman War, when King Unako fled south and murdered thousands in the first mass, organized genocide this continent—perhaps this *world*—had ever seen? What was your role then, if this is mine now?"

Omma narrowed her eyes. "We had just suffered the loss of thousands ourselves."

"So, you let thousands more die?" Tair spat.

"We may always try to remedy our past mistakes."

Tair resisted the urge to scoff. "The King and King Heir—can they not also try to remedy their past mistakes?" She weaponized Omma's own words against her, feeling much like Shianna must have when she had confronted Moss in Braasii, which felt like years ago. Tair shook her head and added, "You did not care for the fate of the Elves and Faeries who had once inhabited the land of Sossoa then, so why now? Why do you care for the fate of Humans who brutally stole the land, who reside there today and undoubtedly harbor hatred for you, just as their ancestors once did? After experiencing firsthand all the pain Humans have caused your kind...why do you care about their fate? Why must I play a part in their future?"

"You..." Omma considered the question a moment before answering. "I have changed in my years. The King and his Heir...they will never change, will never relent, which you would know if you knew what I knew."

"Tell me, then," Tair said.

Omma shook her head. "One day you will find out."

Tair had been told that all her life. She did not want to find out one day. She wanted to find out now. But Omma continued on before she could press further.

"As for your other questions, I have felt and seen the pain, yes. I have lived through the atrocities Humans have committed against my kind, and I have lived through their atrocities against others. Beaten and broken, I could not have envisioned what further defense and war would have solved." Omma took a breath. "But, after all this time of isolation by my kind and Humankind, I have begun to see the potential in unity and total liberation for all beings, across all realms. I have begun again to dream.

"When you have imagined a world such as the one we are

trying to create, it becomes impossible to accept the one we currently live in. It becomes impossible to accept a world where injustice is tolerated because it may not directly affect us—not anymore. We Dwarves are all too aware of the damage that powerful Humans can cause. Only now able to heal, we have come to the conclusion that none should live in bondage, including potentially hate-filled Humans, if it can be helped. If we sit idly by, what did our freedom from Humans in the Doman War mean? If that freedom cannot be felt by all, is it truly freedom?"

Tair bristled. Omma had turned from the past in the hopes of a brighter future, and Tair knew that, no matter the sacrifices she made, there would always be a greater impact, seen or unseen. Freedom could one day be felt by all—but only at the expense of her own.

SIX

That night for supper, it was just Tair and Bonn. They sat in a roomy chamber—one that was as far as Tair could manage from Omma and Shianna without venturing into another mountain. Bonn did not question Tair's desire for isolation, nor did they question Tair's request for their company, neither of which would Tair have been able to answer. When Tair had imagined Doman between here and Mirte, she saw large meals amongst large crowds of Dwarves, as Shianna had once described. As crowded with comradery and joy as her imagination had been, Tair was grateful to find this meal to be rather intimate. She was not prepared to be viewed again as an outsider, nor was she prepared to spend any amount of time with those who had betrayed her. There was no betrayal with Bonn; indeed, they did not yet know enough about one another to betray any sense of trust. That was comforting enough for Tair.

No matter the ease she felt with Bonn, Omma's unsettling words rang on in her head. Thankfully, Bonn was not one for needless conversation. The Dwarf seemed to prefer silence, though that silence was not stagnant. Even in this room, the mountain coursed with life. Tair still could not discern where the light in the room was coming from. Wherever the light originated, it illuminated a full table of breads and vegetables and some thick stew—and alcohol. Tair was unattached to the food, instead focused on the comfortingly warm beer, of which there was plenty. She had not drunk any water that day, she realized, but the soft sting of alcohol and its numbing effects—both physical and mental—brought her needed respite from the horrifying thought of killing two Humans. She moved to refill her stein again before Bonn reached out to stop her.

"You have to go slower," Bonn said. "You'll grow ill."

Tair met Bonn's fiery eyes and set down her cup. The Dwarf had not drunk as much as Tair—actually, Tair could not remember if Bonn had had anything to drink at all, dry as their glass was. Instead, they watched Tair curiously, no doubt wondering what she was so urgently trying to suppress. Tair was in urgent need of a confidant, and preferably one who had not planned the course of her life behind her back for eleven years, as Shianna had. If only she could divulge her secrets to Bonn...She shoveled a bite of bread into her mouth and followed it up with another sip of beer to force her silence. She kept her mouth as full as she could and her eyes as averted as possible, desperately avoiding Bonn's obvious curiosity.

Bonn was no fool, though, and saw straight through Tair's avoidant tactics. Instead of pestering the Human endlessly, Bonn ate their food in small bites and considered the taste of every mouthful. Finally, half an hour later, when they both had consumed all the food present and the room began to dim, Bonn leaned back in their seat, unbuttoned the top button of their trousers to make room for their full stomach, and said, "There is more to you than you're telling me."

Tair stood to leave, but Bonn stopped her by reaching out their hand. Though they did not touch Tair, Bonn's gentle, silent request for her to stay was effective. Tair sank back down in her seat with a huff, crossed her arms over her chest, and took another drink from her stein. She kept her eyes in her lap.

What could she have said, anyway? That everyone in her life found some way to betray her? That her family had been lying to her for years? That she was destined to assassinate both the King and King Heir of Sossoa? That her life ultimately meant nothing if not determined by someone else? Bonn had no claim to that information. Distantly, Tair realized that she, too, had not had a claim to that information until very recently.

As though they could hear Tair's thoughts, Bonn said, "I understand that I may not have a right to know what is happening, but I can still be here to help you."

Tair so desperately wanted for that to be true. Without any evidence to prove otherwise, Tair actually believed that Bonn wanted to help her. As it stood, though, the Dwarf would have to remain ignorant while Tair protected the integrity of an entire revolution. In hopes of changing the topic of conversation—and in hopes of getting her mind off of the information so indelicately shared with her only a few hours earlier—she asked, "Do you have family here?"

Tair's diversion did not go unnoticed, but Bonn was not one to press when their companion was visibly uncomfortable. They chewed the inside of their cheek a moment, then answered, "Dwarves' family structures are a bit more complex than you might be used to—or, at least, I have a more complicated family than you might understand."

Tair raised an eyebrow.

"I suppose one could say I have family here," Bonn said. "Shianna may not have ever mentioned another parent or parents besides Omma—that is only because she never truly had one. If a Dwarf is capable of becoming pregnant and wants to become pregnant, they can will it so; if they wish to no longer be pregnant, they can will it so. It is a very self-determined process, you might say. And quite laborious. The process forces the prospective parent to truly confront their preparedness for pregnancy and birth. Of course, this is not information non-Dwarves know or even truly understand. We are...secretive about many of our affairs."

Tair nodded. As Shianna explained it, Dwarves were not meant to share their magic with non-Dwarves. This little piece of information was more than the whole picture of Dwarven magic that Shianna had painted in eleven years. Tair felt grateful for this divulgence; it displayed a degree of trust that now felt mutual. And, though she did not know why the thought came to mind, Tair wanted to ask if Bonn themself ever wanted to become pregnant. Not that it mattered much to Tair, of course, as her own future had always felt predetermined in one regard or another. She had never once stopped to think about the generations to come, nor had she considered a part of herself living on in those generations. She resolved just to listen, if only to avoid the absurd thoughts about the future that always came up when she was around Bonn.

Tair was curious, though, having previously thought that only Faeries and Elves seeking to produce Fel could reproduce without partnered intercourse. Dwarves, according to Bonn, were apparently much more powerful; they could choose to become pregnant if it suited them, and so it would be. It seemed that only Humans were confined to the dual-partnered sexuality, but Tair could not accept this as fact. There had to be something else lingering within her and other Humans that they had not yet been able to discover. Something that had perhaps laid dormant for generations.

The Dwarf continued, "In that respect, sex and family structures can get a little muddled: one might find their mate, or mates depending on the circumstances, and they may choose to raise a child with that Dwarf or Dwarves. Other times, like with Omma and Shianna, it may be safer to raise a child on one's own.

"As for myself," Bonn continued, "my parents were mates, but they decided to have a child together before they even truly understood that they were mates. It is like...they already knew who they were to one another when words failed them." They paused. "I lived with them for the first decade or so of my life, but I never truly grew attached to them. When I left, there was no struggle. Family is safe like that here; we can choose which one suits us best at which times.

"I found Shianna and her friends when I was still young and, in many ways, they're more family than my parents ever were—or ever have been. I do not miss them, as you might expect me to, so much as they are a part of my blood and I am a part of theirs. I believe I have a few siblings, too, who are much closer to our parents, but they are no more my family than I consider the whole of Doman to be my family. Besides, family is who we choose, who we form our intimate bonds with. Does that make sense?"

It made sense to Tair, who did not feel connected to the biological concept of family as others had described, like Silaa or Alyn. Of course, Tair's idea of biological family had shifted—had been complicated by—all of the information Omma had shared. Was family her parents, whose legacy she apparently had to honor? Or, like Bonn had said of Doman, was family the whole of Sossoa, divided from them though she was, divided though she sometimes wanted to remain? No, Tair did not yet consider Sossok Humans family like she did Shianna, Alyn, and Silaa. The one thing Shianna had never hidden from Tair was that she was not amongst her blood family, evident enough when no one around her resembled her in the slightest. Still, there was something to blood relation that Tair felt drawn to but did not have a grasp on. Tair savored the thought of Moss, the first Human face in her memory—the first face that could have been family. She had later felt guilty for that thought; Moss was essentially a stranger in comparison to Shianna, Silaa, and Alyn; even so, betrayed by those three beings, she looked to find kin wherever she could. She remembered Alyn's words then: *I want you to let me know if you ever need to be Human.*

"I understand," Tair finally responded. "Family is who we choose, and family is who has also chosen us."

Bonn nodded.

Tair appreciated the validation but could see something else in Bonn's eyes that made her pause. She kept eye contact as long as she could before she directed her attention back to her empty plate of food. She asked, "Why are you looking at me like that?"

"I think," Bonn said, "you are endlessly intriguing."

Tair flushed. Tentatively, she nodded and agreed, "I have thought the same of you."

Bonn grinned and said, "Come with me." They held out their hand for Tair. Without second thought, Tair had grabbed ahold, and the two set off for—where? Bonn led Tair through passageways, down two flights of stairs, turned down two additional corridors, and then Tair began to lose track of where she was, their movements all too frantic for her level of intoxication. As Doman wound on and on, Tair marveled at how easily she trusted Bonn. How, twice now, she had trusted them to provide her refuge and to confront her with questions and truths and care. And care was a confrontation now; with someone to worry about her, to give her kind and gentle attention, to distract her from a life she felt she had no claim to, Tair was forced to confront her sense of abandonment and apathy. Toward herself, her kind, her family. She wanted to belong, and Bonn offered her belonging.

Finally, the two arrived at a wall marked with a sigil designed to look like the trees in Doman's neighboring forests. Bonn pressed both Tair's and their hands there and the wall opened up to a great, impossible garden.

Even more questions raced through Tair's head, the first

one she voiced being, "How is this possible?"

"The mountain feeds it," Bonn said. And the mountain fed it generously; all kind of fruits and vegetables grew on trees and bushes Tair had never seen before and a cool breeze blew through the room from some unknowable source—perhaps it was the mountain's own breath! If the mountain breathed, that was. A deep purple color illuminated the space around them. Tair paced up to and placed a hand on one of the trees that reached the ceiling. As she did, a red vegetable fell into her hands, perfectly ripe. She sniffed it, likening it to a kind of sweet potato, though all the potatoes she knew grew underground and not at the tops of trees. She brushed the skin of this new vegetable as she gazed out over the lush garden that spanned perhaps the entire base of all the mountains.

"This is," Tair breathed, "amazing." Too amazing to have also been the site of the hurt she had experienced hours earlier.

Tair could feel Bonn smiling behind her, still stood at the entrance to the garden with their hands folded behind their back. The Human turned around as the Dwarf continued what they had tried to say earlier, their orange eyes now ablaze: "I think you are the greatest Human I have ever met."

Tair scoffed, more shocked than anything else. She shifted her weight as she paused for the Dwarf to continue.

"In all truth," Bonn said, "you are the only Human I have ever met."

What a representative Tair was, only Human by fault of blood. She was also willing to abandon her Humanity in retaliation for their abandonment of her. Selfish, Omma had said. Tair shook her head. "I do not think you would say that if you knew what you do not know."

Bonn frowned but closed the gap between the two of them. In an unspoken request for permission, Bonn looked into Tair's eyes and held out their two palms. Rather on instinct, Tair clasped Bonn's hands.

"Raak kaanosa'aa-yia jssa kias?" What can't you tell me?
Tair loosely translated.

"I cannot tell you what you do not already know."

Bonn chewed on the inside of their cheek and gripped
Tair's hands harder, though without hurting the Human. In
fact, this touch even felt gentle, welcome, warm. Bonn asked,
"Do you feel it?"

Tair immediately knew what the Dwarf was talking about
and wanted to pull her hands away, but there was something
holding them together. She averted her eyes, a slight tear
slipping down her cheek before she nodded.

Confirming what Tair dreaded, Bonn said, "We are
mates."

The next morning, the mystery of the unknown light source
was solved. It was far too dark inside her room the night
before to discern anything in particular. Now, Tair blinked
through her hangover, wondering whether the alcohol was
stronger in Doman or if she had drunk much more than she
had originally believed. Through her haze, she saw thousands
of small crystals inlaid into the walls and ceiling, every single
one helping to mimic the light of day. The quality of light was
so accurate to the suns that it had taken Tair a moment to
realize that she had awoken another morning outside, that it
was not the Red Sun and the Yellow Sun warming her. The
crystals were quite beautiful, flickering between red and
yellow and pink, smooth to the touch and worn by time.
Doman was truly as magnificent as Shianna had always
described. There was a degree of peace to that thought—one
thing that Shianna had *not* lied about.

Tair had been allocated a plain room in one of the smallest
mountains, one of her first quarters as she slowly acclimated
to this foreign land. There was no door, unlike the room she
had eaten in last night, but there was a sigil—one that only
responded to Tair's touch, affording her a kind of privacy she

had not ever known. In Mirte, she had a simple doorknob with no lock. It was not uncommon for Shianna to stroll into her room for random conversation. When Tair was younger, she loved the closeness; as she grew, though, she found herself spending a lot of time outside, trying to create a sense of privacy afforded to her only when no one knew where she was. Sometimes she would venture a little farther than she had intended, but she never would have purposely run off. Stuck now in this predetermined life, she wished she had.

Tair had almost forgotten her fate, distracted instead by the majesty of Doman—distracted by the light and the rock and the *magic* that permeated the mountains. She wished she could have savored that waking moment of obliviousness, but reality afforded her no such refuge. She slumped back in her bed, pulled the sheets over her eyes, and let out a deep huff. She was so forlorn that she lacked tears; for tears, she would have had to believe herself capable of a fight.

Just when she thought she could sleep the day away, she heard a low hum not from someone on the other side of her wall but *from the wall itself*. She sat up in her bed and watched the wall glow brighter than it had moments earlier, swelling when the hum grew louder and dulling when the hum quieted. Tentatively, she stepped out of bed, pressed her hand to the sigil on her side of the wall, and let the rock open up before her.

On the other side stood Bonn. *"Dong'ga."*

Tair blinked. Suddenly the events of the previous night had returned to her. In the same day that she had been told that she was bound to turn assassin, the same day she had experienced such a severing of love with Shianna—that very same day, she had found her mate, which she had never envisioned possible. For much of her life, she had believed that she was not bound to anyone, unbelonging. Never to be known.

And here was Bonn.

Tair registered their words to mean *good morning* in Domani; Shianna had used it often enough. As minimal as Tair's understanding of the language was, she had always loved to hear it used—to use it herself. Domani had always offered this private form of communication between Shianna and her, especially at Elven dinners. It had been a kind of game when she was younger and a safety as she grew older. She bowed her head to her chest as she repeated the greeting to Bonn.

Bonn extended the glass of water to Tair and asked, "*Rako'kaana gon'na?*"

Tair took the glass in question and sipped, desperate for something to excuse her from speaking. If she could not speak, then they were also unable to talk about being mates.

Bonn frowned as the wall began to close up in front of them, the living rock reacting to Tair's anxiety. Tair set down her glass of water and placed her hand on the wall to keep it open and keep Bonn in her sight. Desperate to avoid acknowledging the truth of them being mates and then, too, having to share who she truly was, Tair still was unable to deny that she immediately relaxed whenever Bonn was near her. She let out a deep breath.

"How are you feeling today?" Bonn asked tentatively.

"Hungover," Tair said a little too quickly. Though it pained her, she lied, "I didn't have enough on my stomach before I drank and I—well, I can't remember anything after dinner."

"Oh," Bonn breathed. Their face fell, and Tair halted the instinct to say that she was joking. As monumental a moment as it was to meet one's mate, as exciting as it was, this revelation had come at the worst possible moment. Frightened of what would happen when the powers that be discovered she was mated with someone who would pull her away from her duties, Tair knew she had to protect Bonn from the world's unbearable weight.

No matter the cost.

Eventually, Bonn steeled themself and asked, "Nothing?"

Tair stiffly shook her head and, in attempt to change the subject, she asked, "Was this all..." She flinched back tears, her lie paining her more than she thought possible. How had Shianna managed it all those years with Silaa? She shook her head and continued, "Was this—Doman and all this life—here when Dwarves first arrived?"

Bonn recovered. Their desire not to make anyone uncomfortable had served Tair's lie, but she could not help but hurt as Bonn's saddened features shifted into a smile, one that accepted Tair's denial all too easily. "It is said the mountains created us. We arrived because we were created." Then Bonn began to loosely translate the familiar creation poem, one which Tair had previously believed only the Northern Elves held true:

> *"In Doman's loneliness,*
> *the mountains created life,*
> *the first of which were the Dwarves;*
> *The Dwarves were offered the gift of creation same as their*
> *own Creator,*
> *able to birth life by will..."*

Bonn cleared their throat before their added, "Well, I am not quite sure how to translate the rest, but you likely know there is more."

Tair did know, but part of her wanted to hear the rest from Bonn's lips. She could have listened to Bonn speak for days on end, never tiring. She could not say that, though, and she maintained silence until Bonn straightened and said, "Let us progress onward with our day."

Tair asked, "Our day?"

Bonn smiled. "I am to teach you how to fight."

Tair's eyes went wide. If Bonn was to teach her to fight, then what did the Dwarf know of how she was meant to use those skills? What did *her mate* know? Tentatively, she asked, "What for?"

"I did not ask," Bonn said as shook her head. "I have found you to be rather...private. No matter the reason, Shianna asked me to train you in her stead with the simple explanation that you may need time away from her."

Tair scoffed at the understatement.

"My training, I have been informed, is dependent on yours; as you learn, so will I. My reasons for education are different from yours, different still from what I have told Omma and my family. Perhaps you will learn the true reasons one day, as I will learn yours."

Tair almost asked for Bonn's reasons—and then remembered she had hidden so much from Bonn just in the past few days, including a truth that directly affected them and their relationship to Tair. If Bonn did not have a right to information on Tair's life, how did Tair have a right to Bonn's?

She was too distracted by Bonn's next statement to question them in the first place, though: "I also could not have said no to an opportunity to spend more time with you."

Tair flushed and looked away, feeling eternally watched in the Dwarf's orange eyes. She distracted herself with the matter at hand; simply, her mate was training her to fight; complicatedly, training her to *kill*. Tair did not know if she could manage either.

SEVEN

"*Kaosoa'aa!*" Bonn shouted as they ran toward Tair. The Human lunged at Bonn after their Domani command *move!* They had spent most of the day training with a dagger, which offered Tair the best room for control. She took to it quickly, but now they were working on dodging another's attack, which required far more endurance than Tair was prepared for. This was still an important part of the process, Bonn said, as they were trying to uncover Tair's strengths and weaknesses before they were able to move into more specialized training. She could not, of course, tell Bonn why it was so essential for her to learn and be well-versed in all of these tactics, but the Dwarf no longer asked questions and instead closely observed their sparring mate. Tair did not know if that was for the better, especially given how perceptive Bonn was. She feared that soon the truth of her responsibilities—the truth of their relationship to one another—would be revealed. And what then?

Tair wiped her brow of sweat. Three hours in, her clothes were thoroughly soaked, her rather weak muscles ached, and her exhaustion was nearly crippling. All the same, she found the physical fatigue to be a worthy distraction from the disturbing intent of that training. All that pent-up anger being released in her fighting, Tair thought she was rather rough with Bonn—or just as rough as someone who did not like fighting and who had never trained could have been—but the Dwarf never tired. When Tair believed to have finally seen a bead of sweat drip down Bonn's forehead, it was only the light shifting on their temples. Even when they had been training with a dagger and Tair had nicked Bonn, the Dwarf had healed far quicker than their Dwarven kin in the hall, quicker than Tair had ever thought anyone possible.

"You feel no pain!" Tair exclaimed through huffs. She was growing frustrated with Bonn's endurance, making her feel inadequate in the eyes of the one being she so desperately wanted to impress.

Bonn smiled. "I dull my senses."

"Why?" Tair blurted, though she wanted to also ask *how?*

"I awake with pain," Bonn said simply, their hand over their stomach. "Every day, I awake with pain. Years ago, I discovered that the mountain may take my pain and help me heal quicker than most, but it comes at the cost of dulling many of my physical senses. My daily life is a little more bearable, but..." They shrugged. "We all must make sacrifices."

Bonn's last statement pained Tair—why did they have to make sacrifices to live comfortably? Then she wondered, too, what sacrifices she had made, if any. She said nothing.

At some point, Counselor Denon had quietly arrived in the training hall. Though some other sparring Dwarves were curious as to why Tair, a Human, was in their midst, they seemed more troubled by Denon's attention to this strange Human than by Tair herself. Omma's counselor took notes as Tair attempted to duck Bonn's attacks and tried to land blows of her own. Tair ducked Bonn's punch, landed one of her own, and received a shout of encouragement or praise from Bonn:

"Ong!"

"You're sure?" Tair asked, despite herself. Though Bonn could heal quickly, she still worried every time she attempted to hurt or succeeded in hurting her mate. Bonn only nodded, unperturbed and ready to spar again.

Half an hour later, the crystals in the walls growing brighter as the Yellow Sun apparently rose outside, Tair finally collapsed on the mountain floor. She indulged in the sensation of the cold stone beneath her back, took some deep breaths, and eventually managed to peer up at Bonn standing over her.

"Done for the day?" Bonn asked.

Tair nodded and shut her eyes again as Bonn sat down next to her with a huff.

"Raak kaana'a ong," Bonn said to mean *you're good*, a phrase which Shianna had used with Tair plenty of times when she was younger—mostly to urge the Human not to do something bad. Now, the phrase was not used to scold, but to express admiration. Tair flushed. "We have a lot to learn, yes, but you have the determination."

Or she had the fury. Tair had been averse to fighting all her life, but she had to admit there was a kind of pleasure in being able to exorcise her frustrations. In an effort to believe that she did not like combat as much as she did, Tair had argued to herself that fighting was just another skill to develop, like cooking. And, quietly, Tair felt a degree of pride to know that Bonn thought she was good. She wanted to be good, especially after Omma had accused her of the exact opposite.

Tair turned to ask Bonn what areas she needed to develop further, but Counselor Denon came to stand over the two of them with his notebook in hand. Tair sat up, thin indigo tunic stuck to her back by sweat. Her hair, too, fell in strings across her arms, having grown significantly since they left Mirte. She was desperate to bathe, but it seemed that Denon had other plans for her.

"Have you completed your session?" Counselor Denon asked, in his rather peculiar way of pronouncing every Nossok word with intense precision.

Bonn glared at Counselor Denon. They asked in Domani, "*Raaka gkansa'aa jsa Domankana rak'ak kioo?*"

Counselor Denon pursed his lips as Tair struggled to translate in her mind what Bonn had said, something roughly like, *Why won't you speak Domani with me?* Shianna had once explained that there had been fear of losing the Domani language with the introduction and integration of Nossok, but many young Dwarves surprisingly took to Domani with new fervor, if only to keep it alive in the collective Dwarven consciousness. Counselor Denon, though, did not use the language at all—and especially refused it with those he believed to be beneath him. As superior to Shianna as he clearly thought himself to be the day before, he undoubtedly set himself an entire world apart from Bonn and did not appreciate their challenge.

"I will assume you are finished," he said, "and I will take the Human from here."

Knowing she was pushing the boundaries but wanting to express quiet solidarity with her mate, Tair asked in Domani, "*Ak-kiso?*" Where to?

Counselor Denon turned red in the face, caught between embarrassment and anger. His mouth pressed into a firm line, he forced himself to answer, "You have more training to do."

"I don't think I'm ready for further training at the moment," Tair said with a yawn.

He folded his arms behind his back and took a step away. With a slight bow—a bow that meant was meant to silence Tair, a bow that suggested he knew exactly who Tair was and what she was meant to do, a bow that silenced the rest of the training hall and Bonn, too—he said, "You will join me."

Counselor Denon intended to draw attention and so force her to follow him, and it had worked. Tair stood on achy legs and hurried after the Dwarf, who was already shuffling ahead. Wherever they were headed next, she hoped it would provide her adequate refuge from her complicated relationship to Bonn, hoped it would be less physically draining.

She had also learned not to hope for much.

The last thing Tair had expected Counselor Denon to lead her to was another Human—a Human who was undoubtedly the reason Tair was not an entirely foreign sight to Domani Dwarves. Definitely Tair's senior, though younger than Moss, Tair might have placed the Human somewhere in their forties, though their graying roots suggested slightly older. They had a tired smile, one dependent on every genuine smile that had come before it and existed only in muscle memory. Their skin was a bit darker than Tair's and their arms were covered in permanent black ink, which the Elves of Mirte called *eematt*. Plenty of Elves wore them, and Tair had even seen some Dwarves with them in Doman, but she never imagined that Humans could don permanent designs, too. The Human's *eematts* were of some kind of flower Tair could not initially place but quickly remembered when the older Human introduced themself: "Rose. I'll be your cultural guide and eventually escort you to Sossoa." Tair noted that they did not offer their pronouns, so she kept with the Nossok neutral and chalked it up to cultural differences, ones that she assumed she would learn in time.

This was the tutor Omma had spoken of, she resolved. Rose drew Tair into a strong hug, which caught the younger Human off guard, as had every moment of this interaction. The past couple days of Tair's life had felt like a whirlwind, and even now she could not catch up. She swallowed the lump in her throat as she pulled out of the hug. Omitting her pronouns in accordance with Rose's precedent, she introduced herself: "Tair."

"Not anymore," Rose said without hesitation. "You'll need

to choose a new one."

Tair had considered this on their journey from Braasii, and she had resolved that she did not want to change her name. As she stared into Rose's stern yet kind eyes, she knew that refusal again would not be an option, just as it had been with Omma. Admittedly, Tair understood what kind of problems arose when she revealed her name, one that immediately revealed that she had not gone through the Human tradition of naming oneself. As important as it was, she could not think of a name she identified with more than the one she already called her own.

Rose sensed that Tair had gotten wrapped up in thought and waved Denon out of the room. It was only when they were alone that Tair realized the sheer size of Rose. The older Human, though their name suggested otherwise, was anything but delicate. They were at least a foot taller than Tair, a height that Tair associated with Elves. Their height was only made more intimidating by their strength, their *eematts* highlighting their muscles. They were so strong, in fact, that their clothes strained against their muscles, their sleeveless top no match for their broad shoulders. If only due to stature, there was no way Tair could imagine them blending in here, amongst the Domani Dwarves—or blending in anywhere, really.

Even if they could have, it did not seem that Rose would ever want to fade into the background; they commanded space and attention. Without instruction, Tair knew to sit down across from the older Human as they took their seat. Tair unconsciously tried to match Rose. She squared her shoulders, tilted her head up ever so slightly, and ensured her back was erect.

Rose smiled again at Tair. Then they said something in Sossok—which Tair could only place because it had a similar melody to Moss's words in Braasii. Out of Rose's mouth, each word flowed, soft and melodic, into the next. It had the distinct sound of...

Not belonging. Tair felt she did not belong.

"I don't..." Tair paused from the humiliation. "I don't know what you're saying."

"Nothing then?" Rose said in Nossok, accent akin to Shianna's.

Tair shook her head.

Rose nodded and pulled out a clean sheet of paper. Carefully, in Nossok characters and then Sossok underneath, they wrote out what they had asked, turned the paper to Tair, and said, "I asked: *So'ahllo-aso ano Sanak?* Or, how much Sossok do you know?"

Tair nodded. It was all she could do; no words came to her, her humiliation tying her tongue.

Rose waited a moment, then tapped the paper. "Try it aloud."

Tair struggled but was able to manipulate her mouth to pronounce the words correctly by the third try. Rose did not congratulate Tair effusively, but their pleasant, genuine smile was enough of a reward. Tair traced her fingers over the letters on the page, familiarizing herself with the parent tongue that had never parented her.

"Now," Rose continued as they relaxed back in their chair, "what do you know of our kind?"

"Only what Shianna—the Prime Heir—has told me. Or Alyn, my Fel friend who..." Tair's heart suddenly dropped when she mentioned Alyn's name. She felt as though she had not seen the Fel in weeks, but it had not been one full day since their last interaction. Unfortunately, since the last time they had been able to truly speak with one another, a lot had changed—her newfound responsibilities to a realm she had nearly no personal connection to, then the revelation of her mate, and now she was meeting another Human. Tair felt desperate for Alyn's input and advice, unaware of how much she depended on him until they were apart. She cleared her throat and said, "Alyn, a well-traveled Fel, and Silaa, an Elf, have also shared what little they know."

"And of Sossoa on the whole?"

"I know it was founded after the Doman War, that it is our homeland, that it is where most Humans live..." Tair answered, trailing off where her knowledge stopped. Because she did not know how much Rose knew, Tair did not add that her knowledge of Sossoa also included her task to kill the King and King Heir, nor did she mention how she had come to Doman in the first place by way of abandonment to the Darkwoods.

"We thought his cruelty would not reach us," Rose began without warning. A little belatedly, Tair realized the older Human referred to King Usnaso. "He has been in power seventy years now, beginning his reign when he was around your age. The King Heir was born around thirty years into his reign, and thus began the devolution of an already corrupt and declining nation."

Tair remained silent at the mention of the Humans she was set to kill—the Humans she had refused to kill, even though she had not refused the training that set her down that path. Of course, her training also involved Bonn, so she may have had ulterior motives. She cringed at her priorities, more importance placed on her personal relationships than an entire realm of beings.

"I was born into this declining world. By then, of course, there had long been no non-Humans left; slaughtered, imprisoned, or enslaved almost five hundred years earlier. Our homeland, as you call it, is founded on genocidal homogeneity under the guise of peace, of safety in numbers," Rose explained. Tair swallowed as her words were turned against her. And, distantly, she recognized that the same claims of homogeneity breeding peace and safety could have been said about Doman, too, though for entirely different reasons. It was easy for Shianna to claim Doman as her homeland because her kind had had to fight for the land, fight for their freedom; conversely, Tair could not in good conscience claim a realm that originated in genocide and oppression.

Despite Tair's justified and necessary discomfort, Rose forged on. "Any non-Humans who appear beyond Sossok borders are immediately imprisoned or killed—and protecting them is futile. When I was five years of age, my family had been protecting a Faery child who had strayed from the Darkwoods and ended up further south, but a soldier discovered the youth and killed them without question, without hesitation." Tair shivered. "Unfortunately, when expectations are met, there is not much conflict raised—and we had come to expect, and accept, non-Human death. We were apathetic, fearful of ending up amongst the dead.

"Things first changed with the establishment of Rolt. In the past, the Darkwoods had been free to all Sossok Humans to roam, an important spiritual and environmental border that was the last space that was distinctly *not* Sossoa. Rolt, though, served to correct this; a physical border between Sossoa and the Darkwoods and, thus, Nossoa, too. The wall was finally completed as a gift to honor the birth of King Usnaso's son, a symbol for his future as king."

"Rolt has not been there since the founding of Sossoa?" Tair was shocked at this; she had taken the border for granted, something she had assumed Shianna and Alyn and Silaa had all grown up with, too. To find out it had been built and completed within their lifetimes, that it was closer in age to her and Bonn than it was to Silaa...Tair felt another chill run up her spine.

Rose shook their head. "Countless Humans died in the construction of it. Again, expectations were met—the dead were all enslaved traitors to the throne. They *deserved* punishment—or so we were told. Though when treachery means simply glancing at a soldier the wrong way, everyone is a traitor. Even still, no one posed any challenge because they thought themselves to be above treason, as I once did."

Tair did not push here, but she realized immediately what that meant; Rose had once been amongst the enslaved. The younger Human then noticed the scar across Rose's breast and collarbone, a thick gash about as wide as Tair's finger and long as her whole hand. As much pain as Rose has experienced in their life, Tair was meant to bring an end to that pain, to any future pain Humans would experience. Tair shook her head, denying the fleeting thought that she had any responsibility to a land and a kind that had once cast her out—and to a land whose origins were so vile.

Rose continued, "It is only when expectations are *not* met that any challenge is raised. Food stores were hoarded by greedy soldiers, land was stolen and redistributed only to those willing and able to fight and kill for the realm, and entire families began to disappear at random, my parents and siblings included. I still do not know what happened to them, but I was spared, as they put it. They always left alone those who could produce new generations of Humans."

Tair winced. On instinct, she asked, "Why are you telling me all of this?"

Rose merely glanced in Tair's direction, acknowledging that they had at least heard the question. Even if they had heard it, what they said next indicated that they did not intend to answer. "You cannot imagine the pain—most of which I have yet to mention—that we have all endured throughout his reign, nor what our ancestors had endured before us. You cannot imagine how much can change in one lifetime.

"But, as with all things, resistance comes in waves. We who survived found new ways of living and educating ourselves, contrary to what we had been taught. Even then, no resistance in the face of immeasurable power is complete without an army—and no resistance can survive without a fight. We had the drive, but we did not have the power. That is how"—Rose gestured to the mountain around them, the crystals dulling as the Red Sun set outside—"the kingdom of Doman has become an essential ally."

Omma's words from the day before echoed on in Tair's head: *I have begun to see the potential in unity and total liberation for all beings, across all realms. I have begun again to dream. When you have imagined a world such as the one we are trying to create, it becomes impossible to accept the one we currently live in.*

"As for me," Rose explained, "I was later discovered stealing food from storage to help feed my family and community. I spent five years enslaved, shipped all around Sossoa, until a rebel had finally infiltrated the soldiers' ranks and helped me from Rolt. I ran through the Darkwoods and came North."

Rose went on to explain how they had become a refugee in and around Doman for ten years now, and how they had helped many Domani Dwarves better understand Humanity and the reasons they were fighting. Even still, they planned to return to Sossoa to continue the fight, a sentiment which made Tair question the Human's sanity.

Tair interrupted, "You would return?"

"It's home," Rose said. "Even after all the bloodshed, it is home. If I am to never return, what was the fight for? Why continue living on?"

Tair suddenly felt tears lick her cheeks, so completely unprepared for the agony she had just been exposed to. After a full day of physical labor, she found the emotional labor to be all the more draining. She hung her head in her hands, her shoulders shaking. *What was the fight for?* Tair thought again to Omma's statement: *Your parents, too, had to make hard choices—choices their world also forced them into. Evidently, they did not refuse as you have.* What were those choices for, if not in hopes of the very future that made Rose want to live on? Tair could not fathom that nearly twenty years of revolutionary action would culminate with her ultimate decision: whether or not to take the lives of two Humans. Two Humans of royal blood, two evil Humans, yes, but two Humans, nonetheless. The future would either be born from or die in her hands.

Over Tair's tears, Rose said, "I tell you this to say: to be *Sanak*, you must know what that means in its entirety. The language is nothing without the history; the resistance is nothing without the future. You must know what you come from, and why you have been chosen to finally end it. And you *will* end it."

EIGHT

So went the course of many of Tair's days for the next eight weeks, which she tracked in the notebook Rose had given her for their lessons. She started with a brief breakfast with Bonn on their way to physical training; then, usually without break to bathe or recuperate, she attended Sossok lessons with Rose. Though private dinners with Bonn were at least a weekly occurrence, most of Tair's days concluded in large dining halls amongst Dwarves who encouraged plenty of substance use and ate plenty of hearty food. It was there, in the joyous chaos of the dining halls, that Tair most effectively dodged Bonn's infrequent but probing questions, usually meant to gauge whether or not Tair knew they were mates. Or was ready to admit that they were mates. Tair believed herself to have gotten very good at lying and supposed she had gained the ability from her years with Shianna. Desperate though she was to dull the stress of caring more for Bonn but knowing that their lives would soon be divided if Tair did what the world expected of her, she now found herself queasy at the sight of intoxicating substances, perhaps spurred by Bonn's abstinence.

Her growing distaste for alcohol was well-timed, too, seeing as she had to be aware of and maintain her lies at any given moment.

One night, Bonn and Tair found themselves at the end of a long table in a dining hall. They had acclimated to the third innermost mountain, only one left before they arrived at the final and most daring one. Crowded as the hall was, the two sat close to one another but kept flinching whenever their thighs brushed. They had taken to eating in silence in recent weeks, each more and more dejected by the truths hidden. Even still, even in their silence, they learned about each other and their relationship, for which Tair was endlessly grateful.

And, despite her outward silence, Tair's head was now full of many languages: her fluency in Nossok, her casual knowledge of Northern Elvish, her growing fluency in Domani, and her flourishing understanding of Sossok. The constructed language of her kind had been created to distinguish themselves from non-Humans; ironically, some Domani words had been modified or else stolen entirely for Sossok. Despite the language's deplorable origins, Tair relished in the ease with which it came to her. All of the languages buzzing about in her head provided plenty of vocabulary to process her circumstances and plenty of space for silence.

That silence always shifted once Shianna, Silaa, and Alyn arrived. Though Silaa had disappeared in recent days for some reason unknown to Tair, Shianna still came bursting into the halls full-force, ready to converse. Alyn usually followed closely behind with new stories of his daily adventures—and, as always, was eager to hear any stories the Domani Dwarves had for him.

Tair still had not told him what she was bound to do, but at least she knew that he had not been in on the horrible secret, too. The Human had resolved early on to ask Shianna outright if anyone besides her and Omma had known, a question Shianna had been somewhat surprised by but answered in the negative. It was settled then; Alyn had betrayed her (perhaps reluctantly) when he hid information about their departure from Mirte, but he had never known that he was raising a Human child that would one day become an assassin.

Alyn and Shianna now sat down across from Tair and Bonn, crammed in at the end of the table like any other latecomers. As Shianna had explained, there was no serious attention paid to formalities in Doman, but Tair had not expected it to be to this degree. Even in Mirte, organized in a nonhierarchical political structure, there was a general plan as to how dining halls would be arranged, with the elders at the head of the room and the children at the back. In this way, as one matured, they also received greater physical freedoms within the community. Though the Prime Heir received a few nods here and there, Tair had found that few acknowledged Shianna any more than they would have another Dwarf in the room. As important as she was to the future of Domani Dwarves, Shianna was firstly *Domani*; she did not receive special treatment for a quality she shared with a million others.

"*Rak kaana'a janasaau!*" Shianna said in Domani, a phrase often used to convey extreme hunger. She pounded her fists on the table, which indicated for someone further down the line to pass one of the shared dishes along to her. There were few, if any, personal utensils and dishes in these dining halls. Most ate with their hands, often using bread as a way to transfer the food from the plate to their mouth.

Alyn, too, took his fill. After he swallowed a large mouthful, he sighed in Northern Elvish, "*Eeshanna...*" He closed his eyes and sank back in his chair, which earned a giggle from Shianna and a slight smile from Tair. Bonn, on the other hand, never seemed to know how to feel around Tair's companions. They often looked to Tair for indication of her feelings, but Tair filtered herself a great deal around the Prime Heir and the Fel these days. With the weight of Sossoa's collective future on her shoulders, her personal opinions toward individuals felt rather foolish. Still, she instinctively scowled whenever Shianna walked into a room, which Bonn picked up on and responded to in tandem.

Alyn and Shianna spoke to one another in between their bites of food, slipping easily between Domani and Northern Elvish and back again into Nossok. Bonn had trouble with the use of Northern Elvish. After all, only the Elves of Mirte spoke the language still; Bonn would not have had a reason to learn it.

"What do they mean?" Bonn whispered into Tair's ear, tickling her skin. Alyn and Shianna laughed hysterically at something the Fel had said.

Tair flushed and glanced into her lap. Hiding that she knew they were mates had become particularly difficult in recent weeks. Hiding anything from Bonn was difficult. Even the matter of language created new lies; a few weeks prior, she had told Bonn that she picked up her knowledge of Northern Elvish from Alyn, completely omitting the fact that she had grown up using the language. Now, she explained that Alyn was referencing a time he had been stopped by Domani troops while passing the northern side of the mountains after having used casual magic to amplify his voice while singing. Apparently, they had heard him coming from miles away. At first, they wanted to know why he was projecting so much (sometimes he simply liked to be loud); then they wanted to know if he could teach them the trick. He explained that he could not teach what he had done, dependent as it was on his ability to manipulate the air. This had invited a whole slew of new questions concerning his being a Fel and a lot of misunderstanding...Tair was not quite sure why Alyn and Shianna were laughing. Alyn's encounter sounded tiring, but he was amused all the same. As he told his tale, he twirled his finger in the air, sending little clouds of blue and gray smoke above his head.

Now it was Tair's turn to ask Bonn, "Where does the smoke go?"

Bonn shrugged as they grabbed another roll of bread from the center of the table. They said, "The mountain takes it."

"Where?" Tair pushed.

"Where does any air go?" Bonn countered.

Tair considered this a moment. She had never paid much attention in her classes in Mirte because Shianna undid all of her knowledge anyway. The Elves had explanations for nature that she did not recall, so she just said, "There is more space outside. Shouldn't we suffocate in here?"

"The mountain takes it," Bonn repeated. They turned fully to face Tair now, their legs straddling either side of the bench they both sat at. Tair unconsciously mirrored the movement and leaned in when Bonn did. Quietly—almost too quietly, Tair had to angle herself to hear the Dwarf over the sounds of the dining hall—they said, "I must tell you something."

Tair almost jumped back. She had figured Bonn would reiterate the revelation that the two of them were mates at some point in the near future, but not here and not like *this*. She glanced around to the other Dwarves in the hall nervously, her heart beating rapidly in her chest. Finally, she asked, "What is it?"

"I spoke to Rose," Bonn said.

Tair was surprised; she did not think Bonn even knew who Rose was. Then again, she supposed, when only two Humans inhabited Doman, they were bound to stick out. The Dwarf was smart enough to deduce that they had probably had something to do with one another.

And, Tair hated to admit it, but there was some Human quality that they both shared, too, that would have united them even if they had not come together in Doman. Tair and Rose both understood the roles they had to play in their respective lives. They did not fight reality. They simply saw what life gave them and coped, in one way or another. It was this quality, perhaps, that made Tair prefer the older Human to any teachers she had in the past, all of them Elves who had, on occasion, doubted Tair's ability to absorb any information at all, just by fault of her Humanness. To Rose, Tair was another Human. To Tair, Rose provided access to a world that the younger Human had never been able to engage with. There was a kind of ease with which they existed in each other's space, no matter what loomed at the end of Tair's path which led to an impossible and dark horizon.

Tair tried not to pay too much attention to the version of herself that had become so complacent in her own life.

But she had something else to think about now; if Bonn had spoken to Rose, that probably meant that Rose had told them something that Tair would not have wanted to be revealed. Before she could control herself, Tair had sprung up from the table and run out of the dining hall.

Tair had spent the better part of the night trying to find Rose, but after many fruitless hours and with her growing physical fatigue, she resolved to meet them the next morning for their regularly scheduled Sossok lessons. Storming into the room, she said a curt, "*Aesolo-aso. Asos ahkji—*"

Rose shook their head, cutting Tair off and silently commanding she get up and try again. After four frustrating attempts at entering and exiting the room, Rose seemed satisfied. They finally returned the greeting and gestured for Tair to sit down. Tair knew better than to dawdle any longer and took her designated seat. Desperate to receive some clarity on what Rose had said to Bonn, she was not particularly keen on waiting for their lessons to commence so she could hear more about the pain of her kind, or so that she could learn more of a language she felt she could intuit at that point.

"*So arrha ran'ayie ano?*" Rose asked in Sossok. Though

Tair had believed she could intuit the language, she now blankly stared back at Rose. As they did whenever they realized Tair had not understood something, Rose wrote the phrase down on a sheet of paper, passed it across the table, and said aloud, "It is the informal way to ask how someone is doing, only to be used when someone is clearly not doing well."

Tair nodded and tried the words out on her tongue. She also relished in Rose's passing remark—informality conveyed friendliness. There was something rewarding about the fact that they had grown so close in a language that Tair had only been introduced to two months earlier. The two had bridged an unspoken gap. Tair tried to suppress her smile as she said in Nossok, "*Asos ahrra...*fatigued."

Rose smiled at Tair's slip into Nossok and shook their head. They wrote *hahtas* in Sossok characters—which Tair assumed meant fatigue—and had the younger Human repeat it a few times before they decided to use Tair's native Nossok to ask, "And why is that?"

Tair furrowed her eyebrows and asked, "Why do you think?"

Rose remained silent.

Frowning, she asked, "What did you tell Bonn?"

Rose sank back in their seat, crossed their arms over their chest, and said, "Oh, yes, Bonn approached me to ask questions about you a few days ago."

"*Days?*" Why had Bonn kept silent all that time? She shifted in her seat.

Rose nodded and pursed their lips, then said, "They asked if I knew anything about you."

Tair leaned forward. "And I am sure you didn't tell them anything?"

"They're your mate," Rose said, as if it was any kind of answer.

Though Bonn had not confronted her about being Tair's

mate since that first night in Doman, Tair was surprised to find that Bonn was telling others. Or, at least, that others knew. Maybe they already knew that Tair was lying. That hurt her more than she wished to say. With more pressing issues on hand, though, she repeated, "Tell me you did not tell them anything."

"They would have found out eventually."

Tair buried her face in her hands.

After a moment, Rose said, "I understand why you kept them in the dark, but I cannot imagine hiding such a thing from my mate."

Tair grumbled, "You wouldn't understand."

Rose narrowed their eyes and stood to think and pace, a tick which Tair previously assigned to Bonn. Tair wanted to be angry at this Human; indeed, only a few weeks earlier, she would have likened this to another kind of betrayal. However, she felt no kind of rage as she watched Rose move around the room, their long gray hair drifting when they pivoted. Maybe it was their kinship, maybe it was the kindness with which Rose treated her, but the older Human was one of the only beings left in Tair's life that she deeply trusted. She did not know when or how she would have told Bonn—or if she would have *ever* told Bonn—and, in a way, this breach of confidentiality offered Tair an out she had not considered. More importantly, Rose knew, perhaps better than most, how sensitive Tair's circumstances were. Something like pride swelled in Tair's heart when she realized that meant that Rose found Bonn to be trustworthy.

Rose stopped pacing, gripped the back of chair they once sat in, and looked Tair right in the eyes. They said, "I believe I do understand. I never told my *semsuna*"—which Tair believed to mean mate in Sossok, some combination of "we" and "Human"—"that I was a part of the revolution, if only because I thought it would keep them and our children safe."

Tair had never imagined Rose to have voluntarily had

children, especially after their comment about how the Sossok army had spared their life simply because they were able to reproduce. Tair partially revised her image of Sossoa, but it still was not generous. She did, however, find herself in even deeper reverence for Rose. All that they had sacrificed...And what was Tair sacrificing? Her life had been designed so that she never got attached, never needed anyone besides Shianna, Silaa, and Alyn, and so she had nothing to lose. Nothing to gain, either. Now, she supposed, she could have added Bonn and Rose to that short list. She could not decide if attachments made her want to fight harder or to give up easier—for Rose, evidently, attachments meant *fight harder*. She averted her eyes as she asked, "I thought your family was taken?"

Rose nodded and said, "Yes, when I was a child, my parents and siblings were taken from me, but I was free. Well, as free as one can be without anyone beside them—which is to say not free at all. Still, one day, I had a family of my own, a family I had to feed and defend and imagine new futures for. My mate did not know I had been stealing to provide for them all, but they also knew that neither of us had the resources to sustain all that we had. We never spoke of it. We kept our silence because we foolishly believed we would be safer that way. In the end, it did not matter. I was imprisoned, never to see any of them again, and escaped here. I don't know if they are still alive, nor if I compromised their safety by keeping them in the dark. I wish, though," Rose said in a saddened tone, "I had told them what I was doing. That way, we could have planned for the worst."

Tair met Rose's eyes again. "The worst?"

"To be apart from each other."

Rose understood, then, why Tair suddenly stood from her chair, left the room, and set out to look for Bonn. She lost her way a couple times, nearly sure the mountain was purposely disorienting her, but she finally arrived at the sigil behind which she knew Bonn would be. She placed her hand there, shocked that the wall opened to her, and stepped inside without announcing herself.

On the floor before them, Bonn had hundreds of sheets of crumpled-up paper strewn about. Though that may have been an exaggeration, the room was, without a doubt, a *mess*. The paper was not the only clutter; their bed was unmade, their belongings thrown about haphazardly, and their clothes a heap in the corner of the room. The Dwarf was silent, calculating, and clever—all signs that did not fit the disorder all around them.

Bonn did not notice Tair come in. When Tair cleared her throat, then, Bonn stood and turned around with those fiery eyes that the Human had grown endeared to. Holding another sheet of crumpled paper in their hand, Bonn said, "I was waiting on you, *dorra!*"

Tair blushed at Bonn's casual use of the Domani word for love. Tair was certain now that they knew she had been lying, and they had hit a breaking point, desperate to know why Tair had been so secretive all this time. Tair could not help but smile at the fact that someone was so concerned with her life. She moved to sit on the edge of Bonn's bed, instinctively altering the sheets to bring some order to the chaos. She asked, "What's all of this?"

Bonn said, "I'm trying to figure out a way to get you out."

"Out?"

"I know you," Bonn said, with as much conviction as one might declare there were two suns in the sky. They came to sit down next to Tair, who kept her attention averted.

"No..." Tair hung her head. Unsure of how to continue, she resolved to blurt out, "I've been lying to you."

"I know," Bonn said. "And I...I think I understand why."

"I did not want you to get hurt."

Bonn smirked, an expression behind which they undoubtedly hid pain. "You did not want me to *get hurt*, so you hurt me."

Tair nodded.

"In a different way," Bonn added. "You hurt me a different way."

"I know," Tair said. She switched to Domani for her apology, hoping that Bonn also felt that the expression held more weight in the Dwarven language than Nossok could have contained: "*Rak grasora'a.*"

Bonn nodded. Tair did not feel that anything was resolved, but Bonn continued onward anyway, saying, "I know you do not want to live the life they have designed for you."

Tair sighed.

Bonn offered an explanation, "We are mates, Tair. As much as you want to avoid that fact, it remains true. And, as much as you may accept your circumstances, as much as you tried to protect me from that truth, I know you would change them if you felt able. I have no qualms with what you have to do." The Dwarf was certainly a proponent of self-defense, as many Dwarves were. Tair supposed what she had to do was still self-defense, though to a different degree. Bonn continued, "No matter my opinion, though, it is a matter of what you are capable of, and you cannot kill."

"You have trained me to," Tair mumbled. "I have to."

Bonn tentatively put their hand over Tair's. Tair, surprising herself, did not pull away. They said, "You have been told you have to, yes, but what if there was a different way?"

Tair wanted to laugh at this, but the question was so sincere that she kept listening.

"Violence is at the root of this problem, and violence may help solve part of it. Violence on your part, I think, would only make you vulnerable to further violence."

This, Tair had already accounted for—this little detail that everyone seemed to neglect: her life. How they expected her to kill two high-level Humans and escape unscathed, Tair did not know. It had been two months since she discovered her fate—two months since she realized that no one intended for her escape, her life bound to end before it had truly become hers at all. All the time she had imagined escaping from the bondage of her existence necessitated that there was somewhere to escape to. As soon as Omma had told her what she was meant to do, any future she had hoped for evaporated, whether she had been able to admit it to herself or not. Nonetheless, though Tair could not see herself killing, she also could not imagine that all the pain her parents and her *kind* had gone through would amount to nothing.

"Besides," Bonn continued, "the Human revolution, just as any revolution, is more than a battle, more than death. They can kill the King and King Heir, but what of the oppressed generations taught to hate? How do they heal their bigotry in the generations to come, outside of one singular event in the grander course of a revolution? Would violence truly heal them?"

"Yes, would it?" Tair was curious as to what Bonn had in store, as impractical and imaginative and impossible as it all sounded.

Bonn only chewed the inside of their cheek, waved a hand. "These are just questions. I haven't arrived at any answers— yet."

Tair dropped her head in disappointment. As the crumpled-up pieces of paper suggested, Bonn did not have it all mapped out, but Tair had hoped there was *something*. Bonn hooked a finger under Tair's chin and raised the Human's eyes to meet their own. Tair felt bare in Bonn's eyes, a surprisingly comfortable feeling. She blinked hard and did not wipe away the tear that escaped from the corner of her eye.

Bonn said, "I have not arrived there yet, but I have to care. I *want* to care, I felt inclined to care before we even knew each other's names, before the lies. Just...like when you fall and scrape your knee; sometimes you feel it before you see it. And there's so much there, skin and blood and bone, but now you see it and you cannot unsee it. There are always these hidden layers that are only revealed when laid bare."

Tair smiled. "That is a bit vulgar."

"But it's true," Bonn said, returning the smile. "I cannot look away now, not from Sossok Humans' pain and not from your pain. I am here for you now—have been, will continue to be—and I cannot live in a world where I sit idly by while your life is stolen away from you, one second at a time, until you waste away. What if it were me? What would you do?"

A great question that Tair did not know the answer to. Morally, she did not believe she could let what was happening to her happen to anyone else. She hated the idea of watching while the world took all it could from Bonn, who watched her now with blazing eyes. She stirred in her place, maintaining eye contact. Though it barely began to scratch the surface of her true feelings, Tair said, "I would fight it."

"So why would you let it happen to you if you would not let it happen to me?"

The answer flashed in Tair's mind: she was not worthy, not worthy of the fight from herself but especially not from Bonn. She had come to terms with the idea that she did not have any say in her own life.

Bonn was different, though. They had, as far as Tair knew, always been free to choose their life. If they had not known what choice to make, they had friends and family and supporters around them, willing to give them advice and help them *keep fighting*. Tair envied Bonn's ostensible abundance of choice that freed them to fight for the choices of others.

Tair searched Bonn's eyes as the Dwarf added, "What is this new world if it is not rooted in consent, in a truly collective desire for freedom?"

Tair grabbed hold of Bonn's wrist, her mate now cupping the side of her face.

"I would do this for you because I know you would do this for me," Bonn resolved, despite the lies, despite the pain Tair had caused them. They still cared for Tair. The Human now broke eye contact, frightened of the passion in Bonn's eyes. Over their shoulder were piles of crumbled paper, soaked with drying black ink meant to end Tair's suffering. She shifted on the edge of the bed as she considered her next move: to follow Bonn and determine her own life, or to succumb to the wishes of the world and effectively end her life, abandoning her kind in the process.

Softly, hands still cupping Tair's cheeks, Bonn asked, "Can I kiss you?"

The abrupt question startled Tair. She had never heard anyone ask it before, nor did she exactly believe it relevant to their current circumstances. Yet as the words met her ears, she tried not to nod too eagerly. Bonn ducked down to Tair on the edge of her bed. A hand at the back of the Human's neck, a careful focus on each other's eyes, and then—when their lips met, Tair felt it *everywhere*. In the usual places she expected, and in the places that she did not; energy coursing through her fingertips, her legs buzzing, her hair on ends all over. And, distantly, she thought she could feel how Bonn felt it, too. As if, with one kiss, they were able to become one. She had never felt anything quite like it, wished she had felt it sooner, and knew, deep down, that she never again would.

Foreheads pressed to one another, Tair realized that she wanted to fight. She said, "Whatever you're planning, forget it. I know how to go behind Shianna's back better than anyone."

Perhaps years of growing up with the Prime Heir would pay off after all.

NINE

Alyn arrived at Bonn's room later that night, when the crystals in the wall were turning a sunset pink as the Red Sun set outside. Beautiful as it was, Tair barely paid the colors any mind, distracted instead by the frazzled Fel who sat atop a mountain of crumpled paper on the floor. When Bonn had let him in, Tair smelled that he had been smoking. Even still, his averted eyes, hung head, and tense shoulders expressed a deep worry that whatever he smoked evidently could not remedy. Tair felt for the red crystal in her pocket. He had gifted it to her months ago now, and the small object had become so much an extension of herself that she barely registered its presence until Alyn appeared to her in tears.

After many minutes in silence, he simply said, "I did not know."

Tair let out a breath and nodded. She did not have anything to say.

Alyn did not conceal the tears streaming down his face. He was tired and inebriated and had just found out that his sole mission for well over a decade had an objective that he had never accepted. What Alyn had expected to happen once he brought Tair to Doman—what Tair had expected to happen, too—was unknown, but neither of them could have imagined that the Human he was raising would one day have to commit murder. His aversion to violence was palpable, unwavering, and it lived on in Tair.

Tair and Bonn gave him more time to process, sat silently by each other's sides. Tair was relieved for this outpouring of emotion from Alyn. She struggled to stay committed to this fight for herself. Tears felt like an unnecessary use of energy. Bonn, on the other hand, had wasted little time before they jumped into action. Alyn needed a moment. Tair found that she did, too.

"I would have never brought you back to this place," Alyn muttered. His pale cheeks were wet and puffy. He fiddled with one of his silver rings, then he wiped his face and tried to take on a more neutral expression. He said, "I don't know what would have happened, nor what would have come to pass, but you must know I would have never brought you to Doman had I known your fate."

Tair nodded.

Bonn asked, "Who told you?"

Alyn looked to Bonn then as if it was the first time he had seen them since he entered the room, despite the fact that they had been the one to admit him entrance. His eyes grew wide, settled in recognition, and calmed in a matter of seconds. A mutual respect passed between them.

"Shianna told me only an hour ago now, and I have been trying to find you ever since. I can't be sure, but the mountain might have turned me around," Alyn said with his eyes trained on Bonn. "I know about the two of you, too."

How had he found out? As if to voice Tair's own thoughts, Bonn asked, "*Kiio?*"

Alyn smiled softly as he wiped his cheeks of his drying tears. He said, "It is obvious, is it not?"

Tair hung her head. It was obvious, and she had avoided it—for what, really? So much time had been wasted trying to maintain distance, and still she had grown close to Bonn. She wanted nothing more than to have that time back but hoped they would one day be able to make up for it.

Alyn continued, "I believe I figured it out that day I found you both outside, Bonn confronting you and you taking it in your stride. You are not usually one for confrontation, Tair."

Bonn beamed.

Alyn then gestured to the hundreds of crumpled pieces of paper strewn about the room as he asked, "What's all this?"

"Making plans," Bonn said. A new idea popped into their mind, so they took to sketching it out, paused, and then crushed that one, too. They let out an audible sigh and buried their face in their hands. Through their makeshift mask, they added, "Clearly, none of them are working."

"Yes..."

"Yes?"

Alyn paused a moment. He stood, crossed the room, and pressed his ear to the external wall to make sure no one stood outside. When satisfied, he turned around and returned to the floor across from Tair and Bonn.

Finally, he said, "You should have come to me as soon as you found out what you are meant to do."

"I didn't know who to trust." Tair paused, huffed. "And I didn't know if it would have made any difference."

"I understand," Alyn said with a nod, then continued on, "And, though I am sure you have thought of every possibility you could, I believe I am the only one who can get us all out of here, safe and far away. Not running, but..." He sighed, "Running."

Bonn raised an eyebrow at Tair as if to question his trustworthiness, to which Tair nodded. She had no choice but to trust the Fel. So much of Tair's life had been lived in the shadow of his hopes for a better, more unified world, one in which Tair, too, would have been safe and free to live her life as she saw fit. Though that path had been muddied with lies and betrayal, Alyn's goal could not have changed so radically—his morality could not have changed so radically. At his core, Tair knew, he wanted what was best for all beings and, more than that, he wanted what was best for Tair herself. He could not have accepted her as an assassin, not when he knew it would also cost her own life.

"Running where?" Tair asked.

Alyn only asked back, "Have you considered Lawe?"

It was safe to say they had *never* considered Lawe. Perhaps ironically, the inhabitants of Lawe had decided long ago on the translation of the land's name into Nossok as a variation of "law" to refer to their lawless land far to the northwest. Lawe was known to be diverse, uncharted, and ungoverned. Tair, from Mirte, at least understood a nonhierarchical realm, but there was still structure to the way that problems were to be solved and community decisions were to be made. Bonn, hailing from Doman, had come to understand government as an essential part of maintaining culture and unity and all the things that Domani Dwarves had relied on for centuries as a part of their collective identity. Tair's and Bonn's shared ignorance concerning and misunderstanding of Lawe had pushed the land to the far reaches of their mind, never reaching full consciousness.

Lawe had once been the site of a long range of volcanoes that had made the area largely uninhabitable. It was later repopulated when eruptions slowed and the land became fertile enough for settlement, about ten centuries prior. At present, as far as Tair knew, Lawe was an anarchial territory comprised of Dwarves, Faeries, Elves, Fel—and Humans. After the Doman War, dejected and defeated Humans mostly left Doman for Sossoa, while a smaller faction settled north of the Darkwoods. An even smaller faction, made up of those who did not agree with the genocidal foundation of Sossoa and who did not want to remain so close to what was once their homeland in Doman, left for Lawe.

Beyond that, Tair knew Lawe was Alyn's homeland, but he did not speak on much of his early life, distancing himself instead with elaborate tales of his adventures in other lands. When it came to Alyn's life before the adventures, Tair had learned to accept only what little information was offered. And, assuming he had experienced some sort of trauma there, Tair was surprised to find that he was now willing to return; more importantly, he believed a return to Lawe would be *safe*, among the family and friends he had not seen or spoken to since he left over seventy years prior. No one would have ever expected the three of them to go to Lawe, he argued, and then they would be able to plan for the future. A future Tair could determine.

"But..." Bonn said. When they had arrived at Doman months earlier, Bonn had said that they could not have imagined being away from their homeland for as long as Shianna had. Now, the three were speaking of the indefinite future. Tentatively, Bonn asked, "But what does that mean, really? If we were to go to Lawe?"

"What would it mean for you?" Alyn returned the question.

"I don't know," Bonn admitted. "Reinforcements, maybe? To be honest, I do not believe...well, I *know* I could not live away from Doman for so long."

Tair averted her eyes to avoid Bonn's search for acknowledgement. Tair herself hated the thought of living in—or near, for that matter—Doman for the rest of her life. Not only did the physical environment weigh on her soul, but she associated so much pain with the region that she was not sure if she could ever remedy her relationship with it. Whatever Tair and Bonn were, whatever they were becoming, could not survive if they were so divided on the space they shared. Then again, Tair wondered, who were they together, at present? Who would they become if apart?

"Nor could I live in Lawe for the rest of my life," Alyn said with a smile. "I'm too restless."

Tair smiled to herself and decided to turn back to Bonn, who searched their mate's face. Tair pulled Bonn under her arm. Instantly, the Human felt an unexpected sense of relief at this physical contact—a feeling she knew Bonn shared with her. The prospect of being separated from them completely... Tair felt a chill run down her spine and pulled Bonn tighter.

Alyn continued, "The idea of reinforcements is optimistic at best, naïve at worst. Lawe does not operate under the rule of a particular government or organizational structure. I do not know of anyone who would fight for a cause that would necessitate their involvement in such a political affair."

Tair frowned, unsure of how true Alyn's claim was, and then remembered a further complication: "And what of the Sossok revolution if I were to disappear? Apparently, the rebels have some power in Sossoa and have support from Doman. Even with the optimistic hope for reinforcements from Lawe, what would happen to the revolution in my absence?"

Alyn nodded, thought a moment, and said, "A revolution dependent on one solitary action is no revolution at all."

"That is a matter for debate," Tair said. "Right now, though, we are presented with the very real truth that they are dependent on a solitary action to help bring a close to centuries of strife. I could be their only option."

Alyn shook his head. "Right now, Lawe is *your* only option."

Tair was surprised by his dismissiveness, but also his assuredness. He knew something she did not. She pressed, "What is it?"

"For so many years, I have tried to naturalize for myself lying to you," Alyn said as he hung his head. "No more, I believe."

Tair and Bonn leaned in.

He continued, "While I acknowledge that your task is one of extreme importance, there are...motivations beyond the revolution that the kingdom of Doman is invested in strengthening—in *reinforcing*. Namely, if you were to take out the Sossok king, who is to stop another, perhaps more powerful, empire from commandeering that vacancy in the interim?"

To learn Shianna was the Prime Heir to the throne of Doman was a shock, but for her to have claimed that she was uninvested in maintaining that monarchy...Tair blanched. Was she really meant to kill a king so another Prime could take his place? Shianna had to have been conscious of the attempted expansion of her own monarchy's influence, one which would have undoubtedly strengthened its power in the years to come. Was she truly willing to put Tair's life on the line, only to expand her empire? What of the Humans she and Omma had deceived, what of their years of planning and preparing and hoping? The future that Sossok Humans were constructing was founded on a Domani conspiracy to ensure that it never materialized. They had entrusted the Dwarves with so much—they had even entrusted the beings of Nossoa to care for Tair, yet another symbol of hope—but they had not, apparently, accounted for betrayal in the way Tair had become all too familiar with.

And Omma. Omma claimed to want to remedy the past, but she was only looking to establish a newly oppressed future. All that death and violence, all that she wanted Tair to do—it was all meant to strengthen her own power. Tair felt her cheeks warm in anger.

Worse than the betrayal Tair had felt before, this one cut deep—it was not just about her. All the Sossok Humans who had been planning for their liberation for over a decade—and probably centuries longer, underneath the surface—had planned for conflict from their oppressors, but not from those in their ranks. A soldier of the opposing army's malice was to be expected, but what of the duplicity in one's own legion? Tair wondered how many Dwarves believed they were actually a part of a cause for liberation when, in reality, they too were a part of a much more nefarious battle of revenge. Tair shivered at the thought of her Human kin in Sossoa who relied upon her as an assassin and on the Domani kingdom as an ally, now crushed on both fronts. If Tair disappeared now, she would weaken the Domani plot—but she would also weaken the Humans' rebellion.

She could not tell which was worse.

According to Alyn, one solitary action alone could not make a revolution. There were movement creators and leaders without a doubt, but the revolution lived in the hearts of the collective. That faith could not have been entirely dependent on Tair's existence, she believed. Too many variables could have complicated that vision in the span of eleven years for the Humans not to have accounted for any and all possibilities.

Including the one where Tair rejected her task and escaped for Lawe.

Lawe felt impossible, but it was also the only alternative they had. Tair considered this a moment and asked, "Of Lawe...you believe it is worth a try?"

Alyn thought for a moment as he watched the wall before him. He studied it as one would study a mural, trying to take in all the elements and colors in order to get an idea of the bigger picture—but, the further away one got from it, the better their perception became. Alyn was much too close to it all, invested not only in Tair's fate but also in the fate of the world he had been personally devoted to for years and in the potential of what a refugee life in Lawe would mean for Tair, Bonn, and himself. Whatever Alyn said next would have ripples and *waves* into realms and upon lives that he had never encountered.

Or was it meant to be Tair's decision? She felt selfish placing this weight on him, but it was also his suggestion—and only he could understand the consequences. Tair was new to making these kinds of decisions and had had no practical experience with it at that point. Her own life, in her own hands? Tair's heart raced at the thought.

Finally, Alyn said, "Yes, it is worth a try."

TEN

Alyn, Bonn, and Tair stayed up through the night, planning in hurried, nervous whispers. It was only when the crystals in the wall began to shine a warm orange color, indicating that dawn was upon them, that they finally decided to disband. All three agreed that they would be much more productive and coherent with a little rest in their systems, but, when she arrived back at her room, Tair found that she could not fall asleep. Her body was too alive with hope—something she had, quite honestly, not felt before. Eventually, she fell into a dreamless sleep.

When she woke up, she did not know how long she had been unconscious. She had an intense headache and aching limbs. Worse yet, as quickly as hope had come, it had also gone, replaced instead with dejection. She had tried to put that terrible hopelessness out of her mind, but she was so tired that she later realized she had slipped into and out of consciousness from the effort. It was only when the light in her room mimicked the full-rise of both the Red Sun and Yellow Sun that Tair finally gathered the strength to swing her legs over the edge of her bed and will herself to stand up. Bonn usually awoke her if she had slept in too long. Tair reasoned that the Dwarf had been sleeping in, too. Otherwise...Tair did not want to think about an otherwise. She took the red crystal Alyn had gifted her, glimmering in the internal lights of the mountain, and placed it in her pocket, just as usual. She did not bother to change from her plain nightwear as she staggered to her wall and pressed her palm to the sigil. She nearly fell through the hole that opened up but instead steadied herself on a passing Dwarf she accidentally crashed into.

"Are you okay?" they asked in accented Nossok, concern in the lines of their forehead.

Though she attempted to smile, Tair cringed. The words that fell out of her mouth next were Sossok. When she realized her mistake, she corrected herself in Domani, answering, "*Raos, vasskos.*"

The Dwarf nodded. Clearly in disbelief of Tair's affirmative answer, though, they stayed to help her stand on her own two feet. After a moment's pause, the Dwarf decided to leave Tair on her own. She was both grateful for and upset by this privacy—grateful because her present condition felt rather humiliating, and upset because she did not know how she would arrive at her next destination alone. She huffed as she propped herself up against the wall, her legs only now beginning to regain feeling. Not quite consciously, those legs began to lead her toward Bonn's room.

She practically slammed into the sigil just outside her mate's room. She expected it to open for her as it had only hours before, but she soon realized that the room was now closed off to her. She struggled to open her eyes wider—not even noticing how near closed they were—and discovered that the sigil that had once protected Bonn's room had been replaced. Bonn's pattern had sharp points to it, and the one before her now was a curved spiral. Tair traced it with her finger. She figured that she must have remembered the symbol incorrectly, or perhaps that she had gotten turned around in the mountain due to her disoriented state. When the wall opened up and an unfamiliar Dwarf stood confused on the other side, though, Tair knew in her heart that the room had once belonged to Bonn.

But Bonn was no longer there.

Tair's heartbeat quickened. She suddenly saw clearly, her feet were more assured in their direction, and her headache cleared—slightly. A little way away, closer to the fourth innermost mountain, Tair arrived in front of Alyn's room, the sigil for which had also been altered. His sigil had been less of a symbol and more of a piece of art, a grander piece depicting a storm over what Tair had assumed to be the Eastern Great Sea. Now, the etching had been replaced by three overlapping triangles. Tair struck the wall with some mixture of confusion and anger. It opened eventually, when the mountain surrendered to her frustration, but it had been cleared of all belongings. It was now only an empty room between inhabitants. Tair waited a moment by the wall, just to see if Alyn would, for whatever reason, return. No such luck. Tair hurried back to her room.

After ensuring that the wall was shut behind her, Tair slumped over onto her bed. A million thoughts raced through her mind. A million horrible thoughts, all with a common theme: Bonn and Alyn were gone.

"Not gone," Tair said aloud to herself, "just currently out of my reach."

But it was more than that, was it not? Tair could have very well looked for them all over Doman. They could have gone for a midday meal in one of the dining halls, or perhaps they were off doing their own tasks. They could have been outside the mountains, a world that was so foreign now that the thought of leaving Doman almost frightened Tair. They could have been doing any number of things—but none of them made sense. Most, if not all, of Bonn's time in Doman was spent with Tair. As for Alyn, the Fel had promised to stay nearby in case that they had to leave more suddenly than they had planned, should their plan have been compromised. Most worryingly, all of their belongings were gone. Even when they had moved rooms as they ascended through the mountains, Doman usually helped them to locate each other—on its terms, of course. There had always been this sense of *presence*; now, where that presence once lived, Tair found nothing.

And then there were the physical repercussions of Bonn's absence in particular, presenting themselves to Tair as rolling headaches and a tired body. She could not connect either of those sensations to any other cause; she had not trained with Bonn for three days now, and she had not consumed any alcohol or drugs that might have accounted for her pains. No, this hurt was deeper and previously unknown, only under-standable now that Tair was experiencing it.

Tair flipped over onto her back. The crystals at the top of her room glimmered with a life she could barely understand, just as one could not truly comprehend how the *missai* birds could see all of the world at once. But there was something peculiar about the light now, arranged into a kind of pattern that had never been there before. She sat up on her elbows and squinted at the light as it rippled. Forgetting to blink, the mountain almost looked like it was breathing—and perhaps it was. As the crystals swelled with color, Tair realized that they were directing her to exit her room. She did as she was instructed, not even half reluctant, and was surprised when the wall opened up for her without pressing her palm to the cool stone.

The corridor outside her room had shifted in an almost undetectable way, but Tair now saw something in the walls of the mountain that was akin to communication. Alive as it was, it also had its own motivations, just as it had the night before when it had tried to direct her away from Bonn's room. She followed the designated path through the hallways as they got narrower and narrower, shorter and shorter...

Then Tair began to hear—and *smell*—wind. Up ahead, the Red Sun and Yellow Sun beamed. She shielded her eyes as she stepped outside onto a balcony the mountain had whittled out for its inhabitants. Tair took a deep breath. She had not smelled fresh air in months.

As her eyes acclimated to a flood of natural light, Tair realized she was not alone. To her side, Omma sat in a chair with wheels on either side, taking deep breaths of her own. Tair was surprised at her sudden sense of spite. Tair had directed much of her anger toward Shianna—which felt fair— but now that malice was more complicated. She was not angry at a singular being, but what that being represented, who and where she had come from, and all of that history that had created her. Shianna was as much a part of Omma as Omma was of Shianna. Now, in their first encounter in over two months, Tair's fists balled up at her sides and an uncontrollable scowl spread across her features. She kept her eyes trained forward, inhaled the early summer air, and tried to calm her hammering heart.

For her part, Omma sat with a calm smile as she overlooked the mountains and the lake below. Distracted by her current company, Tair had not taken a moment to truly look upon the world. Now that she did, though, she realized why most inhabitants of Doman had never chosen to leave. Over the crest of the eastern-facing mountains, the Yellow Sun overlapped the Red Sun and cast a warm glow over the world. It was not a particularly cloudy day, though wispy clouds still hung only inches above them. Fulfilling a childhood dream, Tair reached up and could not help but smile as the clouds shifted around her fingers and dissipated in the air. It was not hot, not cold, but a perfect temperature, in part maintained by Doman itself, Tair imagined. Below, the lake was as still as ever. A small group of Dwarves sat along the shore with their fishing rods out. Tair took another deep breath. Her headache cleared; her ailing body numbed.

"Beautiful, isn't it?" Omma asked in Nossok.

Despite herself, Tair nodded.

"Doman knows us like no other," Omma said. She spoke of the mountains as though it had the same consciousness as either of them; Tair realized, after her extended stay there, how much truth was in that sentiment. Or, at the very least, there was no other way to communicate how alive the mountains were. Tair did not overthink it: she let it be; it let her be. Omma continued, "It knows what we need—and knows how to communicate to us what we do not need. Have you noticed that?"

Tair thought back to the garden Bonn had led her to at the base of this mountain. How, as soon as she had stepped in there, she had finally recognized something unspoken that Bonn was able to put into words. The crystals had indicated that the Red Sun was setting outside, yes, but they had also reflected a turning point toward a potential life that Tair did not want to turn her back on now. There was no need to answer Omma's question; there was only one possible answer.

Tair's voice was quieter than she had intended when she finally asked the question she had been dreading, the question Doman had already answered: "Where are they?"

Omma sighed. "Away."

Tair bit her lip. A tear slipped from the corner of her eye. She repeated, "Away?"

Omma folded her hands in her lap.

"Why?" Tair choked out. She was angry—was she not? She cursed her tears, cursed how weak they made her feel.

"There are bonds of which I was not aware," Omma said. "For that, I apologize. I know what it is to lose your mate, as I lost one when I was very young. The war...well, we were torn apart long before he was able to see what parts of him I imbued into Shianna."

Shianna had never mentioned a second parent. Tair

167

supposed she did not have to; Omma created Shianna from the essence of her being, but that did not negate the fact that those one loved were always a part of them, even if only in memory. Tair felt Bonn in her blood from the moment they had declared themselves to one another. She had run from that feeling. She had not appreciated it for what it was, when it was. Even still, Tair knew that there had to be a part of Omma's mate within Shianna, a part that Shianna may or may not have ever been conscious of. Tair felt a kinship with Shianna then, a feeling that had been absent for far too long. Tair, too, did not know her parents, but knew that there was a part of them that was a part of her. There were parts of her that were distinctly Human.

"Nevertheless," Omma continued after a moment's pause, "there are tasks you must complete that they might have made impossible, Alyn and Bonn both. As much pain as this may cause you—"

"We all have a role to play?" Tair echoed Omma's own words from months ago.

Omma nodded. As much anger as Tair harbored toward Omma, she knew she could not muster true fury. She knew, too, that if she had the fight left in her, she would have challenged Omma. The fight was not worth it, not with the Prime, not anymore. Was the fight worth it at all? A decade earlier, she had found out about her abandonment in the Darkwoods and how that had represented a greater future than she could possibly comprehend. Now, she knew that the future she represented was one she would have a direct hand in, as an assassin to two Humans she felt she could claim no firsthand hatred of, no direct bond to. After only one night of hope, Tair presently understood that there was no point in running, in fighting, in dreaming. One way or another, she would always continue down a path she had not chosen.

Tair stood out on that balcony with Omma until the Yellow Sun set in the distance.

Whether or not the Dwarf knew of what Omma had done, Shianna had insisted that Tair join her for dinner that night. Tair reasoned that, after all Shianna had hidden, after all she had lied about, she must have known of Omma's actions. Part of her that wanted to be rid of this awareness of Shianna's deception. Part of her wished she could have lived only in the lies. Truthfully, she just wanted to be rid of the ache of loss, distrust, hatred; rid of the hollow, apathetic feeling in her chest.

Unfortunately, that feeling remained as Tair sat at a long table across from Shianna. The dining hall was particularly eccentric that night, almost mockingly so. The Dwarves present were raucous, eating the most food Tair had seen in the course of her time in Doman and uninhibited by a plentitude of alcohol. Though bothered now, Tair knew she would miss that abundance when she left, however soon that was. She remembered back to her plans with Alyn and Bonn and all their considerations as to how much food they would have to bring with them for their journey to Lawe. How much food could they have stolen without drawing suspicion? And then how many belongings could they have packed without raising question?

No matter. Now they were both gone. All hope had gone with them. Tair stuffed a piece of *senip* bread into her mouth, grateful for the calming herbal properties folded into the dough. Shianna spoke to a Dwarf on her right after countless failed attempts at starting a conversation with the silent Tair. And, as Shianna was in the middle of telling a joke, Silaa appeared.

The Elf looked gaunter than when Tair has seen her last, which had been...Tair actually could not recount when she had last seen Silaa—perhaps a month ago now. The sides of the Elf's hair had been shaved into a flowing pattern and left long at the top, then what was left was contained into a long, intricate braid that snaked down the middle of her head and over her shoulder. It was not a hairstyle Tair had seen Silaa wear before. Particularly striking was the new scar under her left eye, gnarling otherwise smooth skin. She also no longer wore her loose-fitting attire, replaced instead with the kind of thick, tight-fitting, and quilted clothing that Shianna preferred. Unrecognizable, too, was the smile she wore as she approached her mate. The two embraced and held each other in a kiss that garnered plenty of attention from surrounding Dwarves. When they pulled back from one another, Shianna looked similarly as confused as Tair, while Silaa beamed. The first question that came to Tair—that is, where Silaa had been—was answered before she could even ask.

Silaa exclaimed, "Nothing like home to set one in good spirits!"

Tair's eyes grew even wider as she realized what that meant; the Elf had returned to Mirte. Despite herself, Tair blurted, "Home?"

Silaa nodded, her smile still wide across her face. She rubbed Shianna's freshly shaved head, placed a kiss there, and grabbed a spoonful of stew. She sank down into her own seat and piled up an empty plate with a variety of foods, with particular attention paid to the multicolored, still-steaming vegetables.

Tair shifted in her seat. Silaa's response to her question had been too vague. There was an undefinable feeling in Tair's chest that the home Silaa spoke of was not, in fact, Mirte. *Which home?* Whose *home?* Tair had wanted to ask, but was instead interrupted by Shianna tracing a finger along Silaa's scar and inquiring, "Where'd you get that?"

The Elf blinked at the touch. In a softer tone than she probably intended, "A conflict."

"That's all?" Shianna prompted. There was worry in her eyes as she tracked Silaa's movements: ravenously eating all the food she could stomach, forcing it down with a long swig of beer (her previously least favored alcohol), and then back to get more food. Finally, Shianna stopped Silaa with a gentle hand on her shoulder. The Elf slowed, placed her last handful of food back on her plate, wiped her hands on her pants in lieu of a napkin, and turned to meet her mate's curious eyes.

Shianna asked again, "What really happened?"

Silaa scoffed. In a hushed tone, just loud enough so Tair could eavesdrop, she said, "Training."

"Training?"

"We're headed into a war, are we not?"

Shianna dropped her hand from Silaa's shoulder. She frowned and responded, "That is not your fight."

"Isn't it? Your battles are my battles," Silaa said as she glanced into her lap. She then obviously corrected herself: fixing her posture, neutralizing her expression, and looking into her mate's eyes yet again. "Your wars are my wars. Your life is my life. We cannot choose these things."

Shianna opened her mouth to say something but decided against it. Instead, she stuffed her mouth full of food and water and folded her arms over her chest.

Tair frowned. This Silaa was not the Silaa she knew. She said, "You have never believed that before."

"We all change," Silaa said. She drank a sip of beer and shrugged. "My mate is the Prime Heir—one way or another, I will be involved in fights I may not agree with but that I am obligated to. You know something about that, don't you, Tair?"

Tair winced. The Elf had teased her many times, but this was cruel. Of course, Tair agreed with the premise of the Sossok Humans' revolution, but she did not agree with the apparent path that the Domani Dwarves—and, in specific, the monarchal structure that ruled those Dwarves—had set them on. With Omma having sent away the only two beings willing to fight for Tair and Tair accepting it, though, she now felt obligated to her responsibilities. Worse yet, she had resigned herself to her responsibilities, barely posing a challenge to Omma. Tair had stood with the Prime as if no transgression had transpired, as if the Prime was not the same being restricting her freedom.

Unconvinced of it herself, Tair muttered, "You should at least get a choice."

That sentiment was new on Tair's tongue. Bonn and Alyn had offered Tair the opportunity for freedom; now, she felt a newfound responsibility to ensure that others had it, especially those as close as Silaa. She thought back to how things had changed through the years: the Elf had been Shianna's mate and Tair's earliest infatuation—but no change compared to the rate at which things had changed since they left Mirte. There were parts of Shianna that Tair knew Silaa would never be able to accept. Now...she had been roped in, seemingly enthusiastic about war and monarchy and all the systems she once despised.

"I chose this a long time ago," Silaa answered.

"You do not have to adhere to your old choices," Tair countered.

Shianna bit her lip, uncertainty plain across her features. She was clearly surprised by Silaa's disappearance and reappearance as this new...thing, but there was something else that Shianna knew—something else she was hiding. Tair worried that Shianna had played a hand in Silaa's disappearance herself.

Silaa narrowed her eyes and said, "You do not know the first thing about my choices."

"I know you would not choose this," Tair said.

Silaa stood and smashed her empty beer stein on the ground behind her. A few nosy Dwarves glanced over at the rowdy Elf, but, as usual, none were any more concerned with what was going on around them than what was happening right in front of them. Those who did glance at Silaa quickly averted their gaze with disinterest.

Shianna whispered in her mate's ear. Silaa took a deep breath and left the dining hall as suddenly as she had arrived. Tair watched as this shadow of Silaa disappeared from view. She turned her attention back to Shianna, who pushed the last pieces of her meal around on her plate.

"I cannot explain, but..." Shianna trailed off. Tair was unaccustomed to seeing the Dwarf vulnerable; it brought back the memory of their last shared private moment at the top of Braasii. Shianna's guilt permeated the air as she sighed and let her shoulders cave. She said in Domani, *"Rak grasora'a ak'raak."*

"Apologize to me for what?" Tair could count at least five things the Prime Heir needed to apologize for—all apologies that Tair could never accept, not anymore. And why now? Tair imagined that Shianna only wanted to apologize because of whatever she had just seen in Silaa.

Tair must have looked shocked because Shianna said, "Please, it is not so absurd. I must apologize for all I have put you through. Ever since we uprooted you from Mirte, your life has been unpredictable, to say the least. All the lies told, all of it—I hope you can understand that it was in the greater interest of your kind, in the dream of a unified future."

Shianna did not apologize as Shianna, but as Prime Heir. She was vague, removed, political. And, importantly to Tair, she had given no indication that she knew about Omma exiling Bonn and Alyn, but she also did indicate that she was free of guilt.

Tair sighed before she said, "I don't know what you expected of me. You raised me. You taught me there was never a future resolution that justified present oppression. You knew who you were turning me into. All the while, you knew where I was going, and who I would have to become once I got there."

Shianna chewed on the inside of her cheek. Tair winced as she remembered Bonn's own tick, wherever they and Alyn were. Shianna then said, "Despite what you may think, I

173

wanted you to be smart and self-sufficient. You have become that and so much more—though perhaps to a fault, for our purposes. I wanted you to have the future as a point of hope. I believed, rather selfishly, that such a hope might have translated into one for the future of your kind. I could not take that hope from you, not in those early years."

"So, you took it away all at once?"

"Some things are not so simple. Some things require unknown sacrifices that only become known in those moments we feel least prepared to sacrifice. Silaa..." Shianna shook her head as she grimaced, then continued, "Some lives require more pain so other lives can experience pleasure. What you have to do is not about you, so much as it is about the future. I do not know how Silaa has arrived at that point, but I assumed you would one day arrive there, too. I now see that is an unfair assumption."

Sacrifice for the greater good was something that the Prime Heir had always raised Tair to believe. Even still, Tair could no longer bear the thought of complete submission, not when she had been offered an alternative. Not if it meant losing herself, as Silaa had. She no longer wanted to speak with Shianna, no longer wanted to argue, and so she stood and left the dining hall.

The crystals in Tair's walls rippled to life, their red light sharp and far too bright for the previously sleeping Human. Not particularly driven to discover the root of the disturbance, Tair pulled her blanket over her head and squeezed her eyes shut. It was probably just a Dwarf wandering the halls in a drunken stupor, which had happened enough times in the past. Most nights, she was able to sleep through it. That night, however, the crystals' light undulated again.

And again a minute after that.

After the day she had suffered, Tair felt that the world at least owed her a restful sleep, but she supposed even this was too much to ask. She stood from her bed and pressed her palm to the wall, prepared to tell whoever was on the other side to go away.

But it was Shianna who stood on the other side. Tair considered telling her leave anyway, but the Dwarf's eyes were tired and brimming with tears. She still wore the clothes Tair had seen her in earlier, but they were disturbed and carried the faint smell of ash, just as Alyn had the night before. The scent reminded her far too much of hope.

Shianna whispered, "I don't know what to say."

Tair admitted Shianna entry despite her learned distrust of the Dwarf. Her posture weak and her neck hung, Shianna paced over to Tair's bed and sat on the edge. Tears poured down her face, but she did not wipe them away.

"*Rak kaja'a-yia akk-kias rak kosao'a kaguus*," *I do not know what I am fighting for anymore*, Shianna said as she placed her head in her hands. "It's all coming apart."

Shianna's eyes suddenly snapped up to meet Tair's. The Human's legs acted before her mind; when she finally registered her movements, she found herself sat down next to Shianna, hands folded in her lap. Though she hated to admit it, she could not help but feel for this Dwarf who was the closest thing to family she had left.

"I thought back on...how we left things earlier," Shianna began, "I suppose there comes a point where it all passes into cruelty, and you have to wonder what this is all for."

Tair knew enough not to ask any questions until the Dwarf was finished. Shianna took up the space that she needed and only then made space for others; Tair had admired that when she was younger. She was not so sure what she admired about Shianna now. A crying heap on the edge of Tair's bed, Shianna did not the right to emotional turmoil, seeing as she had created much of Tair's. Nevertheless, Tair did not have the heart to stop her.

Shianna picked at her nails, a nervous tick Tair had never

noticed before. Her shoulders slumped, her tears slowly stopped, and she explained, "I went looking for Alyn after dinner."

Tair sighed.

"I did not know what Omma had done until then. When I asked, I discovered that she sent both him and Bonn away. Bonn—your mate. I could not...I hope you know I would not have agreed to something like that," Shianna explained.

Tair winced in the realization that she did *not* know if Shianna would oppose such a thing.

"And Silaa..." Shianna fell back on the bed and covered her eyes with her hands. "I do not know what happened to my mate, but I do know that she did not return to Mirte. Though she poses her challenges to my status as Prime Heir, I would much rather a challenge than whoever—*what*ever—she is now. I asked Omma..." She sighed. "She spoke only of duty and obligation. She spoke of all the things I, too, have learned to weaponize, all the things that could never justify the actions she has taken against you. Against me. The two of us losing them all...our world is shrinking, Tair. What does it mean to fight for a shrinking world?"

Tair had been wondering that for weeks now. But why had their world shrunk so much before Shianna recognized her error?

Shianna continued, "If I had known that any of this would happen, that this would be the cost, you must know I would have stopped it."

"If you had known..." Tair scoffed and shook her head. "And yet you would have allowed all this to happen to me anyway?"

"It's not—" Shianna cut herself off. "Well, it is the same. I just...I thought you could handle it. Of anyone, I thought you could handle it."

"Why me?"

"I raised you."

Tair slumped. As much as she hated to admit it, as much as it was a real part of her, as betrayed as she felt—Shianna was family. Now Shianna claimed that she had put all this weight on Tair's shoulders because she had instilled strength in Tair? The thought would have been laughable, if it had not had such real consequences.

Shianna had indeed raised Tair knowing she would uproot the Human at a moment's notice, so why had she taught Tair about the importance of stability? She had raised Tair knowing the Human would one day assassinate the King and King Heir, so why had she taught the Human about the sanctity of life? She had raised Tair knowing that the Human would one day return to Sossoa, so why had she not prioritized Tair's knowledge of the culture she was born into? Shianna's logic was inconsistent, but then again, so was her existence; she had to envision a free future for not only Sossoa but all realms across the continent—a free future, that was, if united under the Domani empire. She was born into, rooted in, and actively upheld the very systems that restricted the freedom she sought for others. It was no wonder she had lied for so long; the truth did not make any more sense.

Tair's sympathy could only extend so far, though. She had spent her entire life telling Shianna the whole truth, only for the Dwarf to reveal that she had shared as little of her own truth as possible. Had Shianna not been spurred to apologize by Silaa's sudden change or by Bonn's and Alyn's exile, she would have still thrown Tair into the grave unknown, asking the Human to do the unspeakable in the effort of the unimaginable. As much as Tair wanted liberation for Sossoa, as much as she wanted freedom for her kin by blood, she also felt herself an intruder in the cause. Truthfully, she could not even comprehend the end goal; freedom was abstract to her, something she could not achieve for herself but that she was meant to fight for anyways. And, Tair had found, when freedom felt unattainable to the individual, collective liberation was even more of an impossible reality.

"Ultimately, you knew what this would do to me," Tair finally responded. She stared at the crystals in the wall, glimmering a soft orange that reminded her of Bonn's eyes. "You know who you raised—and you created my sense of right and wrong. This...you once would have taught me that this all was wrong. I at least had to try and fight back."

Shianna took a long pause. She was quiet for so long, in fact, that Tair almost wondered if she had fallen asleep. Ultimately, she said, "I think you should continue fighting."

Tair stood from her seat on the bed and moved to face the Dwarf face-on. She gripped the wall, her heart thumping, thumping, thumping in her chest. Shianna's permission to fight was one thing Tair had never expected. Dumbfounded, Tair clarified, "*Now*?"

"That was your plan, wasn't it? Alyn would lead Bonn and you to Lawe, where you would avoid the reality of this world— a world that is having a difficult time achieving freedom." Shianna inhaled deeply, then continued, "But as free as you might have imagined Lawe to be, free from politics and hatred and conflict, no world is absolutely free yet, Tair. I believe you would have been rather disappointed by your circumstances."

Tair huffed and folded her arms over her chest.

"You expected, perhaps, kindness and refuge—as if the beings of Lawe would risk their political isolation for your freedom. You seem to forget that the entire reason they divorced from this world was to escape our affairs."

"At least it is freer than the world you want to build," Tair mumbled. "Freer from what you would have me do."

Shianna either did not hear Tair's remark or did not want to dignify it with a response. "The inhabitants of Lawe want freedom as any other being does, and they know what kind of sacrifices freedom takes. But you must be a fool if you expect them to sacrifice it all to get you your own individual freedom, which I do believe you rightfully chase. Sadly, if Omma threatened to turn her troops against them for your release into our custody, they would send you back in an instant."

"That's not what would have happened," Tair said defiantly. It was not particularly wise to tell Shianna her plans, even if they would never come to fruition, but she also did not like to be called a fool. She clarified, "Once I was safe, I would have someone send word that I died in the journey to Sossoa, knocked out to sea by wind. The Humans would go to war with you—a war you believe you would win in the effort of total dominion—and all would be safe again for me to come out of hiding."

"Wishful thinking," Shianna scoffed. "Your task as assassin is meant to weaken Sossok defense, not be the absolute end to the revolution. You are simply meant to put the Sossok army in a position where the rebels could overcome their oppressors with our aid. We have never desired war, for we know the kind of loss that path necessitates."

Tair derided, "You don't even know what Omma's plans are."

Shianna frowned. "*Kias?*"

"Alyn told me that Omma does not plan to liberate the Humans, but to conquer them—replace one monarchy with another, replace one oppressor with another. The world she fights for is not one of liberation, but of further subjugation. Do you fight for that same world?"

Shianna's shoulders caved in. She did not seem to know about Omma's intentions, but she conceded easily. There were some things her parent would do that she would not agree with—and still she would have never challenged the Prime. She finally admitted, "There are flaws to the plan, yes, but there are far more dangerous flaws in your plan."

Thousands more lives lost. Sossok accusations of Domani Dwarves executing Tair themselves. Discovery of Tair by Sossok-allied Humans in Nossoa. No resources, no direct relations outside of her insular structure that crumbled more and more each day...Tair knew the flaws in her plan. At least she could admit to them. This was the first time that Tair had heard Shianna—or any Domani Dwarf—admit to fault in the Domani regime. What Shianna said next was the biggest surprise, though.

"I have not come to debate with you. I have been raised to think one thing, have come to believe another, and now live in this reality that has shown me how much these mindsets must battle to survive one another. Nonetheless, there is one thing I am sure of: you have to leave tonight, with Rose. I will get you out."

Tair sank to the floor. Shianna felt a duty to Tair now. *Now?* The plot had the faintest presence of Silaa's now-distant influence. Whatever had happened to the Elf, Shianna still thought, in part, with her mate's rebellious lens. Betrayed far too many times by the Prime Heir, Tair could not tell whether or not Shianna was lying. If a lie, Tair would have no reason to trust Shianna again; if the truth, why could Shianna not have arrived here sooner, before they had even set off for Doman? Before Bonn and Alyn were exiled? Tair only stared at Shianna, who seemed to recognize the absurdity in her statement, and allowed Tair to move through the motions of shock.

Tair saw no other appropriate reaction than *no*, if only because she could not envision a reality in which Shianna would actually act in her favor after so many months and *years* of betrayal. But she could not muster up the word, two letters that felt so impossible to put together. She bit her tongue, almost willed herself to say it, but part of her held back. She got the sudden, overwhelming sense that this was Shianna's last attempt to save Tair, to make up for all the pain she had put the Human through, and to give her a chance in this world. When she looked into Shianna's eyes, she could not help but remember the Dwarf as her kin. Those feelings of family, one she was tied to indefinitely and irrevocably, washed over her. She looked at Shianna like she was seeing herself for the first time; these were her true kin—Shianna and Silaa and Alyn and Bonn—by fault of circumstance, by fault of life. Shianna was now willing to put herself at risk for Tair. And, too tired to conjure disbelief, Tair could only muster one simple question: "What's your plan?"

Rose was rather confused as to why they had been awakened in the middle of the night, not unlike Tair had been only an hour earlier. When their wall opened up and they saw Shianna and Tair standing on the other side, the latter with a small sack of belongings strung across her shoulders, Rose silently packed their own belongings and followed without question.

Moving through Doman at night was a challenge, though not insurmountable for Shianna, who knew the land as well as she knew herself. The crystals in the halls were dimmer at this time, the halls themselves somehow narrower, but they moved swiftly and without challenge, the mountain supporting their attempt at escape. Even if they had been seen, no one would have stopped Shianna from moving as she pleased. Despite Shianna's privilege, there was no time to break; at any moment, a guard could pass through and discover them, then share word of their movements to Counselor Denon—to Omma. They hurried through the third innermost mountain, to the second, to the first, and then finally made it outside; by that point, Tair's legs ached and her lungs strained, but she carried on without complaint.

They exited Doman through the small opening between the first two mountains that had once served as Tair's formal introduction to the realm. They then followed the curve of the nearby Dessoa River that stemmed out from Doman's lake. The summer was heat thick as the night deepened and, later, steadily turned into dawn. Though they relished in the cold, refreshing water that lapsed at their shoes, they were careful not to lose their footing. In the receding darkness, the water was their only guide—along with the rising Red Sun and the retreating moon. Tair had been so long without them that they now took on a new beauty. She was so busied by the interlocking beams of light above that she lost her footing more than once and drenched her shoes.

By late morning, they came across a small raft that Shianna said was available for any Domani use. The three rowed for a few hours, stilling when they all tired. Sooner than Tair had expected, the river began to narrow as it traveled out east. They tied the boat so that it did not float out to sea. Looking out around them, Tair felt herself in a distinctly different world that was not confined to stone. Out in the west, a few lanterns sparkled—the Human settlement Tair had originally believed to be her origins, now just on the horizon. She thought back to herself at seven years old, how excited that version of Tair would have been to be so close to those who she had once thought were her kin. Now, they moved away from that potential, using the smooth, moss-covered rocks as steppingstones to get across to the other side of the river. There, low-hanging trees and shrubs led into the Darkwoods. Tair ran her hands through the foliage and welcomed the cool feeling of the leaves against her skin. She could feel Faeries around them, all too accustomed to their presence now, but she had a strong sense that they were not out to hurt her and her companions, merely there to observe. She smiled to herself.

Despite their proximity to the Darkwoods, there was no fear in Tair's heart. Sixteen, almost seventeen, years later, Tair arrived back at the land that she had first been abandoned to. The light foliage got denser as they merged into the Darkwoods, creating its own sense of night. Small lights glittered throughout the woodland and nocturnal animals made their nightly sounds. It was there that Shianna said, "This is where I leave you."

"Where are we meant to go?" Rose asked as they glanced

around, all too familiar with the woods after having to escape north through them all those years earlier. Whatever those woods represented for them, whatever they represented for Tair, was nothing in comparison to the world that laid on the other side. Tair and Rose both shivered.

"I have brought you here as a midway point, if you will. To have gone directly east or west from Doman, we would've immediately been discovered," Shianna explained. Tair realized that she had not thought to ask Shianna much of her plan after *away from Doman...Rose...tonight...*In the cold, she questioned her innate trust of Shianna, even after all the lies.

That swelling sense of distrust was quelled when Shianna said to them both, "It would be hypocritical of me to direct you, so you may go wherever you see fit."

It was clear that the choice was in Tair's hands. Surely, Alyn and Bonn had gone to Lawe, if only in the hopes that Tair might have come looking for them both. For that same reason, Tair knew Lawe was no longer an option for her; that would have been the first place Omma would have gone looking. To return to Mirte was also no longer safe, it was now some radical impossibility in her memory rather than any tangible place. It seemed that the safest place for Tair to run to was, ironically, the very land that was unsafe for everyone she had ever loved—the very land she had desperately avoided for months now, for much of her life. There, she could at least attempt to blend in amongst her own kin, using a language she had just been introduced to two months earlier and employing a cultural knowledge she had never experienced firsthand.

Tair had asked if Rose would ever return there. Without hesitation, they had responded: *Even after all the bloodshed, it is still home. If I am to never return, what was the fight for? Why continue living on?*

She placed her hand on Shianna's shoulder and said, "Thank you." Then she and Rose turned into the Darkwoods and set off for Sossoa.

ELEVEN

The forest was dense—not only in foliage but in *air*, too. As tough a time as Tair had acclimating to the air in Doman, the Darkwoods were further complicated by the fact that they had to get through the land quickly, before anyone realized they were gone. Tair kept her pace swift and tried to emulate Rose, who controlled their breath with expertise. Deep inhales, longer exhales, again and again. As much as she tried, Tair was heaving by the time the two of them stumbled across a clearing in the woods. The Yellow Sun was setting in front of the Red Sun, so it was maybe late afternoon.

Tair's bag on her back was light, packed with the bare essentials, such as a small carafe of water and a loaf of bread. She had not even prepared a change of clothes. As empty as it was, the pack seemingly grew heavier as Tair fatigued. She was grateful to relieve herself of it as she collapsed in the grass. Even though she had trained well enough with Bonn in the short time they had together, her endurance was still lacking. She was much more suited for hand-to-hand combat or lifting heavy objects than she was for a cross-country journey, unlike Rose, who did not look the slightest bit tired.

Rose said, "We'll have to keep moving."

Tair struggled to stand again, huffing and groaning the whole way up.

Rose added, "Though, before we continue, you should probably eat."

"I'm not hungry."

Rose shook their head. "It's not about your true hunger but providing yourself the sustenance to support you in the rest of our journey. It only gets tougher from here."

Tair frowned. So far, they had not encountered anything particularly mystical nor harrowing in their journey through the Darkwoods. She might have missed the magic, though, as distracted as she was by her physical suffering. Thus far, the most absurd thing they had come across was a bug with two heads, which was nothing really to Tair. Throughout her life, Tair had seen Alyn produce smoke from his fingertips; Silaa had, on occasion, lit a fire with her hands; and, as much magic as Tair knew Shianna contained, the Dwarf refused to use it outside of the comfort of her own kind, as was Domani custom. Tair herself did not know if she contained any magic, did not know if Humans were even *capable*, but she had decided long ago not to test it. In all truth, it did not seem important to her. Either way, the use of casual magic—or casually magical creatures, like that bug—was insignificant at best.

Tair had to admit that she was disappointed, having expected the Darkwoods to course with mystical energy after all the tales she had heard throughout her life. After she had learned that she had been abandoned there, Tair had spent many nights of her youth staying up to conjure imaginations of glimmering lights and frightening creatures unheard of in any other realm. For the time being, these woods were no more unique than any other forest she had traversed.

Tair took out a small piece of bread from her sack and

forced herself to swallow. She should have been hungry, her last meal having been the evening prior, but her nerves masked her appetite. Once she had stomached her bite, she asked, "What makes the rest of the journey any more difficult than the start?"

Ignoring the question, Rose looked to the sky, back down at their feet, and kicked at the grass. Raised in Mirte, where the grass and the soil were to be respected, Tair winced. That wince settled into a smile of wonder, though, when the small patch of grass floated up above their heads, seemingly carried by a small orange light. She reached up to touch it, but Rose grabbed her wrist before she could do so.

"Don't do that," Rose said just as the patch of grass dissolved into thin air. Tair looked back down to the ground and marveled at the patch of grass that Rose had kicked at, having already mended itself. "We're standing on a threshold."

Tair looked around the two of them. In the haze of her exhaustion, she had not noticed how extraordinary the clearing was: not only was it a natural clearance, without obstruction from a single stray weed or overhanging branch, but it was also a perfect circle. Tair walked along the unflawed tree line, so perfect that she dizzied after one round. She sat back down in the grass.

"Though we have been walking for a while, we have only walked twenty feet," Rose said. "In the Darkwoods, we could be anywhere and nowhere, and the only way to know is to make it to the thresholds."

Twenty feet? Tair looked back into the woods behind her, suppressing a groan. No wonder Rose said the rest of the voyage would be difficult. The trees seemed to stretch on for miles and miles. Both horrified and mystified, Tair asked, "How many clearings are there?"

Rose considered a moment as they remembered back to their last trip through the Darkwoods. "I believe I last passed through twelve or so. These are the only places where time and distance function as we have come to understand."

"So, it is truly midday?" Tair questioned.

Rose nodded.

"It took us well over an hour to get twenty feet into the forest," Tair mumbled, mostly to herself. She was making calculations in her mind. Louder, she said, "At this rate, we could be in Sossoa by next week."

"Depends," Rose said simply, still watching the sky. "These woods are as alive as Doman is—as alive as we are. It may treat us kindly if we show it respect."

"How do we—"

Rose cut Tair off, raising one finger to their lips. Just as Tair was preparing to ask for explanation, she heard it: similar to the ominous low hum of Shianna's friends in the forests surrounding Doman, Tair now heard the faint, disarming sound of drums in the distance. Instead of waiting to fight, though, Rose silently urged Tair to stand up and then led them both back into the forest—

And toward the noise.

Tair now saw the Darkwoods she had always imagined. Before her, the air shimmered in the light of the two suns. The woods housed all kinds of life, flora and fauna alike, that Tair would not have been able to name even if she tried. She was unsurprised to find a *missai* bird perched up above her—but she did have to admit shock when she saw so many, as populous as the crows in Mirte. These *missai* birds were not their usual multicolored pattern but were instead black as night. Tair preferred this black plumage; beautiful as it was, the birds could effectively (and enviably) disappear. Indeed, the only identifying *missai* trait were their many eyes shining in the light at the top of the trees.

Preoccupied by the birds, Tair did not see the warped tree that stood in her path. Nearly crashing into the blue bark before her, Tair caught herself just in time to place her hands on the tree and steady herself. The thick, scarred bark was cold as ice beneath her touch. When she tried to tell Rose to wait, she realized that she could not move her mouth to form the words, nor could she see any farther than the tree before her. All that was before her—all that ever seemed to be—was this deep sapphire tree that clung to her, or otherwise that she clung to. As frightening as this was upon reflection, she presently felt welcomed, invited, *akin*...

Rose yanked Tair off the tree, which disappeared as soon as the younger Human removed her hands. She blinked to make sense of what she had just experienced, but, before she could comprehend or question any of it, Rose rushed them both through the forest. Tair felt a little lighter on her feet, almost as if the tree had removed any physical exhaustion. She did not know if she should have been grateful for that gift, manipulative as the tree might have been, but she did not think on it long as the drumming noise grew nearer.

And nearer.

And nearer.

The next clearing was another perfect circle as the last, though much larger. A crowd of Faeries stood there, all as tall as the two Humans who just intruded. Where Tair might have expected hair, instead a crown of light danced around their heads in a dense pattern that varied from Faery to Faery. This was not as surprising as the fact that they were all nude, save the three with small drums held at their hips. Their quite literally golden skin glistened with sweat. The beings paid the intruders no mind as they hunched over a figure at the start of the group. Up in the air, a small constellation of drums thrummed on. Tair did not have a moment to ask Rose what was happening before the older Human pulled her to the front of the group.

Laying just before them all was a much smaller Faery, clearly not a child but littler than their observers. Unlike their observers, though, they were draped in a fine white cloth with silver lacing; they were not dead, but they were clearly dying.

And no one was doing anything to help.

Tair almost knelt down to help the Faery, but Rose said, "*Sanas.*"

"But they're dying—"

"It is not our life to save."

Tair looked back to find that the Faery had a pleased smile on their face. Their eyes were still open but closing slowly, their features settling into forever. Their body relaxed, the suns shone, and then they were gone. The ground swallowed them whole, leaving nothing but the white cloth where they once lay. Despite herself, Tair squatted to touch the fabric. It was soft to the touch but felt like a *greeting*. Tair drew her hand back.

One of the Faeries touched her shoulder, their eyes kind and gentle. They knelt next to Tair and showed her how they folded up the cloth. When they had finished, the material formed a perfect circle, just like clearing in which the smaller Faery had passed. The one beside Tair gave her the cloth to hold, which the Human accepted gratefully; they then kicked at the dirt, just as Rose previously had. A small patch floated up and, on rightful instinct, Tair quickly placed the cloth in that vacant space in the grass. Then the ground healed itself again, and all traces of the recent death passed, too.

"Greetings," the Faeries said in unison.

"You speak Nossok?" Tair asked, rather stunned.

The Faery that had knelt down with her chuckled and said, "Language ceases here; the woods provide us open communication free of arbitrary distinctions."

"You're speaking Nossok, though," Tair countered.

"Or you are speaking Papopon," the Faery said.

Tair blinked.

"Forgive her," Rose cut in. "It is her first time in these woods."

Tair resisted the urge to scoff. In part, it was true; she had no conscious memories of these woods, so it felt to her like her first time; on the other hand, it had been the start of her life as she knew it. To suggest she had never been there before felt like an affront. Even still, she would not have had any other way to describe her relation to the land, not in all the languages she knew, nor the Papopon she was apparently using now. She pulled herself to her feet on her own, despite Rose's attempt to aid her, and dusted herself off.

Tair watched all of the Faeries with wide, curious eyes, but they did not return that same surprised look. Rather, they seemed enthralled in conversation with Rose, familiar and friendly. It was clear that they had all met before, however many years earlier.

"I heard the drums," Rose said with a smile—a wide smile which revealed to Tair, for the first time, the gap tooth the older Human had. They continued, "I rushed to get here."

The Faeries nodded collectively. The one that had guided Tair, who seemed to be most inclined to speak, stepped forward and pressed their forehead to Rose's. The light that acted as their hair engulfed and danced around Rose's head. When they broke apart, so did the little lights. The Faery said, "We are glad to have you again, though we apologize for your loss."

"I am glad to be here, Bopnaa," Rose bowed. "But...my loss?"

Bopnaa—the Faery who had folded up the cloth with Tair—said, "That was Panook."

Rose drew their hands to their mouth.

Tair asked, "Who was Panook?"

Rose explained, "Panook led me to Nossoa. He was...he was very fond of Human refugees. This is a loss for all."

The Faeries all nodded again.

Rose wiped away their tears, then drew their eyebrows together. They asked, "Why was he so small?"

Bopnaa nodded. "We start small, we grow large, and we end small. A perfect cycle."

A perfect cycle. Tair marveled at the way they described life, as far from her reality as it was. If she had to describe her life thus far, it would have been an unpredictable valley, never having any say in whether or not she would ascend or descend another hill. Now, these Faeries spoke of perfect cycles. Tair wanted so desperately for that.

"What brings you here?" Bopnaa finally asked.

"We are on a return journey to Sossoa," Rose answered. There was an assuredness in their voice that Tair could not have claimed herself, as much as she had been the one to decide their destination. Sossoa existed in her mind only in story. Even now, she could not quite wrap her mind around her own choice, nor could she comprehend Rose's conviction that it was the right choice for themself, too.

It was home to Rose, Tair supposed, and she had never had the chance to understand the true concept of home.

Bopnaa pressed their lips into a hard line. Their face and body went so still, so suddenly that Tair almost thought they had turned into a statue. When she glanced around, she realized that the other Faeries had done the same. Then, after a moment, they all came alive again, and Bopnaa nodded. "We will provide you safe passage."

"We cannot ask that of you—" Tair started, but Rose cut her off with a gentle hand on her shoulder.

"We would be eternally grateful," Rose said. Then, into Tair's ear, they whispered, "It is rude to reject a collective offering."

Tair furrowed her eyebrows. "Collective?"

Rose nodded.

"How..." But then Tair understood that in their momentary stint as statues they were not, in fact, lifeless; in that small span of time, they had been telepathically communicating. Tair had never seen anything like it. She now had a million questions and no particular sense of how to verbalize them. She resolved to echo what Rose had said: "Yes, we would be grateful."

The Faeries all smiled. Then, without another word spoken, they clapped their hands to disappear the drums floating above their heads, turned in unison, and strode back into the Darkwoods.

Tair constantly had to remind herself that time did not pass the same in the Darkwoods as it did outside, as much as her body wanted to reject that fact. Again, she wished she and Bonn had spent more time building her endurance, but she wished for a lot of things in hindsight. Perhaps, more than wishing for more practical endurance training, she wished to be *with* Bonn—and Alyn. The two were most likely in Lawe, a land just as unimaginable to Tair as the Darkwoods she now strode through—as unimaginable as Sossoa, her final destination. Her present reality was something like a dream, she realized; if she pretended, she could hear Alyn singing behind her or feel Bonn beside her. Different as they were, the Fel and the Dwarf had provided her optimism in a time when she needed it most, only for it to be stolen away and then regifted in completely new form by Shianna and Rose; unexpected but so needed.

She was lost in thought when they came to the next clearing, the fourth they had come across. This one was much wider in diameter than any other. Travel between clearings was much easier with these Faeries, the forest recognizing them and giving them the freedom to move as they pleased. Tair dropped into a crouch and took a few deep breaths.

After all, just because it was easier, did not mean it was easy.

The Faeries were well accustomed to the Darkwoods and would not have heaved even if they had to cross the entire distance of the land three times over. Some were toned, some were bulky, some were round—but all of them were far better equipped to this journey than Tair, including Rose, who was still relatively unaffected by their travel. Even though rest was only taken for Tair's sake, none hurried her.

And what time those breaks took up! When she finally looked up at the sky through blurry eyes, the Red Sun was setting in the distance and the moon chased after it. A few stars speckled the sky, visibility somehow not as strong as Tair remembered in Mirte or even at the edge of the woods. Tair wondered what impeded the light.

"We will rest here for the night," Bopnaa concluded, after another silent moment with their Faery kin.

"I can keep going," Tair insisted.

Rose shook their head. "It's not about you. These woods are not safe at night."

"Not safe?"

"We do not want to find out."

Tair conceded without another word, feeling no need to question further.

The Red Sun fully set half an hour later. In the precise moment that the sun disappeared, a chorus of insects erupted. That sound itself was not so disturbing, but it was compounded by the stomps and echoey roars of a loud, large creature somewhere behind them. At the perimeter of the clearing, at the sound of that animal, a million little lights flickered on, just as bright as the stars. Had the stars come down to live among them?

When she looked to ask, though, she found that all the Faeries had disappeared, small drums now abandoned on the threshold floor. In the middle of the clearing, Rose lay with an arm draped over their eyes to block out the bright lights. They took steady, meditative breaths, but this did not stop Tair from interrupting to ask where all the Faeries had gone.

"To sleep," Rose answered simply.

"Yes, but where?"

Rose smirked. "They are the light."

"You mean..." Tair looked wide-eyed again at what she had

thought were stars but now understood to be Faeries. Somehow, the concept of the stars living amongst them was easier to comprehend than the reality. She wondered if these Faeries sometimes lived in the sky as stars, or if they contained stars within them, or if...so many outlandish possibilities ran through her head, but she did not seek further clarification. There was a childlike mystery to it all that she did not want to spoil—a childlike mystery that she wished she could have shared with Bonn and Alyn, too. She let out a sigh in awe as she laid back in the grass next to Rose.

"Are you asleep?" Tair asked after a moment of staring up at the sky. A dark cloud passed in front of the moon.

Rose answered, "I do not sleep here."

"Are you resting, then?"

Rose hummed.

"I am sorry to disturb," Tair said, though she did not stop speaking. "This is all new to me. Newer than the Faeries who imprisoned my family and me in Braasii, newer than Doman on the whole...Is this what it is like in Sossoa? All this magic and life?"

"Sossoa is nothing like this. Nothing at all," Rose said.

Rose nudged Tair awake. She stirred and sucked in a deep breath. At some point in the night, she had turned onto her stomach, so now she had to pull a few stray blades of grass from her mouth. Passingly, she remarked the faint taste of mint, and then stood and fixed her clothes. The previous day having been particularly physically taxing, sweat was now pungent on Tair's clothes, and she wished she had packed an extra outfit. The thought did cross her mind to strip down, but she ultimately decided that she was not as comfortable in the nude as her Faery counterparts.

The Faeries had rematerialized around them and began to help one another stretch as they once again grew accustomed to having a body. As they stretched, Bopnaa said, "We will arrive today."

"Today?" After how long the journey had taken them thus far, Tair had a hard time believing that they would be out of the Darkwoods by the end of the day. She stretched out her legs in anticipation.

"Not in the way you might be accustomed," Bopnaa said.

"Oh?" Rose prompted.

"Last time you journeyed with Panook alone. Our way is not possible individually. Now we move together, so we may traverse the woods at a much quicker rate."

Tair blurted, "Why did we not do that yesterday?"

Bopnaa smiled. "Our ability to break you down into your core elements was not possible without your first having spent some time in the forest. You had to collect some of the energy, if you will." They gestured all around themself, to this energy they spoke of that Tair could not feel distinctly. They then continued, "Besides, we needed to rest."

"Break us down? As in, we will be as you were last night?" Tair asked.

Bopnaa nodded with their Faery kin simultaneously.

Tair considered this a moment, with Rose standing next to her and not raising any question. Rose apparently trusted these Faeries and what they were proposing, as strange as it sounded. The younger Human felt a little warier; she could not decide if she wanted to stay intact and endure the pain of another day's travel, or if she wanted to be broken up into a thousand different pieces of starlight. It thrilled and horrified her all the same. As she considered, though, she began to feel herself fragment...and fragment...and fragment...

Tair could no longer see, nor hear, nor speak, nor smell, nor feel. All her senses ceased to exist; indeed, "she" ceased to exist. She was, in that moment, a part of a whole she could not comprehend because there was *nothing to comprehend*. She simply was. There were insects, but they passed through this army of light without fear. There was movement, yes, but it felt nothing like movement, fluid and unimpeded as it was. There was above and below and forward and backward, but she was not conscious of direction. There was light—but she was light, too.

As abruptly as the feeling had come, it had gone. Tair came back into herself with a screeching halt. She expected to feel dizzy, but she felt more whole and grounded than ever before. She leaned back to stretch, felt another Faery grasp her wrists to help her, and then she did the same for them. All around they went, putting their bodies back together again. They had become individuals again, though now part of some unspoken whole Tair could not articulate, even to herself.

Tair realized, too, that she no longer had her belongings, though somehow her (still unclean) clothes had traveled with her, just as the drums had traveled with the Faeries She reached into her pocket and sighed in thanks—the red crystal Alyn had gifted her had remained, too. She was not particularly concerned to have lost what little water and food they had left. For a brief moment, all concern eluded her. She also was not upset that the Faeries had foregone her consent, though she might have preferred to give it. Their decisiveness had propelled them forward into another clearing, only minutes passing.

Tair grew accustomed again to her tongue in her mouth, such an odd thing to be aware of, and finally managed to ask, "How far have we come?"

"The next clearing is right at the border to Sossoa," Bopnaa said with a kind smile. They remarked, "You do not seem surprised by how we have arrived here."

Tair stretched her neck, shook her head, and responded, "It is only surprising in theory."

"It was beautiful," Rose added.

Bopnaa nodded in agreement. Then their smile faded as they said, "As wonderful as it is to see—and meet—you both, we hope not to see you again."

Tair frowned. She felt they had all shared something impossibly intimate, and still they rejected her. She inched closer to Rose on instinct. The Faeries all laughed.

Bopnaa raised a hand to halt the sound. "I only mean," they said, "that we hope you will have found home."

SOSSOA

TWELVE

The last stretch of the journey had been surprisingly easy—surprising only until Tair had noticed that every tree they passed had been slashed through the middle. The trees, both marvelous and treacherous, brought life and magic to the woods; now, those same beings had been gutted, their internal rings exposed and the ground at their feet burned, weeded, broken. Tair was sure that nothing could grow there for the next century, at the very least. As they had neared the border, the birds and insects grew quieter, life disappearing with the trees. Rolt served as a border for the Humans seeking to travel north, the non-Humans seeking to travel south, and then ensured that nature, uncontrollable though it was, conformed to the constructed boundaries Sossoa created, too. Tair sucked in a sharp breath to still her pounding heart.

Rolt was over one hundred feet tall and stretched all the way to the Great Seas on either side. It was made of packed dirt that seemed entirely unsustainable, even with the countless enslaved Humans shaking on rickety supports to repair the wall's gaps with more plaster. Perhaps that was their torture: performing a futile task meant to maintain arbitrary boundaries that contained the world that oppressed them. To watch over them, hundreds of guards stationed themselves across the top of the wall, evenly spaced out for miles and divided by the red-gold flag of Sossoa. To match their flag, each soldier wore some variation on a bright red uniform, the color that had once meant independence and love to Tair now warped by Doman and Sossoa alike. Red only meant pain. And pain surely would come if they were not careful; every single soldier in Tair's eyeline had their arrows drawn on Rose and Tair.

Tair shielded her eyes from the Red Sun and the rising Yellow Sun as she peered up. She whispered, "What should we do?"

Rose did not answer and instead placed a protective hand in front of Tair as the heavy steel door before them swung open. Rose beckoned for Tair to follow them into the dark hallway. She rushed in, heard the door shut behind them both, and discovered that the only light source was on the other end—in Sossoa. She braced herself, finding comfort only in the fact that she knew that she was safe as long as she stayed with Rose.

On the other side of the wall, a shout sounded, and then thirty or so Humans were pulling them out of the tunnel and down onto their knees. Rose placed their hands at the back of their head, and Tair followed suit. Whatever Rose did, Tair echoed, finding security in united movement.

Rose said in Sossok, "*Sem ahggii raisto-anas.*" *We mean no harm.* Tair sucked in a breath; the use of Sossok clearly delineated that she was, in fact, in a new world.

The Human soldiers chuckled. Their apparent leader— dressed in a fully red uniform, too, though with distinguishing gold lacing and jewels sewn in throughout—indicated for the soldiers to search Rose and Tair. Tair distantly remembered the red crystal Alyn had gifted her in her pants pocket, distantly hoped they would not confiscate it, distantly acknowledged their disregard. She felt somewhat out-of-body, the soldiers' brusque hands tugging at her clothes and pulling her from presence.

To distract herself from the soldiers' hands, Tair took a moment to observe her surroundings. She tried not to be too obvious about her disorientation with the land, but it was unlike anything she had seen before. It was brown everywhere. The buildings, placed on stilts above the muddy ground, were made with a dark bark that too closely resembled the trees of the Darkwoods. The mud around the buildings was so matted down that, even if a lone weed had tried to grow, it could not have survived long. Tair saw only one tree in the distance, also brown with wilted branches and dead leaves. Stranger still was the weather; though Tair had assumed that the seasons would behave differently in Sossoa, she never thought it would be so stark. There had been a severe chill in the air ever since they had crossed over from the Darkwoods, and it only grew colder by the minute; contrastingly, when they had left Nossoa, the world was nearing summer. Tair imagined that the Darkwoods created a natural barrier for weather, but she did not know exactly how. In the distance, Tair saw the border of a grand lake, though the water there looked much murkier than the clear blue that she was accustomed to in Doman, in the whole of Nossoa. In truth, she may not have distinguished it as a lake were it not for the Human who waded out, a large net of fish trailing behind them.

The Humans not occupied with the search said nothing and moved little, expressionless and intimidating. As she watched them, Tair realized then that she had never really met anyone with her exact skin tone; brown as it was, there was always something just slightly different to hers than to those she had been raised around. Shianna and Silaa were beautifully dark in their own ways, and Alyn's pale tone was unique and distinctive, comforting to Tair now that they were apart. Bonn's skin, too, was a marvel to Tair, an even, near-black shade that made their orange eyes appear even brighter. But Tair's brown skin always had yellow undertones where the others were warm or cool; now, she found herself surrounded by those with skin just like hers. They all had scars across their bare arms (apparently unaffected by the cold) and faces. Their hair, too, was similarly as curly as hers and Rose's, some wearing braids as intricate as the ones Tair had seen on Shianna's friends and some maybe a month from their last shave.

When the soldiers finished searching Tair and Rose, they merged back into the crowd behind them, nodded, and then took up arms again.

"*Sem ahggii rainto-anas*," Rose repeated. Their muscles flexed beneath their shirt, menacing to Tair and the soldiers all the same.

Rose then told them something else in Sossok that Tair distressingly did not recognize. She worried that Rose had not taught her enough of the language but was quickly distracted when the apparent leader called the soldiers all into a huddle, voices so quiet they blended in with the sound of the wind. Instinctively switching to Nossok, Tair asked Rose, "What's happening?"

"*Sa-anas*," Rose answered in Sossok. *Not here.* "You cannot use that language here."

Tair internally reprimanded herself but hid her shame as the circle unraveled. The leader stuck his spear into the mud at his feet. The other men followed suit, lowering their weapons starting from the middle out. Tair, grateful for the reduced aggression, let out a breath she did not know she had been holding.

"*Moela onsam*," the leader said. *Welcome home.*

It did not feel like home. Then again, Tair thought, did

anywhere? In Sossoa, there were beings who looked like her, yet she was still unsure of whether or not simply looking like someone made anywhere feel like home. There was also a dangerous comfort in this newfound sameness—a comfort Tair did not want to admit to herself, lest she also accept the unequivocally evil foundations of Sossoa.

The guards led Rose and Tair across the mucky ground. The leader, named Aloe in Tair's Nossok translation, led them toward one of the buildings she had seen from afar. Rose had once clarified to Tair that, though they and other Humans used the non-gendered pronoun "*mes*" ("they" in Nossok), soldiers like Aloe and his men did not. Rather, soldiers went by the Sossok pronoun "*mus*," loosely translated to "he" in Nossok. The pronoun was the same the King and King Heir used, which associated them closer with the power structures they participated in and upheld. Where this divide in pronouns had been intended to instill and maintain hierarchy, Sossok Humans had instead turned the common pronoun into one of unity, a badge of honor that said they were part of a distinct group from their oppressors.

Aloe led the pack, his soldiers close behind—not to intimidate but to protect. There was apparently an understanding that, if any Humans were to arrive from Nossoa, soldiers were to embrace them with welcoming arms. Tair feared what that reception was rooted in.

There were three buildings, though more spread out across the distance, stationed at what Tair had assumed were other passageways between the Darkwoods and Sossoa. They arrived at the middle building of the three, guarded by a tired young Human—a child, really—who welcomed Aloe with the formal greeting, "*Aesolo-aso*." He then opened the door and beckoned them all inside.

Tair nodded to the young soldier in thanks. He stared back at her with wide eyes, then shook his head to neutralize his expression. The other soldiers that trailed in behind Tair teased the child, so she felt she had done something wrong. She made a mental note of that but was distracted from her error when she came to full awareness of her new environment. The room was wide and without interior walls. There were a few firepits throughout the room, which would have been rather risky for a wooden building if it were not so wet both inside and out. It would have been difficult to start a fire at all. There was a staircase leading to what Tair assumed were the soldiers' quarters, the only indication that there was more to this building than just the common room. There were plenty of sofas inside, all full of guards who stood when they noticed Aloe had entered the room. Not until he indicated that they could relax did they return to their quiet conversations and meager meals.

Though Tair had expected some kind of welcome party—being Sossoa's lost child and all—she realized now that no one had any reason to recognize her. She was nothing special to them—to anyone, really. She was a pawn necessary to carry out the will of the rebels, but she was also only one pawn of many, and she would not have meant anything in particular to these soldiers. The *idea* of her had more power than her face, than her name, both to the oppressors and the liberators. She was simultaneously comforted and disturbed by her mundanity, also unsure of if it put her and Rose in any more danger.

"Your journey?" Aloe asked as he turned around, eyes locked on Rose but the question clearly directed at Tair.

"Uh," Tair stuttered. When she realized he was asking how their journey *had gone*, rather than what the intentions of their journey was, she answered in Sossok, "*Seh*," with the intention to mean "well." She knew something was off when Aloe smirked at her and the men behind her snickered. She folded her arms over her chest.

Rose explained in Sossok, "They have been around the *raiso* for so long, please forgive their mistakes." Tair realized

206

that she now had to grow accustomed to her new Sossok pronoun. Also unfamiliar was that word—*raiso*. The way Rose had said it indicated to Tair that it was not a kind word. That hypothesis was only strengthened by the fact that Rose had never taught it to Tair in the first place—clearly not a word worth spending time on, nor a word she needed to repeat—and by the fact that the soldiers had all grunted in understanding.

Aloe directed some soldiers sitting by a pot over a firepit to serve their guests some food. Before she could reject the offering, Rose stopped her with a shake of their head.

Knowing from her experience with the Faeries from Braasii that she should never again accept unfamiliar food from strangers, Tair reluctantly took the bowl into her hands. She was extremely hungry, though, and she had to admit that the stew smelled amazing. She let the scent overtake her: rich mushrooms and plenty of pepper and *spice*. Oh, she missed well-seasoned food. They had plenty in Mirte, as Elves love as much spice as they could stomach. In Doman, though, the food was mainly seasoned with salt, the intention to taste the food as purely as the mountains intended. She sipped some of the soup and was nearly overtaken by flavor. She stopped herself from making her pleasure too obvious, not wanting to seem like she was enjoying her time. She decidedly was *not*—even though she did not know these Humans personally, she knew that they did not share the same values as her, knew what they and their ancestors had done to stand on the ground they did today. She did not want to share any pleasure with them, but she also needed to eat. She waited for Rose to swallow a spoonful of the stew first and, after they seemed unaffected by the contents, Tair took small bites of her own.

"You will leave tomorrow," Aloe announced, after a moment of conversing with some of his men. "A farmer brings us their produce then, and they will take you wherever you need to go. For tonight, you will stay with us."

Rose bristled. Tair questioned how Aloe were so sure that the farmer would be willing and able to fulfill the task, but then she remembered that their choice was irrelevant in a choiceless world. She kept quiet, offered a slight smile and nod in thanks, and tried her best to avoid saying the wrong thing again.

Tair and Rose ate their meal in silence on a vacant couch toward the far end of the room. Rose had angled their body to protect the younger Human—from what, Tair did not know. Though aware of herself, Tair did not yet feel unsafe. Having lived with non-Humans her entire life, she had expected to face the same amount of overt violence she knew her loved ones would have had they joined her in this journey. Thus far, these soldiers had surpassed Tair's expectations: she had not found even a hint of hostility beyond that gruff introduction, and they were feeding her well.

But she slowly came into the awareness that her Humanity was a safety in itself. Had it been Bonn with her instead of Rose, Tair did not believe the two of them would have received such a warm introduction. Even then, Tair could sense that the soldiers were acting contrary to how Rose had expected. The older Human clearly felt some hesitation at the thought of a night spent amongst these soldiers, shifting in their seat and eating their soup in gulps, barely tasting it.

Aloe then placed a hand on Tair's shoulder. She whipped around to meet his eyes, these soulless green things, as he stated, "Your travel companion is wanted for treason."

Tair set down her bowl of soup calmly, not too alarmed by the statement. Rose had anticipated it long ago. After all, their goal had always been to travel to Sossoa together, though perhaps under different circumstances and in a less roundabout way. Rose had explained that Tair would have a responsibility to excuse their apparent grievances. The soldiers would not ask Rose themself for vindication; as the older Human had explained, anyone wanted for crime was stripped of their Humanity and was incapable of representing themselves. In preparation, Rose had devised a script for Tair. Originally, she was meant to say that Rose would serve a translator between Tair and the King to atone for their crimes against the throne.

That story now had no place. Tair had to improvise.

Her Sossok slow and calculated, she asked, "Have they not proven their loyalty to and reverence for the realm by abandoning life amongst the *raiso*, just as I have?" Though she had not known what *raiso* meant just yet, she felt that it worked in this context. Rose appeared pleased with Tair, especially since she had proved that all of their language lessons had not been wasted. The two watched for Aloe's and his men's reactions.

Aloe raised an eyebrow and sneered. Rather than respond, he directed their attention to the northernmost wall of the building. There stood three heavy wooden doors that Tair had not noticed before, seemingly without any way to get in—or out. Tair felt a shiver run down her spine. Aloe led the pair to the doors.

Then he said, "This is where we keep our prisoners."

"Prisoners?" Tair asked before Rose could stop her. Tair felt this to be a deliberate tactic to put both her and Rose further on edge. And it was working, as much as she wanted to deny it. She instinctively took a step closer to Rose.

Tair's fear obviously pleased Aloe. With a wide, malicious grin spread across his face, he gestured for one of the guards to unlock door. The soldier followed his directive without question. He pulled a key out from under his tongue—small and easily swallowed, which might have been a safety precaution in itself—and unlocked the middle door. Immediately, the heavy stench of rotting flesh and feces and urine infected the air so thoroughly that Tair had to cover her nose in order to see clearly. Even then, there was not much to see, dark as it was inside. Only a thin strip at the top of the outward-facing wall allowed in the smallest sliver of natural light, just wide enough to pass a rope through but not enough to get anyone out along with it. There were at least fifteen decaying bodies in the cell, drained of hope and life. There were a couple Humans, but, for the most part, the prisoners were Dwarves and Faeries. They may have come to Sossoa just the same as Rose and Tair, in search of a land of refuge but looking in entirely the wrong direction. Why had they not gone to Lawe, gone somewhere where they had a fighting chance? Tair shivered—Sossoa might have been their only option.

Startling Tair, someone paced at the back of the cell—a young Dwarf, some years Tair's junior. They repeatedly mumbled something in Domani to themself.

Tair wiped the tears that welled up in her eyes. Before she could stop herself, she whispered, "What...why?"

The Dwarf flinched at the sound Tair's voice and darted toward the open cell door. On instinct, Aloe drew a dagger strapped to his belt and scratched the young Dwarf's skin. They jumped back with a yelp, covering their new, shallow wound on their bone-thin arm. They sounded more animal than Dwarf, and Tair supposed that was the point of imprisonment: to animalize one's captives. Aloe chuckled at the Dwarf's pain, again avoiding Tair's question. This was a demonstration, not a time for inquiry.

A soldier came up behind Tair and tossed the dregs of the hot soup into the cell. The Dwarf recoiled from the steaming soup, but they did not hesitate to crouch down to the ground and salvage what they could. Tair averted her eyes. The Dwarf's conditions would certainly only worsen as they ingested an inordinate amount of toxic waste mixed with that cruel meal, if it could still be considered a meal. Only moments earlier, she had consumed her soup in peace, had remarked at the exceptional flavor, and now it had been weaponized. As desperately as she wanted to do something—*anything*—she knew that if she tried....

Rose was already wanted for treason, and Tair had no authority to free the Dwarf, as badly as she wanted to. She thought about Shianna in that situation, or Bonn, or any other Dwarves she had met in Doman—or any of her family, really, Alyn and Silaa included. Grateful for their relative safety, Tair still knew that this would not be the worst violence that hatred could create. She held back her tears as she realized that she would have to accept most, if not all, of these horrors to find safety for Rose and herself.

But then, what did her individual safety mean if others were not safe? A flood of guilt and shame washed over her.

Rose, on the other hand, watched the scene with a hard-set jaw and steely eyes. Though disturbed, they clearly knew how to hide their revulsion better than Tair. Finally, after what felt like an inordinate amount of time, Aloe indicated for the soldier to shut the door once more. All sounds of the Dwarf lapping at the pool of soup and waste disappeared.

Tair suppressed her nausea.

Aloe waved for another soldier to come over. He was younger than Aloe but much more muscular. He held a red cloth with a large black mark across it. Aloe took the fabric, turned to Rose, and offered it to them. They took it with a hung head. Aloe said, "You may have decided to abandon life amongst the *raiso*, but you are not absolved of guilt. You must travel with this mark visibly attached to you at all times, or else face a similar fate."

Tair grimaced, but Rose nodded for the both of them, acknowledging that they were aware of their current conditions. They recognized the cloth, recognized what it represented, much more than Tair ever could have.

Aloe shouted for one of his soldiers, startling Tair and Rose both. He smirked at the two of them as the Human he called for arrived, young like the other but taller than he was muscular.

"Show them to their bed," Aloe demanded. With a slight upturn of his nose, he added, "And get them a change of clothes."

The clothes in question were much too big, though unsoiled, and the single bed much too stiff, though just large enough for both Tair and Rose. It would have had to do for one night. In the span of mere minutes, Aloe had gone from threatening to imprison Rose to offering them his own bed. Rose relaxed when they realized that two of them had their own walled-off space at the back of the second story quarters, past about thirty bunk beds. Tair reasoned that this demonstration of welcome had to do with repatriation; a sign that they were, in fact, welcome in Sossoa.

And she would always be welcome here, the realm having been designed with the specific intention of keeping Humans separate from non-Humans by any means necessary. When Tair thought to Bonn, though, she worried that the Dwarf would never receive repatriation, exiled from their homeland of Doman and separated from all that they had ever known and loved. Alyn, in his own way, was also without home; he had been exiled from Doman where part of his chosen family lived and unwelcome in Sossoa where another member of that family now found herself. Now, likely returning to a home he had chosen to leave decades ago, he undoubtedly felt himself without place. Tair felt grateful for the privilege of place—and then she felt guilt for her gratitude.

Though Tair had tried to distract herself from that guilt by starting conversation with Rose, they only sunk back in the bed and shut their eyes against Tair's chattiness. They released their breath fully for the first time in hours. It was the sound of Rose's even breathing, the clinking of glasses below, and the pattering of rain outside that eventually lulled the antsy Tair to sleep.

What woke her, though, was not the rising of the Red Sun,

as she had expected it would. Later that same night, a shriek sounded outside. Tair shot up and waited. Another shout sounded two minutes later. More silence followed. Finally, after the third shriek rang through the air, Rose awoke alongside Tair. The two peeked out the overhead window and found nothing out of the ordinary, save an empty wooden wagon with two animals Tair could not identify attached to the front. Animals Tair had never seen before and did not have the language for. The wagon itself would not have been cause for concern were it not for the growing fear that someone new had arrived by it—and the confirmation of that fear when the sounds of conflict erupted below.

Tair stirred to get up and—what? All her training with Bonn told her to fight, to struggle for her life, but her natural instinct was still to run and hide, avoiding conflict at all costs. Before she could decide, though, Rose stopped her and whispered, "Just wait."

Tair did as she was told, however anxious she was to react. Metal clashed and dishware clattered. Loud moans and sharp screams echoed through the floorboards. Whatever transpired below them was far from pleasant. Soldiers clambered from their beds just outside Tair's and Rose's temporary lodging to check on the noise. One final skreich, one final holler, and then all sound ceased.

Rose rustled around beneath Aloe's bed and was obviously relieved to find that he had tucked a spare battle axe there. Tair had never imagined the older Human wielding a weapon—then again, Tair had not imagined much of Rose's life outside of the information she received in their lessons. Upfront as they were, Tair always assumed Rose would eventually tell her what she needed to know. Admittedly, too, she had been preoccupied with her own life. Rose was certainly strong enough to wield the weapon, and they had to have picked up something in their time as a rebel all those years ago, so Tair had no choice but to trust them. In fact, she *admired* them, the confidence in their stride and the strength in their axe-wielding hand. The two were careful to shuffle out of the room, trying to avoid any creaky floorboards.

The soldiers' quarters were in shambles. Those who had been sleeping had rushed from their beds, with the trunks at the start of the room splayed out. It was far too dark to discern anything, not a single window nor a lit torch in sight. The only light came from below, interrupted by a number of shadows. Hushed, hurried voices traveled through the air. Tair gulped and, in that moment of dread, tripped over a raised floorboard, falling face-first onto the ground. Rose winced, laid down their axe, and helped Tair stand. A Human covered in blood that was evidently not their own stumbled up the stairs to find the source of the noise, their crossbow slackly pointed at Tair and Rose.

"Identify yourselves!" the young Human shouted. They fidgeted, their eyes still adjusting to the dark as they looked between Tair and Rose. In the time it took them to adjust their bow, Rose had picked their axe back up.

"Identify yourself first," Rose said.

The newcomer gulped and held their arms up. Though the Human could have easily shot Rose at that distance, they conceded at the slightest threat of a defeat. There was no way that they had participated in the battle below, Tair resolved. She almost laughed before her nerves returned. She shifted another step behind Rose.

Finally, the nervous fighter answered, "*Asosso Ami.*"

Ami...Tair translated the name to Oil in Nossok.

"Not your name," Rose sighed in exasperation. They dropped their axe an inch. "Who are you allied with?"

"Oh," Oil said with a grimace. "That...that depends on your allegiance."

"Only a rebel would answer that way," Rose resolved. "You need to work on your script."

Oil nodded and flinched as Rose finally dropped their axe

to the floor. They strode over to Oil with a renewed confidence, Tair close at their heels. Then they introduced themself and Tair, using a name for the younger Human that she did not recognize. She decided to ask later what her new name meant, somewhat relieved that she did not have to choose her own chosen name—and still frustrated that Shianna and Silaa had once tried to do the very same thing. How she wished they were still in Braasii, still worrying only about where Alyn had gone before their entire world had been turned upside down.

Tair was brought back to reality when someone called from below, "*Ahrra-messos oopa?*"

"They're friendly!" Oil responded back in Sossok, though Tair did not believe they had nearly enough evidence to verify their claim. Oil gestured for the two of them to follow down the stairs.

When they arrived at the bottom, ten more rebels came into view, bloodied weapons drawn in Tair's and Rose's direction. Rose did not surrender and, instead, held their head high. Tair stood two steps behind, her first defense Rose and her second her own two trained fists, which would have been no match against all the weaponry that threatened them: maces, swords, double-edged daggers, and bows and arrows. Clearly, Oil's trust was no reflection of the group's, perhaps a trainee themself. Unlike Oil, these rebels could have killed Rose and Tair in an instant—they had already killed many that night. All the once-living soldiers now laid in a gory heap in the middle of the room, eerily similar to the Dwarves and Fel and Humans hidden behind the prison door to Tair's left. Tair swallowed back that first feeling of awe. As opposed as she had been to fighting three months ago, as much as she could not have imagined a world in which something like this could happen, she had to admit that the rebels had garnered a degree of admiration in her eyes, killing the soldiers that had committed far more evils than Tair had been exposed to.

Committed evils against entire kinds for not being Human—
and who would have committed evils against beings whom
Tair loved.

Then again, Tair had to remind herself that the rebels had
just murdered fifty Humans in five minutes' time—amongst
those fifty, she could not have been sure that every single
death could have been justified. What of the young soldier who
had held open the door? Had he yet committed any violence
in his short life to warrant such a brutal end? Tair was not yet
decided on whether or not death could have ever been
justified. Allied with the rebellion, though, Tair hoped they
were at least on the right side of history, hoped this was
appropriate retribution for a wider system of cruelty. For her
own sake, allied with the rebellion both by obligation and by
choice, she *needed* them to be on the right side of history, if
history were to be told in binaries.

"Identify yourselves," the leader said—or, at least, the
Human who seemed to lead. Authority was always more
plainly defined in Mirte and Doman. Already in Sossoa, it was
clear that authority was assumed rather than defined. Similar
to Aloe, the rebel leader never outright declared their title,
their authority instead explicit in their presence. Unlike Aloe,
though, this apparent leader wore no distinctive clothes, nor
did they bear any kind of badge. They stood at the far end of
the group, no desire to be front and center. Their graying
temples coupled with their large, twinkling eyes made their
age imperceptible. Their skin was close to Tair's own color,
though with plenty of black *eematts* like Rose's. Their *eematts*
were of trees, permanently stretching all the way up their
arms and onto their neck. Their tightly coiled black hair
almost served as a treetop.

"We have already done that for this one here," Rose said
as they gestured to Oil, who now weakly drew their bow at
Tair's side. This version of Rose was foreign as any, having
taken on this new role that far too closely resembled the one

Shianna had taken on when she revealed that she was Prime Heir. Rose's role in the rebellion seemed to have been much larger than Tair had originally understood. Tair bristled; she did not know whether to be angry at this lie—or angry at herself for never asking. She decided on the latter. She could not feel betrayed by yet another trusted companion.

Confirming Tair's suspicions, Rose added, "I suppose they are much too young to know me by my name."

"Which is?" The leader stepped forward as they sheathed their dagger at their side. The hostility in the room lessened only slightly; the rest of the rebels still had their weapons drawn and their expressions steeled as they waited for instruction.

"*Osaa*," Rose said.

The weapons slacked around them all.

"You were killed," the leader breathed, their eyes wide.

"Imprisoned, yes. Set to be executed, yes. But killed..." Rose gestured to their body as they smiled wide. "Not yet."

The leader sighed in relief as they pulled Rose into a tight hug, if only to feel that they were still real, still breathing. One by one, the rest of the rebels approached and pulled Rose into long embraces. Rose may have filtered themself in Doman because they never knew who was listening in, but...How much had they really been hiding from their student? After so much time spent with Rose, Tair felt rather self-centered for never asking for more details on their life, the extent of her knowledge of Rose's involvement in the rebellion being that they had stolen supplies to support their family and community. Tair had thought herself to hold an important role in the balance of the rebellion, but Rose, too, had been so significant that the rebels had immediately recognized their name, perhaps an uncommon one, and laid down their weapons.

After all the hugging, Rose rocked back on their heels and beamed at the group, their arm slung around who Tair assumed to be the leader. Rose asked, "What is all of this?"

The leader looked to the pile of bodies in the center of the room, then motioned to the wall to Tair's left. They answered with a shrug, "Liberation."

Rose chuckled—a sound Tair did not recognize became she had never yet heard it. It was deep and rich and it contagiously echoed throughout the room. They said, "You have made that rather difficult for yourselves by killing the only one with a key."

"Oh?"

Rose nodded to the body of the soldier who had unlocked the prison cell earlier. He had undoubtedly swallowed the key during the struggle. Tair could not imagine that it would have been worth the effort to cut him open and search for the key that way. He was already a mess; blood poured from his chest and mouth down over his face, and his eyes were open and blank, drained of all life. Tair turned away from the sight, unaccustomed to death in general but especially unaccustomed to such gruesome death. The more she observed the ramifications of the rebels' violence, the harder time she had stomaching her meal from earlier. Fighting seemed to come naturally to these rebels. As for Tair, she had struggled to justify simply *learning* to fight, using it primarily as an excuse to spend more time with her mate, and she had also denied her murderous duty to Sossoa. She tried to focus on the fact that soldiers had committed the same amount of, or far more, violence throughout their lives in the name of a far worse cause than the rebels. Did that make it right? Tair did not like how complicated her feelings were on the matter. She made sure not to look at the gore again.

The leader asked, "Any ideas?"

"Break it open," Rose said with a shrug. They went back up the stairs and descended with their axe in hand. They then hurled the weapon over their head and slashed at the wall. For a few minutes, there was no give, not even a slight splinter in the wood, but still they did not tire. It was not until a few other Humans joined that the wall began to crack. When a space wide enough for an arm to reach through had opened up, Rose began to tear at the wood with their bare hands, unconcerned by the blood that poured from their palms. The other rebels began to work at different points in the wall, opening up two places for the other cells to be torn apart. When they had finally finished, perhaps half an hour later, they all held torches into the cells and looked for any signs of life.

The Dwarf Tair had seen earlier curled into a fetal position in the corner of the cell, undisturbed by the breaking of their cage. They snored and scratched at the air, scratched at the hand that now reached in free them. When they finally opened their eyes, they stirred onto their feet and pressed back into the wall. Twelve Humans stood outside of their broken-down cage and, behind those Humans, a heap of bloodstained bodies shone in the center of the room. A large tear slid down their cheek, and Tair could not blame them for their fear.

She was afraid, too.

Rose said something in Sossok as they reached out to the Dwarven child, who cringed at the touch. Tair imagined herself in the young Dwarf's position—imagined anyone she loved in the Dwarf's position. Here was a Human who looked exactly like their captors and spoke the language of their captors. Careful to avoid stepping in puddles of waste that made her eyes water, Tair pulled Rose back with a gentle hand and stepped inside the cell. The older Human considered following, then stepped out with a slight nod. Tair inched closer to the Dwarf, though maintained a comfortable distance so as not to frighten them further.

"*Rako grasora'as ak'raak,*" she said. *We are sorry* in Domani, hopefully a comforting remedy to Rose's misguided use of Sossok. "*Raak jsa'aa Domankana?*" *Do you speak Domani?*

The Dwarf stared back at her with fearful blue eyes but

nodded. In a strained, unused voice, they asked, *"Kiina kaana'aa-raako?" Who are you all?*

Tair looked over her shoulder to find the rebels watching her with keen eyes, unsure of a Human who could speak a language they had never encountered and could not understand—a language they probably could not even label as Domani. Tair sighed and whispered, *"Akros kojsajo'so akk'raak." They fight for you.* Tair had chosen her words carefully, not wanting to claim responsibility for the damage done. Even her choice of *kojsajo* had been deliberate, using the Domani verb "to fight" that did not refer to self-defense. More accurately, she had said: *They kill for you.*

The Dwarf nodded and took Tair's now outstretched hand. Then they switched to Nossok to ask, "What's your name?"

Tair bristled. She should have asked Rose immediately what her name was meant to be in this new world. As if hearing Tair's anxiety, Rose stepped forward and helped the two of them get over the bodies on the floor of the cell. They answered, "Her name is Missai."

Missai. Tair beamed. It had a different translation in Sossok, which Tair remembered from earlier because she had not recognized it. And, though Rose's translation used the Northern Elvish word for the bird, the Dwarf recognized it easily.

The Dwarf looked at her in wonder, as if to ask why someone else had answered for her. She could offer nothing more than a nod. They said in Nossok, "My name is Iom, he."

Tair acknowledged the change in pronouns, comforted by this little detail. The Dwarf was young enough to have learned the Domani cultural trend that Tair had seen amongst Shianna's friends. She felt a twinge in her heart as she remembered Bonn's introduction, confident and upfront. Tair placed a hand over her heart and said for herself, "She."

Iom nodded.

"So ahllo raiso?" The leader asked in Sossok, a language

that made Iom flinch. Tair noted the use of the word *raiso* again—and then finally realized that it was a demeaning and all-encompassing Sossok word to refer to anyone and *anything* non-Human. Indeed, the leader had asked if Tair "knew *raiso*," which implied that any of the many languages used in Nossoa had been homogenized into one word, in spite of the realm's incredible diversity. Tair flinched; all that she had ever known, all who she had ever encountered, *everything* was the same to the Humans of Sossok, their very language inadequate to describe the lived realities of millions.

Tair had probably made a mistake, then, in choosing to speak Nossok. A stranger to the rebels, she should not have been able to communicate so easily with the Dwarven child. Still, she would not have made a different decision if she had been able to speak to her past self; solidarity with Iom came easier to her than solidarity with the rebels, his face more familiar than those that looked similar to her own.

Tair struggled to hold up the Dwarf at her side, despite the fact that he was nearly all bones. She shifted her weight so Iom could lean against her better. With a huff, she answered in Sossok that she spoke Nossok and Domani: "*Sunos. Asos ahllo Nossok esya Domani.*" She had to use the Nossok words for the languages, knowing that their translation in Sossok would simply be "raiso," which she never wanted to say again.

The leader frowned, undoubtedly confused. "Domani, *esa nahhs?*" *What's that?*

Distracted by the child propped up on her hip, Tair again answered without thought, "*As ahsan.*" *A language,* Tair said, and explained further, "*Asos ahllo* Domani, Nossok, Sossok, *esya* Northern Elvish."

Rose winced.

"How's that then?"

"What?"

"How did you learn all those...languages? And the words for them?"

221

Tair considered her answer for a moment. She obviously should not have had knowledge of so many languages, even if she had been raised in the Human colonies to the north of the Darkwoods. In that case, she would have known only a little Sossok and her primary language would have been Nossok. Domani could have been justified, as those colonies sometimes interacted with Dwarves, but Northern Elvish? Few who lived outside Mirte had reason to speak the language without ancestral ties to it.

"Braasii," Tair finally decided. She knew enough about the land to claim it as home to amongst Humans who had never, and probably would never, venture there and return to contradict her tales. "Rose and I met in their travels across the north in a mountain called Braasii. Many live there, and many languages are spoken."

Rose slacked their shoulders, pleased with Tair's answer. The justification would likely require further explanation, but for now it was all they had. And, apparently, it was enough: the leader stepped up to Iom and Tair and said, *"Asosso Klauseh."*

Tair translated the Sossok to Nossok for Iom, "Their name is Crow."

Crow slowed their next statement down, as if it would help Iom understand any better: *"Sem so-akar."*

"They liberate you," Tair tried in Nossok, but then decided it would make more sense in Domani. She repeated what she had said earlier, *"Akros kojsaoo'so akk'raak."* This time, though, she switched verbs from *kojsajo* to *kojsaoo*, now meaning self-defense for oneself *and* the collective.

Iom nodded with a soft smile, Tair's use of Domani easing him. His shivering had lessened and the wrinkle between his thin eyebrows smoothed with every passing second. Still, he was fatigued, his body certainly only days away from death.

At least he was alive, unlike his fellow prisoners. Not one other had survived.

Tair, curious now, asked Crow, "Liberate them to where?" Tair used the Sossok common pronoun for Iom, not wanting inadvertently associate him with the dead soldiers piled up in the middle of the room.

Crow frowned. "Nossoa, of course."

Tair frowned, too, but, when she looked around the room, she found no one else thought this solution worrying. She adjusted Iom in her arms. It seemed clear enough to her that all the non-Human prisoners had fled to Sossoa for a reason. Nossoa had no longer been an option for them and, despite knowing that Sossok Humans posed worse threats than whatever they were fleeing, they had fled here, nonetheless. Tair asked, "Why do you think they came here in the first place?"

Crow looked around the room for answer. When no one else had a better explanation, they asked, "Is that not where they belong?"

"Who is to say they do not belong here?"

"They are not safe here," another rebel proudly offered up, as if they had come up with the perfect reasoning to send Iom to Nossoa.

"They *were* not safe here, yes," Tair said. "Until you liberated them into our custody. Again, why do you think they came here in the first place?"

The rebels were silent, Rose among them. Rose had seemed confused by Tair's words at first but, after a moment of consideration, appeared almost *delighted* with Tair. They smiled wide, revealing again their gap tooth. Rose said, "Missai brings up a good point. Is that not one of the goals of total liberation for all?"

The rebels grunted in agreement.

"Liberation may one day mean the ability to move freely between lands, to determine for oneself where they belong and what they will do with their lives once they get there," Rose continued on. They turned to Iom and Tair again and asked the Dwarf in Nossok, "Would you like to stay here?"

Without a moment's pause, Iom nodded. No matter the harm done unto him, it must have been better than whatever he had escaped, the exact details of which did not matter as much as the fact that he had to leave. Tair would not force him to relive his trauma, but Crow wanted to know: "*Saano?*"

Rose shook their head. "Now is not the time for stories. Let us get him—and ourselves—to safety."

THIRTEEN

They waited until morning to leave Rolt. Everyone had been required to contribute to the cleanup, save the severely fatigued Iom. Tair had been unable to bring herself to organize the soldiers' bodies in the central building for burning, so she had chosen instead to help loot the ramshackle barracks for essentials, like food, clothing, and weapons.

The fire meant to burn the bodies and buildings had been hard to start, with the wood of the barracks so damp from the rain, but the corpses provided morbid kindling. The resulting fire was a sign; a sign that soldiers and the regime they served were not safe, so any who did not wish the same fate upon themself had to defect or face the same future. It was also, in Tair's mind, a sign that the rebellion's power was strong and had spread to some of the throne's major holdouts, like Rolt.

By the break of dawn, the Red Sun burned just as red as the fires that blazed under its watchful eye, and the rebels had killed and cremated over one hundred soldiers, totaled between the three barracks. The ten (eleven, including Rose) of them had not lost one of their own. Tair wondered why the

Sossok rebellion needed help from Doman when they seemed fully capable of defending themselves. She especially wondered why they needed help from *her,* relatively untrained and incapable of carrying out what was expected of her. She wondered about a lot of things—how the rebels dealt with the guilt, if they had any, or they justified it in the name of war—but she stopped her wondering because her opinions were already far too muddy.

She was not prepared for uncertainty. Not yet.

The land had transformed in the early morning light. The fleecy clouds overhead were gray and pink, some mixture of the Red Sun and the plumes of smoke traveling high. Bugs called *fhani,* with long, slim bodies and six wide wings, flew low to the ground and landed on each and every Human they encountered. Tair flinched when one first touched her but quickly realized it was far too delicate a thing to cause concern. Rose had even said they were a symbol of good luck. Tair doubted (if they were good luck, why were they everywhere, landing on everyone?) but appreciated the sentiment.

Their transport was simple: a wagon led by two *dusoo,* the name Rose had just taught Tair, that the younger Human had seen bucking about the night before. The *dusoo* had hooves, like the deer Tair knew of in Nossoa, but were much stronger and had much thicker coats of red-brown fur. There were so many new creatures in Sossoa, in fact, that Tair began to marvel at how diverse life could be across the continent of Gosso, despite how much the Sossok empire had tried to eliminate diversity. Tair knew, too, that the Darkwoods distinctly separated Nossoa and Sossoa from one another, the worlds divided both by culture and environment. One of the younger rebels, *Saani* (roughly Fawn, in Nossok), apparently the child of a farmer, spoke to the *dusoo* with care before they allowed their passengers to climb into the back of the wagon. Finally, the party rode away from the barracks until the fire was small in their eyes, and the smoke became the only indication that they had ever been there—until all that laid before them was a land Tair was only truly meeting for the first time.

The wagon was rather cramped with everyone packed in. The rebels had planned for ten travelers and now had three additional passengers to fit in. Crowded together like that, Tair could not help but notice that most of the rebels had speckles of blood crusting over their clothes and skin, which they picked at occasionally as it dried in the early afternoon sun. Something about the ease of their actions worried Tair, so she distracted herself with other things, like Iom sleeping on her arm, heavy and snoring, and the sky overhead. The sun kissed her skin, the sound of the lake to the west a kind of lullaby. Tair fell into sleep, which she had lost the night before. Every once in a while, she distantly registered laughter, or a bump in the road, or a *fhani* landing on her forehead. None of this woke her, though. It was the Yellow Sun that brought her back.

As little room as there was, the Human across from Tair made space for her to stretch out as she woke. She nodded in thanks. Tair asked in Nossok, "Where are we?"

The lake was a little way behind them. From this angle, it looked much more like a sea, not unlike Doman Lake. The water was much more inviting now, too, as though the storm from the night before and all the bloodshed that had come with it had cleansed the once murky and unpopulated water. Today, families floated aimlessly across the clear blue water in small boats and groups lounged about the shoreline. As it once had in Doman, leisure centered around the water surprised Tair. In Mirte, the nearest water had been the river through the woods, or the Eastern Great Sea, neither of which were suited for restfulness. In contrast, the Sossok Humans saw the water as naturally as Tair and Silaa saw endless grassland, or as Shianna and Bonn saw the landscape of Doman, as naturally as Alyn saw the world. She observed Sossoa for all of them.

When Tair focused back on Rose, she found them chewing their bottom lip, unnerved by Tair's instinctive use of Nossok. Their Braasii lie would only hold up for so long, and Tair's persistent use of the language that came most naturally to her prompted question as to her true origins—and as to how and why she had ever gone north, and why she had come back now with Rose.

Rose rubbed at their bandaged hand, injured the night before as they tore through the prison cell walls. Eventually, they answered in Sossok, "We're heading South."

Of course, that was the best answer they could give: Tair would not have recognized any names of precise locations in Sossoa, but their vagueness still made Tair frown. The concept of "South" only further disturbed her, her only reference being that it was where the King lived and that it had been where Rose had spent their tumultuous childhood. Tair did not press, despite her confusion.

The wagon navigated the eastern side of an extensive mountain range and passed through a forest to the southeast of the lake. As they passed under the sparse canopy, Tair adjusted Iom on her shoulder. The more he slept, the more comfortable he became, and the more Tair realized just how young he really was. She had originally assumed he was a few years younger than her, but he could have been at least a decade younger, perhaps around ten years of age. Tair realized then that she had aged another year in her time spent confined to Doman, the day passing without all the fanfare it once had in Mirte. She smiled when she thought of how Bonn might have celebrated with her, if only she had not lied about knowing the two of them were mates for so long. She wondered if Bonn now forgave her: for the lies, for inadvertently exiling them from their homeland, for not chasing after them.

To distract herself, Tair cast her gaze into the thicket and *swore* that she saw a small, isolate green hand wave at her—unmistakably Faery. She sat up quickly, Iom rolling off of her, and strained forward to look through the dense brush of trees. The same hand waved at her again, now ten feet away. Careful to use Sossok so as not to alert the rebels who undoubtedly questioned her identity, she whispered to Rose, "Did you see that?"

"*Es* Faery?" Rose responded nonchalantly as they adjusted themself. They used "Faeries" in Nossok, rather than "*raiso,*" which comforted Tair. No one noticed, having passed into their own conversations.

Tair's eyes went wide. Quieter this time, she asked, "There are Faeries in Sossoa?"

"Of course," Rose said.

"But I thought Humans had killed—" Tair began but stopped herself when some of the rebels glanced over at her. She offered them a half-smile.

Rose shrugged, obviously more comfortable now that they were in the company of allies, and now that Tair was being diligent about her use of Sossok. "Soldiers cannot kill those who can disappear in an instant—those who can disguise themselves as Human."

"Faeries can disguise themselves as Humans?" Tair was only a little too loud when she asked this, and all the rebels around her laughed.

Crow nudged Rose as they teased, "Braasii, huh?"

Rose did not look so amused, but they smiled to appease the group. They explained to Tair, "I've seen it before. They walk among us as kin. You all have seen it, too, no?" They asked, posing the question to the group.

The rebels all nodded. Tair, too, nodded. She had seen Faeries disguise themselves as Fel, but Humans? In Sossoa? She thought the risk far too great, but she supposed that if Faeries had been living in the land for generations, they must have found ways to adapt. Still, Tair feared...

229

Crow confirmed those fears as soon as Tair thought them. "You have been away for a long while, *Osaa*. Many *raiso*"—Tair bristled—"have now been found, imprisoned, or killed. There are still some amongst us, but they are...they are Human now."

Rose scratched their chin. "Permanently?"

Crow nodded. "For their own protection, yes. They're indistinguishable from the rest of us, but at what cost? Imagine disguising yourself your entire life...*Kias!* Another freedom we fight for, I suppose."

All the rebels grunted in agreement, something Tair had seen in Shianna's Dwarven friends. Tair also noted the use of the Domani word for "what" as a filler word in Crow's statement. Remnants of Doman lived on in Sossok culture even five hundred years later. Tair quelled the sadness that entered her heart when she thought of Doman. When there, she had been desperate to leave and never return, but now she wished to be amongst beings she recognized, whose morality and values she shared; more than that, she wished to be with Bonn and to relive all the days they had spent in each other's company, even the days clouded in lies.

She set aside her wishes for the future.

Tair was still settling into the idea that she was completely surrounded by Humans here in Sossoa, so to find out that some of them may not have been Human at all...It was mildly (and perversely) amusing. Sossoa had been founded on the desire to create a land separate from non-Humans under a shared trait of Humanity, and even that had not been totally accomplished centuries later. The Faeries' continued presence brought Tair comfort; a land so rooted in violent and oppressive homogeneity would always falter, always fail.

Tair sank back in her seat and rolled Iom's head onto her shoulder again. The Dwarf snuggled into the crook of her neck. She tried breathing deeply, as Rose often did, and was surprised to find a familiarity in the air, perhaps lingering from all those years ago. Her body remembered even when she could not. That warm air settled her, and she fell asleep once more.

Tair felt their next stop with a jolt. Once her eyes adjusted to the bright afternoon light, she found that she and Iom were the only ones left in the wagon. She shook the child awake after his almost twelve-hour sleep. Rose, Crow, and the others stood and stretched just a few feet away in dried, brown grass.

"You stay here," Tair said in Nossok to Iom as she crawled off of the wagon. Not that Iom had much choice; he was still rather weak and could not have stood without some help. Tair tried not to shiver every time she looked at him, every time she wondered back to his imprisonment. As grateful as she was to see him freed, she knew that he was certainly no safer wandering around Sossoa. She realized, too, that she was no safer than him. There was an unspoken tension in the air, something she had not let herself acknowledge. As strong, as powerful, and as determined as these rebels knew themselves to be, they never spoke of the King and King Heir, the roots of their oppression and their ultimate targets. They never spoke of an assassin meant to kill those Humans. Even then, Tair knew that her true identity could have been used against her if she had accidentally revealed it to the wrong Human at the wrong time. On top of that, now she had taken on the responsibility of a Dwarven child in an all-Human land, just as Alyn, Silaa, and Alyn had once raised a Human child in an all-Elven land. As misguided as that might have been, Tair knew now their sense of obligation: she would never have left him there, nor would she have approved of abandoning him to the Darkwoods against his wishes. She felt a weight now, a need to protect not only herself but also this child. It was a weight she somehow had no trouble accepting.

Perhaps three miles behind them was the forest they had passed through, still visible in the mid-evening light around the bend of mountains. Another hundred feet in front of them was a wall surrounding what Tair assumed was a town.

"Is that where we're stopping?" Tair asked. She pulled on another's—*Kansii,* or Slug in Nossok—arms to help them stretch out. Slug had perhaps the most beautiful hair Tair had ever seen, locked and braided into an intricate pattern down the back of their head. Since they used a bow and arrow, they were one of the few rebels who had not needed to get involved in hand-to-hand combat. The only blood on them was from moving the bodies.

Rose nodded and answered, "We would not be able to make it to Raaha in a day."

After they had fully stretched one another out, Slug gave Tair a kind smile, full of crooked teeth, which Tair returned in kind. The image in Tair's mind of Slug or any one of the rebels as murderers faded; as she spent time around them, their deeds became normalized. Death was a part of life, murder a part of war—or so she began to tell herself.

"What about...?" Tair tentatively asked, gesturing to Iom, who lounged back in the wagon.

Crow frowned, as did Rose. The two looked to one another in silent conversation before Rose concluded, "*Sem ahkji mesesaka.*"

"Disguise?"

Rose went over to the wagon and greeted Iom. He sat up slowly and looked to Tair to see if he could trust the older Human before him. Tair nodded and came to stand by his side of the wagon for reassurance. Rose then set about attempting to camouflage Iom. For now, his height would not reveal him, as he was about as tall as Tair had been at his age. As he grew older, though, his height would have been an obvious problem; at most, he would maybe grow half a foot taller. The only thing that distinguished him now were his abnormally large ears, which Dwarven children grew into as they aged. Rose tore a piece of fabric from their undershirt and tightly wrapped it around Iom's head, then took off their hood for him to sling over his head. His skin was lighter than any other Human Tair had seen thus far, perhaps due to his time in a sunless cell, but it would not have raised too much inquiry, Rose said. Finally, when they seemed satisfied, Rose presented him to the rest of the group, who nodded in approval.

"*Raak kaana'aa kasa,*" Tair said as she brushed Iom's head. *You're good.* He smiled at her and asked her to help him down off of the wagon. It seemed that, with every passing moment, he somehow grew skinnier. She turned to the rest of the group and asked in Sossok, "Can we get him some food?"

Crow scoffed. "We can all get some food."

Tair had not realized it in the moment, but Crow had only scoffed at her question because it was not a matter of *if* they were able to get food, but rather a matter of accepting all the food they received. Apparently, these rebels were very well-known and, thankfully, well-liked. Humans from all corners of the small town congregated to greet Crow and their troop and to offer them an overwhelming amount of food and drink, a convention Tair likened to gift-giving in Mirte. Children pulled at Iom from all directions, all wanting to know what it was like to travel with such famous rebels. Though clearly overjoyed by the company of those his own age, Tair feared for his safety and clutched him close to her side as their group pushed through the crowd.

Not one of the rebels had thought to mention their celebrity to Tair. If their skill was any indication, Tair supposed she should have assumed their acclaim. After all, they had to have had previous successes, having taken down an army ten times their size in one night. She was rather embarrassed to admit how little she had tried to learn about them.

Someone handed Tair a large loaf of dense multigrain bread, probably the weight of an infant, and she took a bite for herself and gave the rest to Iom. The Dwarf tore at it as he walked on unsteady legs; the more food he consumed, the more his stomach grumbled. Tair realized that she, too, had not eaten much in the past few days. She quietly hoped that someone would hand her another free meal.

The group proceeded into a pub where a few Humans had already set about moving tables together for their guests. Before they had even all taken a breath, they had full steins of beer placed in front of them—Iom included. Tair pushed the glass away from him as he reached for it. Dwarves had different kinds of alcohol for children to drink, much less alcoholic than their elders' drinks. And, even though they had a much higher tolerance for alcohol starting at a younger age than Humans, Tair did not think that Iom should have only bread and beer on his sensitive stomach. He whined as the glass was taken from him but was quickly distracted by a bowl of some steaming potato dish placed in the middle of the conjoined tables. Tair portioned him out his own plate, then her own, and the two of them ate as quickly as was safe.

When she had finished, Tair leaned over the corner of the table to speak to Rose. They were rather absorbed in their own conversation with the townsfolk and only turned their attention to Tair when she began to tug on the older Human's jacket. They asked, "*Nahhs?*"

"Is this normal?" Tair asked. More Humans began to pile in, ordering drinks of their own and overcrowding the rather small space. Tair stiffened as someone knocked into her, spilling a little of their beer down the back of her shirt.

Rose grinned. "Not to me."

Tair smiled despite herself. All of the tales Tair had heard about the Sossok revolution—from Domani Dwarves and Rose alike—had been, for the most part, aged. Rose's tales were all of the past: tales of revolutionary action driven underground or severely punished; families torn apart at the mere idea of treason; and rebels were supposedly unknown, unsuccessful, untrained. Rose had not been home in over a decade and, in that time, so much had changed. If not of the past, Tair had heard tales of the future: Dwarves saving Humans with their military might; Tair killing two men in order to bring it all to a close; and strength in growing numbers. Even Moss in Braasii had only spoke of rumors, but there had been no tales of the present. Now, the revolution was celebrated openly before their eyes. Change was not only on the horizon, but also a current reality.

And Tair was meant to be a part of that change.

When she saw the beaming faces of her kind, the hope in their eyes, her duty to them became much more real. Where before it had all been theoretical, she now saw directly what the revolution was and what it meant. She was expected to kill King Usnaso and King Heir alike; Humanity practically depended on it. Whether or not they knew she was sitting right in front of them, she was their future—or, at the very least, part of their future. The air grew heavy with sound and smoke as she wondered at her denial of her responsibility. She looked to Iom, then tugged at Slug's tunic and silently asked them to watch him. When Slug nodded, she stood and exited the anxiety-inducing pub.

Outside, the Red Sun loomed over the horizon and purple clouds streaked the sky, broken up by a high-flying black *missai* bird Tair did not know the name of. The exterior pub wall was cool at Tair's back as she sank down in the mud. She placed her head in her hands and breathed, but the air provided no comfort. Even though she had earlier recognized the feel of it, just a distant memory from a life she could not remember, it now felt as though it was not *her* air, it was not Mirte nor Doman, nor even Braasii; it was not Nossoa. Here, she was another Human in the masses, though entirely unfamiliar with her newfound sense of belonging through homogeneity. Oddly enough, she almost missed not belonging; she missed having a clearly defined position in cultures that she could not claim neither through ancestors nor blood but perhaps through experience—and in cultures that did not have such dreadful histories. She missed her *family*, those who did not look like her but who felt far more tied to her, despite their many betrayals, than the Humans around her, who were far more complicated than Tair had ever anticipated.

Unfortunately, outside the pub was no respite from her discomfort. Someone sat down beside her in the mud and said, *"Aesolo."*

Tair looked up from behind her hands. Beside her sat a Human perhaps five years older than her with tanned brown skin, dark brown eyes, and black hair. They had a broad, flat chest, their muscles straining beneath their light tunic that did not seem appropriate for the chill in the air. Tair blinked away the memory of her own inappropriate clothing in the Mirte valleys, that fated night before her entire life was turned around. Instead, she focused on the Human's freckles, covering their face from forehead to chin but disappearing at their neck. They sat not even an inch away from Tair.

"Aesolo-aso," Tair mustered, clearing her throat of nerves. She averted her eyes.

"Aso?" They laughed heartily at Tair's formalization of hello—she had clearly misread the situation. Then they asked in a friendly, light tone, *"So arrha ran'ayie ano?"*

Tair scoffed and gestured to her current circumstances. She answered in Sossok, "How does it look like I'm doing?"

They frowned, glanced at Tair through the corner of their eye, and nodded. Then they reached out a hand to introduce themself, *"Asosso Lokya."*

Hawk. Tair clasped their hand and lied, *"Asosso Sayias,"* using the Sossok word for *missai*. After one shake, they broke contact—contact that, admittedly, was rather comforting in Tair's anxious state.

"Would you like to smoke?" Hawk asked. From their pant pocket they pulled out a small pipe and some ground purple leaf Tair had not seen before. She was not one for smoking, as much as she had seen Alyn and Shianna partake in the activity over the years. She winced at her last memories of the two, both with the heavy scent of ash lingering their clothes and both with tears streaking their cheeks. In a perhaps misguided effort to feel closer to them, she wanted to indulge herself, so she nodded.

Hawk smiled and packed their pipe, lit the end, and inhaled. They held the air in their lungs a moment, moved their cheeks around, and then blew out a puff of air in the shape of a tree. Tair's jaw dropped as she asked, "*Ano?*"

"Lots of practice," Hawk said with a smile. Their teeth were crooked like Rose's, their jaw slightly forward and softly rounded. Their muscles suggested their facial features to be a little more defined, but Tair found their soft angles rather gentle and reassuring.

"How much practice?" Tair asked as she watched the smoke dissolve into the air.

Hawk considered. "Four years."

Tair nodded and took the pipe in her own hands. Though she wanted to try out a fancy shape like Hawk had shown her, her body denied her, and she inadvertently hacked up her smoke. It was far sweeter than she expected—and far drier. She rubbed her throat as fresh air entered her lungs again. Once her eyes had stopped watering and her ears ringing, Tair was grateful (and a little surprised) to find that Hawk was not laughing at her inexperience.

"Practice," Hawk said with a wink. They took the pipe back into their own hands. Tair felt the anxiety of the previous moment begin to melt away already, but she could not decipher whether it was from the intoxicating effects of the smoke or the company of a kind Human to distract her. Perhaps it was a combination of the two.

Hawk continued, "See here..." They tapped their chest. The cooing sound of a bird came out. Tair smiled. "If I become a bird in part, the smoke becomes a bird in whole. It's almost like you're tricking your body, then tricking the smoke, and then..." They pulled in a breath of smoke again and then appropriately released the shape of a hawk.

Tair clapped. She briefly wondered about Humans' magic and whether or not Hawk was employing their own. Distracting her, the Human at her side spoke again.

"So," Hawk began. They passed the pipe back to Tair cautiously; she took it in her hands, waited a moment, and inhaled a smaller cloud of smoke. Though she did not make any shapes, she also did not choke. The two smiled at each other before Hawk asked, "What are you doing out here? The fun's inside."

"Too much noise," she answered. She remembered then her first private conversation with Bonn, which felt like years ago now. Her mate had pulled her from the chaos of the barrack to confront her, but it did not feel so much like a confrontation. Tair was glad to have had new company, to have had someone who cared about her without question. She turned away from Hawk, trying to divert her eyes before they again started to well with tears.

Hawk asked, "Islander?"

"*Nahhs?*"

"You're from the Southern Islands?"

Tair had not known that there were islands to the South of Sossoa; truthfully, she knew nothing about Sossoa's geography beyond Rolt. When she looked within, she realized she did not know much about the whole of contemporary Sossoa, her information mostly secondhand, either from sources with either biased or dated information. Hesitating slightly, Tair asked, "Why do you say that?"

Hawk shrugged. "The accent. Your hair is like theirs, too, but I suppose everyone's hair is like that toward the south. It's said...well, I'm sure you know what's said."

Tair nodded, though she did not know what was said

about islanders. She was unsure, too, if her nod was meant to validate their incorrect suspicions, or to acknowledge that she had heard what they said. Of course, if they had asked any questions about the Southern Islands later, Tair would have had nothing to say, so she did not elaborate on her nonverbal response.

Hawk did not mind that she did not answer, though. Instead, they continued onward, "Too much noise, *sunos*?"

Tair did not answer, not liking how they intoned her words. The Red Sun set in the distance, and the moon hung over their heads. The air grew colder around them, purple clouds fading to gray as they traveled across the land and prepared to rain. Sossoa's nightly storm was only minutes away. The sounds of foreign insects filled the silence.

"You came with the liberators," Hawk stated, "but you are not one of them."

"Oh?" Tair could not manage any more than that, finding it rather difficult to lie.

"You do not agree with what we have done."

Tair stayed silent.

"You do not like how we have chosen to move toward freedom, though you do not abhor us for it."

Tair then, very suddenly, felt Hawk's thoughts infiltrate her mind. Thoughts of fear and shame and pain and longing. Memories of their family being torn away from them when they were still a child, before they knew their parents' names. Tair had lost her parents' names, too. She felt their anger and their rage and felt the lives they had taken, the necessity of those deaths—the pride in those deaths.

She stood from the mud. The night wind breezed her legs and made her shiver, but her blood had again grown warm with anxiety. She asked, "What did we smoke?"

Hawk shook their head and stood. "I know who you are..." They shut their eyes, turned their head toward the sky. "I *feel* who you are, Tair."

Tair's breath hitched at the declaration of her name.

"You fear and reject what you must do because you do not know what it means for anyone but yourself. You feel your denial of responsibility to be selfish—rightfully so. You have yet to recognize that how we arrive at liberation for our kind does not matter, so long as we arrive there."

Tears spilling from her eyes, Tair asked, "Arrive there with a trail of blood in our wake?"

"Arrive there with blood on our *hands*," Hawk spat defiantly. "You are not Human like us. You have no care for us, for our fates. You ceased to be Human the day you decided to turn your back on us."

Tair's nostrils flared as she took a step back from the Human. *Human?* No, Hawk was a Faery. Tair felt this with certainty. Their face warped in the haze of whatever drug she had consumed, the brown of their cheeks turning as red as the sun that had been in the sky minutes before. They had seen within her, claimed the Human identity for themself, and told her that she was not Human like them. A Faery, more Human than her? Words she had never let surface were now laid bare in front of her.

"I cannot be your salvation," Tair choked. If she did what she was meant to do—if she *killed*—she risked putting Sossoa at the mercy of the Domani empire. Of course, she could not say that exactly, so she only said, "There is worse to come if I take up your sword."

"I see that future in your head," Hawk said as they tapped their temple. "I would walk through that world a hundred times over if it would release us from this one."

FOURTEEN

Though the two of them had separated, Tair felt Hawk's consciousness linger in her mind hours later. Thankfully, their consciousness had gone by the next morning—but their words remained, haunting her. Tair, despite her prior disdain for violence as solution, would have preferred that they just fight her—or she fight them—and then they both could have healed without ever having to think of one another again. The mental infiltration was worse, far worse. *You ceased to be Human the day you decided to turn your back on us...*

Tair shifted in her bed, Iom tucked tightly against her chest. The group had received free room and board for the night, even received open access to the town's food stores to replenish their stocks, but no amount of welcome from these Humans—her *kin*—made her feel any more like she belonged, not after her confrontation with Hawk. The more they indulged her, the guiltier she felt. She was not Human, she thought, not like the others who snored and hiccuped around her. Even then, she was not non-Human. She...she was an ever-outsider to the cultures she was born into by blood, raised in by community, and familiarized with by family. She felt that she belonged to none of them.

Tair stood from the bed suddenly. Iom groaned as he rolled onto his back, a child losing the warmth of the one being who sought to protect him. She had taken on the responsibility of Iom without second thought, but she had immediately rejected the idea of protecting or defending or even taking up arms with Sossok Humans. She remembered Omma's harsh scolding of that rejection, remembered the sting of finally feeling reunited with family only to, moments later, feel rejected by that same family.

Alyn and Bonn had also offered their opinions on the matter: they wanted her to do what she was capable of and had risked so many comforts to free her from doing what she was incapable of, an easy enough route when removed from the context of centuries-long oppression and dawning liberation. Now, embroiled in the reality of the beings she was meant to help liberate, Tair had to confront a far more complex reality than she had previously been able to imagine. So many had fought for and risked their lives for the very *idea* of Tair, just to ensure that their kind (her kind, she corrected) could one day be free. She did not know where her loyalties lay, and so she did not know how to decide what her responsibilities were.

And what of Rose? They had been exiled to Nossoa and, without question, had riskily followed Tair back to Sossoa, not once bringing up Tair's responsibility to Humanity. They clearly had their own opinions on what needed to be done for the fate of the revolution, but they had stopped sharing their judgements with Tair long ago. Tair had preferred the clarity in Hawk's aggression; with Rose, she could have already failed the older Human in a hundred different ways, and they would never have said anything.

Almost as if on cue, Rose awoke. They stretched out their arms as they sat up in bed and said, "Let's go home."

It took another half-day, the Yellow Sun at its peak in front of the Red Sun, to get to Raaha, Rose's home. The townsfolk had not cheered them on as they left. Instead, the calm, cool morning rain had seen them out, tickling their cheeks. According to Crow, it now rained almost every night in the wintertime, a recent development. No one knew where the rain had come from, but their crops were starting to thrive and the earth was a little softer to travel by, putting less strain on long-distance journeys, so none complained.

When Raaha came into view, Tair's jaw went slack. It was not a town but a *city*, completely unlike anything she had ever seen before. Tall buildings and bustling streets stretched on for miles, a thick, smoky air set over everything, and new Human faces breezed by on their way to unknown lives. Tair was overwhelmed by all the smells—bakeries both sweet and savory, tea and smoke shops, and the passing scent of feces that wafted up from what Rose called a sewage system. Tair indulged most in the sounds, though: singing, joking, yelling—and all in Sossok. Metal pots and pans crashed, children cried, merchants shouted in passing. There were endless new sounds for her ears to enjoy. Even Iom, having spent far too long imprisoned, was thrilled by the stimulation. Raaha made the two of them, Iom and Tair both, feel that the world had come alive again.

The ground was paved, something that Tair had never seen before but likened to the solid, smooth rock in the mountains of Doman. The land only got sturdier and the paths wider as they journeyed to the city center, where they would relieve their tired *dusoo* and finally part with their wagon. Tair was not particularly eager to relinquish their only means of transportation and instead wanted to remain observer for as long as she could manage. Unfortunately for her, they quickly arrived at a grand fountain at the city center, with a statue in the middle that was at least two hundred feet tall. At the center of the fountain was a golden statue of a Human looking east toward where Tair knew to be his appropriated home.

Iom asked in Domani, "*Kiina kaana'saa-akr?*"

"The first king of Sossoa," Tair answered as she gazed up at the figure. "King Unako."

As little as Tair knew about Sossoa, she did know him: Sossoa's first king, King Unako. There was nothing great about that Human, though his statue implied otherwise. Not only had he been the one to incite and organize the capture of Dwarven children at the start of the Doman War, but he was also one of the first soldiers to take up arms against the Dwarves to justify that enslavement. When they had lost, he fled south with hundreds of loyal Human followers to found Sossoa. Then, he had ordered the slaughter of non-Humans living in the land he had stolen, successful or not, and so established a homogenous Human nation—a nation entrenched in blood. The Humans who disagreed with the evils committed against their non-Human neighbors were assimilated, enslaved, or exiled. Most assimilated, which Tair never understood. How could they have tolerated evil and chosen complacency?

She stopped that thought in its track. Was she not doing the very same thing?

King Unako had also developed the Sossok language and culture, forced upon his new subjects in an effective attempt to divorce themselves further from their Domani origins. He changed his name from Unako to "Usnaso," thus arbitrarily creating a bloodline that still reigned in Tair's day, five hundred and twenty years later—the very bloodline Sossok Humans now rebelled against, and the bloodline to which Tair was meant bring a conclusive end.

Though the statue itself was impressive in size and material, it had not been respected throughout the years. Before their arrival, Crow had explained that Raaha was now a known rebel holdout, the first town—the first *city* rather—to be taken from the Usnaso regime. As such, the golden statue had been (rightfully, in Tair's mind) neglected. Well, not neglected so much as outright disrespected, smelling of both Human and animal feces, caked in a thick layer at the base and then aimed further up the statue. The fountain's water no longer danced, suppressed instead by garbage and rodents. No matter the disrepair it was in, taking down a statue of that size would have put the surrounding buildings, and countless lives and livelihoods, at risk of collapse, too. So, high up in the sky, King Unako's crown still shone in the light of the now-rising Yellow Sun. One day, it would be torn down, Tair knew, but for now it served as a reminder of what they were fighting against.

The *dusoo* slowed to a stop and all of the passengers scooted off of the wagon. Iom was beginning to gain back some of his strength, but he still wanted to be near Tair, which she did not mind. The child was comforting, Tair thought selfishly, and she liked to feel responsible for once in her life. They all stretched out while Crow negotiated with the Human that they had rented their transport from, arguing that they deserved a discount because they fought for the revolution.

"So do we all," the vendor said as they rolled their eyes. They were clearly young, but they had undoubtedly dealt with many like Crow and their troop. Some other employees began taking the *dusoo* back to their stables while another two wiped down the wagon and secured two horses—those Tair recognized—to the front. Then they were off to put the cart to use again.

"Not everyone else has killed one hundred and sixteen soldiers in the span of one night," Crow argued, their head held high. "And what do we say of soldiers?"

The merchant huffed, their nostrils flaring. Reluctantly, they said, "A good soldier's a dead soldier."

Crow smirked and nodded. "So, about that price..."

Rose came over to Tair and Iom with three pieces of warm

bread in a small paper bag. Tair thanked the older Human, took a bite into the offering, and nearly spit it back out. It was delicious but it was *hot*. Tair had burned the roof of her mouth in her carelessness and fanned at the sweat that sprang out across her forehead. Iom and Rose giggled.

"What are you laughing at?" Tair asked with tears in her eyes. Though she had used Nossok, she knew it would not draw too many wandering eyes. Everything else was so loud that a couple foreign words would have passed as mishearing.

"A hot pocket," Iom laughed.

Tair frowned and glanced into what Iom called a "hot pocket," full of vegetables and some brown cubed things. She took a small piece out and chewed on it, but was rather put off by the texture and flavor. She asked, "What is that?"

"Pastry and meat," Rose answered before they took a bite.

Tair's frown deepened as she passed her meal back to Rose. "You can have mine."

"You don't eat meat?" Rose and Iom asked nearly at the same time. They seemed to have grown close to each other in their own way. Tair suppressed the jealousy that bubbled up in her heart. Iom was not her child, but she did not like the feeling that he did not truly need her.

Tair shrugged. "Not like this. Perhaps fish in Doman or in Braasii, but there was little of it eaten in Mirte and—"

"Mirte?" Crow chimed in as they came up behind Tair. "*Ahrra-noas esa?*"

Tair tensed but was thankful for Rose's quick rescue: "A land to the north of Braasii where some visit if they want to get away from the mountain."

That was far, far from the truth, but Crow was none the wiser. They nodded, a grin still spread across their face, and said, "I got them down to three *pas*."

Rose had told Tair that *pas* was a kind of money—or simply another way to trade. In Nossoa, the system varied but usually depended more on what felt like a fair trade, rather than prescribing a fixed point of value to a coin or sheet of paper. Three *pas* sounded like absolutely nothing, so Tair readjusted her knowledge of the money. *Pas* had to have had a much greater value than she had originally calculated. Three *pas* had been enough to help keep the merchant in business, otherwise they would not have accepted the price, but it still seemed too good to be true. She tried not to reveal her shock at this trade and instead opted to ask, "Where to next?"

Rose smiled, turned around, and began walking. Confused, Tair stared on, then realized Rose intended for her and Iom to follow. Tair ensured that Iom's headscarf was still wrapped tightly around his head and hood secured to the wrap, tucked him under her arm, and followed behind the older Human. Crow and the rest of the rebels stayed behind or split off to go on their own adventures. Clearly, Rose was not too concerned with their separation from the group, not even taking a moment to say goodbye. Their lack of acknowledgement had briefly startled Tair but then she remembered back to one of her lessons with Rose in Doman. Goodbye—or "*olosae*"—was a rarely used word in Sossoa. It was more polite to leave without a sound than it was to say goodbye; a farewell implied that they did not desire to encounter each other again for some time.

As tall and sprawling as the city had seemed from the outside, it was even bigger inside. Winding streets with shops and restaurants and pubs, residential areas, passing wagons with patrons loaded up on the back—everything felt disorganized but there were clearly rules, unknown to Tair though they were. It was as if everyone *wanted* to live in chaos. It became more overwhelming by the second, and Tair and Iom quickly fell behind Rose's wide gait, only catching up to them when they decided to pause for their companions.

Though the two fell behind, Tair felt no need to slow Rose. There was too much joy in their confidence to interrupt. They weaved through the streets with the same familiarity that

Shianna had on her approach to Doman—the familiarity of *home*. They strode by shops that they mentioned they had frequented as a child, pointed down the alleys they had first smoked in, and teared up at the outward rebel support they noticed across the city. Wherever they looked, the traditional Sossok flag, originally red with three vertical golden lines equidistant from one another, was coated over with the rebels' black. The only sign there had ever been another flag were the fallen flecks of black paint on the city streets, dried out by the two suns.

Though risky to use the language in those narrow and underpopulated streets, Rose chose to speak in Nossok for Iom's sake. Still, their voice was quiet as they reflected aloud, "When I was a child, all demonstrations of rebellion were quickly suppressed. Curfew, families dragged out in the middle of the night, screams unanswered, shops that would not sell to those without associations to a soldier or to the crown...It was a whole different world. Now, look at everyone—so free, even before the battle has been won."

So much had changed. Rose had once said that they had spent their childhood in Raaha but moved to a small township to the northeast when they grew older. They had been radicalized in that town, imprisoned there, exiled from there. They had never seen what had come of their hometown and their neighbors—had never been able to imagine that the world they had grown up in could change so thoroughly, so quickly.

Tair wondered, though, where all the soldiers were. As much of a rebel stronghold as Raaha might have been, Tair thought it impossible that the city was completely free of enemies. Everyone she passed could have been an infiltrator. She feared every remaining sign of the Usnaso regime, feared every lingering glance. She held Iom close to her at all times, wishing desperately that they would arrive wherever Rose was taking them sooner rather than later.

The older Human stopped up ahead. They had turned onto another residential street, this one far quieter than the last—no, not quiet, but deserted. Tair and Iom neared Rose, who stood in front of the most dilapidated house on the street. Tair said nothing, noticing the tears in the corners of Rose's eyes.

"This was my childhood home," Rose muttered.

Tair went wide-eyed and dropped her grip on Iom. The Dwarven child peered up at her a moment and took his freedom in his stride, exploring this deserted bit of the city on his own. Tair did not stop him, the house before her distraction enough. It had somehow been burned without turning to ash, the red wood on the outside now blackened and the roof caved in. A fire had been set to smoke the inhabitants out, without actually burning down the structure they resided in or any of the nearby households. Not even the surrounding grass had been burned. Such an act required an unprecedented amount of magic—a kind of magic only Faeries or Dwarves possessed. The Usnaso regime and its soldiers—who had they tortured and stolen from in order to commit such a horrid act? Wherever they had gotten the power, their goal of total devastation had been achieved; what had once been Rose's childhood home was long dead; what had once been their neighborhood, now deserted.

"*Rak grasora'a*," Tair said in Domani. Rose had been colloquially familiar with the language, living so many years in Doman, so Tair felt comfortable using the Domani word for "apologize," which held the most weight in Tair's mind. She could not find another way to portray her deep sorrow in any other language she knew. Without a second thought, she took Rose's hand in hers. They clutched on.

"It was me," Rose choked out. "They did this because of me."

Tair said nothing. It was probably true. Tair remembered that Rose's family had been taken from them at a young age, but they had stayed a while in their home in the hopes that their family would return. They left in their teens, later starting a family of their own, but they had probably never predicted that any and all lifetime relics would be destroyed in the aftermath of their imprisonment. Rose had been discovered for thievery and held captive as punishment— enslaved until they had been able to flee. When they had left for Nossoa over a decade ago now, soldiers had likely combed the whole of Sossoa to destroy whatever they had left behind, whatever they held dear, so that they had nothing left to return to. Anything they recognized must have been destroyed—and if the soldiers had done this to Rose's childhood home...

It did not bode well for Rose's mate and children, nor the town they had resided in.

"They're okay," Tair said. It was a lie, she knew, but it was better than the alternative—the total annihilation of everything Rose held dear. She repeated, "They're okay somewhere out there, safe and looking for you."

Rose nodded despite themself. "They are okay. They have to be."

Just then, Iom screamed.

Tair whipped around, but the Dwarf was nowhere in sight. He screamed again, this time more distinctly to Tair's right— toward the edge of the residential area, the edge of the city. She took off running, Rose close at her heels, but she still could not find the child. She cried out his name and was met with a soft groan of pain behind the house she stood in front of. She ran down the side and found...

Iom, laying in a puddle of his own blood, his hood pulled back and headscarf thrown to the side, and a bloodied soldier standing over him with disgust on his face. "*Raiso*," he spat as he kicked Iom where he was most bloody. Rose instinctively knelt down to the child—a parent themself—which Tair would have done if it were not for the uncontrollable rage that rose up within her.

She stared at the soldier, who only looked between her and Rose in confusion. Iom was just *raiso* to him, and therefore deserved to die by fault of birth. All Tair and the other rebels had risked saving him had been for naught. She had no time to check Iom for a pulse nor comfort him before her instinct to attack got the best of her. In a half-second, she lunged at and straddled the soldier, his dagger twisted out of his hand and into hers. She punched him, slashed at him, *stabbed* him. Blood and gore and all the things Tair had thought herself averse to in the abstract were now caused by her own hands. A tear streamed down her face—

Or was it blood?

Tair did not stop until Rose shouted for her. She pulled herself off of the soldier, his blood sticking to her thighs and torso and nearly everywhere else, and crawled over to where Iom and Rose sat. Now she was sure it was tears on her cheeks, but she could not stop them from coming. Iom whimpered in her hands as she held his face, begging him not to shut his eyes. Rose clamped down on his wound, but it was much too big for his still-healing, still-growing body to repair in time for them to get help. And who in Sossoa would have helped him— a Dwarven child who had escaped to the land in hopes of a better life, a gaping wound now in his side and blood pouring out of his mouth? Iom was already weakened by his imprisonment, still healing and unable to cope with such a wound. No matter the revolution, Sossok Humans were too unfamiliar with Iom—and all those they called *raiso*—to willingly offer care. Non-Humans were still an abstract in the revolutionary mind; non-Humans still represented an impossible world that Humans were indoctrinated to hate, their own language betraying their best efforts. They would send the Dwarven child away before they would heal him.

Iom died within minutes, never having said another word.

Tair awoke the next three mornings with blood on her hands.

Not literally, though that might have been easier to cope with than the imagined blood that clung to her no matter how much she scrubbed herself clean.

Following the murder, Rose had found the two of them a public bath to clean in. Tair had scrubbed and scrubbed and scrubbed her skin until it nearly broke—had scrubbed until the image of Iom's and the dead soldier's bodies lying in the mud left her mind. They were food for flies now, nothing but flesh.

And Tair wanted nothing more than to be out of hers.

Rose had not been concerned about being questioned, whether by a stray soldier or the organized rebels, no matter the incriminating blood on their clothes. After all, they had said, there were few Humans who questioned blood, something that had not changed since Rose was a child. No one bothered Tair and Rose because they had, evidently, been the victors.

Tair did not feel like a victor. She and Rose had joined the rebels again later that fateful night to dine and to find room and board, apparently much more affordable for a bigger group. Rose had described what Tair had done as everyone cheered on. Tair might as well have heard a story told about a savage killer—even only hours later, the events did not feel like actions her hands could have carried out. When Tair had tried to direct attention to Iom instead of the act of vengeance committed for him, there were no condolences, only simple acknowledgements that some had to die in the course of a war.

Iom had not been at war, though. Tair certainly did not feel herself a part of any war. Yes, she had been forced into one, lived during the course of one, but she was not actively at war. *Rak kojsaoo'a*—the concept was simpler in Domani: she had lost someone she cared for and had fought for them. Or, at least, fought for their memory.

Of course, the last being Tair wanted to see and still the only being she wanted at her side when she woke was Shianna, the same being who had lied to her for over a decade—who had lied to her family for over a decade. Despite the betrayal, despite the pain, Shianna was the only one in Tair's life who would have understood completely, who would have fought for her family no matter the cost, too. To Shianna, Iom would not have been a casualty in the course of a war but instead a precious life lost too soon.

How many had the rebels lost that life no longer felt precious? How much loss had they endured, not grieved, steeling themselves against the pain so that it might hurt less? How many had they killed or let die in the name of war?

Tair had not want to become them, not in action, and yet she could not deny that she now had. She remembered Bonn saying that she could not kill; now, she had *killed*, past tense. Fearful as she was that Bonn would not have ever forgiven her for her lying, she was especially frightened of what her mate would think of her now—if they would turn Tair away because she, too, had turned from herself. They had said that violence was at the root of the Sossok Human's struggle for freedom, and that violence could have resolved, perhaps, part of that struggle. But violence had only magnified Tair's grief. Something had taken over her when she attacked that soldier, she had told herself in attempt to distance from her actions. As much as she hated him—hated what he had done—she could not say that she felt any better for retribution. She did, however, feel some elusive power in killing the soldier, his life representing something so much larger than just himself and instead representing the whole of power that had allowed him to become the Human he did, the Human that killed a Dwarven child without question and without remorse. Worse yet...

Worse yet, Tair now had no justification for shirking her responsibility to the rebel cause. She had not thought herself capable of killing a Human—no less, two Humans of royalty, two unreachable, impossible Humans—and yet she had. Capability had not been a part of her decision to attack; she had acted on instinct, on fear and rage and hatred and all the emotions she had avoided as she sunk into apathy and complacency.

She stood from the bed she now shared with Rose after another sleepless night. She had already forgotten the feeling of Iom grasping close to her in the night, forgotten his fear. He lingered in her memory like a ghost. Instead of Iom, Tair had slept with the red crystal Alyn had gifted her clutched in her palm, and now it lay on the floor, probably tossed out at some point in the night. Though she knew Shianna would have validated her actions, she thought then to what Alyn would have done in her situation. And Bonn? Silaa?

She picked up the crystal and wondered what she was meant to do. Hoped someone would tell her, as she had grown accustomed. All her life, Tair had followed the path that others had laid out for her. In this most infrequent moment that she had to think freely for herself, her mind came to a screeching halt. Even when she had possessed some responsibility, like in the course of her imprisonment in Braasii, there had still been Alyn to communicate for her, and Shianna to ultimately save them—but it was a mistake to think about Braasii, the origin point of her slow and steady downfall. Shianna had saved them, yes, but only by revealing a truth that had permanently altered their family. And it was from Braasii that she had later found hope and care in Bonn, unconditional familial love in Alyn. Tair placed her head in her hands. The crystal cut into her forehead. A small drop of blood trickled down and affected her vision a moment. She blinked hard, a slight bloody tear slipping out.

She felt hollow, if hollow was an emotion at all. Tair had once been able to justify her inability to help Sossok Humans—her kin, whether she admitted it to herself or not—with her moral stance against violence and murder. Trained to fight, trained to kill, and now a killer—the question on her mind was not if she *could* kill two Humans, King Usnaso and King Heir, but *would* she? Would she kill them and, in the process, kill their horrible dream of homogeneity? Would she kill them and end the legacy of hatred and violence that would undoubtedly repeat itself if it went without intervention? Would she kill them, knowing what could come to her kind if she did what was tasked? Did the rebels have the strength to achieve liberation not only from their current empire, but from Doman, too?

An eternity of the present world, or the vulnerable future of the next. Tair felt she had the ultimate judgement.

Rose awoke. Tair heard them before she saw them; when she met eyes with the older Human, she had her answer. She placed the red crystal in her pocket, fastened her shoes, and left the inn.

The Red Sun was only beginning to rise, the early morning air was brisk, and the nightly rainstorm had ceased. She had grown accustomed to the Sossok rain over the course of her five days spent in the once known, now foreign land. As much as she had tried to run from her past, this world had a particular way of reminding her of her own history in and with it.

Tair only stopped walking when Rose caught up to her. They grabbed Tair's shoulder and spun her around. They did not say anything as their eyes searched Tair's for an answer to an unspoken question. Rose's grip was tight, and Tair knew they would not let go until she told them to. She said nothing.

"You killed the soldier," Rose stated. Of course, Tair already knew this, and so she nodded. It was reassurance, if nothing else, that Tair was capable of what she had to do.

Rose chewed the inside of their cheek. Tair blinked away thoughts of Bonn, who would have stopped Tair. Or Alyn, who would have found a way to help her no matter what choice she made. Now, no one stopped her, no one offered help—it was only Rose. Rose, with whom she felt she had spent a lifetime, even though it had been a little less than three months. Rose, who had let Tair come to her conclusion before they imposed their own. Rose, who knew what Tair had to do, knew that they had to release her, and still their grip tightened. They asked, "Where will I meet you after?"

Tair looked down at the ground. A tear fell into the puddle that bridged the gap between the two of them. What Tair had to do...there was no after, she thought. There was nowhere she would one day meet Rose—or Bonn, or Alyn, or Silaa, or Shianna. She would never again see her loved ones. She shook her head and managed, "I don't—"

"*Sanas*," Rose snapped. "*Noas?*"

Tair glanced at the inn—aptly named *Es'ann Unas*, or the Final Inn, in Nossok—and then back at Rose. Tair had lost as much as she could bear, and even then she could not imagine all that Rose had lost: their life, in all the forms that life had been manipulated and abused; their family, twice over. And where were their children now? Tair imagined herself one of Rose's children and placed a hand on over the older Human's on her shoulder.

She answered, "Right here."

Rose released Tair's arm. Tair turned to leave Raaha—and Rose—behind.

FIFTEEN

The path to the King's castle and *Es Mmas Rrakas*—the Hunting Grounds, Rose had once called them in Nossok—was not a challenge to navigate. Tair simply had to walk straight through the eastern quadrant of Raaha to find the river that trailed out to the Eastern Great Sea and stopped by the castle along the way. At least, that was what she had heard mention of as she had trailed the streets of the city in the wake of Iom's passing, trying to distract herself from the gore that haunted her memories—and desperately trying to figure out what she had to do next. Now, with her decision made and settled upon, Tair trailed the foaming shoreline of her guiding river and hoped that her destination would soon become apparent. The river had raged so constantly in Raaha that Tair had originally assumed the sound to be the wind whipping past the city's innumerable buildings. Seeing the waters clearly now, she knew that this river had a mind of its own, much like the Doman Mountains and the Darkwoods.

She followed the curve of the river for miles—east, a little northeast, and east again—until Sossok flags began to crop up, this time free from the rebels' black paint. Tair could not understand why the King allowed the rebels to have such a stronghold in Raaha, only miles west of his front door. It seemed ludicrous to her, until she realized that he might not have seen any reason for concern. That frightened Tair—a being with no reason for concern was dangerous.

Tair subconsciously slowed her steps as unmarred Sossok flags became more frequent and her destination clearer. There, through the canopy of trees that made up the Hunting Grounds and just across the horizon, she saw the peak of a great tower. She had not seen it before, not in Raaha. Tair supposed that, from where she stood, she was not meant to see it; rather, King Unako's statue was meant to gaze upon his legacy in the Hunting Grounds, and his legacy would look back at him, too.

The castle towered over the world, a wall half its size to match. All along the top of the wall, she could already see sentries poised in anticipation of a battle. They probably had not expected an army of one at their front door.

The wall surrounded a small pocket of the Hunting Grounds that the castle had been nestled into centuries prior. A manufactured moat had been dug into the ground just before the wall. Not yet near the edge of the trench, Tair could nevertheless hear the snapping jaws of beasts below. Though growing more fearful the nearer she got, she could not stop herself from glancing over the edge, where she saw a fifty-foot drop and then, thrashing about in shallow water, unknown wild creatures with sharp teeth and long, scaly, and limbless bodies. They were just as eager to tear apart each other as they were anything that happened to fall into their trap. Whatever they were, Tair knew she did not want to die by their wounds.

Before she could register where the whistling sound in the air had come from, Tair felt an arrow pierce her left thigh. She dropped to the ground, clutching at her wound, but found that it crippled her without releasing any blood and without causing an insufferable degree of pain. Suddenly, though, her tongue felt loose in her mouth, so uncontrollable that she could not cry for help—not that she would have received it. Inside the wall, wide and large enough to house an army of at least five hundred, the clanging of weapons sounded. The drawbridge then lowered in front of Tair, and two soldiers ran across to hoist her up by her arms.

Tair tried to focus on anything but the arrow sticking out of her thigh and found the tower before her to be a worthy distraction. Intricate golden lines laced throughout the cracks in the building, both magnificent and essential. Indeed, without the precious metal Tair wondered if the building could even stand. Even still, she knew that gold was not as strong as was often assumed—knew that something else, something magical, must have been there to support the aging building. There were hundreds of large windows, some with mosaics also laced with gold. In contrast to the muddied and gray Sossok world she had been introduced to upon exiting the Darkwoods, this was perhaps the most vibrant and luxurious building she had ever seen. There was no mud around it, just a patch of fine, trimmed grass, a stone pathway that led toward the castle from various directions, and a semicircle of stones just past the wall where they dropped her limp body. As the Yellow Sun began to rise overhead, the castle glowed red, not quite unlike the crystals in the walls of Doman. The guards here were dressed far nicer than the first ones Tair had encountered—and the ones Tair had later seen killed—fitted in vibrant, skintight reds and golds so golden that Tair wondered if it was even a fabric and not just some trick of the eye. Every guard here seemed important; every guard here protected King Usnaso and King Heir—the very same Humans Tair was here to kill.

As soon as she had been dropped onto the stones, twenty men flanked her. They stripped her of her belongings—or singular belonging, Alyn's gifted crystal—and jostled the wound that did not hurt as much as it should have. Though the arrow did not cripple her completely, the soldiers' hands were excessively violent, with little care as to where and how they slapped and punched her. Tair struggled against them; after all her training with Bonn, her first instinct was to defend herself. Bonn would have defended her. She sighed when she remembered two things: first, that the soldiers had already demonstrated that they felt no hesitation in hurting her; second, she had to remain compliant if her hastily crafted story was going to work, if she did not want to present as a rebel or even rebel aligned. They finally stopped searching her—*attacking* her—and then organized themselves into a defensive pattern, as if Tair would have been a very worthy opponent with an arrow sticking out of her leg, with the growing bruises on her body, and with tens more arrows aimed at her. She was defenseless. She tried to keep her shoulders squared and her confidence alive, but this confrontation alone was enough to drain her. From behind the group of soldiers, one who seemed to be the leader emerged. His outfit was the most elaborate, with the most embroidery and decorations and jewelry—much too elaborate for true conflict. Even his sword's hilt was laced with gold. How much gold did this place have?

"*Aesolo*," he said casually, as if there were not countless weapons pointed at Tair's head.

Tair gulped and responded, "*Aesolo-aso.*"

"*So ahrra oopa?*"

Tair took in a deep breath. She glanced down at the arrow in her thigh and finally registered that it was enchanted to encourage the truth, which she certainly could not give. She needed to lie—for the sake of the rebellion, for the sake of her own life, but the truth felt...appealing.

Tair knew she had to make herself seem assured, as shaken as she was, and so she stood on shaky legs. When she had steadied and dusted herself off, she looked up to find that all the soldiers had advanced upon her. One of the soldier's swords now cut into her upper arm. She winced as she pulled back, realizing too late that she could have earned their respect without trying to demonstrate physical strength.

Finally, she answered in Sossok, "I am Tair, child of Sossoa." That was the truth. So far. The soldiers only laughed, having no knowledge of why this fact was significant in itself, and all drew in closer, predators trapping prey. She swallowed and continued, more confident this time, "I was young when I was stolen away from my home and raised by *raiso* in the kingdom of Doman." Stolen from her home by her own parents, raised by non-Humans for a couple of years in Doman. She would have winced at the use of the derogatory term *raiso*, but she had to feed into the lie. The arrow wanted more, so she said, "I have finally escaped and wish to seek refuge in the kingdom of Sossoa with the great King Usnaso." *Escape* and *refuge* were their own kinds of truth, desperate as she had once been to leave Doman. She sighed as the arrow loosened its hold on her.

The swords drew back only the slightest centimeter and the bows slackened. The leader paused a moment before asking, "*Sem kassiis saano-so?*"

Tair braced herself. Why did she have to prove herself if she was already enchanted to tell the truth? She relented, though, and said, "I know there are few among you—us"—Tair quickly corrected herself—"who know their language and their ways, but I do. They had accepted me as one of their own. I have news of their present and future transgressions against the kingdom of Sossoa...and I have news of the rebellion."

"You are not a rebel yourself?"

Tair could not answer this question, even if she was not enchanted to tell the truth. She did not believe she had put in the work nor had the experience to classify herself a rebel, but here she was doing the work of the rebellion. She shook her head—it was all she could manage, and it was still its own truth.

"If we kill you now, what difference would it make?" The leader was testing Tair. She knew he would—or someone would—and yet she had not prepared herself well enough to answer.

"No difference at all," Tair lied. "But I have information that the King might like to hear with his own ears, and I would not want to make the wrong decision to turn me away—to kill me—on his behalf. Would you?"

The leader shifted a step back, as did the rest of his soldiers. After quiet conversation among their ranks, one of the soldiers yanked the arrow from her thigh, the wound healing immediately but the shock a pain of its own, and then they all ushered her into the towering castle.

There were no gates nor doors for the tower's entrance; rather, there were grand archways that showed no fear of invasion. If Tair had thought Doman was a complex web, alive and ever evolving, this castle was designed to be unconquerable. The disorientation she felt upon entry, probably from an additional enchantment, was quickly overtaken by the head-clearing ache in her legs as she ascended countless flights of stairs. Added to that ache was the still-lingering hurt of the soldiers' attacks and of the arrow being pulled from her thigh.

The first flight of stairs, though unremarkable, was plenty difficult to overcome after having walked many miles earlier that day. Those stairs then opened up to a second story with two rooms down the hall. The flight of stairs after that opened up to a longer hallway. As they moved higher and higher still, more rooms appeared on each level, all with varying degrees of activity. And, with each rising level, Tair noticed that there were more and more servants and less guards. She lost count of how many flights they climbed, the air thinning around her. Her breath became more difficult to regulate and she dizzied as they spiraled ever upwards. The guards took her on random turns, too, without first indicating their direction. Had they just taken a right, or a left? She stumbled a few times and assumed—*hoped*—their destination would present itself soon. Unfortunately, at the start of each staircase she looked up to find, even still, an endless number of stories ahead. Tair was beginning to understand why they were not concerned about attack up here; if someone had made it all the way to the King, they would have been so physically fatigued and disoriented that they would not have been able to compose themselves for at least a few minutes before they caught their breath.

"One more," Tair heard one of the soldiers behind her say. Sweat poured down her back and her heart drummed in her chest. Her hair clung in tendrils on her forehead, and she thought distantly: How long had it been since her last haircut? Would she ever receive another one?

The guards, unaffected as they were, must have made this journey daily. Once they got to the top, they stopped at the end of a hallway for Tair's sake. Then they opened a locked door—one that opened up to a descending staircase. So much for one more flight.

"W—wait," Tair stuttered in Nossok, slumping to the floor. She forgot to correct herself. The use of the foreign language made the soldiers nervous, but she could not indulge herself in her slight reclamation of power as she was too busy collecting herself.

When Tair was finally able to stand without tipping over, the guards wrongfully assumed that she was also able to move at their previously established pace. She struggled to keep up as they led her through the door and down more stairs. Descending was much easier than ascending, Tair was glad to find, but her legs still tired under her, desperate for a break that she feared she would never receive. In contrast to the many stories that they had passed on their way up, these stairs went on without break and seemingly without destination. There were no branching hallways with closed rooms, nobody bustling about—just endless stairs. Before she lost track, Tair had counted about three hundred steps in a vain attempt to familiarize herself with her new environment. At some point, the guards stopped and said in Sossok, "On your way."

Tair raised an eyebrow at them. They said nothing more, so she steeled herself and began to descend the other hundred or so stairs on her own before she found herself at a wide-open hallway that culminated in two grand doors. Etched into the wood was a scene of great hordes of Humans, all their eyes turned overhead, where a golden Human contorted in a fetal position rested in the center of the Red Sun, with the Yellow Sun rising inches to the right.

Tair took a deep breath. Before she could knock, the doors swung open, and the most blinding natural light illuminated within, the intensity enough to attract Tair in without second thought. She practically glided across the marble floor, also lined with gold, her eyes slowly adjusting to the light.

And the doors shut behind her.

The room was sparse for the most part but, there, at the head, was a great glass box. It was flanked on either side by two heavily armed soldiers in red uniforms and matching red masks, just enough space for them to see and breathe through. Beyond the steady rise and fall of their chests, they may as well have been statues. Tair thought her eyes were deceiving her when she saw, inside that box, one Human morph into two. Or was that just a trick of the eye? No...one sat on a grand red velvet throne, interlaced with even more golden thread and atop a matching gold frame; the other paced around the cage of their own making. Tair knew immediately that the one on the throne was King Usnaso—the other one was, without a doubt, the King Heir.

King Usnaso, however old the world perceived him to be, sprung up with life when Tair entered. With a big clap, his soldiers rested their weapons and knelt. The King Heir came to the edge of the box, hands clasped behind his back, and stood with his head held high. They were identical. Literally. At first glance, Tair thought them twins. They had the same long golden hair cascading over their shoulders and down their backs, the same golden-brown eyes, the same golden-brown skin. They were...*magnificent*. Tair hated to admit it, but they could have very well argued that they were gods and faced little argument.

"Semas scese ogo!" Our lost child, King Usnaso exclaimed, in a voice most like honey. Apparently, he had communicated with the soldiers who had so cruelly welcomed Tair—but when? And how?

At the realization of a larger problem, though, Tair silently cursed herself; King Usnaso spoke in Sossok, under the impression that Tair knew what he said. Of course, she did know, she had revealed as much to the soldiers who unkindly greeted her; however, as the lost child, supposedly kidnapped and raised in Doman amongst Dwarves, her knowledge of Sossok should have been nonexistent. She had not considered that when she had spoken Sossok earlier and now worried that she had revealed herself too soon.

King Usnaso was surprisingly unsuspicious. Instead, he smiled, one gold-capped tooth shining in the light. He placed a hand on the glass and passed right through it. The King Heir followed in tow, though a degree less friendly than the King — like he was still growing accustomed to encounters with other Humans, well into adulthood.

These were the Humans Tair had to kill, the Humans who had committed all the atrocities Rose had described, the Humans ultimately responsible for the oppression and violence and hatred, the Humans responsible for the world in which Iom needlessly died in the name of prejudice. Tair almost thought it impossible—impossible to believe that such beautiful beings could do such terrible things.

King Usnaso stood before Tair without her totally registering his appearance. He cupped either side of her face and made her meet his eyes. With a wide smile, he embraced her.

"We are eternally grateful to liberate you from the *raiso* of the north. We hope what you have seen has not turned you against us," King Usnaso practically hummed. *Grateful, liberate, hope*—he used the language of rebels, yet he was no friend to the rebellion. Tair steeled herself in an effort to conceal her false intentions and the truth of her arrival.

Tair had also been so taken aback by his general demeanor that she barely registered his use of the *raiso* slur. And then she registered it. She braced herself, shut her gaping mouth, and squared off her shoulders, trying to regain the confidence that she lost in his and the King Heir's presence.

Then the King said, "Please, let me present to you my son, *Scosso Sankoj Usnaso*." *Scosso Sankoj*—Rain Storm, Tair translated to Nossok in her head.

Rain bowed in front of her and took her hands in his, pressing his shockingly cold lips to her knuckles. She tried to stop herself from recoiling too fast, but she could not hide her instinct to wipe her hand on the side of her pants. Rain took a tentative step closer, still holding her hands, still staring into her soul. His hands were ghosts in hers. Across all his fingers, he wore gold bands. On his wrist was a golden cuff, delicate clouds of rain carved into the metal. Without realizing, she had drawn his hand closer to her face in attempt to see the jewelry closer. She took a step back, unsure of what had drawn her in. *Why* she had been drawn in.

She focused her attention instead on how the two Humans towered over, so similar to Rose. Where his parent grinned, Rain struggled to bring a smile to his face but, when he did, Tair again got an uncanny sense of his similarity to his parent—too similar to not be the very same. There was surprisingly no doubt in her mind that they were the same Human physically, despite the fact that King Usnaso was supposed to be, at the very least, thirty years older than his apparent child.

And then she wondered, in the uncomfortable silence of their stares: why had they not asked her any questions, neither of Doman nor of the rebellion?

Just then, in the back of her mind, Tair sensed that something had infiltrated her thoughts. She looked to the two Humans, wide-eyed, and attempted to steel herself against what she assumed to be their invasion. She blinked her eyes once, twice. Harder a third time.

"What's happening?" Tair stuttered.

King Usnaso laughed the same laugh as King Heir Rain. She wondered if it was all in her head, if they could truly cross the threshold of her mind and see her thoughts, or if they only had to *convince* her that they were lingering there, in that most private space. Neither answered the questions that plagued her mind; instead, the two of them simply paced over to the wide window that spanned the entire length of the southern wall. They had the same strides and same posture. They looked over a great forest cut through by veining rivers and culminating in a lake out on the horizon.

The Hunting Grounds. About four hundred feet below them.

"Isn't it beautiful?" King Usnaso said. "This world...we are quite proud of it."

As if they had crafted it with their own hands. Tair furrowed her eyebrows and came to stand by King Usnaso and Rain. In the face of two unbelievably alike Humans, of an impossible world, Tair saw what they saw, felt what they felt—

And wondered if they were anything close to mortal.

As if hearing her thoughts, Rain sighed and placed his hand on Tair's shoulder, his touch no longer a ghost on her skin. He was real. He was Human.

And Tair would have to kill—

Interrupting her thoughts, Rain asked, "Would you like to see your room?"

King Usnaso had a guard lead her to her room, only one level lower than the room she had met these two Humans who were, she constantly reminded herself, only Human. She strolled behind the guard who guided her, her steps slow so that she could pay close attention to her new environment. After just one flight, though, she felt disoriented, but still she tried to shake off her sense of defenselessness, of weakness. She was alone, so she would have to be her own safety.

When they arrived at Tair's room, she began to wonder why they were welcoming her so easily. Had they seen something in her that she had not meant to reveal? Was she some plaything to them? All the questions that raced through her mind clouded the realization that her room was the only one on the floor, like the throne room had been. The guard opened a heavy wooden door and ushered her inside. Inside, the room was simple but made distinctly for someone of importance. Made for her. Who had arranged it? And *when*?

Tair furrowed her eyebrows as she stepped inside. There was a bed dressed in fine white and gold-laced sheets. A couple of torches framed the bed, though they did not seem necessary with all of the natural light flooding in through the large window that spanned the south-facing wall. At the end of her bed, there was a small trunk, atop which the crystal Alyn had gifted her sat. She scrambled toward it with a sigh of relief and clutched it to her chest. It was the only thing she had left of the life she had to leave behind—the only reminder of family and of the world she was fighting for while confined to the world of those she was fighting against. She hung her head as she rocked back and forth on the trunk, missing her family.

Missing the life she had left behind.

Hours later, Tair sat cross-legged on the cold hardwood floor in front of the window. The Hunting Grounds stretched out east into the horizon until it met with the Great Sea, then south where it met that lake Tair had seen earlier. Over it all, the Yellow Sun began to set in front of the Red. And then a surprising thought: was this all home, these woods and this land—this perspective of the world? Tair had never truly grasped the concept, not in all the time she had been in Mirte, nor Doman. There was a familiarity in the wider Sossoa, if only due to physical resemblance. The way that had come to be, though, did not bring Tair the same amount of comfort. Deeper still than familiarity, there was something in this particular area of land that made Tair feel akin—something, or someone, looming just over the horizon.

For the first time in a long time, Tair wondered where her biological parents were. Maybe the Southern Islands, like Hawk had suggested. Or maybe much closer. Maybe she had passed them in Raaha. Maybe they had been in the ranks of soldiers she encountered. And maybe they were dead. All the possibilities in the world did not comfort Tair; she understood that she would never meet them. She had come to terms with that fact as soon as she discovered that they had left her to rot in the Darkwoods.

Or left her to live...

The birds settled into their nests in the treetops.

Tair pressed the red crystal to her heart. It was warm now, after she had held it for so many hours, just watching the suns set and the forest move and trying to clear her mind. As inexperienced and unprepared as she was, Tair also tried to train herself in protecting her mind from intruders. King Usnaso and Rain had a peculiar quality to them that unsettled her. For now, they seemed able to hear only the little things at the very surface of her mind. She put that together with what else she knew: they drew her toward them without a word spoken; they had moved through glass as if it was air; and they were the exact same Human.

Tair had concluded this in the hours after meeting them. There was no other explanation for it. Rain had entered the world at the time they had asserted, Tair decided—but he had not been *born*. No, he had been *created* from the very fibers of King Usnaso's being, like Bonn had once said was a Dwarven ability. There had not been a new king in Sossoa since the very first, King Unako. Indeed, though she could not see his exact features so high above, Unako's statue's features were near enough to Usnaso's and Rain's that Tair had a hard time convincing herself otherwise. Unako had simply created continuous versions of himself to convince the world that he was passing authority over to his successors, when in reality he was only passing it to himself. As convinced as she was of her conclusion, Tair knew she was only speculating, indulging herself in conspiracies that fit a little too well. Of course, she had (briefly) entertained the idea that King Usnaso and Rain were twins, but that failed the test of logic more than the admittedly outlandish theory that King Unako was King Usnaso was King Heir Rain Usnaso.

Still, Tair did not have all the answers. In fact, she had more questions than answers, as she often found to be the case. She could not quite understand how they decided when one would die before the other one took up the mantel. How did they exist in the same space, at the same time? Did they hold the same memories, thoughts, feelings? In part, it helped her to believe that, in killing King Usnaso and Rain, she was only killing one Human, rather than two. One Human who had extended himself through time by endlessly creating new versions of himself...

Tair shook her head. She had not figured it all out yet; her ignorance frightened her more than her theories. As far as she knew, there was no one being who could give her the information she sought—besides the very Humans she was set to murder.

The door opened and, on instinct, Tair tucked her crystal into her pocket. Her clothes were rather disgusting after a day of intense travel (and intense *sweat*), but she had not been offered a bath. She also did not want to change into the clothes she had found in the dresser. They were all gold or red or otherwise much too similar to King Usnaso's, Rain's, and their soldiers, and she did not want to associate with them.

Two guards stood in her door, masked like the ones who guarded the glass box in the throne room. These two, however, had their red uniforms patched back together with gold lace, as though they themselves were torn apart and sewn back together again. Tair found that idea both horrifying and magnificent, as everything in this castle was. As everything in Sossoa was. They did not speak to her, nor did they seem to see her. Without instruction, Tair knew to follow them. She picked herself up from the floor with a soft sigh and prepared herself for more stairs.

They ascended without sound—well, save Tair's huffs and calls for pause. Her legs ached beneath her. Thankfully, they came to the top of the castle before she had even registered it, her body so tired it barely comprehended the movement. They then descended what Tair counted as three stories before they stopped. The guards gestured for her to continue down the hall without her. She hesitated, if only because, the last time that happened, she had met King Usnaso and Rain for the first time, but she knew not to reject their directive. The door at the end of the hall opened as she neared it.

This was the dining room. There was no doubt about that. But where Tair expected a long table covered in food and crowded with hungry Humans, not unlike Domani meals, she found a small round table with only enough seats for King Usnaso, Rain, and herself. There were three plates, pre-portioned, and a set of golden cutleries around each. Only four torches lit the sparse room. All the gold and red and luxury of the rest of the castle, even the throne room itself, seemed to be a front; indeed, her bedroom and this sparse dining room both reflected a general trend toward minimalism. It seemed that they did not need all the frills they adorned themselves with reflected in their decorations. They could exhibit power in other ways. Tair had found that, the more power someone had, the more they tried to hide it—like Omma had, like the King and King Heir did now.

"Please, sit with us," King Usnaso said as he stood to welcome Tair. She shuffled to her seat, careful to avoid his outstretched hand that attempted to pull her in for another one of his odd embraces. When she denied his advance and sat down, he did not press her.

"I hope the room is to your liking," Rain added with a smile. Something about the way he moved...he seemed unaccustomed to the world, unaccustomed to the power he held. Tair could use that against him, she thought. Over her thoughts, he continued, "I designed it myself, for your pleasure."

Designed? There was not really much design to it, Tair thought. And, besides, she was more distracted by Rain's anticipation: either they had both known she was coming, which was frightening in itself; or, more worryingly to Tair, perhaps they had access to a magical cache that, in this case, they had exploited for spatial creation, as she had once seen Faeries do in Braasii. If they were using Faeries for their magic, where did the imprisoned reside, and how long had they endured their torture?

Tair suppressed a grimace, forced a smile, and said, "It is very nice."

"Better than any room amongst *raiso,* I imagine," King Usnaso mumbled, though he owned up to his statement with a slight chuckle.

Tair bristled at the slur but tried to calm herself with images of the Hunting Grounds, undoubtedly beautiful but undeniably ominous. She also pictured her private dinners with Bonn, intimate and hopeful. She pictured the valley of Mirte on a warm spring day, the smell of Alyn's hearty *camiit* stew in the air...She envisioned anything and everything that was not here, not now, not where she hated both Rain and

King Usnaso for disguising their hatred with false charm.

She picked up her fork and did not respond to the King's comment. Instead, she pushed around the food on her plate and asked, "What is all of this?"

There was a small beige ball that looked like it had been fried and smelled of something Tair could not place but seemed edible enough. Next to it were vegetables, she was sure of that, but she had never seen any that were *pink*. In the center of the plate was some kind of meat. They ate plenty of meat in Sossoa. Staring at all this food, she did not know exactly what it was or, truthfully, how she was meant to eat it.

"Would you like something more familiar?" King Usnaso said, half-annoyed and half-amused.

Tair, thinking it to be a test, only shook her head no. She picked at her food a moment and then decided they would not poison her—so soon, at least. Anyways, royalty was supposed to eat well, were they not? They had the same plates as her, so they had not given her something they did not deem fit for themselves. Tair took a deep breath and took a bite.

Evidently, they did poison her—in a way. She woke the next morning with a heavy head and no memory of what had happened after she took her first bite of food. She remembered liking the taste, she remembered King Usnaso's and Rain's laughter, she remembered...nothing else. She wore new, clean clothes that she could not recall dressing herself in, and she smelled as though she had been given a bath. She pressed the spot over her eyebrow where it hurt most, scraping a little at the slight scab that had developed where she had cut her forehead with her crystal.

What had been done to her? She felt...the only word she could think of was *studied*. Tampered with. She shuddered and dragged her bedsheets over her head, hoping that no one would disturb her for the rest of the day.

No such luck. Just as she had begun to overcome the

mounting anxiety that filled her chest, her door swung open. Drawing the bedsheet back from her head a bit, she saw Rain step inside the room, his expression a little harder, a little more solid, than it had been the day before. He clenched his teeth, his jaw flexing. His eyes bore into Tair's without actually seeing her.

Finally, he said, "*Aesolo-aso.*" The formal greeting, unlike the one he had offered her the day before. Also, unlike the day before, Rain was sure of himself. Did he and King Usnaso trade bits of consciousness that allowed one to feel more grounded while the other idled? Tair contained her sigh. Too many questions, and no one to answer.

When Tair did not return his greeting, Rain huffed and said, "*Sem ahmoe.*"

Tair raised an eyebrow in question. *Go where?*

Rain sternly repeated, "Let's go."

Tair stretched out her legs but made no move to stand up, her body still aching from all it had endured the day before. Rain did not tolerate her defiance, though. He sighed and stepped back from the door, welcoming in two guards. They wore red masks and uniforms, but each one had a line of gray stitched down the sides of both arms that marked them as lesser in rank than the ones in the throne room. They approached her so rapidly that she could not fend off their aggressive hands yanking her out of bed and onto her feet. Her legs wanted to collapse beneath her, bruises and scabs littered across her brown skin, but the guards did not let her fall, two hands under each of her arms. She struggled to gain footing and shake them off and, after a few seconds of trying, she could not fight any longer. She slumped in their grasp.

Rain turned around and left, so the guards and Tair followed, though Tair herself had no choice in the matter as the guards carried her down an incalculable number of stairs and out of the tower. She was grateful to not have to descend the steps herself, but her gratitude quickly dissipated when they unceremoniously dropped her into the mud—*where?* Tair looked up to see the Hunting Grounds a little walk away.

A long bridge linked the castle and the forest. The river raged beneath it, just as loud as Tair had come to expect. She clawed at the mud beneath her, the ground soft from the rain the night before—rain that Tair had unknowingly slept through. In fact, she did not feel like she had slept at all, her mind and body were so tired. She felt entirely exposed and far too unsafe. Her clothes, too, were no defense against the rather frigid temperatures that blew from within the forest over her skin. As quick as she could manage, she tried to stand and dust herself off, though it turned out to be more of an ordeal than she had originally thought. Thankfully, it was only Rain and herself—the guards had already departed—and she decided that she had nothing to prove to him. Still, she felt rather embarrassed when her legs gave out on her once, twice, and then on the third time she was finally able to hold herself up on bent knees and unsure feet. The cold muck clung to her knees and hands, but it kept her alert, something that was rather comforting after her blackout the night before.

Rain said something in Sossok that Tair did not understand. She stood taller.

Then Rain repeated the previously incomprehensible Sossok, "*Sem ak'rrakas.*"

The words weaved through the air and, once they reached Tair's ears, she knew exactly what he meant. *We will hunt.*

SIXTEEN

That was not what Tair wanted to hear. She did not know what she wanted to hear, but she knew it was not that. Her legs went slack beneath her, and she half-hoped that she would disappear into the ground. Rain, though, would not let that happen. He grabbed her shoulder and held her up. His grip on her was harsh but Tair understood what it meant; she was not meant to display any more physical weakness for the rest of the day. She nodded with downcast eyes in acknowledgement of his unspoken demand.

Rain let her go, wiped his hands on his otherwise pristine emerald-green pants, and repeated for a third time, "*Sem ahmoe.*"

Tair shuffled over the bridge to catch up to Rain, who had already started for the woods. She did not want to follow him, but he at least knew the Hunting Grounds better than she ever would, no matter how much she had tried to map it all out from her view in her room. He could keep her as safe as he deemed fit, and she hated him for it. Tair chose not to look over the edge of the bridge and see what lurked in the raging water five feet below her. It would undoubtedly heighten her fear, just as it had when she had glanced into the moat just before the castle. There were all kinds of strange creatures in this new environment—Rain included. She did not need to meet all of them.

Seeing the forest from overhead or standing across the bridge, Tair had not been able to understand how *alive* it all was until they crossed the threshold. As much magic as there was in the Darkwoods, Tair immediately knew that there was just as much here. Perhaps, at some point, the Darkwoods had covered all lands—but there was no one left to tell tales that tall.

All kinds of bugs and birds sang around them. The trees buzzed at the caress of the wind. It was somehow brighter beneath the canopy of leaves than it had been outside. Tair realized then why Rain wore such a deep emerald color that day, in contrast to the standard red and gold she had seen elsewhere; it was a form of camouflage in these bright green woods. Tair felt all too visible in her beige clothing but looked down to find that, with all the mud, she now wore a similar enough color to the tree trunks around her. She felt somewhat comforted by the fact that her skin was similarly as dark as the trees, too, like the trees were her kin more than this Human she felt nothing but spite for. She pressed her hand to the nearest one, partially to steady herself on the uneven forest floor, and partially to develop a sense of harmony with the disharmonious world she felt trapped in.

When she placed her hand on the bark, she knew immediately that there were Faeries nearby. She had become familiar enough with their presence, first in Braasii, but then more thoroughly in the Darkwoods. She felt comforted by the fact that there was one kind of non-Human that the Usnasos could not rid themselves of, even in their most immediate environment. They had to find some degree of peace with the Faeries' presence in order to even enter the woods at all—

right?

That was true to Tair until Rain pulled a bow and arrow from his back and shot ahead of them. A thud sounded, and Rain went running. Unfamiliar with her environment and lost without a guide, Tair tried to keep up with the King Heir, but he deliberately ran faster than she was able. The sound of Rain's feet trudging through the mud and the heavy footprints he left in his wake were the only indication of the direction in which he had gone. She finally caught up to him to find him hunched over something on the ground, humming to himself. Tair knew—she just *knew*—she did not want to see what his back hid from her view. Unfortunately, a morbid curiosity took over as she peered over his shoulder to see what he had shot.

There, in Rain's murderous hands, was a Faery. Their green skin was covered in sweat and, evidently, blood. The arrow had somehow splintered in the air before it hit their chest, a chest now heaving under the pressure of their body trying to heal them. There were five entry wounds that Tair could see, and even still they were not dead.

They were not dead.

Tair wanted to puke. And then she did.

Rain laughed, then pulled a dagger from the sheath at his side. Tair heard the most horrible squelch in her life. It was one thing to talk of murder in defense of oneself or the ones they loved—Tair had become very personal with that opinion when she killed that soldier who slaughtered Iom. It was another thing entirely to hear the sound of a body being torn apart and hear the Human she was trapped with *laugh* as he set about his psychopathic mutilation of a living Faery's body.

Tair had not yet noticed the pack Rain carried on his back, but now he rustled around in it. She heard the sound of small bones breaking and water trickling and then Rain's groan as he stood and cracked his back. She was still turned away from the scene, bowed and heaving against a tree nearby, but the sounds of Rain's actions were just as bad as, if not worse than, the sight.

Rain came to stand next to Tair, holding out a bloodied cloth for her to see. In it were three small bones, which Tair figured were from the Faery's ribcage, and an organ. An organ not unlike the meat on her dinner plate the night before...

She threw up again, though this time it was just leftover bile. No wonder she had been poisoned; she had consumed the magic of a once-powerful, once-living Faery. She had never felt so repulsed by herself—not even when she had come to terms with her murder of Iom's killer—let alone repulsed by another being. Rain only sneered.

Rain tied the cloth closed and stuck it in his pack. Over his shoulder, Tair could still see the Faery's body splayed out across the forest floor and, without thinking, she started running. As fast as she could. As far as she could. Anything to get away from the horror in front of her. Rain howled as he chased after her, blood still on his hands, blood still his motivator. She could not, under any circumstances, hunt and kill a Faery, if that was his goal in all this. She knew that she had killed that soldier, but she was able to justify it out of a sense of duty to Iom; she knew that she had to kill King Usnaso and Rain, but she was able to justify it out of a duty to her kind. There was justice in that, was there not? But this...she could not stop to think about her own morality, nor Rain's, nor anyone else's. She just kept running.

And Rain kept chasing her. He did not seem to tire as she did and, with that realization, Tair remembered how tired her body was. How desperate she was to stop...

Just as instinctively as Tair had started running, she stopped. Her heart thumped in her ears and her lungs filled up her entire chest and her eyes clouded with tears and...Rain was beside her, his own breath silent. *Inhuman.* Just as he had that morning, he stood with his hands folded behind his back and his eyes patient. He knew he could break her eventually, and he did not seem to care about the challenges along the way. He said something, but Tair did not hear him.

Suddenly, Rain slammed a hand against Tair's back. Instead of feeling pain, the younger Human stood up straight, sucked in a deep breath, and finally heard what Rain was saying. In Sossok, he asked her if she could hear the river.

She met his eyes, somehow finding more comfort there than she might have if she looked for the origin of the horrible waters in the distance. As loud as it had been from outside, as loud as it had been crossing that bridge, the rivers surrounding the Hunting Grounds now felt suffocating from within the forest. It was...it was an *evil* that screamed and would not stop screaming until it had been satiated. It was so loud that Tair wondered if it was truly a river and not a waterfall or perhaps the middle of the Western Great Sea. She had imagined waves high as a mountain out there, but it seemed that these rivers contained that very same impossibility. Rain began walking in the direction of the noise and, without second thought, Tair followed him, careful to watch for his hands. If he tried pulling his bow again, Tair planned to subdue him. Of course, that plan was not fully formed, but she could not handle the pain it caused her to hear his cruelty, let alone imagine what it felt like for the actual victim. She kept close to his heels in case she would have to act fast.

They arrived at the river—the rapid, feral, wrathful river. The water frothed at the shoreline. Fish leapt up and out, full of teeth and even faster than the waters they called home. It was as if the river saw within Rain and King Usnaso, saw the evil there, and wanted a bit of that for itself.

Tair could see the other side, though. Just barely. It was so wide that she knew, if she gained the courage, it would be at least a ten-minute swim for an inexperienced swimmer such as herself. It would probably take more time than that, too, considering her deep physical ache that had not let up since she left Raaha. No matter the risk, at least it was a way out. She let out a breath and relaxed her jaw and shoulders.

Then Rain grabbed the lapel of her shirt and leaned her over the edge of the river. She could barely see her own reflection in the water, it was so fast, but she felt the forest ground begin to give beneath her feet and the water spray at her face and—a fish leapt out and scraped the side of her cheek. She let out a yelp, struggling at Rain's hand at the base of her neck. She shouted, "*Vassos! Vassos-aso!*"

After nearly a minute of her pleading and screaming, Rain threw her to the forest floor by his feet. She coughed, clutched her knees to her chest, tried to reclaim her body. When she could manage it, she childishly yelled, "*So ahtas-nasaj os saano?*" *Why are you trying to kill me?*

Rain only grinned down at her and Tair *swore* that, for a second, he was, quite literally, King Usnaso. But then he was back, in his own distinct way. Whatever held him and his supposed parent together, both of them took great pleasure in her misery. She coughed once more, pulled herself up onto wobbly feet, and gambled, "You cannot kill me."

"We can do anything we please with you," Rain countered, his grin lingering. "You die; we bring you back. You try to kill us; we kill you first. You will watch next time, as I tear your precious *raiso* to pieces. You will learn to hate them as you should."

Tair nearly spat at his feet. Instead, she stood and coughed once more. She barely knew who she was dealing with at that point, barely knew what to say. They did not trust her, and they did not need to, as far as they knew. She had not yet proven her worth nor had she been offered the opportunity, even as the *scese ogo*, the forgotten child. All she could say was "You need me to trust you."

"Oh?" Rain smirked.

"I still know something you don't," Tair said. "If I do not trust you, you will never learn the Domani plans for war."

There was a hut somewhere ahead, much less luxurious than the castle but still fit for royalty. Two guards stood in front, with their own cabin just past the wall of trees that surrounded the shed. Rain dismissed them and opened the door, pushing Tair inside. He had been incensed ever since Tair claimed to know what war plans were being made but had said she would not tell him until she felt safe, until he could be trusted. And, though Tair knew King Usnaso and Rain both could see the surface of her mind, Rain seemed frustrated to find that she had steeled herself against any further mental invasion—exactly how, she did not know, but she was happy to find that her efforts had been effective. For now, she was simply stalling for time, stalling for her life.

Tair knew she would not, under any circumstances, tell him what she knew. Not that she knew much beyond her own role in the Domani plot, nor beyond Omma's vague plans for the aftermath that Alyn had spoken of. Everything else had been kept private for Domani safety—and perhaps her safety, too. She convinced herself, though, that she *did* have something that he wanted, convinced herself that she had those war plans lurking in her mind. That way, whatever Rain saw at the surface could convince him that she held more truths than she actually did.

There were two beds inside the hut. It had the same sheets as her bedroom back at the castle, however far back that was. She could not pinpoint exactly where they were in the forest, not after her aimless running and Rain's series of odd turns that could have taken them any direction in the world. Besides the beds, inside the cabin there was also a small wood-fired stove, two big lanterns and a fireplace, and a map of Sossoa that abruptly cut off at Rolt. Nossoa was not even acknowledged nor considered a part of the continent.

There was a door at the back, which Tair had not expected because the building had not seemed so large from the outside. From behind that door emerged a being in a long, loose-fitting blue dress that rippled over their lithe frame. Their skin was brown and rather weathered. As old as their skin made them out to be, their long hair seemed unaffected, as stark black as the depth of night. Their rather gentle eyes sunk back into their skull, a sign not of malnourishment but of deep sorrow. Still, they beamed when they saw Rain and approached him with open arms. Rain embraced them, sucking in a sharp breath. The two were...mates. Tair felt it just as clearly as she had when she had seen Shianna and Silaa together, or when she first met Bonn.

The being unraveled themself from Rain and looked to Tair, the stranger in the room. Where Tair expected a scowl, they held their smile and asked in Sossok who Tair was.

Tair responded, softly, "*Aso—*uh...*Asosso* Tair." She had dropped the false name Rose had given her, as she was already known as the lost child to King and King Heir. There was no use in pretending any longer. Still, her name was distinctly *not* Sossok, Tair knew, and the being under Rain's arm could tell.

They raised an eyebrow at Rain, who seemed somewhat pained by the interaction. Tair would have never guessed the same hands that now cradled his mate could have, only minutes earlier, carved a Faery's body open and then threatened to drop Tair to her certain death into a raging river. She kept in mind that his love for one being did not negate his hatred for Tair, nor did it negate his hatred for all non-Humans.

The two had an inaudible conversation in Sossok as Tair shifted her weight in the doorway. She wanted nothing more than to run out the door. She knew, however, that Rain or his guards would catch her before she got even ten feet from the cabin and that she would have been in even greater trouble than she already was. She cleared her throat.

Rain whipped around to meet her eyes, shoving his mate behind his back. He growled, "*Nahhs?*"

Tair had nothing to say. She did not mean to startle him

as much as she had, but she liked the idea that, if only for a moment, he was frightened of her.

"You want to trust me," Rain said. "Well, this is *Silee*. She would not be in your presence if I did not trust *you*." *Silee*—his mate's name was Isle. Tair also noted the wholly distinct pronoun used for her in Sossok: *esu*, or she. Tair arbitrarily replaced it with the Nossok pronoun, since "*esu*" was not one that Rose had taught her. Perhaps Rose had never learned it; perhaps it existed for Isle alone.

Rain did not trust Tair, she knew that much. But this was a display of...something. Vulnerability? He could not have possibly contained one ounce of vulnerability in his being, but if he did, it would have been Isle. He still clutched her behind his back. Tair recognized that this was an attempt at getting her to trust him, impossible though it was. Maybe then, her mind would be more susceptible to him. So, what had they done to her the night before? She had originally assumed that they were trying to infiltrate her mind further, but Rain could decipher her mind no more than he could now.

"The lost child," Isle muttered, in just about the heaviest Sossok accent Tair had ever heard. Clearly, Sossok had been a second, learned language for Isle, in contrast to Rain's ease with the language his ancestors (or he himself) created. Actually, Isle's accent sounded rather similar to Omma's...

Tair nodded, unsure of herself in this situation, as her eyes darted between Rain and Isle. Her legs begged her for a break and, careful not to make any sudden movements, she shuffled over to one of the beds and sat on the edge. Almost instantly, her body thanked her. She could have fallen asleep then and there, if it had not been for Rain's palpable anxiety, Isle's curiosity, and her own bewilderment at the two of them. Tair kept her arms folded across her chest and refused the urge to sink back into the admittedly plush mattress.

"We'll eat," Rain announced. Isle sprang into action at the command and took Rain's pack from him, setting to work with the organ he had just taken from a Faery, alongside a plethora of vegetables that seemed to appear out of thin air. Tair wondered if Isle knew how the flesh had been obtained, whose body it was once a part of. Did she even know half of the atrocities Rain had committed for the food she was about to eat, the atrocities he had committed against the Humans of Sossoa and any unlucky non-Humans who ended up in his realm?

The food cooked quicker than Tair thought it would have and, in only a short while, they all sat on the floor around their full plates. Isle spoke a quick, silent prayer that Tair could not translate, but knew it was not quite Sossok. Rain did not participate in the prayer but listened lovingly, nonetheless. Tair watched them both with curious eyes. She had about one thousand questions she wanted to ask, but she knew that Rain would not allow his partner to answer them.

Though she was hungry, Tair did not touch her food, both out of principle and out of an extreme sense of caution. She could not have forced herself eat a Faery now that she knew what the meat was, and she still could not figure out whether she had just an adverse reaction to the flesh the night before, or if she had been intentionally drugged. All she knew was that she had definitely been inspected, and that she would not allow it to happen again. She kept her food at arm's length in front of her. She watched as Rain and Isle ate together, exchanged food with one another, laughed over something silent that passed between them. Tair noticed then that they wore identical rings. Indeed, now that she thought about it, she did not think she had seen Rain without that ring the entire time she had known the Human. And King Usnaso had one of his own.

Was Isle Usnaso's mate, too? Were Rain and his supposed parent and all the generations before them so much the same being that they shared a mate?

And, if Tair's theory was true, how old did that make Isle?

Tair tried to convince herself that Isle just represented some repressed side of Rain, incongruent with his cruel exterior. Rain did, indeed, seem softer around his mate. Not that it excused any of his grievances, but Tair imagined that, if she had the gall, she could have killed him right then and there. Something held her back, though. She knew if she killed Rain now, she would have no way to return to the castle without losing her way in the forest or otherwise getting caught, and from there she would have been killed. Her mind spiraled as she thought of the irreversible damage her actions now could have on her (admittedly nonexistent) plan, so she knew now was not her moment.

Tair opted instead to keep a diligent eye on Rain. He fed Isle a few times, which made both of them giggle. Tair was disgusted by his apparent indifference to—rather, his enthusiastic embrace of—what he had done earlier that day, how easy it was for him to put aside the memory of a brutal murder and make space for these acts of love. Tair still could not decide whether Isle knew of Rain's transgressions, or if she even cared to know. Tair thought of Silaa and Shianna; how Silaa had felt impossibly betrayed by Shianna after the revelation of all the lies, but how the Elf had been somehow convinced in the end to accept them. Silaa had become a wisp of who she had once been. And, to make up for what had happened to her partner, or at least appease her guilt and shame, Shianna had released Tair and Rose. Released them to this world...

Tair felt both grateful and saddened that she had only been with Bonn so long, only allowed herself to truly care for them for so long. Tair heaved at the thought of her mate. Her chest ached so suddenly that she realized how quickly and easily she had ignored and suppressed thoughts of Bonn since she had arrived in Sossoa in an effort to avoid the hurt of being apart. Now, she could not help but wonder about her own mate—and then wonder about them all: Bonn, Shianna, Silaa, Alyn...Rose,

Iom...everyone she had left behind. Everyone she had ever loved.

When she doubled over, Rain asked, "What's wrong?"

Tair shook her head, braced herself on the floor, took a few deep breaths to calm her pounding heart. Slowly, Isle pulled all the plates away from Tair as she continued to hyperventilate. Somehow, this pain was deeper than the physical ache of having climbed thousands of stairs, or running over uneven ground, or even the trauma of her life hanging by a thread over the river. No, this was a *severing*. A loss.

Then, in some sort of miracle, Isle held a piece of *senip* out for Tair, the purple Domani bread with calming herbal properties. It was stale, probably a few days old by that point, but Tair devoured it as quickly as she could without suffocating. It was not until she was done and felt less consumed by grief that she realized that she had just eaten a Dwarven recipe. She looked up at Rain's mate and recognized something she had not before: Isle was part-Dwarf.

Her eyes widened as she looked between Rain and Isle and Rain and Isle...and landed on Rain, who seemed to understand what Tair had just realized. He hung his head, somewhat... humiliated? Tair wanted to laugh in his face. Or hurt him. There he was, mutilating and consuming the flesh of a Faery, and then, too, hand-feeding his half-Dwarven mate. Somehow, he managed to love her and hate her kind.

"What—" Tair started but was cut off by Rain.

"We met before—" the King Heir scrambled to explain.

"Before what?" Tair spat.

Rain glared at her. Then Tair knew they had met before *everything*. Before Sossoa, before the Doman War, before the schism between Dwarves and Humans. Dwarves had much longer lifespans, so Isle very well could have been the Usnaso mate for centuries. Unako was as much Rain as Rain was Unako. King Usnaso, then, was the same. He had created Rain from himself, or Rain had created himself from Usnaso, or Isle had been coerced into creating all of them, or she had created them willingly...Tair still could not piece it all together, did not know the exact mechanics of it, but the fact that they were the same Human was enough to make Tair grin. She had another piece of Rain that made him vulnerable—and he knew it, too. He wanted her to trust him, desperately. And his desperation made him weak.

The biggest, lingering question in Tair's mind arose again: if the King and King Heir were, indeed, the same Human, would she have to kill them both, or would killing one result in the other's death, too?

And Isle...Isle must have been driven insane. There was no other explanation. Unako had battled, enslaved, and *killed* Dwarves—her kin. He had done the very same to every other non-Human, perhaps including those who were also part-Dwarf, like herself. Had she convinced herself that, the more iterations of her original monstrous Human mate, the less he was that same Human who had killed her kin? Still, that did not explain his present evils.

Isle clutched onto Rain's arm as if he could protect her from— who? Tair? Or Usnaso? Or Rain himself? Perhaps she protected herself from the mere memory of what she had once been, the Dwarf in her so dissociated that she may not have even registered it until Tair stared at her with wide, horrified eyes. Isle knew Rain's prejudice against her own blood, knew the repercussions of such prejudice, and still loved him. Tair did not know if she could truly speak to it, but she knew this much: if Bonn had done even one of the things that Tair had seen Rain do, or one of the things that she had even *assumed* he had done, she knew she could not ever look at her mate in the same way again. Even Silaa, up until she had been split from who she had once been, had a hard time looking at Shianna after the revelation of her mere political status. There were things that mates did not have to get over. There were pairings that sometimes broke. Nothing was eternal. So, Rain's actions against Isle's kin must have broken her—or had they?

Tair stood, brushed herself off, and began to pace the room.

"She's a Dwarf," Tair said. It was reductionist, but she felt the need to point this out to Rain, make his own hypocrisy known to him.

"She is, but she's also..."

"Your mate," Tair finished for him. The room felt like it was spinning around her.

Tair stopped pacing and said, "I'm going to—I don't know—I have to clear my head."

Without a word from Rain, she left the shed and headed into the woods. He must not have been concerned about her departure because, after a few moments of walking, she realized he was not following her. In fact, no one followed her.

She began to run.

Tair did not know where she was going, but the woods were dark and the sounds of the day had faded to a quiet lull and she felt that, even if she had known her way around the Hunting Grounds, she still would have gotten lost. It was a different world at night, nearly pitch-black if not for the occasional patch where the full moon shone down through the trees.

After a while, the particular reason she had wanted to clear her head in the first place left her. These woods distracted—*protected?*—her from the chaos. Tair had a very clear sense that she did not know how to get back to the cabin, even if she had wanted to. The only thing that started to feel familiar about the environment was the river. She heard it distantly, but she realized soon that she had unconsciously neared the waters, unable to stop her feet from taking her there.

Tair...

She whipped around.

Tair...Tair...

Tair looked through the thicket of trees, even kicked at the dirt beneath her feet. The origin of the voice, though, was ahead of her. She followed it.

Taiiiiiiirrrrrrrrrrr...

The voice grew louder, even louder than the water. She felt those rapids when her foot dropped into the water, and she was whisked away by the tide.

SEVENTEEN

Tair awoke on the shore of the river. She did not appreciate waking up and not knowing what had happened to her in the hours she had lost, and it had happened to her two nights in a row. The last thing she could remember was running—from what and to where, though, came only in pieces. She assumed that she had fallen into the river at some point. Her clothes were still rather damp, and they only made the cold Sossok air even harder to bear. Even assuming that she had gone for a dip, she could not recall why she had entered the water, nor how she had gotten out. The rivers around the Hunting Grounds were feral, so she could not imagine why she would have gotten close enough to even *look* at the water. Then again, she had clearly survived the rapids and, from what she heard, the ferocity of the river had now quieted to a low trickle. However foolish the thought was, Tair felt that something in the river had become a part of her. Her fingertips ached, but other than that the only thing that bothered her was the Red Sun in her eyes. She groaned as she sat upright, careful not to rub her eyes with the mud all over her hands.

Though she could not see them, she knew someone stood near her and, before she could even guess as to who it was, they spoke.

"You did not get too far," Rain said.

Tair blinked her eyes and found the King Heir leaning against a tree in front of her. She could have rolled back into the river in that moment, tried to swim away to spite him, and hopefully make it to the other side before the waters got too wild again. She glanced over at the water and stretched out her hands. They still ached but were slowly regaining feeling. Despite the pain in her hands, her legs were fine—in fact, she could no longer remember the pain of her now disappeared bruises nor the pain of the arrow in her thigh, nor the ache of all those stairs, all that running. It was as if someone had, thankfully, taken all that sensation away from her. She felt well-rested for the first time in well over a week, and she was ready to fight, she thought.

And her target stood just before her with a horrible smirk on his face.

"I was not trying to run away," Tair admitted. "I just wanted to think."

"How did that go?" Rain asked.

"Great, apparently," Tair said.

Rain chuckled. Tair did not like that she made him chuckle. She did not like the ease with which they communicated—the ease with which she could conduct herself around him now. She had sequestered off a part of herself so that she could make him believe she now trusted him.

She stood up, which was a big mistake. Her aching hands were still unprepared for any strain, so when she pushed herself up from the ground, a sharp pain shot up her arms and grabbed hold of her heart. She clutched onto her chest, doubled over, but refused to fall into the mud again. She had done so far too many times in Rain's presence, and she did not intend to do it again.

Tair glanced up. Rain seemed surprised by her current state. His meticulously constructed features had contorted into a harsh frown, one which distorted his face into something that far better matched to his personality. A hard line formed between his furrowed eyebrows, his lips pursed, his jaw hardened, and his nose scrunched up. Tair was rather amused at this. As invincible as he and his supposed parent seemed, they were not perfect.

Now it was her turn to smirk. Both of them knew that something had changed in Tair. Something was different. Different, not wrong. Not wrong but changing. She could not place what it was, but she at least had a secret now—something she could not, and would not, allow Rain to see.

He paused as he often did when he was displeased. His frown hardened and, in that moment, Tair could actually *feel* him tapping around at the surface of her mind. A new wall had been built there, though, a wall that she had not built herself. One that did not have a door, and one that he could not climb. She stood up straight, folded her arms over her chest, and looked him right in the eyes. After a moment, his frown softened.

"*Sem ahmoe,*" Rain finally said, with no mention at all as to him visiting her mind. He loved that phrase—*let's go*—as if it were something that Tair had any choice in.

Rain did not run ahead of her this time. Instead, he took very careful steps, pausing constantly to ensure that Tair was following him, and never made any sharp turns without first announcing them. In all her following, in all her running, Tair had not yet had an opportunity to map out any part of the Hunting Grounds, now found herself somewhat grateful to become acquainted with the land. She appreciated, too, that she did not have to ask him to tell her about the trees or the animals or the insects. Instead, she would look at something long enough, let it breach the wall in her mind, and, without even glancing back, Rain would explain what it was.

For instance, there was a tree they kept passing. Tair only knew they had passed it multiple times because of a spiral carving that had been made into its bark, toward the top where the leaves began. She pushed that thought past the wall in her mind and, still lingering, Rain knew to answer.

"We are not going in circles," he sighed. "We just have to pass it four times before we are allowed to move on."

"So, we *are* going in circles?"

"No," Rain said. "Not circles. It's just part of the path."

Tair did not fully understand, but she knew that she was testing Rain's patience, and she did not want to push him too far. After all, he was still the Human he was, he was still the King Heir, and he was not going to tolerate her insolence forever. He seemed rather disheartened by the fact that he could only hear what was happening in Tair's mind when she let a thought pass through her newly constructed wall. What passed, of course, were basic questions as to the forest, but never anything she deemed precious—and nothing that she could not understand herself. That wall, she knew, had been built not by her own hands (her own mind, rather), but by something else that had learned to protect itself for Tair's sake. When she tried to look into it, she received a sharp shock to her fingertips, so she knew not to root around. It would reveal itself soon enough.

And Tair understood that she could not reveal it herself. Rain tried—she felt him trying—but he too could not get past a certain point. Tair smiled at his tense back. Whatever was within her was currently doing no harm, though it was clearly causing Rain mental turmoil. She protected it as it protected her.

Whatever had happened, happened in the river. She knew that much.

And so did Rain. However many years he had lived near those waters, it had never offered him this power—it had never taken his power, either. Tair had known immediately how alive those waters were, but she had never thought that it would be a part of her, that she would be a part of it.

They arrived back at the cabin. Those same soldiers from the day before stood out front, having only taken a break, apparently, to sleep. Rain could have defended Isle better than any soldier could have, but, while he was away, he must have known that Isle was not safe in the Hunting Grounds on her own. Safe from what, though, it seemed Rain himself did not even know. There was no way any stray Sossok citizens would have been able to cross the rivers surrounding the Hunting Grounds in the first place, nor would they have survived a second in these woods without experience nor guide. Danger, then, came from something Rain had never been able to figure out about the forest—something he could not *find*—that he felt warranted a degree of precaution. It was not the forest that unnerved him now, though; it was Tair. She felt his fear as he rustled around in her mind.

When they entered the lodge, Isle stood from her spot on the edge of a bed with a wide grin on her face. "You found her," the half-Dwarf, half-Human said.

Rain nodded as he crossed the room toward his mate. They whispered a moment before Isle looked back at Tair with wide, intrigued eyes. She nodded at the last thing Rain said before he turned around, walked past Tair, and left the cabin behind. Clearly, he was not threatened enough by this new Tair.

Tair spent another week in that cabin alone with Isle. She could not bring herself to explore further into the forest on her own out of fear of getting lost. As afraid as she was of the Hunting Grounds, she was no more comfortable here, with Isle, who barely spoke to her but watched her constantly. Even when Tair left to relieve herself, Isle followed; when Tair traced her path with Rain from the river out to bathe herself in the still-calm waters, Isle followed; when Tair went to sleep at night, she felt Isle watching her. As uncomfortable as it made her, Tair never said anything against it for a few reasons, most of which she could not particularly place. She was, of course, curious as to Isle's attention—which no doubt had something to do with what Rain had told her before he left. There was also a degree of safety to the constant shadowing; if Tair's assumptions were correct, Isle had been living in the Hunting Grounds for centuries at this point, and probably knew how to lead Tair back to the cabin if Tair ever lost her way. All those centuries, too, must have seen Isle locked up to this small part of the woods, only to be comforted when her mate decided to visit her again. She must have been so terribly lonely. Tair took pity on Isle if nothing else, so she had a hard time convincing herself to confront the being.

That was, until their eighth night together. Isle always cooked supper without question, and never asked Tair what she would like that night. It did not particularly matter to Tair. This was the way Alyn had raised her—to eat whatever he decided to make that night—and nothing Isle made was ever as inedible as it had been that first night with Rain. Once the King Heir had disappeared, so too had the meat on their plates. They ate a plentitude of vegetables and nuts and breads and whatever else Isle quite literally conjured up. Sometimes Isle's casual use of magic shocked Tair but, then again, she was not accustomed to it from Dwarves. Shianna refused to use her magic in the presence of others, and even Bonn's details were sparse, though they were far more forthcoming than the Prime Heir ever had been. The only other use of magic Tair had seen like this was from Faeries. Tair reasoned that Isle had no use in hiding her abilities because she was, for the most part, alone.

Isle laid out the food between the two of them and sat down on the floor across from Tair, then said her usual prayer. The more Tair heard it, the more she understood it to be some odd mixture of Sossok and Domani. King Unako had constructed the language and culture of Sossoa to make a clear distinction between the Humans of the land from those non-Humans and Humans alike who remained in what had become Nossoa. Tair wondered if Isle had been one of the first to hear this new language. Isle's prayer, though, was stranger than using Sossok words then Domani then back to Sossok; it combined words entirely, switched up sentence structures. To Tair, it seemed that Isle had deliberately made it incomprehensible. For whom, Tair did not know, though she could guess.

"...*vak'kaja'aa Rakasos ahrra'a kassa'go goksa*," Isle finished. *Please know I am still here.* It had taken Tair those first four days to translate that last line in her mind, jumbled and nonsensical as it was. Once she had, she wondered who Isle prayed to, who needed to know she was still "here." Was "here" the Hunting Grounds? No, Tair had the distinct feeling that Isle's "here" was not about that exact location they found themselves in, but something more elusive, more profound.

Much to Isle's surprise, Tair had echoed that last line with her, for the first time since the younger Human had translated it to herself. Isle smiled at her demurely as she glanced down at her lap. She asked in accented Sossok, "How did you figure it out?"

Tair shrugged as she began to pile up her plate. "I speak Domani."

"So does Unako." Isle cleared her throat and added, "But he does not speak it with me."

Tair noted Isle's reference to Rain as Unako. They were the same in Isle's mind, no more distinct from one another than Tair was to herself. Tair asked, "Why not?"

Isle finished a few bites of food before answering, "He does not like the Domani language." *Does not like?* An understatement, Tair knew.

"*Nak raak? Raak kinnana'aa jsa Domankana?*" Tair asked.

Isle's eyes went wide. If she had been eating, Tair was sure that she would have spit out her food. Instead, Isle turned pale and violently shook her head. "You cannot speak that here," she said in Sossok. "Not so brazenly."

Tair furrowed her eyebrows but obliged. As invasive of Tair's privacy as Isle had been, she had never been unkind, and Tair did not want to make her feel uncomfortable. After all, they were stuck together for however long Rain was away.

Still, Tair knew now that Isle was not averse to challenge, just surprised by it. She tested her luck and finally asked the question that had been plaguing her for days now: "Why do you watch me all the time?"

Isle continued to eat.

"Why?" Tair pressed.

Isle said nothing.

With a force that Tair had not expected from herself, she shouted in Domani, "*Kiio?*" The cabin shook a little around them and that aching feeling returned to Tair's fingertips. She balled up her fists and fought back tears. She did not intend to grow so angry, did not intend for whatever energy she now contained to be released, but Isle's refusal to even acknowledge that Tair had spoken upset her more than she thought it would.

Isle finished eating a little more slowly now and repeated, "You cannot use that language here."

Tair looked down at her food.

"Rain asked me to watch you," Isle finally answered. "He thinks something is wrong."

Despite herself, Tair asked, "Is something wrong?"

Isle considered this for a moment. She did not attempt to root around in Tair's mind like Rain would have, nor did she move any closer to Tair. No, Isle went inward, turning so stock-still that Tair wondered if she had the same communicational magic that both the Faeries of the Darkwoods and the King and King Heir had. Between Rain and King Usnaso, though, they had been able to communicate with each other because they were, for all intents and purposes, one entity. Isle seemingly communed only with herself, isolated to her own mind as her eyes rolled back in her head and her mouth hung open. Tair did not move, though she was almost frightened enough by this display to go retrieve the guards in the cabin past the row of trees surrounding her and Isle. As if they would have been able to do anything. Tair simply continued eating and waited for Isle to come back to their shared realm.

Finally, Isle blinked and glanced around the room to reorient herself before her eyes finally landed back on Tair. With an amount of resolve Tair had never yet seen, Isle said, "*Sanas.*"

Tair furrowed her eyebrows. "No, as in, 'nothing's wrong'?"

"Not wrong," Isle said. "Changing."

Tair sighed with relief, but then tensed again as she recognized those words from her own mind. "Who told you that?"

"The lost child," Isle said as she shut her eyes. "You believe you were left a mere two decades ago; I have been waiting for you for centuries—waiting for your return."

"My..." Tair flinched back from Isle instinctively. "My return?"

"The woods could only protect you so long before the world was ready to change again." Eyes still shut, Isle stood and crossed the room. From a dresser, she pulled out a small dagger and then came to sit back down across from Tair. She then added, "Before things had to change."

There were tears in Tair's eyes that she did not realize until they dropped into her open palms. Isle twirled the dagger in her hands, the sharp edge of the blade making small incisions in her skin, over and over and over again. Tair did not move to stop her.

"And now you have returned," Isle sighed. She opened her eyes—her eyes, Tair's eyes, *the same eyes*. Tair gasped.

Together, they said, "*Vass'kaja'aa Rakasos ahrra'a kassa'go goksa*."

Isle smiled. Before Tair could stop her, she had plunged the dagger into her chest.

It did not take long after that for Rain to return. When he did, he found Tair still sitting across from Isle's corpse. The dagger stuck out from her chest and, from that point, a flower of blood blossomed out from where her beating heart should have been. Rain screamed when he saw Isle's body, a guttural, angry, horrible scream. He did not hurt Tair—not yet. He ran over to his dead mate's body and held her in his arms, rocking and sobbing. The guards did not enter and, somewhere in the back of her mind, Tair knew they were dead, too. Not by Tair's hand, but by Isle's mind, when she had entered that inaccessible state. No one but Tair heard Rain's cries. Even in her ears, the sound was distant.

Tair said, the words moving her mouth more than she moved her mouth, "She wanted me to know that she was still here."

"What did you do?" Still clutching onto Isle's limp body, Rain repeated, "*So aht'se nahhs?*"

"She did it to herself," Tair breathed. Contained to the walls in her mind, she still felt safe, but now trapped behind what had once felt like a line of defense. Rain still pushed against the wall, this time harder, this time desperate, but it would not budge.

This enraged him further. He stood up and, on instinct, so did Tair. They stood now, face-to-face, Rain silent and frantic to hear what Tair thought. Tair understood two things now: firstly, he could not breach those walls because the river had planted them there; secondly, he could not breach those walls because, in a way, centuries ago, he had built them without even knowing.

Tair was his and Isle's child.

This fact came to her only distantly. Instead of the ache

that had once been in her fingertips, a sharp feeling now sunk through them. When she glanced at her hands, she saw talons, black and long as the *missai* birds' in the Darkwoods. Rain glanced at her hands, too, and looked back at her with rage in his eyes.

"You would try to kill *me*?"

Tair would not try. She would. She sent this message to him through the wall.

Rain tried to take a step back, but Tair had rooted him in place. He never feared, only raged. Between their minds, Tair felt Rain thrash in her hold, but his body would not budge. He struggled to say, "You kill me, and another one takes my place."

Tair shook her head. "You are the last one. The parent lives on through the child's continued life." Recognition flashed across Rain's face—and so it was. It had not been too difficult to piece together, not when she realized that a part of him still lived in her. That supposition had been passed to her without him even intending to share it. Isle had taken it, put it in Tair, and then sequestered this child of theirs away to one day return. To find that, yes, her parents were still here. Still alive.

And her arrival would kill them both.

Rain gained a little control over his movements, but only to move closer. He drew Tair's face in close to his own by her chin, his long nails piercing her skin. He said, "You do not even know who you are, but I know what I am. I am what you could never be—what no one will ever be again if I die—I am eternal."

"I know what I am." Tair smiled. "I was unaccounted for, unbelonging and unknown. I am..." Tair glanced over Rain's shoulder at Isle, laying in death with a pleased, final smile. She said, "I am defined by your end—I *am* your end. It is there that I finally find belonging."

Rain's eyes went wide as he tried to draw back. He could

not. "If you kill me, you kill yourself. You are your own end."

Tair knew this. And still, she plunged her talons into Rain and let their lives go.

AFTER

It was a dark night, and no inch of the continent was free from it. A storm rolled over every bit of known land, stretching out as if awakening from a long nap. Traveling over borders, manufactured and not, the rains could not have been governed. And, gentle as a talon piercing flesh, Bonn, Alyn, Shianna, and Silaa all awoke to the sudden feeling that, somewhere far away, Tair had gone where they could not reach.

ACKNOWLEDGEMENTS

I am eternally grateful for the entire team at Atmosphere Press. When I was twelve, I dreamed to publish a book by the age of twenty and, as the years went on, that fantasy felt more and more impossible. With all of you, that dream has been actualized. I am particularly grateful for these four people: Albert Liau, for first helping me believe in my book; Ronaldo Alves, for creating my dream book cover; Alexis Kale, for all your edits, encouragement, and enthusiasm; and Nick Courtright, for your dedication, endorsement, and care.

I am grateful for all my earliest readers. I am grateful for my teachers, especially Mrs. Winston and Mrs. Cordell for teaching me how to write before I decided what to write; and I am grateful for Matt Schultz, for gifting me my first ever publication. I am grateful for the online audiences who read my fanfiction and short stories—and who first taught me how to receive criticism. I am grateful for all the readers who read *Where the Rain Cannot Reach*, reviewed it, shared it, and allowed it to be a part of their lives. My writing means nothing until you give it meaning.

I am grateful for Kim Vance and all her amazing work on the map that appears at the start of this book.

I am grateful for Alienor. I am honored that you are a part of who I am.

I am grateful for SK. Thank you for dreaming with me.

I am grateful for Joshua.

I am grateful for my grandparents and their unconditional love.

I am grateful for Oliver.

I am grateful for my younger siblings Negasi and Bakari. Thank you both for surviving with me, healing with me, thinking with me, and creating with me.

I am grateful for my mom. Thank you for trusting me to create my own path; thank you for making that path a possibility. I am grateful for everything you have done, continue to do, and will do. I am grateful for everything you are.

ABOUT ATMOSPHERE PRESS

Atmosphere Press is an independent, full-service publisher for excellent books in all genres and for all audiences. Learn more about what we do at atmospherepress.com.

We encourage you to check out some of Atmosphere's latest releases, which are available at Amazon.com and via order from your local bookstore:

Twisted Silver Spoons, a novel by Karen M. Wicks

Queen of Crows, a novel by S.L. Wilton

The Summer Festival is Murder, a novel by Jill M. Lyon

The Past We Step Into, stories by Richard Scharine

The Museum of an Extinct Race, a novel by Jonathan Hale Rosen

Swimming with the Angels, a novel by Colin Kersey

Island of Dead Gods, a novel by Verena Mahlow

Cloakers, a novel by Alexandra Lapointe

Twins Daze, a novel by Jerry Petersen

Embargo on Hope, a novel by Justin Doyle

Abaddon Illusion, a novel by Lindsey Bakken

Blackland: A Utopian Novel, by Richard A. Jones

The Jesus Nut, a novel by John Prather

ABOUT
THE
AUTHOR

Adesina Brown writes prose and poetry in a room full of books
and plants, which is to say: Adesina Brown reads and tends to
their plants, and sometimes writes prose and poetry. *Where
the Rain Cannot Reach* is their debut novel. To learn more,
please visit their website adesinabrown.com.

CPSIA information can be obtained
at www.ICGtesting.com
Printed in the USA
LVHW041638161121
703500LV00015B/607

9 781639 881383